PROUD AND ANGRY DUST

PROUD AND ANGRY DUST

PROUD AND ANGRY DUST

KATHRYN MITCHELL

UNIVERSITY PRESS OF COLORADO

Copyright © 2001 by the University Press of Colorado
International Standard Book Number 0-87081-608-X

Published by the University Press of Colorado
5589 Arapahoe Avenue, Suite 206C
Boulder, Colorado 80303

The University Press of Colorado is a cooperative publishing enterprise supported, in part, by Adams State College, Colorado State University, Fort Lewis College, Mesa State College, Metropolitan State College of Denver, University of Colorado, University of Northern Colorado, University of Southern Colorado, and Western State College of Colorado.

The paper used in this publication meets the minimum requirements of the American National Standard for Information Sciences—Permanence of Paper for Printed Library Materials. ANSI Z39.48-1992

Library of Congress Cataloging-in-Publication Data

Mitchell, Kathryn.
  Proud and angry dust / Kathryn Mitchell.
     p. cm.
  ISBN 0-87081-608-X (alk. paper)
  1. African American boys—Fiction. 2. African American teenage boys—Fiction. 3. Petroleum industry and trade—Fiction. 4. Murder—Fiction. 5. Texas—Fiction. I. Title.
  PS3563.I767453 P76 2001
  813'.6—dc21

                                                                00-013139

Design by Daniel Pratt

10 09 08 07 06 05 04 03 02 01   10 9 8 7 6 5 4 3 2 1

For my mother, Bessie Simmons, with much love;
and to the memory of my friend Dr. Henry McBay.

ACKNOWLEDGMENTS

I would like to thank the following people, whose encouragement and support have been invaluable: Karin Bell, Emily Carmain, Carol Johnson, Ginger Kaderabek, Sandra Wilmore, The Professor, and all my other friends and family, who are a continuing blessing to me.

PART ONE

KNOX PLAINS

CHAPTER ONE

I never knew anybody who liked to laugh as much as Barnett Lindsay did. He'd break up over about anything. Back in 1924, when we were in sixth grade, we were reading aloud from a book about Sinbad the Sailor, and there was a man in the story named Hinbad. Barnett thought "Hinbad" was the funniest name he'd ever heard. Every time somebody said it, he'd just about fall off his chair laughing. Mrs. Davenport would beat him with a leather strap, but it didn't matter. He'd still laugh every time. It sounded to him like "hen-bad." "That man must be named after chicken stink," Barnett would say and start laughing again.

Another time he got Wesley Wilson and me in trouble when he got us to go along with a prank during morning devotion. After prayer we would go around the room in order, and each pupil would recite a verse from the Bible. Wesley was after me, and then Barnett. Just when the teacher was starting, Barnett whispered to me, "When they get to you, Moose, say, 'Jesus wept.'"

"That's a baby's verse," I protested. "I know lots of verses longer than that."

"Just say it, okay?"

I knew he was up to something, but curiosity got the best of me, so when my turn came, I said, "Jesus wept."

Wesley solemnly pronounced, "Moses slept."

Then Barnett added, "And Jacob fell down the back doorstep."

It took Mrs. Davenport twenty minutes to stop the laughter and restore order. The whole class had to stay after school and listen to a lecture from the principal, and Wesley, Barnett, and I took a beating with the strap and had to write five hundred times, "I will not mock God's Word."

The next day Rosetta Nesbet, who had been out sick all week and still wasn't feeling well, decided to take the easy route when it came her turn to say a Bible verse. She said, "Jesus wept." When everybody laughed, Rosetta thought they were all making fun of her for saying a simple two-word verse. She ran out of the room crying.

The little school for colored in Knox Plains, Texas, would have been the dullest place on earth if Barnett hadn't been there to liven things up once in a while, especially in the summer, when the class-room was hot as a ginger mill. Big-city pupils were out for vacation, but we had to start the school year then so we could take a two-month break in the fall to help harvest the crops.

That was a big joke among the black people in Knox Plains be-cause none of us had a crop that couldn't be harvested in a week, even though we had land. Land was plentiful and cheap in Texas after the Civil War and well into the early years of the twentieth century, so most people, black included, had big spreads. My pa never bought much land, just the little plot our house and store sat on. He said there wasn't much point in buying land on the south side of Knox Plains, and that was the only land the Knox Plains Land Allocation Council would let us have.

Pa said you couldn't raise a fuss on that south-side land. So, in-stead of farming, he had made money driving cattle and running a small general store built and stocked with money from his father, an Irishman named Tyrone O'Malley. When Pa was fourteen, Grandpa O'Malley and my grandmother moved to Louisiana, where people were inclined to leave interracial couples alone as long as they didn't flaunt the relationship in society. But by then, Pa had fallen in love with life on the range and chose to stay in Texas and be a cowboy. Grandpa O'Malley worried that a cowboy's income was too uncertain for a family man, so when Ma and Pa married, Grandpa O'Malley gave them the money for the business as a wedding present. The store, which was just a few feet from our house, turned out to be a smart idea. We were far from rich, but we lived better than most of our neighbors, in a two-story house with a wide wraparound porch, nice furniture, and a set of china from England.

I was just eight when Pa died in an accident on a cattle drive. Of the pictures I hold in my head of him, I don't know how much is actual memory, how much is stories I've heard people tell, and how much I just made up in my childish need to have a father to look up to. I remember that he had light skin, hazel eyes, and curly brown hair. He looked more like a white man who'd been out in the sun all summer than a man with the blood of Mother Africa flowing in his veins. He wore boots and a big cowboy hat and would come riding up to the house on a golden-brown horse. He'd reach down from the horse, scoop me up with one arm, hold me high in the air, and put me down in front of him. Then he'd scoop up Barnett the same way and put him in the back. We'd ride off down the road, just like cowboys.

After Pa died, I started going with Barnett to the moving-picture show to see the cowboy features the theaters ran every Saturday afternoon. Seats in the colored balcony were just a nickel, and I liked sitting far from the screen, taking in those expansive shots of the western plains. Tom Mix was my favorite cowboy. More and more, he seemed to look like my pa. I started to imagine that Pa really wasn't dead at all—he'd gone off to California to pass as a white man and make movies under the name Tom Mix. I told my mother that one day and she said, "Roosevelt, I don't know where you get these ideas. Your father's dead. I'll take you and show you his grave if you want me to." I was sorry I ever said anything to her.

With Pa gone, the only grown man in the house was Uncle Will. Will Lindsay wasn't really my uncle. He was my mother's stepfather. She called him "Uncle" Will to suggest a close family relationship without implying that he had replaced her father. Barnett, his only son, was my mother's half brother, making him my uncle, even though he was only a year and three months older. My grandmother had surprised everybody by marrying Will Lindsay after all her children by Grandpa Patterson—my mother being the youngest—were grown and married. Everybody thought Granny Patterson was ready to settle into quiet widowhood when she went to Muskogee, Oklahoma, to spend a few months with some relatives. But she came back with a husband. And a year later she died giving birth to their son—that was Barnett. I was born a year and three months after that.

Ma just raised us both as though she had had two sons. So while Barnett was actually my uncle, we grew up as siblings. Barnett and I didn't look much alike, but no two brothers could have been closer. Barnett was black and velvety like Uncle Will, and he had handsome features that I'm told he got from my grandmother. I was coffee with a heavy dollop of cream, just a little darker than my half-white pa. Folks around there referred to people my color as "bright." Uncle Will liked to call Barnett and me Midnight and Daylight.

Nobody called me Roosevelt but Ma, my teachers, and the grown people at church. I was always Moose to Barnett and my schoolmates, even though Moose is a funny name for a short, skinny little fellow like me. My full name is Theodore Roosevelt Bullmoose O'Malley. I was named after the man my ma admired most next to Pa and the nickname of the party that tried to get Roosevelt elected after he broke off with the Republicans.

Ma liked two things about President Theodore Roosevelt. Like Pa, he loved manly outdoor things—riding, hunting, and fishing. Ma also read an article that said Roosevelt was "committed to improving race relations in the United States" and was working with Booker T. Washington to find highly qualified black people to fill high federal posts. Roosevelt talked of change and progress. He continually attacked the status quo with big, bold actions. He shouted to the crowds about "fair play and a square deal for every man and every woman in the United States." Wasn't that what black Americans had been crying for since the end of the Civil War? Roosevelt was the leader we needed to improve our lot, if not bring us into full equality with other Americans, Ma argued. President Roosevelt was even fond of quoting an old African proverb, "Speak softly, and carry a big stick."

Ma's friends kept pointing out that Roosevelt had plenty of opportunities to help black people, and he didn't do it. But once my ma decides she likes somebody, or doesn't like them, it's hard to turn her around.

I was only five years old on a bitterly cold January day in 1919 when my mother read the news that her beloved President Roosevelt had died. Ma had been certain that Theodore Roosevelt, only sixty years old at the time of his death, would run in the 1920 presidential election and win. Wrapped in a quilt in the front parlor, she curled into a ball like a small child and wept all day as though she had lost a dear family member. Nothing my baffled father could do or say would console her. Many years later I understood that for my mother it was not just a man who had died on that gray winter day, it was the best hope that black Americans had seen for many decades.

Grandma Patterson had sent Ma all the way to Nashville, Tennessee, to Fisk University just so she could find a professional man to marry. Instead, she came home with her degree and married John Patrick O'Malley, the good-looking cowboy she'd been wild about since she was nine years old. In that same stubborn fashion, Ma named me after Theodore Roosevelt even though I was born in 1913, a full year after the "Bull Moose" party had failed to return its candidate to the White House.

Barnett and I were in the same grade because I got so far ahead of my class that I skipped a grade. Barnett was smart, too, but his grades weren't as good as mine, mostly because teachers kept marking him down for all the mischief he stayed into.

In Texas history class, for example, he'd done a fine job of writing a research paper on the area where we lived. He went into detail about Cornell Barrimore Knox, who had owned a huge estate there when Texas was still part of Mexico, and how Knox had been great friends with Antonio López de Santa Anna until the Mexican president threw aside his country's democratic constitution and made himself dictator. Barnett told all about how Knox sided with Sam Houston in his fight to free Texas from Mexico, making a bitter enemy of Santa Anna, who was once his friend. Barnett had created a lively and colorful yet historically accurate account of the early history of Knox Plains. He probably would have gotten an A on it if he could have resisted throwing in his own editorial comments when he presented the paper in class.

"Knox Plains was founded soon after the Civil War, which really wasn't all that civil, on some land where the Caddo Indians once lived," Barnett's oral report began. "Back when squatters could have any land they could defend and do something with, pioneers killed or chased off all the Indians and took the land for themselves. The interesting thing about all that is that the name 'Texas' comes from a Caddo word meaning 'friendship.' "

Mrs. Davenport reminded him that personal opinions were not appropriate in a history report, but still Barnett couldn't resist telling everybody what he thought. "After the war, lots of people, white and colored, moved west looking for a better life, but I don't have to tell you which group life got better for. Even though the land was supposed to be available to whoever claimed it, Old Luke Dayton set up the Knox Plains Land Allocation Council that his family's been running ever since, to make sure that coloreds and Indians and even poor whites stayed on the side of town where the bad farmland is." All of this was true, but his saying it in class annoyed Mrs. Davenport and knocked Barnett's grade on the paper down to a C.

Ma always said that nobody gets an education in school. School, she said, teaches you how to get an education. People really educate themselves by reading and by doing. Ma often told us she preferred Pa to those college boys she met in Nashville because even with his ninth-grade education, he was smarter and more knowledgeable than anyone she knew. Pa read everything he could get his hands on and often amazed far more educated people with his storehouse of information. "Brains are where you find them," Ma liked to say, "and your pa had brains. There are plenty of educated fools out there."

She insisted that Barnett and I read when we were small. By the time we were in about fourth grade, she no longer had to insist. We had more books, magazines, and newspapers than anybody I knew. We subscribed to the Dallas paper, which arrived by train the day after it came out. Barnett and I would also go down to the train station and pick up magazines and newspapers that riders from other cities had left behind. We found papers from Chicago, Kansas City, St. Louis, and other distant and exciting places. We learned about things we'd have never have heard of around Knox Plains.

As one of the few college-educated people in town, Ma set a high standard for Barnett and me. She insisted that our math skills be sharp and that we use correct grammar, no matter what we heard around us. With our friends, Barnett would slip in an occasional lapse in grammar just to be one of the boys. I never dared. I was downtown with Ma once when I was about six. We saw a group of men putting up telephone poles along the main downtown street. I pointed and asked, "Who they is, and what they doing?" Ma lit into me as if I'd stolen something.

By the time I was ten years old, Barnett and I were just about running the store by ourselves while Ma did housework. We didn't stock much other than basic groceries and such household items as thread and soap, but we could special order almost anything you wanted, and most of the black people in Knox Plains would rather do that than put up with rudeness from the downtown clerks. At first I had to stand on a crate to reach the cash register, but Barnett and I were both sharp at arithmetic and made all-around first-rate store managers. Barnett loved running things except when his least favorite customer stopped by.

Whenever Miss Violet Nesbet would come into the store, Barnett would hide in the back and let me handle her. Miss Nesbet was a tiny woman about my color who wore her long graying hair pulled back in an unflattering ball just at her neck. She wasn't really that difficult to deal with, but she and Barnett didn't get along because they had such different personalities. He saw the humor in almost anything. She saw humor in nothing. It also got on Barnett's nerves that Miss Nesbet watched him like a hawk did a chicken when he had to measure a purchase for her. In fact, when she narrowed her light-brown eyes into slits and pointed her sharp little chin to watch the needle on the scale, she looked a lot like a chicken hawk. We sold prepackaged sacks of flour, sugar, corn meal, and the like in standard sizes—ten pounds, twenty pounds, fifty pounds—but if a customer wanted an odd amount, we measured it out ourselves from hundred-pound drums.

"That old biddy acts like we're going to cheat her if she doesn't stand right over us," Barnett complained. "We never cheated anybody in our lives. If anything, we give folks a little more than full measure. She's the only one I won't do that for. It makes me so mad when she stands over me with that sour look while I'm measuring that if she orders eight pounds of meal, she gets eight pounds and not a grain more."

Another thing that made serving Miss Violet a chore was that she kept two separate accounts, one for family food and the other for company food. She even kept two stashes of staples in separate cabinets at home. "Don't we need sugar?" she asked her brother, Mr. Seck Nesbet, one morning in the store.

"We got twelve pounds of sugar last time," Mr. Seck declared crankily. "You need to pay attention to what you're doing, Violet, and quit wasting money."

"That was company sugar," she snapped. "Roosevelt, add fifteen pounds of sugar to the order, and be sure you put it on the family account. Don't you cheat me, boy, I'm watching you."

If the Nesbets were expecting guests, Miss Violet would take out the company flour and sugar and bake a cake. If the cake was for family, it would be made using supplies from the main cabinet. The only reason I could think of for this peculiar system was that it allowed the tight-fisted Nesbets to know to the penny how much they spent on guests. One January first, following Emancipation Day service at church, I heard Miss Violet tell everybody she greeted, "Last year we spent eight dollars and fifty-three cents entertaining company."

Miss Violet was a spinster who lived with her sister, Miss Ella, also a spinster, and their brother, Mr. Seck. Mr. Seck was the survivor of twins named Timothy and Second Timothy—shortened by their pa to Tim and Seck. Mr. Tim died of influenza in 1918, just days after his wife.

Mr. Tim didn't marry until he was nearly forty-seven years old. He'd been keeping company for sixteen years with Miss Alberta French, a schoolteacher who was then approaching her thirty-sixth birthday. People say she'd decided the relationship was never going anywhere and it was time to cut her losses, when one summer night in 1908 on Miss French's front porch Mr. Tim suddenly came across with a left-handed marriage proposal. "There was a time," Mr. Tim reportedly said in his usual monotone, "when I would have said I was having too good a time to get married, but I don't know as I can say that now."

That was good enough for Miss Alberta. She and Mr. Tim married quietly in Reverend Esau Brown's study with only Miss Ella, Miss Violet, Mr. Seck, and Miss French's mother as guests. Mr. Tim brought his bride to live with him and his unmarried siblings even though both Nesbet brothers had good jobs with the railroad, and Mr. Tim probably could have afforded a separate house.

Ten years later, the couple were among the victims of a worldwide influenza epidemic. Mr. Tim and Mr. Seck had owned the house and the surrounding acreage jointly. Mr. Tim left his share of the property to his twin on the assumption that he would do what the Nesbet men had always done and look after the females. These included not only the sisters but Rosetta, Mr. Tim and Miss Alberta's plump six-year-old daughter, who Miss Violet and Miss Ella then raised in their own awkward way.

Rosetta had few enough natural charms, but Miss Violet and Miss Ella compounded the problem by clothing their niece in ill-fitting homemade dresses in the ugliest styles and colors imaginable. Rosetta wore glasses but never had a pair that actually fit. They were always askew in spite of her constant efforts to set them right. The two spinster sisters, who both had hair like a curly-headed white person's, didn't have the first notion what to do with Rosetta's kinky locks and tried unsuccessfully to style their niece's hair with dozens of randomly placed hairpins. There were always stray bits of hair sticking out. The overall effect made Rosetta look like she'd just gotten back on her feet after a clumsy fall. To make matters worse, at the first sign of winter, Miss Violet and Miss Ella made a garlic poultice that poor Rosetta had to wear around her neck until spring to ward off sickness.

Miss Ella could be pleasant and kind, even generous, when her sister and brother weren't around to criticize her. If she came to the store alone, she passed out pennies to the children playing out front so they could buy candy. One penny would buy ten jawbreakers, twenty pieces of taffy, or five Hershey's chocolate silver tips. It would for sure buy a grateful smile from the child she gave it to.

I never saw any such amiable side to Miss Violet. I used to swear that woman started every day by drinking a tall glass of lemon juice. The one place her sour nature worked to her advantage was at Ham Smilings. Once in a while the Dorcas Ladies' Handicraft Circle at church would raise a little extra money by selling tickets to an event called a Ham Smiling. At the appointed day and hour the people who bought tickets would sit in a circle around a ham. The idea was to keep staring at that piece of meat with a completely somber face as long as you could. If you laughed, or even smiled, you lost and had to leave the circle. The last person left staring at the ham got to take it home. The contest usually didn't go on for long because any regular person would feel durn silly sitting there staring at a ham. All of a sudden somebody would break out laughing, and two or three others would be right behind. Miss Violet Nesbet almost always went home with the ham.

Ham Smiling was Miss Nesbet's sport, and she could talk as excitedly about the successful capture of a ham as a baseball player reveling in his game-winning home run. "So the man in charge said, 'The ham goes to the little bright lady,' " she'd boast. "There was another bright lady there, but she wasn't quite as bright as me."

In a far corner of the store, we had a desk where Barnett and I did the paperwork. Actually, I did most of it. Barnett could process orders, keep the books, and do inventory as well as I could, but he found it all boring and would put these administrative tasks off until I did them myself. Although the store really belonged to Ma, she almost never looked at the books or the wholesale orders. We'd just tell her when we were having an especially good month or an especially bad one. Then one day she came to the store to get some laundry soap while I was working at the desk.

"What are you doing, Roosevelt?" she asked, walking over to the desk.

"I'm just sending some orders to the wholesalers."

"Let me take a look."

Drat! She never paid attention to things like that. How on earth did she know to look the one time I was trying to slip something past her? I swear parents have the second sight about what their children are up to. Still, I handed her the pile of orders nonchalantly, hoping she wouldn't notice a small irregularity.

She shuffled through the pile, then suddenly stopped. I knew just which order had caught her eye. "Why are you ordering things like sodium sulfate and sodium hydroxide?" Ma wanted to know. I was right. It was the pharmacy order.

"You can use them to make magnesium hydroxide—that's milk of magnesia—and magnesium sulfate, which is Epsom salts."

"You don't have to mix those things yourself, Roosevelt," she explained gently. "We order them already prepared."

I answered in a voice so low she barely heard me. "I've been reading this book that tells you how to make common household medicines. I just wanted to see if I could do it. I wasn't planning to sell the stuff to anybody." I added my final argument. "It's not much money."

"Don't say 'stuff,' unless you mean material inside a pillow. Is this for a school assignment?"

"No," I answered, my voice still small. "I just wanted to try it."

"I ought to punish you for trying to sneak something past me like that. That's no different from lying, you know."

"Yes, ma'am," I responded, trying to sound as humble and contrite as possible.

"I'll let it go this time, but the next time I'm paying for one of your little adventures, I'd like to know about it, you understand?"

"Yes, ma'am."

In fifth grade, I got my first real introduction to science, and I knew from that moment what I wanted to do with my life. Chemistry especially fascinated me. I loved the periodic table. I loved learning the elements and the special properties each had. I loved the way the whole universe could be worked out in mathematical perfection. It baffled me that some of my classmates dreaded science and learned just enough to get a passing grade. To me, chemistry was more fun than shooting marbles, watching trains come in, or even swimming buck naked in the pond on Mr. Power's farm. Before long, I had pulled ahead of my class-mates and was getting special lessons from Mr. Daniel, who was actu-ally the high-school science teacher.

It was Mr. Daniel who first showed me a copy of a monthly maga-zine called U.S. Science. It instantly became my favorite publication and I nagged Ma night and day until she agreed to buy a subscription for me. The other boys I knew who liked to read bought detective magazines and adventure stories. I liked those, too, but U.S. Science was far and away my first choice. Each issue was filled with articles about the latest discoveries in all branches of science and how these discoveries were being applied in the world around us. When I found something really exciting, I'd talk my teacher into letting me give a report on it at school.

"You're just trying to make the rest of us look bad," Barnett griped. "No wonder nobody likes you." It didn't matter what he or anybody else said. I loved science like a drunkard loves whiskey. I couldn't stay away from it if I tried. I spent any spare money I had on science books and laboratory equipment. Mr. Daniel helped me build a small lab in the enclosed back porch where Ma hung laundry on rainy days.

Uncle Will often gave me money to spend on science equipment, but he wasn't just interested in furthering my education. The whole time he had lived with us he'd been going under the house to mix tonics and potions that he sold to his "patients," who called him "Dr. Will." He saw it as a great stroke of luck that just as he was starting to feel too old and stiff to crawl around down there, I built my lab.

He started using my equipment plus some of his own to make his "medicines." Most were commonly available compounds to which he added scents and colorings, then rebottled, attached his personal la-bels, and sold at inflated prices. Also behind the house was a distillery, allegedly part of my science laboratory, that Uncle Will used to make grain alcohol that he flavored, colored, and sold as medicine. No one but Uncle Will and I could tell his illegal medicine factory from my legitimate lab equipment. "Oh, that's just some of Daylight's things," Uncle Will would tell any visitor who asked about the still. "That boy do love his science."

Uncle Will not only looked African, he lived by a lot of the old ways and knew all about ancient African folk doctoring, practices known in this country as witch doctoring and voodoo. He was so full of super-stitious beliefs that even after living with him all those years, the rest of the family had a hard time remembering them all. When I was little, Ma once got upset with me because I was playing in the mud in the clean clothes she had just put on me. "Theodore Roosevelt Bullmoose O'Malley!" she screamed. That made Uncle Will bolt upright with alarm. "Lil, don't you say that boy's full name at one time," he warned. "Haints'll hear you. They kin work all kindsa wickedness on you jes' for the fun of it when they knows yo' whole name. I recollect what happened to ole Clay Dorsey. His wife got put out with him over sump'um 'nother, and she hollered out 'Clayton Forrest Dorsey!' Well, them haints heared her clear as day. They put a pain in his right leg so bad that ever' time he stood up after that, he got a swimmin' in the head. He was lack that 'til the day he died."

There were people around Knox Plains who believed that Uncle Will had the power to do anything. I remember one young woman who walked miles from somewhere out in the country to get Uncle Will to help rid her of some spook she believed was after her. "She ridin' me, Dr. Will, she ridin' me ever' night," the woman cried.

"That so?" Uncle Will said in a voice as soft and quiet as a spring breeze. "Well let's see what the chickydee-whick say you got to do to keep that ole night witch from ridin' you." He pulled himself up on his cane and hobbled across the room, his peg leg dragging slightly. From a shelf he took a large jar of roots in a liquid and shook it vigorously. For a full minute he watched the roots as they settled into their new positions. Finally, still studying the roots, he asked, "Which away is yo' bed facin' now?"

"It's facin' east, Dr. Will."

"Well, there's yo' problem rat there. The chickydee-whick say you got to stay away from that house for three full days, then when you do go back, turn yo' bed so that it'll face south, don't let it face east no mo', you understan'?"

"And the night witch won't bother me no mo'?"

"Not in that house. That'll be fifty cent."

Ma was an educated woman and a Christian and didn't believe in spells and voodoo and all that. She was determined to make Barnett and me Christians, too, taking us to Galilee Baptist Church every Sunday and sometimes during the week. But she never said anything against Uncle Will and his conjuring. I think even after all those years, she still thought of him as a guest in her house, and she was raised not to offend a guest no matter what. Besides, the small change Uncle Will brought in working roots and spells and selling his assorted potions and tonics meant he had his own money and didn't have to ask her for any.

About the only thing Ma took on at Uncle Will about was bathing. She thought people should bath regularly, especially in the summer.

"Now, Uncle Will," she'd say, "I drew you a bath. Come on in here and take it while the water's nice and hot."

"Aw, Jew Baby," he'd answer, "I don't need no bath. Look like I just had one."

"That was day before yesterday, Uncle Will. You need to take a bath every day."

"Jew Baby," he declared. "I wouldn't take a bath every day if the Sabine River flowed hot and soapy."

Ma had finally given up telling Uncle Will not to call her "Jew Baby." Most of the time he called her Lil, but sometimes he called her "Jew Baby," because he said she looked like a Jew. I had no idea whether he was right. To me, Jews were those people in the Bible, and from the illustrations between the Old and New Testaments in Ma's big leather-bound edition, they looked just like regular white people. My mother, a medium-brown woman with delicate features, would hardly be mistaken for one of them. Ma's actual first name was Lillyun. I always suspected that Grandma and Grandpa Patterson had heard the name Lillian and liked it well enough to give it to their youngest daughter, but had never seen the name written, so they took their best guess as to the spelling.

After Uncle Will had had his bath and changed into the clean clothes Ma put out, he'd sit on the front porch, smoking his pipe, relighting it from time to time by striking matches on his wooden leg. He'd brag to everybody who passed by, "I feel lack the angels in heaven. I jes' had me a good bath."

Uncle Will was the closest thing to a grandfather I had. I never met Grandpa Patterson or Grandpa O'Malley, and I really didn't know much about either of them. Pa did tell me one time that Grandpa O'Malley loved black people because everybody gave them a hard time, just like the British had been giving the Irish a hard time for centuries. He told me that back in the seventeenth century an Englishman named Oliver Cromwell hated Irish people so much that he drove them out of the parts of Ireland with good farmland and made them live on the rocky west coast in County Galway. Cromwell liked to say, "There are just two fit places for the Irish—Galway and hell." The only foods that would grow in Galway were cabbages and potatoes. When the potato crop failed in the 1840s, more than a million Irish people, including Grandpa O'Malley, who was a small boy at the time, left for the United States and other countries. Another million starved in Ireland. I sometimes wondered if the Daytons here in Knox Plains were maybe some kin to Oliver Cromwell. I could just imagine old Luke Dayton saying, "There're just two fit places for darkies, Indians, and white trash—the south side and hell."

Ma didn't say much about Grandpa O'Malley except that she didn't approve of the fact that he had made his living importing Irish whiskey. As for the money Grandpa O'Malley gave her and Pa, Ma always said, "The Lord sent it even if the devil brought it."

During one of those long Texas sunsets when the sun seems to sit bright red for hours against the horizon, Uncle Will was in his favorite spot on the front porch and Barnett and I had just finished helping Ma with the supper dishes. I looked out the front door and saw Nate Jackson coming up the steps. "Will Lindsay!" he shouted in greeting.

"Aye-God, don't call all of my name at one time," Uncle Will answered grumpily.

Like most of our friends, Nate Jackson was land rich and cash poor. Mr. Nate had a huge spread, but he couldn't get enough cotton out of it to pay his bills or raise enough vegetables to feed even his own family. He and his boys had to piece out a living doing farm chores for Willis Dayton over in north Knox Plains. Mr. Nate's wife, Minnie, had kept up the Dayton house and two others on the north side, spending two days each week on each of the houses, with only Sundays off, until she died of TB when her two boys were still small.

Mr. Nate was fighting his own personal war with his land. He and his two boys were out in the fields, hacking away at the unyielding soil just about every day from sunup to sundown. Mostly, all Mr. Nate was growing was old.

Every now and then he'd come into the store, waving a copy of *The Farmer's Monthly*. He'd point to a fertilizer advertisement that promised to improve the yield of even the poorest land. "Order me some of this here," he'd say. "This sound lack jes' what I need." But no fertilizer or farming technique could coax more than a few scrawny plants out of the stubborn soil. Mr. Nate's eighteen- and nineteen-year-old sons, Wright and Matthew, had long since been ready to raise the white flag of surrender, abandon that land, and move on to someplace where the earth was friendlier, but they had nowhere to go and nothing to start over with.

" 'Put your money in lan',' my daddy used to tell me," said Mr. Nate, starting a familiar refrain. " 'You'll never go broke. You can farm it, you can build on it, and if you need to, you can always sell it for more than you paid for it.' I wish I had his ghos' back here so I could tell him what a liar he were. I wants to tell him what a po' piece of lan'll do to you, how it rob you ever' day you live. How it laugh at you whilst you works yo'self to a skeleton tryin' to get a livin' out of it."

"Them ole Caddos done put a cuss on this here lan'," Uncle Will explained. "I been tryin' to get it off for years, but the ghos' of them

Caddos is still mad 'cause dem white folks done run 'em off they lan', and they cussed it so's nothin'll grow here."

"You thank you could tell them ole Injun haints that I ain't white and that I ain't run nobody off nothin'?" Mr. Nate suggested. "If they gots to be cussin' somebody's lan', they needs to be cussin' lan' belong to that ole soda cracker Willis Dayton."

"Now a cuss is a powerful thang, Nate," Uncle Will said. "Sometime it take mo' than a notion to git rid of one. But the chickydee-whick say it'll be gone one of these here days, and when the cuss is gone, good times is sho' to follow."

CHAPTER THREE

The farm next to Nate Jackson's belonged to Mr. and Mrs. Benny Gibley, who had four daughters living with them in their ramshackle tin-roof house. The oldest, Glenda, was in the class with Barnett and me, and the others stairstepped down to eight-year-old Brenda. Belinda was my age, but a year behind me in school, and the remaining sister, Linda, was just ten months older than Brenda. Linda and Brenda were both born in 1916, Linda in January and Brenda in November. Pa used to say that made them "Irish twins."

The Gibley girls did their best to help around the farm, but Mr. Benny didn't want them to do harsh farm work. More than anything on earth, Mr. Benny wanted his daughters to be ladies. Mr. Benny himself was never formally educated beyond third grade, and his wife, Pearl, never got beyond sixth grade, but you would never know it if you just saw them walking down the street, especially when they were dressed for church. Mr. Benny had the manner and bearing of a Negro bank president, and Miss Pearl stood as proudly as any king's wife. Although his grammar and enunciation were flawed, Mr. Benny spoke carefully and formally in an obvious effort to overcome the speech patterns he had learned in his youth.

I heard him complain to Uncle Will again and again, "Look like I works all the time and cain't never git a nickel ahead. Me and Pearl, we talks all the time 'bout how we want to git the bes' for our girls, want 'em to have nice thangs and go to college and like that. But ever' time I git a few dollars, seem lack somebody in the house gots to go to the doctor, or somethin' break down and I got to git another one or some such, and there go that little money. Will, ain't you got no roots or yarbs or nothin'll brang a hard-workin' man some money?"

Uncle Will would grip his pipe in his teeth and shake his head.

"If'n I had me somethin' lack that, I'd be livin' in the lap a' lux'ry m'self, Benny. When it come to money, that ole chickydee-whick she let me down ever' time. She don't mine most of the time tellin' me what's done been and what's gonna be, but she sho' don't have no power to change what's got to be. Now she keepa tellin' me better times is comin', and I jes' keep askin' her 'When?' "

I remember once when I was about eight there was a knock at the front door one Sunday afternoon. It was Mr. Benny, still dressed in his church clothes. He softly and politely asked to speak with Ma. Puzzled, Ma came to the door and asked, "Yes, Mr. Gibley, what can I do for you?"

"Ma'am," he said, "I needs some he'p with my girls. I 'spec' you knows my wife Pearl do a fine job with they hair and keepin' up they clothes and all lack that, but there's something else they needs. I'll be glad to pay you, you jes' tell me what you'd charge. I know you been to college, ma'am, and I really needs the girls to learn 'bout poetry and good music and how to read—not jes' reg'lar readin' like folks 'round here does, but them high-tone books with the long words like you reads."

Ma was taken by surprise, but she quickly answered, "Yes, of course, Mr. Gibley. I'd be happy to do that. You don't need to pay me. It would be my privilege to work with your daughters."

Even though Mr. Benny was clearly relieved that Ma refused to accept a fee for teaching his daughters, every Sunday afternoon when he brought Glenda, Belinda, Linda, and Brenda by for their culture lessons, he also brought some small gift—an armload of firewood, a bunch of collards, a bucket of eggs, or some of Miss Pearl's homemade fig preserves.

The Gibley sisters were tall, slender, and dark, traits they had gotten from both parents. All four girls had the best features of each parent—Mrs. Pearl Gibley's long artistic fingers and flawless skin and Mr. Benny's excellent bone structure, which was most obvious in their strong chins, high cheekbones, and chiseled noses. They were very handsome young women. They were also polite and pleasant, which added to their charm. The refinement that Pearl Gibley had worked so hard to give them had clearly taken root.

The job that Ma had taken on as a kindness to a hardworking couple determined to create a better life for their daughters soon became a joy for her. She was thrilled that the Gibley sisters actually liked poetry and would borrow her books and learn poems on their own. Only about a month after they started coming to her for lessons, Ma was so pleased with how beautifully Glenda recited Longfellow's "A Psalm of Life," that she had her recite it for her father when he came to walk his daughters home. Mr. Benny was near tears he was so proud. "You are an answered prayer, Miz O'Malley," he said, "an answered prayer."

In time, the Gibley girls became like sisters to Barnett and me. We gave them free treats from the store once in a while, helped them with homework, and defended them whenever older boys teased them.

One afternoon after school I was sitting on the front steps with Glenda. Our conversation stopped in midsentence when we heard an airplane overhead. We looked up as the curious object crossed the bright blue sky on its way, no doubt, to the new airfield near Dallas. It had become a tiny speck and finally disappeared completely before I spoke again. "When Pa was little, who would have guessed that man would build a machine that could let him fly through the air like a bird? It's things like that that make science so wonderful—working out ways to make things that were impossible possible and even commonplace. There are so many things in God's great and wonderful universe that we don't even have a clue about yet."

"There are people," Glenda commented, "who say that man is not supposed to know everything, that the universe is God's business and He's going to punish us for meddling in it."

"Oh, what nonsense!" I shrieked. "Those people would have us all living in caves and wearing animal hides, probably without even a fire to keep us warm. God gave us amazing minds, and as long as we use them for good and not evil, He surely approves."

She nodded. "I like learning new things, too. Until your ma started letting my sisters and me come over, I was never around books much, except schoolbooks and the Bible at home. There's a lot of good stuff, I mean information, in books." Ma had also taught the Gibley girls that "stuff" is slang, unless you mean material to fill a pillow, and slang is a lazy person's way of expressing himself.

Before the Gibley sisters, no one took much interest in our extensive collection of books except Ma and me, and Barnett when he was in the mood. We had all the classics—*Ivanhoe*, the *Canterbury Tales*, the works of Milton and Shakespeare, and loads of nineteenth-century writers such as Mark Twain and Charles Dickens. Some of the books were from Ma's college days, or volumes she had ordered or that friends had sent her as gifts. The rest of our informal library was made up of books that had belonged to my paternal grandmother. After her death, Grandpa O'Malley packed them up and shipped them to us with a note that simply said, "These belonged to Ida Mae. I thought you might like to have them."

There were books of essays and poetry and fiction that ranged from classics to detective novels. To me, among the most interesting books in my grandmother's collection were her etiquette books. I understood Mr. Benny and Miss Pearl's desire to prepare their daughters to move easily in high society. That was what I wanted for myself—to be able to go anywhere and meet anybody without giving away that I was just a country boy from Nowhere, Texas. Grandma's etiquette books called for behaviors that I had never actually seen anyone exhibit, not even my college-educated ma, but I was certain that one day I would be around people who did. For example, one of the etiquette books said that when you meet a woman or girl that you know, you should always let her speak first so that she can ignore you if she chooses to. But none of the females around Knox Plains seemed to know this rule and thought you were rude if you didn't speak. So around home I just did what people seemed to expect.

There were science books, too. Some were laughably out of date, but others had information that kept me absorbed for hours on end. For some reason there was a book on famous chemists and their work. I couldn't imagine why my grandmother, a woman with no education beyond the sixth grade, would have owned such a book, but it became my treasure. Inside, there were drawings of some of these men. Some showed just their faces, others showed them in white laboratory coats with tubes and beakers and all manner of fascinating equipment. The book, titled simply *The Great Chemists*, stirred an excitement in me like nothing I had ever felt before.

One evening I said to Barnett, "I've decided what I want to do with my life. I want to be a research chemist. Look at this book. I've been reading about these men and what all they discovered. That's what I want to do, discover things in the laboratory, things like new medicines that will make life better for everybody."

He looked at me as though I had told him I wanted to fly to Mars. "Moose," he said patiently, "maybe you didn't notice, but all of the men in that book are white."

"So what?" I asked.

"So even if somehow you got the education you need, you'd need to get a job in a laboratory somewhere, and if you showed your little biscuit-brown face to apply for a job like that, they'd either throw you out or hand you a broom and tell you you could sweep their floors."

I was a little angry at Barnett for poking holes in my dream, but he had a point. I tried to think what a black man could do with a chemistry degree. The two most prosperous black men in town both had jobs that involved the sciences. I sure wanted to make enough money to live well, but more than that I wanted to work at a job I liked so much that going to work would be a pleasure. To me, life was just too short to get up every morning and spend ten or twelve hours doing something you dreaded. I already knew too many men who did just that.

The two men whose jobs included chemistry were Dr. James Billups, our family doctor, and Mr. Cornelius Creasy, the undertaker. One day when I was walking past Cornelius's Mortuary, I saw Mr. Creasy outside, tending to the flowers that lined the walkway. After we exchanged greetings, I asked. "Mr. Creasy, how did you get into this business?"

"Well, Roosevelt," he answered, "a man's got to make a living at something, and I discovered a colored man could make a pretty good living looking after the deceased. Generally, white undertakers won't touch a deceased colored person. In fact, most people don't care for this work, but I don't mind it. I got used to being around people who had passed on when I was young. I had to find work when I was just fourteen, and Mr. Washburn, the local colored undertaker, was the only one who'd hire me. You see, I wasn't big and strong like a lot of the boys."

I could sure sympathize with that problem. Unless I had a growing spurt soon, I wasn't going to be strong enough for most of the jobs available to men my color.

"At first, I just cleaned up around the place, did odd jobs, and bathed folks before Mr. Washburn went to work on them. Back then, we seldom brought folks to the mortuary for embalming. Usually we did it right at their house, then laid the person out in the parlor for viewing. I still do that today when somebody out in the country passes away. Most beds even now are made so they can be turned into cooling boards. That was one of my jobs back when I worked for Mr. Washburn."

I recalled that one of the old deacons at Galilee Baptist Church always said, "And before my bed becomes my cooling board, let me make my final peace with thee, O Lord" as part of his standard prayer.

"I learned most of what I know from Mr. Washburn—not just about caring for the deceased, but how to run a business and lots of other things. He taught me arithmetic and how to speak proper English. I needed both of those to run a successful funeral business. He also let me borrow an old beat-up copy of *Gray's Anatomy* and a book on mortuary science that told all about preparing embalming chemicals," Mr. Creasy continued. "I passed the state examination easily, and I took over the business after Mr. Washburn passed on himself. Matter of fact, I embalmed him."

Delighted that a bright young man had taken an interest in his business, Mr. Creasy invited me on a tour of the mortuary. He showed me a small chapel with gleaming oak seats, a rich muted floral carpet and heavy blue drapes. There were two offices. Mr. Creasy's was neat and smartly appointed like the chapel. Behind Mr. Creasy's desk was a painting of Jesus ascending to heaven with bright angels waiting to receive him. The other office was obviously used for records and accounting. It had file cabinets, an adding machine, and trays of papers.

Then there was the embalming room. In sharp contrast to the building's other tastefully decorated rooms, the embalming room was stark and industrial. The other rooms had the graceful air of an elegant Southern home. Only the embalming room was filled with the ambience of death. The smell of chemicals nearly knocked me over. As I looked around, I was startled by the sight of the only body waiting to be prepared for burial. In the half-darkened room, at first I didn't see the body of a small child, dark, plump, and naked except for a sheet across his middle, on a slab in the corner. He couldn't have been more than two years old. Before I could comment on the small corpse, Mr. Creasy said, "A family from out in the country brought him in on the back of a wagon. We're holding him here until his casket comes. We keep some standard-sized caskets in the back, but we have to special-order them for children. His is due today."

As we continued the tour, the truck delivering the special-order casket arrived. Mr. Creasy asked me to wait in the business office while he signed for the delivery.

Alone in the room, I noticed a shelf behind the desk and below eye level. On it was a hand-painted wooden sign that read, "Whereas ye know not what shall be on the morrow. For what is your life? It is even a vapor, that appeareth for a little time and then vanisheth away. —James 4:14." Below the sign there was a set of ornate little boxes made of gleaming wood. They looked like miniature coffins, lined up as if for a Lilliputian mass funeral. My childish curiosity was stirred, so I lifted one and opened it. Inside I found a twenty-five-cent piece resting on a satin lining. A note inside the box said, "This is a twenty-five-cent piece that Belle Winkfield, a little child, strangled on." I looked inside another box and found a bullet and a note that read, "This bullet was taken out of Dan Madison, a man killed in a hunting accident."

I had just returned the second box to its place when I heard footsteps approach the office. I looked up and saw a woman that I recognized as Mrs. Ruby Nell Creasy. Although I saw her at morning worship every Sunday, I doubt that I had spoken three words to her in my life. She was so aloof that it would be easy to believe she was very rude. I suspected, however, that she was just extremely shy. I said, "Hello."

Without ever making eye contact, she responded coldly, "Please excuse me." She sat behind the desk and started to go over some papers. I walked quickly out of the office, found Mr. Creasy, and thanked him for showing me around. I hadn't decided what my future career would be, but I was certain it wouldn't be in the mortuary business.

Ma wanted me to be a doctor even though she knew we didn't have anywhere near enough money to pay for medical school. In my heart I was certain that wouldn't be a problem when the time came. I had a distinct memory of my pa telling me that he had put aside money for my education. Maybe there was enough for college and medical school, or maybe the money would come from somewhere else. I was always reading books about how God took care of the needs of good people. I had absolute faith He'd take care of my education, too.

PART TWO

EVIDENCE OF THINGS NOT SEEN

If there was anybody who complained more bitterly about the bad farm-land and general poverty in Knox Plains than Nate Jackson and Benny Gibley, it was Amos Wilson, Wesley Wilson's father. He, too, had plowed, hoed, and fertilized himself into perpetual frustration. Wesley was my best friend next to Barnett, so I spent enough time at the Wilsons' house to know how hard they were struggling. Mr. Wilson was working to provide not only for his two sons and his wife, Cora, but also for his wife's mother and two of Miss Cora's sisters.

Some Sundays Wesley would come home with Barnett and me after church and have dinner with our family, and other Sundays Wesley invited the two of us to eat dinner at his house. At the Wilsons', the adults and Wesley's older brother, Louis, ate in the dining room, but a children's table was set up in a little room off the kitchen for Wesley, Barnett, and me. Cora Wilson brought us our plates, which always held the same meal: vegetables, cornbread, and chicken gravy over rice.

One Sunday as we were walking home from the Wilsons', I said to Barnett, "Miss Cora's a pretty good cook, and I like the food she gives us, but I wish we could have some chicken. I don't understand why there's always gravy, but there's never any chicken. If she's serving us chicken gravy, there's got to be some chicken in that house someplace."

"You know," Barnett mused, "Miss Cora's gravy makes me think about what Paul said in the Bible about faith: it's 'the essence of things hoped for and the evidence of things not seen.'"

The whole Wilson family would have packed up and left years ago if not for Mrs. Wilson's mother, Sadie Brown, who wasn't well enough to travel. Miss Sadie was eighty-three. She had been born a slave in the independent republic of Texas and had outlived five husbands, the fourth of whom was Wesley's grandfather. Miss Eddie Mae, Miss Cora's half sister, was well into her sixties and took on most of the responsibility for Miss Sadie's care. Miss Thelma, who was younger than Miss Eddie Mae but older than Miss Cora, took in laundry to supplement the family income.

Once in a while, I'd go to the Wilsons' house just to visit Miss Sadie. I'd read to her and she'd tell me stories about what she called "the olden days" in Texas, right after the Civil War. What made Texas a better place for a black person than most of the South, she used to tell me, was that not all whites in Texas believed they were naturally superior to other races. A lot of them came from the cowboy tradition, where everyone starts out equal in life, then proves their worth as they go along. As long as you worked hard and upheld the law, those folks would be fair to you, whatever color you were.

Even in the 1920s, I found a lot of truth in what she said. Texas was like two different states. Texas the Western state was different from Texas the Southern state. Even though Texas had been officially part of the Confederacy, there was very little fighting there during the Civil War. Texas's main role had been to supply the rest of the South. Because Texas never saw the devastating loss of life and property that the other Southern states suffered, Texans were nowhere near as bitter after the war as Confederate supporters from the Deep South. Miss Sadie, who readily acknowledged that slavery at its best was a cruel and evil institution, believed that Texas slaveholders hadn't been as harsh as those in the Deep South. But soon after the Civil War, planters from Louisiana, Arkansas, and Mississippi, who were deeply embittered by the outcome of the war, dominated the area. "That were the start of a whole heap of trouble heah in Texas," she'd say. "That were the start."

When Ma had more housework than she could handle, she'd send some of our laundry to Miss Thelma so she could get caught up. One time when I was taking laundry to Miss Thelma, I thought it would be nice to stay and read some to Miss Sadie. At the front door I asked, "How's your mama, Miss Eddie Mae?"

"My ma's tired," she sighed.

"Ah stays tired," Miss Sadie muttered from a dark corner.

I walked over to the wizened ebony woman, who was huddled in a shawl even though the outside temperature was in the seventies. I lit the kerosene lamp on a nearby table. "I came to read a little to you from *The Baptist Index*," I said in a voice raised to accommodate Miss Sadie's hearing problem.

"That'd be fine," she answered with a hint of a smile.

After I'd been reading for a few minutes, Miss Eddie Mae came in and put a quilt over her mother's lap. "My ma's cold," Miss Eddie Mae explained.

"Ah stays cold," Miss Sadie said.

I was about to leave when Mr. Amos came home from work at the Dayton farm. "You droppin' off laundry, Roosevelt?" he asked.

"Yes, sir," I answered. "I was reading a little bit to Miss Sadie from *The Baptist Index* while I was here."

"You's a good boy to do that," Mr. Wilson said. Then he added in a distant voice, as though he were talking to the universe generally, not just to me, "I don't rightly see how Mama Sadie keep her faith in God when all she done seen been hard times, poverty, miserable work, an' losin' one husband after 'nother. How come God give so much to a mean ole coot like Willis Dayton and don't give nothin' to folks like me and Mama Sadie?" He waved the two dollars that a week's work at the Dayton farm had yielded him. "Sometime I think this here is the only god there is."

Miss Eddie Mae was adjusting the pillows around her mother. "My ma's in a strain," she said.

"Ah stays in a strain," Miss Sadie responded.

Amos Wilson's only small success at farming was in the chicken and egg business, though most people raised enough chickens themselves to supply their families with eggs and a fryer or two for Sunday dinner. We bought chickens and eggs from the Wilsons for our own use and sold a few of Mr. Amos's eggs in the store, but his best customer was Lula Pendergast.

Mrs. Pendergast was a widow who derived her income from the one asset her husband had left her, a huge house. She rented rooms to a few folks in town, black schoolteachers mostly, and to black strangers passing through. She fed her boarders in the dining room and set up tables in the sun parlor for people who came by just for a meal. Her makeshift restaurant did a brisk business, since it was about the only place between Shreveport, Louisiana, and Dallas that a black person could stop and get a real home-cooked, sit-down meal.

Her only help was Joe Ollie Harkwell, a wiry little coal-black man with effeminate mannerisms. Mr. Joe Ollie had an ageless face that hadn't changed in all the years I'd known him. He seemed to have no family and no personal history that anybody ever talked about. Some people said he was a sissy, but I never knew Mr. Joe Ollie to take a romantic interest in anyone, male or female. Mr. Joe Ollie lived at Mrs.

Pendergast's, where he helped cook, clean, and serve in exchange for a first-floor room too small to rent to a guest. Mr. Joe Ollie could beat any woman you ever saw cooking, cleaning, sewing, and ironing.

What little money Mr. Joe Ollie had he made doing housework twice a week for the Daytons, a job he had taken over after Minnie Jackson died. Laurel Branch Baptist Church, where the Daytons were members, also paid Mr. Joe Ollie a small sum to come in on Saturday mornings and clean the church building. And he picked up money here and there doing cooking, cleaning, and laundry for whoever needed his services. He didn't seem to care anything about money anyway. Mr. Joe Ollie's currency was gossip. If he could get some juicy news before anybody else, he'd rather have that than money. With his ties to Mrs. Pendergast's boardinghouse, the Daytons, Laurel Branch Baptist Church, and Galilee Baptist, where he was a member, Mr. Joe Ollie was perfectly positioned to be among the first to know anything going on in Knox Plains.

Sometimes Mrs. Pendergast had white customers, but they never ate at her house. They took food home and had Mr. Joe Ollie come get the empty dishes the next day. Mr. Junior Potts was one of her regulars. He bought food from her because he couldn't cook and his wife was sick a lot. Mrs. Pendergast felt sorry for Mr. Junior and would let him have a pot of butter beans and some cornbread for a dime if he had it, and for free if he didn't. She even kept his two little towheaded children there at the boardinghouse for him when Mr. Junior's wife was ailing. Mr. Joe Ollie fussed and fawned over the Potts children just as he did over all white people.

Mr. Junior Potts was one of those they called trash. That's what you got for being even poorer than black people. But Mr. Junior wasn't trashy at all. He just didn't have any money. I'll tell you about trash. When we were growing up, there were two white men who sat around in front of the post office all the time drinking whiskey, even early in the morning. One evening Ma had us all dressed up for a big revival meeting at church. A preacher from Dallas was in town, and I guess every black person in Knox Plains, even the ones who didn't go to church regularly, turned out to hear him. On the way to church we walked right past the two post-office drunks. I heard one of them say, "I'm going to 'at thar nigger meetin' afore I go to bed to-nyet."

"Whar?" the other one asked.

"To the nigger meetin'," the first one shouted back.

Sure enough, about halfway through the service, in came those two, stumbling and stinking up the place. Now that's my idea of trash.

Mr. Junior had a good heart, and he seemed to work all the time, but between his wife's being sick so much and the poor yield from that sorry piece of land he had, his family barely got enough to eat. He had a brother, Mr. Ike Potts, who had a good job in a factory in Dallas and would send Mr. Junior a little money from time to time. Then in the spring of 1924 there was an accident with one of the machines at the factory. Mr. Ike's right arm got torn up pretty badly. He recovered to the point where he could care for himself, but he couldn't do factory work anymore, so he came to Knox Plains to live with Mr. Junior and his family. Mr. Ike couldn't do farm work either because of his arm, so he said to Mr. Junior one day, "Didn't I see a lake down the road there? At least I could catch us some fish for supper."

Miss Lucille, Mr. Junior's wife, said, "Ike, you can't eat the fish out of that lake. There's some kinda grease floatin' aroun' in it that gits all on the fish and makes 'em not fittin' to eat."

The next morning, Mr. Ike went down to the lake to look for himself. When he got home, he told Mr. Junior, "You know what, Junior, that grease in the lake, well that's not grease, it's oil. Your ground's full of it, too. That's why nothin'll grow out there. But there's companies in Dallas that'll pay a lots-a money for that oil. Junior, I 'spec' you and some other folks around here is about to be rich."

CHAPTER FIVE

When Mr. Joe Ollie came by the store one day with a story that Junior Potts had sold his land for a lot of money and was moving his family to Dallas, Barnett and I didn't believe it. Nobody else believed it either, not until we saw strangers in town tearing down that old shack the Pottses called a house.

Then Mr. Joe Ollie came in wanting me to change a hundred-dollar bill for Mrs. Pendergast. "Ooo-wee, Mr. Joe Ollie," I said, "Where'd Miz Pendergast get this kind of money?" There wasn't enough in the cash register to break a hundred-dollar bill. I had to go to the safe.

"Don't tell nobody," he whispered in a just-between-us-girls voice, "but Junior Potts give it to her on his way outta town. He say he jes' didn't want her thinkin' he'd done forgot about all the times she he'ped him out when Miz Lucille was ailin'."

"Did he say where it came from?"

"He say he sol' his lan' for a lots-a money. He didn't say how much, but I figger if he's throwin' hundred-dollar bills aroun' now, where he used to sometimes not have a dime for a pot of butter beans, it was a heap. Either he done found a sho'-nuff fool or there's somethin' 'bout that old Potts place we don't know."

Well, the next thing any of us knew, there were white men from Dallas knocking on every door in town and asking, as polite as you please, if they could test the land for oil. It turned out that what little land Ma had didn't have any oil to speak of, but other folks were getting the most outlandish offers from oilmen who wanted to drill on their property. It seemed the poorer a family had been before, the richer their land turned out to be. By Thanksgiving of 1925, a lot of folks in Knox Plains had plenty to be thankful for.

Mr. Benny finally got what he considered to be the only blessing of his life, except for his loving wife, Pearl, and four smart, pretty daughters. He and Miss Pearl were quick to tear down the old house and build a big two-story Victorian-type with enough bedrooms so that each daughter could have her own. He asked Ma to order five or six new dresses and several pairs of shoes for each of his girls. "Git hats and whatever else go with it, Miz O'Malley," he instructed. "You knows what to do. Pick out plenty pretty thangs for 'em. I wants my girls dressed up prettier than them l'il white gals over 'cross town."

Even Miss Violet Nesbet was walking down the street grinning, although the oil strike on the Nesbet property was a modest one compared with the fortunes that had come into the hands of some of the Nesbets' neighbors, and the land actually belonged to Mr. Seck. In a rare generous mood, Mr. Seck allowed Miss Violet to give a Saturday afternoon party for Miss Ella's birthday. Miss Violet bought extra company groceries and baked three cakes and made vanilla ice cream and a big bowl of lemonade. She even came in and ordered a store-bought dress for Rosetta. It was the first birthday party Miss Ella ever had, and she spent most of the afternoon crying and saying how sweet it was of Miss Violet to do it and how sweet everybody was to come.

Nate Jackson got the biggest oil deal of all. I know his first check was for more than ten thousand dollars, because he got me to go to the bank with him. Mr. Nate had never before seen fifty dollars all at one time, and he had never had a bank account. Mr. Nate wasn't scared of much, but those bank men in their dark suits looked scarier than red-headed devils to him. That's why the first few times he went to the bank, he took me with him. He knew I went to the bank all the time to do business for the store. Unlike Junior Potts, Mr. Nate didn't settle for a lump sum and leave town. He just stayed and let the oilmen keep drilling, and the checks keep coming in.

As we walked home from the bank one day, Mr. Nate said, "This here is a funny ole world, Roos'velt. I kept a-tryin' to git them white folks to let me buy some decent farm lan', and they wouldn't do it. They set up that ole Knox Plains Land Ally-cation Council, they calls it, and all it were were jes' a polite way of makin' sho' no niggers or Injuns or po' whites got no farmin' land fit for nothin'. All they'd let me get was that ole lan' where wouldn't nothin' grow, and it turnt out to be worth mor'n all they lan' put together, and then some. Sometime in life the folks that sets out to do you wrong does you mo' good than all them that sets out to do right by you.

"It's kinda like wid slavery. Somewhere way back I guess some white slave traders grabbed my great-great grandpappy or some of 'em and threw him on a slave ship and made him go through all kindsa miseries. I'm sorry as I can be he had to go through all that, and I gots no kind words for them as put him through it. But 'cause they did, I gits to be a rich man in the U.S. of A. insteada livin' in some mud hut over in Africa."

Mr. Henry Ford used to say that you could have any color car you wanted, as long as it was black. Colored people changed all that. Some say a black prizefighter in New York had a baby-blue Cadillac and that's the first car that wasn't black, but that's not true. The first colored cars were twin pink LaSalles with all kinds of extras such as radios and sixteen-gallon gas tanks, ordered by the Jackson brothers right here in Knox Plains.

Before long, those two farm boys were all decked out in fancy clothes from Chicago, New York, and who knows where all. They built a big new house with running water and an indoor bathroom. They got the house hooked up to the power lines so they could have electric lights. All you had to do when you wanted light was flip a switch, just like God saying, "Let there be light."

The Jacksons got Mrs. Pendergast's place wired for electricity and hooked up to the power lines, too, but not just out of gratitude for past favors, though Mrs. Pendergast had been even nicer to the Jacksons than she'd been to Junior Potts. The Jackson boys wanted to eat like the millionaires they were, so they got Mrs. Pendergast a big freezer and had her stock it with big thick steaks, roasts, chops—everything they'd been missing in all those years of trying to cotton farm. They ate every meal at Mrs. Pendergast's and tossed her tips that were more than the price of the food.

Mrs. Pendergast, like a lot of black people who didn't have any oil on their land, was getting prosperous off those who did. She built a big addition onto her house, a huge new dining room and more guest rooms. On the side of the house, she added a wide covered porch that she called the verandah. She put up a fancy sign that she'd ordered from a company in Dallas. It read, "Madam Lula Pendergast's Boarding House and Restaurant." In smaller letters the sign said, "Enjoy Dining by Electric Light." Mr. Joe Ollie wasn't a penny richer, but anybody would have thought he had more money than Andrew Carnegie he was so happy. He had so much to gossip about he could hardly keep up anymore.

I couldn't believe how the money was rolling in to our little store. We started stocking things we never carried before, including Roi Tan cigars from Cuba and Madam C. J. Walker cosmetics from New York. We also got electric lights at the house and the store. We had a telephone put in and got a gasoline pump so we could sell gas for all those new cars suddenly appearing in town.

Our store had always been a gathering place for black people on Saturday afternoon, but now it seemed every Saturday afternoon gathering was a party. The newly rich came by to spend money, and others came by to watch. The highlight of the afternoon was when the Jackson brothers drove up in their twin pink cars.

One Saturday afternoon Wright Jackson pulled up to the gas pump, stepped out of the car, and pointed his bony black index finger at me. "Put in twenty gallons fo' me, boy," he demanded.

At ten cents a gallon, he was talking about two dollars' worth of gas. I never knew anybody to spend that much on gasoline at one time, but that wasn't the problem. "Wright, this car won't hold twenty gallons. Even that special tank you had put in won't hold but sixteen gallons from dead empty."

"Den put in sixteen gallons and spill the rest on the ground." He laughed, handed me a crisp five-dollar bill, and said, "Keep the change."

Just about every Saturday afternoon, the Jackson boys would stand outside the store and let Little Charlie Dunsen shine their shoes. Then they'd come inside and buy chocolate candies to pass out to the ladies in the crowd and factory-rolled cigars for the men.

Regular cigars were a nickel and Cuban cigars were a dime apiece, or three for a quarter. Wright Jackson bought regular cigars for the onlookers, but he always bought six Cuban cigars for himself. He liked to roll up a five-dollar bill slowly, put a match to it, then light his Cuban cigar from it. He'd toss the flaming bill on the floor, but we never had a fire. Little Charlie was right there to stomp out the flames and stick the bill in his pocket.

After a few weeks, Matthew Jackson got tired of performing for the crowd and went back to spending his Saturday afternoons with Dolly Miller, the same quiet girl he'd been walking to church every Sunday for years. He used to keep company with Dolly in her parents' parlor or on their front porch. After the Jackson family got money, Matt and Dolly would still visit on Saturday afternoons, but with cash in his pocket, Matt could take his young lady to supper at Mrs. Pendergast's or maybe to a moving-picture show.

Nate Jackson didn't care anything about showing off. He didn't even buy a car for himself at first. He just let one of the boys drive him wherever he needed to go. He got himself some new clothes and gave a big chunk of money to the church, but really he was just happy not to have to work like an old horse anymore.

Mr. Nate did enjoy eating supper at Mrs. Pendergast's, as much for the atmosphere as the food. Lula Pendergast was always smiling and telling funny stories and pampering her guests like they were all her babies. Some man would shout, "You look mighty pretty this evening, Miz Pendergast," and she'd answer sassily, "I know it." Everybody would laugh when she did that. Mr. Nate loved being part of the fun. Beyond that, he just got a kick out of watching Matt and Wright enjoy the money.

Wesley Wilson's family didn't do as well as the Jacksons, but they definitely got enough money to be "nigger rich." They had a new house built just down the road from the Jacksons and fixed up the old house for Miss Eddie Mae, Miss Thelma, and Miss Sadie. Wesley's mother, who used to slip quietly into her seat at church wearing that same old brown hat she'd had for as long as I could remember, started coming to church in a fabulous new dress with a matching hat every Sunday. She strutted in like Lady Asterbilt's plush horse, and her husband was right next to her, dressed to make a Philadelphia lawyer jealous. Louis became Wright Jackson's running buddy after Matt decided the fast life wasn't really for him. Louis bought a Pierce-Arrow with a rumble seat and some of the same custom touches the Jackson brothers had ordered. Louis had a radio and an oversized gasoline tank put in, too, but instead of ordering some eye-popping color, he had it painted a tasteful midnight blue. Every young girl on the south side of Knox Plains was begging for a ride. Pretty soon, though, there was just one young woman riding in that Pierce-Arrow.

I thought I knew just about every black person in Knox Plains. Then one afternoon Louis walked into the store with a young lady I'd never met. She was so fair that for a second I thought Louis had lost his mind and was walking arm-in-arm with a white girl.

"This here is Miss Lorraine Dupree," he said proudly. "We jes' had some pitchurs struck of I and she, a couple, about six, you know. Miss Dupree would care for a Co'cola this afternoon, and I do believe I'd care for one myself." That was not the way Louis usually talked. He was doing what black people called "talking proper." He tossed a quarter on the counter and said, "Keep the change, my good man." Coca-Colas were just a nickel apiece. He really wanted to impress this lady.

As I pulled two Coca-Colas out of the ice chest and uncapped them, Louis continued. "Miss Dupree is from New Orleans. She's in Knox Plains for the summer, since the doctors say the air here go' do her asthma a whole heap of good. She's staying at Miz Pendergast's boarding establishment." He added with a bashful grin, "Las' night she give me the go to keep comp'ny with her." The first question that hit me was, if the air in Knox Plains is good for asthma, why had Miss

Maggie Gray, who had lived here all her life, died from asthma? But I thought it would be bad manners to mention it. Maybe Miss Maggie had just had a really bad case.

A few days later, I thought I saw Miss Dupree at Mrs. Pendergast's, but it turned out to be another young lady with very light skin who was also boarding there. It wasn't another week before I swear I saw two or three more young women who looked like they could be Miss Dupree's sisters. After a while, I lost count of them. This was the dangedest thing I ever saw. Was there an epidemic of asthma among light-skinned Negro women? And what did Knox Plains have that was so special it could cure them?

Things got to the point where you had to wait on the verandah for a table at Mrs. Pendergast's, especially on Saturday evenings. Every young black boy in town was down there trying to meet those pretty high-yellow girls from Louisiana who were in town for their health. I couldn't help noticing that the boys who wound up with those girls on their arms weren't the handsomest, cleverest, or nicest boys in town. They were the ones whose families had hit it big in the oil strikes. In a way I could understand it. Young girls like having fun, and you can have a lot more fun with money than without it.

Barnett and I got to talking about those new girls one day at the store when we didn't have any customers. "What's supposed to be so special about light-skinned girls?" I asked. "I've seen plenty of really pretty girls who are brown or downright black."

Barnett agreed. "And there're some light-skinned girls I wouldn't go near if you paid me. You take Miss Violet Nesbet's niece, Rosetta."

"No thank you," I said. "You take her."

"She's got ratty hair and a shape like a two-hundred-pound sack of potatoes. She looks like a pig in the face. One time Miss Ella tried putting some face paint on Rosetta, and she looked just like a pig in lip rouge," Barnett recalled. "Now, that girl is just a whole lot of yellow wasted.

"I guess the reason colored boys get so worked up over light-skinned girls is that all their lives they've heard stories about how white men would kill you for looking at white women, let alone touching that alabaster skin. So they figure white flesh must be something really special. A light-skinned colored woman is about as close as they can come. If they touched a real white woman, they'd get lynched for sure. Isn't that right, Pa?" Barnett turned to Uncle Will, who had been smoking his pipe and listening quietly.

"In most cases, I'd say you was right, Midnight. I do recollect one time, though, that a white woman kissed me—kissed me rat in front of a hunnard or so other white folks and nobody did a thang about it. In fact, it saved my life."

"Uncle Will, you're joshing now," I said.

"Uncle Will don't josh," he stated solemnly. "Let me tell you 'bout it. It was back when I was workin' on the railroad. We took great stock in bringin' the trains in on time, boys, great stock. It was a powerful disgrace to an engineer if'n his train was late. I recollect one time—I b'lieve it was on the Wabash Cannonball—we'd been slidin' along smooth as butter when Ole Jim Crawford—he was the engineer—took bad sick. He sent for me. He say, 'Will, the Lord is callin' me home. I can hear angel voices chantin' my welcome song. If I go to my heavenly home before this here run is over, there ain't but one man can bring this train in on time, and that's you, Will Lindsay.' He died in my arms.

"I decided then and there, for ole Jim Crawford's sake, that train would pull into Memphis on time. We fired up the boiler hot as she'd go. Then late into the night, we was coming up on a crossin', and the board was up to let another train pass. Well, you boys don't know nothin' about railroadin', but if the board's up and you got to get through, you can blow your whistle to ask for the board. If they gives you the board, they holds the other train and lets you pass. Well quite naturally, I asked for the board, but they wouldn't give it to me." Uncle Will took a long draw on his pipe. "Then I begged for the board pitiful, and the board dropped."

"Uncle Will, did you get to Memphis on time?" I asked.

He let the suspense build while he relit his pipe. "Let me tell you, Daylight. We was makin' such good time after that I got into a playful mood. I started blowin' tunes on the whistle. The music was so pretty, folks come out of they houses and danced in the moonlight.

"We pulled into Memphis the nex' mawnin' twen'y minutes early. There was a great crowd out by that train. The passengers and all the folks come to meet 'em was bunched up around the engine car. They wanted to shake the engineer's hand for doin' such a fine job bringin' that train in. Then some of 'em saw two men takin' ole Jim Crawford away, dead as an ole maid's hope. A woman screamed, 'Lawd, another nigger done kilt a white man!' They was 'bout to take me off and string me up, when I looked off into the crowd and seen the fattest white gal I ever laid eyes on, pushin' her way through the crowd in a lavender polka-dot dress screamin', 'Take yo' han's of'n Will, ever' las' one of y'all. Will didn't kill my daddy. Ever'body knew Daddy had a bad heart.' When she got to me, she threw them big sausage arms around my neck and kissed me. Ever'body was so shocked, they jes' let me go. That big ole fat white gal kissin' me in front of all them folks was all that saved me."

CHAPTER SIX

The Knox Plains Land Allocation Council had since about 1910 been largely a political and social club. After the oil strikes on the south side, the council's current president, Willis Dayton, grandson of its founder, quickly returned the organization to its original purpose. A full-page announcement appeared in *The Knox Plains Register* that land allocations were being reevaluated. Anyone who had once asked for land on the north side could now be required to buy that land and give up for resale or trade any other land holdings they had in Knox Plains. They even found some jackleg lawyer to phrase it in legal mumbo jumbo for them.

Well, any dunce could see that this was a blatant attempt by Willis Dayton and his buddies to take the oil-rich land. Mr. Dayton himself even started spreading the lie that he had requested land on the south side twenty years earlier and had been forced to accept land on the north side instead. The council decreed that "so everybody could have the land they had originally asked for," some of Dayton's acreage would be exchanged for land belonging to Nate Jackson.

Mr. Nate was incensed when he came by to tell Uncle Will the latest turn of events. He had stopped by the oil field that used to be his farm and found Eli Dayton, Willis Dayton's seventeen-year-old son, looking around. Mr. Nate huffed, "He barely out of short pants good and he got the nerve to come up to me talkin' 'bout 'I'm Mr. Dayton.'

"I say, 'You missed a pot o' slop by not being a hog. That's the onliest mista I sees.' And then he go on about how I gots to give up my lan' 'cause I axed to buy lan' on the nawth side back in aught three. I say, 'Boy, you crazy as you look. This here is the onliest lan' yo' daddy and yo' granddaddy'd let me buy back then, so I bought it fair, square, and legal, and you ain't gittin' it now.' "

What made the Jacksons' newfound wealth an especially hard pill for the Daytons to swallow was that Minnie Jackson, Mr. Nate's late wife, had been the Daytons' maid since before Eli was born. "Why, that woman used to clean out our slop jars," Mr. Dayton bellyached, "and now her husband is trying to take over the town from us and turn it over to such as him. Who ever heard of a bunch of slaves living better than decent white folks." Willis Dayton always talked as if the Emancipation Proclamation and the Thirteenth, Fourteenth, and Fifteenth Amendments had never happened.

Mrs. Henrietta Dayton, Willis's wife, was simply confused by it all. "Why would they want to have all that money?" she asked. "Those people don't know anything about money. Everybody knows that. Colored people are so lucky when they have good white people like ourselves to see that they have what they need, but not enough to get in trouble." Mrs. Dayton firmly believed that she had the most generous attitude toward blacks of anybody in the South. She had allowed Minnie Jackson to bring little Wright and Matt with her on cleaning days when she had no place to leave them. Now and then Mrs. Dayton would breeze through the room where Minnie was cleaning, look at Matt and Wright and say, "They're adorable, Minnie, just adorable. I do believe you have a pair of house servants here. I don't think these boys are going to grow up to be common field hands at all."

There was a story told around town for many years after Miss Minnie's death about the time Miss Minnie asked to leave work early because the Dorcas Ladies' Handicraft Circle of Galilee Baptist Church was meeting at her house. "Why, of course, Minnie, you seem to have everything nice and clean here," Miss Minnie's employer said. Then Henrietta Dayton had an idea. "I'd love to come along as a guest," she exclaimed. "I would just love to meet your girls." It was quite enough that Miss Minnie had to rush home, bath, dress, and prepare refreshments, now she'd have to do it all with a silly white woman in tow. But what could she say? Mrs. Dayton took so long getting dressed that Miss Minnie wound up leaving just twenty minutes earlier than usual.

At the meeting, Mrs. Dayton fairly gushed over the quilts, sweaters, and socks the club members had made to give to the needy. When she blurted out, "Oh, this quilt is so beautiful I could just keep it for myself—it would look so lovely on my four-poster," for one heart-stopping moment they thought she meant it. They were afraid this self-centered daughter of the Deep South might actually walk off with a quilt they had lovingly made for a family even more needy than themselves. When Mrs. Dayton saw their chocolate faces frozen in amazement, she quickly added, "I'm only joking, of course."

During devotion, Miss Minnie sang "Deep River" as a solo while Mrs. Dayton smiled and pressed her hands together in approval. But the white society lady fidgeted like a three-year-old during the business meeting, which had little entertainment value for her.

After they had cake and ice cream and were ready for parting prayer, Miss Minnie asked if her guest had anything to say.

"Everything was just beautiful," Mrs. Dayton responded, "especially Minnie's singing. Minnie sings so beautifully, I declare, when I get to heaven, I'm going to ask the Lord if I can go visit on the colored side once in a while so I can hear Minnie sing."

It was easy to see why Willis Dayton and his family didn't like what was going on. They had once had the nicest house in town, built on the grounds of the old Knox estate and modeled after the mansion where Cornell Knox had entertained General Santa Anna. The version built by the Daytons, however, had the latest conveniences. Now their home looked like a shack next to the ones being built on the south side. Black men and women were walking around in clothes Mr. and Mrs. Dayton couldn't start to afford. The finest cars in Knox Plains were being driven down the newly paved roads on the colored side.

Willis Dayton and his buddies quickly learned that they were no longer the most powerful men in town. William Sullivan, a vice president with Pennant Oil, went around and personally visited all the landowners who had made deals for the oil rights to their property. He assured them that the Knox Plains Land Allocation Council's activities were completely illegal and that Pennant had hired top-notch lawyers to make them cease and desist.

Mr. Sullivan also arranged to speak at a Council meeting. His speech was friendly, full of phrases about progress, community goodwill, and the benefits of cooperation for the common good, but when he sat down, everyone in the room understood that Pennant Oil intended to protect its "local partners" against any and all threats.

It wasn't that Mr. Sullivan or anyone at Pennant had any special love for black people, but this was business. Pennant's representatives had already struck satisfactory deals with the current landowners and had no intention of starting negotiations all over again with greedy new ones. In any contest of color, green usually comes out on top.

Pennant Oil's lawyers succeeded in pulling the teeth of that old beast the Knox Plains Land Allocation Council. The group continued to exist, but the story around town was that its meetings were largely gripe sessions, with members decrying what the world had come to when a white man would take a black man's part against other white men. The old Knox Plains gentry tried to use what poor weapons they had left to strike back. They refused to give work to black people, but no one cared. The south side was generating its own economy. Former farm workers and domestics were earning more in the oil fields than they ever had working for the well-to-do in north Knox Plains. Those who continued as domestics found wealthy black families willing to pay relatively generous wages.

The one black servant the Daytons kept was Joe Ollie Harkwell, who seemed so unchanged by all that was going on that even the Daytons couldn't find fault with him. In fact, their relationship with the obsequious Mr. Joe Ollie came to symbolize the way the Daytons felt things should be between whites and other races. Just having him around helped the Daytons believe that the upheaval they were witnessing was temporary and that things would soon return to their natural order.

Just two years after the oilmen hit town, Knox Plains had changed so much I almost didn't know it. I watched in fascination as men in big wide-brimmed hats and neckerchiefs who reminded me of the cowboys Pa used to work with put up poles and strung electrical lines on the south side. The town became a study in contrasts. The old south-side public well, which many still used, was now just a few feet from the little branch office of the Knox Plains Water Company, which had been built after city water pipes were extended to the south side. Automobile drivers and riders on horseback made an uneasy peace with one another as the smell of gasoline fumes became as familiar as the smell of horse manure. There was even a story going around about a man who bought a Frigidaire and put a block of ice in it every day, and I knew of at least one household with both a wood-burning stove and an electric range in the kitchen.

Around town you'd see fewer women dressed in turn-of-the-century-style dresses with full-length sleeves and skirts that reached their ankles, and more of them in the shorter skirts and sleeves that had become popular during the Great War. Men were adopting the straw hats and striped jackets that young gentlemen in the big cities had been sporting for years.

We no longer had to go to school in a weather-beaten old one-room shack with a leaky roof and a stinking outhouse, or study from books that were passed on from the white school after they had become too worn or out-of-date for the white students to use. When I was in elementary school, it wasn't unusual to be reading aloud in class only to discover that the next page was missing from the book. The teacher would ask, "Who has a book with page seventeen in it?" The reader sometimes had to swap books three or four times just to get through a chapter. The south-side community built a new high school, bought all new books, and offered such good teachers' salaries that professors from Rio Vista State College and Prairie View A&M left those institutions to come teach high-school students. Some say we had the best mathematics and science programs in Texas. While the rest of the high school was excitedly examining the new football stadium—with a locker room and all—I was slipping into the new chemistry lab to finger the beautiful beakers and Bunsen burners and stare in awe at the cabinets of chemicals. A wonderful new south-side library was built just a short walk from our house. I was in heaven.

The broken-down bleachers at Fredericks Field, the south-side baseball stadium, were replaced, the fence was repaired and painted, and a refreshment stand that sold hot dogs, peanuts, popcorn, and ice-cold soda pop was installed. A bright new sign proclaimed, "Fredericks Field, Home of the Black Prairie Dogs." The Black Prairie Dogs got uniforms and new equipment. Before, they had played in their own ready-for-the-rag-pile clothes, with only one hand-carved bat and a pathetic old baseball that had been restitched countless times. There were a few well-worn gloves that I believe had been retrieved from white people's ash bins. Ragtag as they were, the Black Prairie Dogs were the best baseball team I'd ever seen, and several of the Black Prairie Dogs went on to play professional baseball in the Negro National League.

There's a story told around town that a championship Negro League team visited Knox Plains before I was born. They had just won the Negro League Pennant and were touring America, playing exhibition games in various cities. In every town they went to, black people turned out in droves just to look at them. When they came through Knox Plains on their way to Dallas, the Black Prairie Dogs' manager approached the professional team's manager. "We're so proud of you. Our whole race is proud," he said. "It would be a tremendous honor if your team would play one game against our little local team. It would be something our boys would remember for the rest of their lives." He explained that Knox Plains' black population was wild for baseball, and they could easily fill the stadium at twenty-five cents a head. No matter how the game came out, he said, they'd give the professional team sixty percent of the gate receipts.

These were all young men who loved baseball so much they'd play anybody, anytime, for any reason, so the game was set for that afternoon at two. The professional players chuckled when they saw the Black Prairies Dogs' equipment and offered to supply balls, bats, and gloves for the game. Word got around town quickly and by one-thirty that sunny October Saturday, the rickety old stadium was packed. As a gesture of respect and gratitude to the professional team, the Black Prairie Dogs gave their opponents the home-team advantage, allowing them to bat second. Around five that evening it got too dark to play and the umpires finally called the game. It was still the top of the first inning. In three hours, the professional team had been unable to get three outs against the local team. We were all delighted that the Black Prairie Dogs finally had uniforms and equipment worthy of them.

But baseball was no longer the only recreation available to Knox Plains' black population. A juke joint that sometimes featured live blues and jazz singers had been built somewhere off the main highway to Dallas, and a pool hall was now just a few feet from our store. Even though the Eighteenth Amendment was now the law of the land, and the manufacture, sale, and possession of alcoholic beverages was illegal in the United States, it was an open secret that beer could be had at both the juke joint and the pool hall.

New faces were appearing in town and old ones were disappearing. Most of the newly wealthy, black and white, used their money to start over someplace else. They either decided, as Junior Potts did, that they no longer belonged in Knox Plains, or left because they worried about the recent waves of local violence and feared that even the mighty Pennant Oil Company could not protect them from the anger and jealousy of the north-siders.

Reverend Esau Brown, who had been the pastor of Galilee Baptist for as long as I could remember, sold his property and its modest oil deposits at a handsome profit after he decided the Lord had called him to Chicago. He was replaced by a succession of eager young preachers who each moved on after finding a congregation struggling with its new social and economic order too much to handle. These changes at church caused more strain on people than all the others. Church had always been the anchor of the community. It was the one thing you could depend on, no matter what else was going on.

In Knox Plains, church was the center of everything we did. Everybody I'd seen get married, be buried, or celebrate any significant event in their lives had done it at church. It was where people learned what was going on in town, where they met those they would court and marry, where community decisions were made, including those that had nothing to do with church. Even the people I knew who weren't making any special effort to live righteous lives belonged to a church and actually came to services once in a while. Members addressed each other as "Brother" and "Sister" and truly behaved as though we were all part of a very large family. They gossiped incessantly about each other but always stood by one another in times of need. Children obeyed all adults in church as though they were their own parents.

My most vivid early childhood memories are of times spent in church. Maybe my oldest is of a time when I was about four years old and small for my age. My mother took me to a funeral. The church was crowded when we got there and there weren't two seats together, so Ma put me in the middle of a row while she sat in a vacant place on the end. A large woman came in just before the service started and couldn't find a seat. She came over to me and said, "Get up, baby, and let me have your seat. You can sit in my lap." Although I didn't know this woman, I knew the rule: at church all adults are to be obeyed without question. So I did as she said. The woman's well-padded body felt like a pile of pillows to me, and I quickly fell asleep on her ample bosom. I stirred to a semiconscious state as I heard a soloist singing "When We Walk the Last Mile of the Way." The woman holding me must have forgotten I was there, because she threw up her hands and screamed, "Yes, Lord Jesus! We all gots to walk that last mile!" As she did this, she sprang suddenly to her feet, sending me hurtling forward like a basketball in a free throw. I landed about three rows ahead in the lap of a startled deacon. He simply and quietly returned me to my human catapult.

Within Galilee Baptist, change had always been slow and purposeful. When I was little, Reverend Brown decided to follow Dr. Billups's suggestion that we stop taking the Lord's Supper from a common cup and switch to small individual cups. Dr. Billups got up and explained to the congregation that tiny living creatures called germs cause many diseases and could be spread easily if we all drank from one communion cup. He also recommended that we switch from the homemade grape wine Miss Elsie Cotter provided to store-bought pasteurized grape juice. There was a little opposition to the changes, mostly from people who resisted any changes, no matter how sound the reasons for them. I think there were also a few who looked forward to their Sunday morning sip of wine and hated to give it up. I remember the time when the common cup was being passed and old Miss Nellie Renfro, about the third person to receive it, drained it, then announced out loud, "I love my Jesus so good I drank him all up!"

The oil-field work attracted laborers from the neighboring states of Oklahoma, Arkansas, and Louisiana and from as far away as Mississippi,

Kansas, and Missouri. Some of these men spent time in the pool hall, and I'd see them when they popped into the store for cigars, cigarettes, candy bars, or a pint of Uncle Will's all-purpose tonic. Ma wouldn't let Barnett and me go into the pool hall, but Wesley went in there all the time with his brother Louis, and he told us stories about the men who hung around there. Most of them had found work in the oil fields, but there were some, including a gold-toothed fellow named Dillard Lester, who never seemed to work but always had money. Wesley noticed Lester particularly because the others seemed afraid of him.

Dillard Lester didn't bother anybody especially, but that's exactly what made him stand out—that and the fact that he was an abrupt, rude man who never said "please," "thank you," "sir," or "ma'am." Before the oil strike, we rarely had new people moving into town, and when they did, they quickly tried to make themselves part of the community. Every time newcomers settled in Knox Plains, the big question would be which church they would join. About two-thirds of our community belonged to Galilee Baptist, and most of the others belonged to the African Methodist church. There was also a Catholic church on the south side that couldn't have had more than twenty-five members, and some of them were Indians whose families had been converted by Spanish missionaries. Mr. Lester didn't join or even attend a church, even though they had all invited him.

CHAPTER SEVEN

Most of the beautiful fair-skinned young women moving into Mrs. Pendergast's boardinghouse were between eighteen and twenty-two years old, but there was one among them who was around thirty and divorced, I was told. You'd see her any evening at the boardinghouse, having supper with Mr. Seck Nesbet, who had to be nearly thirty-five years her senior. The peculiar thing about this was that I must have heard Mr. Nesbet say a hundred times that divorce was an abomination before God. He said it was the work of Satan, and divorced people should be shunned in polite society. I guess that fair-skinned lady caused him to rethink his views about Christian charity and forgiveness.

There was a lot of courting going on in Knox Plains. You could even see it in sales at the store. Men came in to buy cologne, hair pomade, and boxes of chocolate candies. They put in special orders for suits, shirts, jewelry, and French perfume. There was a fair run on Uncle Will's love potion. He must have been selling fifteen bottles a week. All it was was a mixture of rubbing alcohol and Hoyt's Cologne with a little green food coloring, but he told folks that if they could slip a drop or two into their intended's palm every day for three weeks, they'd find true love for life.

Uncle Will was doing a booming business in his all-purpose cure, too. His sign said, "Dr. Will Lindsay's All-Purpose Tonic—Cures Anything You Weren't Born With and Does Most Any Little Thing." He got me to add a line at the bottom that said, "Good for Asthma Relief." The all-purpose tonic was just grain alcohol that Uncle Will distilled behind the house and mixed with flavored syrup, but nobody taking it seemed to have any trouble breathing.

Even though those near-white girls seemed to be putting a spell on every black boy in town, Barnett and I were still shocked when just a few weeks after they started arriving, Louis Wilson came in and ordered a wedding set—a diamond engagement ring with a matching wedding band. "Miss Dupree done said she'd do me the honor of becomin' my wife," Louis announced, grinning so big I thought his cheeks should be aching.

"Louis, how long have you known her?" I asked. Miss Dupree and her breathing problems had just come to town two months earlier.

"I feel like me and her been keepin' comp'ny for years," Louis answered. "I ain't never met a lady made me feel like she do. Miss Lorraine Dupree's the one, all right."

Barnett chimed in. "Louis, you ain't but nineteen years old. You haven't courted that many girls. Though Miss Dupree is a real beauty. I've had a couple of dreams about her myself." Louis looked for a second like he might slug Barnett for saying that. Then he realized Barnett was just fourteen years old and he was just kidding.

Soon after the rings arrived, Louis and Lorraine were married at Galilee Baptist Church. At the fancy reception in the garden of Amos Wilson's new house, Mr. Wilson stood in the elevated gazebo and announced that his wedding present to Louis and Lorraine would be cash to build a house of their own. He didn't say how much cash, but the rumor around town was that it was twelve thousand dollars.

The very next Sunday in church, Seck Nesbet pulled himself up on his cane and announced that he and the divorced lady, whose name was Sally Lee, were to be married a week from Saturday.

Neither of the Jackson boys jumped into marriage, although they seemed to be prime targets. Wright was enjoying all the attention and didn't want to pick just one flower from the lovely bouquet that surrounded him. Matt was torn between his feelings for Dolly Miller, whom he had been sweet on since third grade, and all the new possibilities throwing themselves in his path. In particular, there was Miss Dupree's good friend Miss Fancy LeBlanc.

It seemed more and more Matt was going down to Mrs. Pendergast's without Dolly. Sometimes he could be seen sitting on the verandah sipping lemonade with Miss Fancy, and more than once he'd been spotted giving her a ride in his pink LaSalle. Miss Fancy also sent Matt to our store to buy Uncle Will's all-purpose cure, which she said did her asthma worlds of good.

Mrs. Sally Nesbet was an even bigger customer for Uncle Will's all-purpose cure. She'd buy two or three pints at a time, and as often as not she'd down a dose before she ever left the store. Sometimes when the tonic had loosened her tongue, she'd complain loudly about how stingy and old-fashioned Mr. Seck was. Of course, all of us already knew that about him, and if she hadn't been in such a rush to get married, she might have figured it out.

Neither getting rich nor getting married changed Seck Nesbet much. He still wouldn't spend a penny that he didn't have to. After the oil strike on his property, Mr. Seck didn't leave his job at the railroad. He worked the remaining seven months until his sixty-fifth birthday so he could retire and collect a pension. Mr. Seck moved his new bride into the same house he and his family had lived in for forty years, and he kept feeding his one cow the same way he'd always fed her. He had an arrangement with Quinn Moore, the groundskeeper at Fredericks Field. Every weekday morning right after Gertie's milking, Mr. Nesbet led the animal down to the baseball stadium and shut her inside the gate. She'd graze the outfield until almost sundown, then the old cheapskate would come get her. That way Quinn didn't have much grass cutting to do and Mr. Nesbet only had to buy feed for those Saturdays and Sundays when there were afternoon ball games.

"We can easily afford indoor plumbing and electric lights," Sally Nesbet would fuss. "In fact, we can afford our own brand-new house, but that old buzzard is so tight-fisted he just keeps saying, 'I don't see the point.' " She also complained that Mr. Seck now expected her to take a turn at cooking from the family groceries instead of taking meals at Mrs. Pendergast's. She started fixing awful food just to spite him, and he kept eating it just to spite her.

Telephones were another "newfangled gadget" that Mr. Nesbet didn't see the point in, so Mrs. Nesbet came down to the store pretty regularly to use the phone. One morning she came in with a big, ugly bruise that spread from her left cheekbone up across her eye and into her hairline. She said Mr. Seck's rusty-hinged back screen door had swung around and hit her, and she needed a pint of all-purpose tonic for the pain. She also asked to use the phone. I thought maybe she wanted to call Dr. Billups to look at her bruise. Instead, for more than an hour she ranted to someone about her new husband's shortcomings, taking large swallows of the tonic from time to time. When she hung up, the bottle was nearly empty. She bought two more pints and walked unsteadily down the street toward her house.

That evening, just as Barnett and I were closing all the bins and getting ready to shut the store down for the night, we looked up and saw Mrs. Nesbet standing in the doorway. I almost didn't know her. She looked like the hind wheels of bad luck. In addition to the bruise, her face was puffy, her eyes were red, and she seemed have trouble standing up.

"Are you okay, Miz Nesbet?" Barnett asked.

In a slurred voice that I could barely understand, she answered, "I needa call a doctor. Somebody shot Seck down by the ball field when he went to get Gertie. I think he's dying."

Barnett called Dr. Billups and told him to meet us at Fredericks Field. We locked up the store and drove Mrs. Nesbet back to the baseball stadium. In the car she told us that she had started to worry because Mr. Nesbet was taking so long getting back with Gertie, so she walked down to the ball field to check on him and found him on the ground, bleeding and gasping for breath. Mrs. Nesbet was reeking of all-purpose tonic.

When we got to the stadium, Dr. Billups was standing just outside the main gate. He had already checked Seck Nesbet. "Is Mr. Nesbet going to be all right?" I asked anxiously.

Dr. Billups shook his head. "He's not gone yet, but he took two bullets in the chest at close range, and he's not a young man. Help me load him into the back of my car, and I'll take him over to the clinic and do what I can. Barnett, you come in my car so you can help me take Mr. Nesbet inside. And Roosevelt, you stop and get Mattie, and y'all meet me at the clinic." Mattie Holmes was Dr. Billups's nurse, who had probably been home from work less than an hour, but Dr. Billups was going to need her help with Mr. Nesbet.

At the clinic, Dr. Billups and Nurse Holmes worked on Mr. Nesbet for several hours. Sally Nesbet sat across the waiting room from Barnett and me, wringing her handkerchief and muttering to herself. Once in a while she would ask us, "What do you suppose is happening? Why is this taking so long?" While we were waiting, I called the sheriff. When he arrived, he walked straight into the room where Dr. Billups was working. He came out a few minutes later. On his way out he said to Mrs. Nesbet, "There's nothing I can tell you. They're still trying to save him." She responded with a groan that sounded more like exasperation than grief.

It was close to ten when Dr. Billups came out. His arms and clothes soaked in blood, his face streaked with sweat, he announced, "We lost him. I'm sorry, Sally."

The next morning, the widow Nesbet was back at the store, this time to call the oil company to say she'd decided to sell all her remaining rights to Mr. Nesbet's property. She signed the papers at the bank the next day and didn't even stay in town for the funeral.

One cool evening in the early spring of 1927 I heard Nate Jackson on the front porch, talking to Uncle Will. I came out to join them, but

Uncle Will said, "It's kinda airish out here, Daylight. I cain't have you boys catchin' cold and cain't go to school. You and Midnight go on to bed and get yo' rest." That meant they were talking about something I wasn't supposed to hear, so, of course, I went inside and scooted down under the open front-room window opposite the front porch swing so I could listen.

Mr. Nate was talking. "I ain't never seen my boy Matt in such a state, Will. He say, 'Pa, I done done it this time. I done got myself in so much trouble I don't know what to do.' I guessed right off the trouble was about that Fancy gal. She looked like trouble the second I seed her. I was on the money. Matt told me Miss Fancy was in the family way and he's the one done it."

"What he go' do 'bout it?" Uncle Will asked.

"Well I's hoping to goodness he wa'n't thankin' 'bout marryin' her. It's bad enough Louis Wilson done went an' married some high-fallutin yellow gal from New Or-Leans don't none of us know nothin' 'bout. But this 'un Matt's mixed up with is so fas' she's droppin' her draw's for a man she ain't knowed but five or six munts."

"Sound to me like Matt dropped somethin' his ownself," Uncle Will observed.

"That's for sho', Will. That's for sho'. But I didn't wants to see Matt's whole life messed up from here on out on account of one mistake. He still want to marry that gal Dolly Miller when the time right, and I b'lieve she the right choice for him, not some fas' red bone from Lu'zanna. I got to studyin' on how I could he'p my boy. So I went down to Miz Lula's to talk wid the young lady," Mr. Nate continued. "Wasn't nobody out on the verandah, so I gets Lula to bring us some iced tea out there. Thank the Lawd Joe Ollie wasn't nowheres 'round. I sho' didn't need that li'l gossipin' sissy in this.

"I axed Miss Fancy right out, 'Does you want for you and my boy to git hitched?'

"She say in that proper voice she got, 'Well, Mr. Jackson, I do b'lieve he need to do the right thang by me, don't you?'

"I say, 'Don't look to me like much thought been give to doin' the right thang up to this point.'

"Well, her eyes gits all wet and she pull out her lace ha'se-ker. She say, 'Mr. Jackson, I been a good girl all my life and I ain't never done nothin' wrong 'til yo' Matt led me astray wid all his fine talk and promises. Now if'n he ain't man enough to do his duty, I reckon I'll have to go somewheres and live out my life in shame.'

"That 'fine talk and promises' she was goin' on about didn't sound a whole lot like Matt, but it's a good thang I didn't study too hard on that or I woulda missed what happened nex'. That yella gal tho'ed open a do' my boy could ex-cape through.

"She say, 'I know 'bout a place back in Lu'zanna where colored gals in my kinda trouble can go and live quiet, out of the public eye, don't you see? There's doctors and nurses to he'p 'em have they babies there, and then they gits 'em adopted into nice colored families wid doctors and professors and what not. But it costs a whole heap of money to go to one of them places, and I ain't got near enough.' "

"So you give her money," Uncle Will said.

"I give her ten thousand dollars," Mr. Nate answered. "I figger that'll go a long way towards Matt doin' his duty."

I almost choked when I heard the figure. It's my guess that Miss Fancy would have cheerfully left town with a tenth of that. Duty is a big thing in Texas, and Mr. Nate was old Texas stock. I knew it was important to him to do the right thing. He asked, "Will, did I do right?"

Uncle Will told Mr. Nate to just sit and think on the matter for a few minutes. My one-legged step-grandfather pulled himself up and hobbled into the house. A couple of minutes later he came back out on the porch and told Mr. Nate, "The chickydee-whick say, yeah, you done the right thang gettin' that light-skinned gal out of town, all right."

There was a widower named Simon Woods who had about thirty acres on the south side of town. He had made quite a bit of money from an oil strike, but he took up with one of the Louisiana women who seemed to have a fondness for jewelry. Before that woman came to town, Mr. Simon had lived simply and almost never put in special orders at the store. The only one I could remember was for a pair of eyeglasses. He brought them back a few days later. "I axed fer readin'," he complained, "and they sont me long-distance." But once he started keeping company with Miss Renee, as she was called, he became one of my best mail-order customers. She had Mr. Simon buying her gold bracelets, diamond ear bobs, a ruby necklace, and I don't know what all. Miss Renee must have come in the store six or seven times and asked to look at the fine-jewelry order book. She'd pick out some outrageously expensive thing and tell Mr. Simon that was what she wanted. Grinning like a kid at a carnival, he'd say, "Go on, order it fer her, she kin have anythang she want." The young woman promised to marry him, but as soon he gave her a big diamond engagement ring, she changed her mind and left town—with the jewelry.

Another one of these women got her fiancé, George Hambrick, to give her access to his bank account so she could buy furniture, dishes, and other things she needed to set up housekeeping so they could start a life together when they got married. She changed her mind and left town, too. The next day Mr. Hambrick checked his bank account. The balance was two dollars and seventy-three cents. The week before, it had been more than fourteen thousand dollars.

Uncle Will felt sorry for his friend Mr. Nate, since it was his son's folly that wound up costing him money, but generally he had no sympathy for the men who were losing their money to the light-skinned Louisiana women. "Any fool wid one eye and half sense could see they's jes' after money," he snorted. "You didn't see no young high-yella gals all over ole Hambrick or Woods neither when they was po' as Job's turkey."

It seemed that everywhere light-skinned women went, trouble wasn't far behind. I got to the point where I was downright scared of any woman who wasn't at least a nice milk chocolate. I'd walk a mile out of my way to avoid passing a light-skinned woman on the street. I've heard some black people say that there's a bile white people have in their blood that black people don't have. They say the bile makes their skin white, but it also makes them evil. Now it stands to reason that if there is such a bile, light-skinned black people must have some of it, and that could explain why light-skinned Negro women are so full of the devil.

The trouble with that notion is that I've known a lot of people with light skin who were as nice as anybody you'd ever want to meet. My own pa is a good example. He didn't have an evil bone in his body as far as I know, and he was half white. For that matter, everything I know about his pa, a full-blooded white man, says he was an okay fellow. He gave us that money to start the store and all. And, of course, here I am, at least one-fourth white, and never had the urge to rob, kill, cheat, or do anybody wrong in my life. But if all I had to go by were people like Willis Dayton and those women staying with Mrs. Pendergast, I could believe in that evil bile, with no problem.

PART THREE

BY MAN CAME DEATH

By the fall of 1927 I was beginning to worry that the whole world had gone crazy. It seemed you couldn't pick up a newspaper without reading about shootings, stabbings, race riots, lynchings, or other horrible crimes. I kept thinking about a murder case that had been in all the papers three years earlier. It seems two students at the University of Chicago, Nathan Leopold and Richard Loeb, had killed a thirteen-year-old boy just to prove they could do it. A famous lawyer named Clarence Darrow kept them from getting the death penalty by arguing that crime is a disease. In a sense, he was saying, the killers were as much victims as the poor boy they had murdered. I found all that hard to understand, since I was raised on the teachings of the Bible, which make it pretty clear that we are all responsible for what we do. But even the Bible talks about people being possessed by demons and not in control of their actions. I really wanted to understand, because it seemed crime was everywhere. Up north, gangs of criminals were slipping whiskey into the country and killing each other for the right to sell it. In our once quiet community there had been a lot of robberies and even a few murders.

Some people got robbed with a gun, and some, like Mr. Benny Gibley, got robbed with a fast, slick tongue and a pile of legal papers they didn't understand. Since their good fortune, the Gibley girls had quit coming to Ma for culture lessons. Mr. Benny hired a private tutor from Dallas, who was teaching them fancy manners and how to recite and whatnot. They also quit spending much time around Barnett and me. They seemed to prefer the company of Wesley Wilson and other boys whose families had done well in the oil strikes.

One day Mrs. Pearl Gibley used their new telephone to call us and invite us to their new house. Mr. and Mrs. Gibley were giving a Sunday afternoon tea for the girls, she said. Ma wasn't overjoyed to get an invitation from a family that had pretty much ignored us since they got money, but she said we'd go anyway. Most of the Gibleys' guests were from the newly oil-rich black families. Besides us, the only other guest who wasn't rich was Mrs. Pendergast.

At the tea, Miss Pearl presented her daughters one at a time and had them walk slowly down the ornate curved staircase in long dresses as their names were called. I hardly knew Glenda in her fancy hairstyle and face paint, but I went over and spoke to her anyway. I remarked on the baby grand piano in the corner of the parlor. "That's really beautiful," I told her. "Now, I guess you can have the music lessons your pa's been wanting you to have."

"Yes," she said, "that's mine. Let me show you what else." She took me by the hand and led me into a sitting room, where I was surprised to see another baby grand piano. "This is Belinda's," she announced proudly.

"Your pa bought two grand pianos?" I asked in disbelief. With a big smile she took my hand again. This time we went into the huge dining room, where there was yet another baby grand.

"That's Linda's," she explained. "Brenda's is just like it. It's in the music room."

"Great day in the morning!" I exclaimed. "I'll bet King George himself doesn't have four grand pianos in Buckingham Palace." Some slick salesman had come by and convinced poor Mr. Benny that each of his daughters needed a piano. In addition to the fact that he had paid about twice market price for the pianos, Mr. Benny also had paid the salesman for a year's piano lessons for each of the girls. Not long afterward, he finally realized that the girls would never get the lessons he paid for. He never saw the salesman or his money again.

But the murders around town were far scarier than the confidence games and robberies. Some people here in Knox Plains were killed by robbers, others were slain by night riders, Ku Klux Klansmen who didn't like the idea of black people having money and living better than white people. They didn't bother targeting their victims. They just grabbed any black man they could catch and lynched him to scare all the others. Pa used to tell me folks joined outfits like the Klan because they were scared of black men who were smarter than they were and could do a job better if given half the chance. The Klan wanted to make sure black men never got a chance at all.

To me, the oddest thing about the Klan is the way they wave crosses around and call themselves Christians. I've read the New Testament from the first chapter of Matthew to the final verse of the Revelation and I didn't see a thing saying it was okay to go around murdering people for not bowing down to somebody else's skin color.

Mothers begged their sons not to go out after dark, but few listened. Even Barnett had taken to coming home late on Saturday nights. As he neared the end of his fifteenth year, Barnett was almost as tall as a grown man, and he spent a lot of his time around older boys. Although Ma fussed at him for his mannish behavior, she realized that her control over her happy-go-lucky brother was quickly slipping away.

One Saturday night we all reluctantly decided to go to bed even though Barnett hadn't come home yet. I lay beneath the covers, but I couldn't go to sleep. Every few minutes I'd turn the light on and look at the clock. In between I'd say little prayers for Barnett's safety, each more urgent than the last. Finally, I heard the front door open and footsteps on the stairs. I got up and met my truant family member in the hall.

"Barnett," I whispered with great irritation, "where have you been?" I was angry that he had let us all worry like that, especially Ma, who loved him more than barefoot boys love summer. Sometimes I think she loved Barnett more than she loved me because he was double kin to her. He was her brother by birth and her son because she'd raised him from a baby.

"Hush," he whispered back. "You'll wake Sister."

"You know she's not asleep. You know she can't sleep with you out."

Barnett tiptoed to Ma's door, tapped lightly, and whispered, "I'm home now, Sister. You can go to sleep."

"When I get up in the morning, I'm going to strangle you, Barnett," she answered.

I followed Barnett down the hall. "I'm not going to wait until morning," I declared. "Where have you been?"

"Stop talking like you're my daddy. I'm your uncle, even if I am just a little more than a year older than you."

I repeated my question. "Where have you been?"

"I went to the picture show with Susie Fletcher. After I walked her home and was on my way back, some man jumped out from between two buildings and pointed a gun at me. He said, 'Give me all your money or I'm gonna shoot you.' So I said, 'Wait a minute, buddy. I'm in the same business you're in. I'm out here to see who I can rob, and right now I'm on the trail of a good mark. There's this fellow who's been flashing money around town all day. He must've had three hundred dollars cash on him. If you help me catch up with him, we can split it.'

"So the fool asked me, 'Which way did he go?' I said, 'I don't know for sure, but he's here in town somewhere. You go toward the north end and I'll go toward the south end and we'll move in toward the middle. That way we're sure to get him.' So he said, 'Okay, partner.' And I ducked into the cemetery and hid out for a while. When I thought it was safe, I came around behind the church, went through Mr. Powers's cow pasture, and slipped on home."

I sighed. "Barnett, will you be careful? Haven't you heard about all the robbing and killing out there?"

"Nothing's gonna happen to me," he said, and went to bed.

The next Saturday night, Barnett went out again. Again it got to be late, with no sign of my fun-loving uncle. The telephone we had put in two years earlier hung on the wall in mocking silence. For about two hours I went through the same routine of praying and clock watching that I had gone through the Saturday before. Then I decided I wasn't going to let him do this to me again, and somehow I put it out of my mind and went to sleep.

The next morning I woke up early and checked Barnett's room. His bed hadn't been slept in. I looked out a front window at a perfect Indian summer morning. The red and orange leaves dancing gently against a deep blue sky created a setting for painters and poets to love. If I could just have seen my tall athletic uncle strolling up the front walk, I would have felt perfect peace with God that Sunday morning. The Ford was still outside, so wherever Barnett went, he must have walked.

Downstairs, Ma and Uncle Will were both in the kitchen, but they weren't talking. Ma was cooking breakfast with such intensity you'd think the fate of the world depended on the biscuits she was rolling and the sausage patties she was shaping. I said what they both already knew. "Barnett didn't come home last night."

At first nobody even looked up. It was as though they hadn't heard me. Then Ma fairly screamed, pronouncing each word slowly and separately, "I told him not to go. I told him there are fools out there who wouldn't think any more about killing him than they would about swatting a fly." Heavy tears rolled down her cheeks, and she dried her face in her apron. "Get cleaned up for church, son. I'll have your breakfast ready by the time you're dressed."

I really wanted to stay home to wait for word about Barnett, but I didn't want to risk upsetting Ma more, so I just took a bath, went upstairs, and put on my church clothes. Ma took a really long time getting ready. As we were leaving the house, I realized why. She wanted to get to church just as the service was starting and not have to greet anybody who'd ask, "Where's Barnett this morning?"

The church seemed unusually hot for mid-October, even with the big ceiling fans turning. The service seemed endless. Every song, every announcement, every collection was tedious. I didn't listen at all to what the preacher and the deacons were praying for. I had only one prayer in my heart: that Barnett was at least still alive.

I found myself getting impatient as Deacon Elias Meadows lined out the hymns. For a long time I had seen no reason for our church to continue this outdated and time-consuming practice, but that morning I found it especially wearing. In old-time Negro churches, where the church owned only one or two hymnbooks and few members could read, a deacon would read each line of the hymn, then the congregation would sing it. We had plenty of hymnbooks, and the few members who couldn't read were old enough to have heard the same hymns hundreds of times and surely knew the words by heart. Nevertheless, true to Galilee Baptist Church's time-honored tradition, Deacon Meadows read, "Amazing grace, how sweet the sound that saved a wretch like me," and the congregation sang, "Uh-uh-uh-maaa-zi-i-ing grace, how sweeet the soun', tha-a-at saaved uh-uh wretch li-ike meeeeee." Compounding the problem was the fact that Deacon Meadows, now well past eighty, took forever with each hymn. He laboriously moved a chair to the front of the sanctuary, eased into it, and searched the hymnbook for the song Reverend Longley had called for.

Then Rosetta Nesbet asked if she could share a poem she had written in her Uncle Seck's memory. She gripped a damp handkerchief tightly as she read. Typical of the poetry refined women of that period churned out, the lengthy, maudlin verse had no meter or regular rhyme scheme and was filled, almost comically, with archaic words and phrases. Still, the congregation was visibly moved. At last, she got to the final two lines:

> And 'though thou now with the angels soar,
> Thou dost soar in our hearts forevermore.

Seck Nesbet had never been popular in the community. While he was with us, no one sought his friendship and nearly everybody joked about his stingy, unpleasant ways. Still, the grief at losing him was genuine. We had lost one of our own.

When Reverend Longley finally got up to preach, I mentally tried to rush him through the sermon. He'd say, "We all know the story of Jesus and the woman at the well," and I'd think, *Yes, yes, we all know it. Could we just move on?*

At Galilee Baptist, as at most black churches in the South, there were members who'd "get happy" during the service and scream and shout for several minutes, sometimes disrupting the service until they could be calmed. Mr. Joe Ollie got happy almost every Sunday. He walked up and down the aisles of the church, shaking everybody's hand and screaming phrases like, "Praise His name, chillun! Don't you know you just gots to praise His holy name!" On that October morning, it seemed Mr. Joe Ollie would never sit down. In fact, he got two or three others started, and Reverend Longley had to pause in his sermon until the shouters could be quieted.

Finally, the service ended, the closing hymn was sung, and we rose and bowed our heads for the benediction. When we opened our eyes, there were newcomers in the room. "'Scuse me, Reverend. 'Scuse me, folks," boomed a voice in the back of the room. I turned and saw a uniformed Texas Ranger standing near the back door. Another Ranger was close behind him. "I'm real sorry, folks," the first Ranger announced, "but we done found some colored men dead early this morning. Look like they was murdered las' night. And whoever kilt 'em took they billfolds, so we got no way to know who we got here. They're in a truck outside. We need you to take a look and see if you know any of these men."

Ma was gripping the pew in front of her so hard her small brown hands had turned bluish purple. I took no comfort in the fact that the Ranger had used the word *men*. It was easy to believe that he could have mistaken Barnett for an adult. I told myself that Barnett was safe. He had the best instincts for avoiding danger of anybody I knew. Still, the facts stood like boulders in front of me: Barnett was missing and some black men had been murdered.

"I'll look," I whispered, although my heart was pounding like a small bird's and my limbs felt like crowbars. I moved as quickly as I could through the crowd. None of the usual after-church greeting was going on. The congregation wasn't even stopping to shake the preacher's hand. Everybody just wanted to know who was in that truck.

Once we were outside, people froze. No one wanted to be the first to look. Reverend Longley seemed helpless. He was so new in town he didn't know the members of his own congregation yet. He certainly wouldn't be able to identify the dead men in the back of the truck. "Come on," one of the Rangers urged. "Somebody's got to look."

"I'll look," I said, and moved quickly toward the truck before I lost my nerve. At first I just saw a tangle of bloody clothes and bloody brown flesh. Then I saw that there were three men stretched out in the bed of the truck, their feet toward the cab. I looked for faces. I was quickly sure that I didn't know two of the men. A lot of strangers had moved into the area recently. But one blood-streaked face lying in profile looked familiar to me. I boldly reached in and turned the lifeless head. It was Louis Wilson.

I turned and walked back toward the crowd that waited for me in anxious silence. My eyes fell almost immediately on Mr. and Mrs. Wilson. Wesley was with them, but Louis's wife, Lorraine, was not. Ma walked up and gripped my arm tightly. I whispered, "No, Barnett's not in there," and tried to shake her off.

She kept holding my arm. "Are you sure?"

"I'm sure," I said as I pulled away from her and walked straight to the Wilsons. Before I opened my mouth, Mrs. Wilson knew. She closed her eyes tightly and spoke his name. "Louis."

"Yes, ma'am," I said. "I'm so sorry."

Then I felt someone shove me so hard I almost lost my footing. It was Wesley. "You liar!" he screamed. "Where do you get off tellin' us a lie like that? My brother ain't dead."

Amos Wilson's face was gray as a tombstone, but he gently took Wesley by the shoulder. "Come on, son," he said. "We go' look together." The three surviving Wilsons peered into the truck at Louis's face, clearly recognizable even through the caked blood and dirt. Wesley turned and collapsed crying in his pa's arms.

Mrs. Wilson looked pleadingly at one of the Texas Rangers. "Kin I take my son wid me?" she asked in a small child's voice. "We gots a car. We could put him in the back seat wid me. I could hol' his head."

The Ranger stared at the ground. "Ma'am," he started, searching for the gentlest possible words, "your son had done been out there a right smart of time when we fount him this morning. After a time, bodi . . . that is, people . . . kinda get, well, stiff . . . and I don't thank . . ."

Mrs. Wilson raised her gloved hand to stop him from saying more. "Thank you," she said with almost tea-party politeness. "If you could jes' carry him over to Cornelius's Mortuary, I'd be much obliged."

No one else from our church knew the other two dead men. So the Rangers moved the truck on to catch the congregation at the African Methodist church before they all got away.

I spent Sunday afternoon searching along the roads that led into Knox Plains. I feared maybe the Texas Rangers had missed Barnett when they were picking up bodies Sunday morning. Ma let me take the car, a used Ford we bought for two hundred dollars from George Hambrick, who badly need cash after the woman he planned to marry left town with the contents of his bank account. Even though I was just fourteen, I could drive about as well as anybody in town, better than some.

By twilight I'd looked every place I could think of. I decided to drive back through town, hoping there might be a clue as to what had happened that bloody Saturday night.

The main street was empty, as it always was on Sunday. Right after I passed the statue of Cornell Knox in the downtown square, I saw a man walking with his back to me in the fading afternoon light. He walked like Barnett. His suit even looked like the one Barnett was wearing when I last saw him early Saturday evening. But I knew the tricks your mind can play when you want something too much. I remembered how sure I'd been that Tom Mix was my pa. I didn't dare let myself believe that Barnett was on his way home, twenty-four hours late.

Still, I pressed the gas pedal a little harder to catch up with him and be sure. When the car was just a few feet behind the fellow, he turned and called out, "Moose?"

I stopped the car. "Barnett?" I asked tentatively.

Then came the laugh I knew before I could walk, the laugh that was always music to my heart but never more than at that moment. "Guess I'm gettin' in a little late, huh?" Barnett asked mischievously as he climbed into the seat beside me. "I thought that must be you.

There isn't another car in the world that sounds like this old Tin Lizzie."

He was dirty. He was disheveled. He smelled like warm hog slop. And he was the most beautiful sight I'd ever seen. I did something I'd never done before in my life: I hugged Barnett.

Suddenly his face grew serious. "Moose," he said, "something terrible has happened. Louis Wilson is dead. He was murdered."

"I know. The Texas Rangers found him early this morning. Do you know how it happened?"

Barnett let out a long breath. "I was with him. He called me Saturday afternoon and asked me if I wanted to go to Jimbo's with him—you know, that juke joint that opened up back off the highway about a year ago. I think marriage, even to a beauty like Lorraine, was making Louis a little restless. He just wanted to spend an evening feeling like a free man. Louis said Lorraine told him he could go out without her and have some fun. I guess he didn't want to go by himself, and Wright Jackson had something else to do, so Louis called me. I didn't tell anybody because I knew Sister would have a fit, me going to a place where they were playing reels, dancing, and drinking beer. Anyway, I walked downtown and Louis met me there in his Pierce-Arrow.

"We knew Jimbo's was back off the highway toward Dallas, but we weren't sure just where. We figured we'd see some sign of it if we headed out there. So we were driving slowly along the highway, looking for lights. After a while, we could just barely make out some light way off to the left. There was a narrow dirt road leading that way, so we turned off the highway and started up it. It was so rocky we couldn't move but about five miles an hour."

Barnett paused and wiped sweat from his forehead. I could see he was shaking. "We had gone about a quarter of a mile when we heard gunshots," he continued. "Louis whispered, 'Hush.' Then he pulled as far off the road as he could. He turned the lights and the motor off. First we heard the hoofbeats of a horse that must have gone right past us toward the highway. We could still see the light we saw before, and once in a while you could hear a noise in the distance like people shouting. Maybe fifteen or twenty minutes later, we heard hoofbeats again. This time there were lots of horses, and the light was coming closer.

"Before long there must have been ten or fifteen men on horseback galloped past us going back down that little dirt road toward the highway. Some of them were holding torches. There was enough light that we could see they were wearing white robes and hoods. They even had hoods on the horses."

"Night riders!" I gasped. "Barnett, that was the Ku Klux Klan. The Ku Klux Klan killed Louis."

"No, let me finish. They never saw us. After they were gone, we went down the road to see what they'd been doing down there."

"Are you crazy?" I demanded.

"I must be," Barnett acknowledged. "At the end of the road, we found two colored men shot to death. We didn't know either one of them." I remembered the other two men in the wagon with Louis, but I didn't interrupt the story.

Barnett went on. "Naturally, we got our black butts out of there. Of course, the only way back to the highway was that same little one-lane dirt road. If the Klan had come back, we would have met them head-on. I believe that was the longest half-mile-ride of my life. When we finally got to the highway, I thought we were safe. We weren't thinking about any juke joint at that point, we both just wanted to go home.

"There was almost nobody on the road, but about three miles out of town a car pulled out right behind us. We thought it was the Klan again. I ducked down in the seat as far as I could go. The car pulled around and ran Louis off the road. Then it sped up. Louis's car cut off when it hit that rocky ground, so we just rolled to a stop. I didn't know who they were or why they were after us, but every instinct I had said they weren't through. I said something like, 'We'd better get out of the car,' then I jumped out and started crawling along in the grass. A few seconds later, I looked up and saw the other car turn around and come back for us. I also saw that Louis was still behind the wheel. I shouted, 'Come on!,' but Louis didn't move. I don't know whether he thought he had a better chance in the car or whether he was just frozen with fear, but it wasn't until the other car stopped and two men jumped out that Louis finally got out of his car. I was crouched down in a shallow ravine, praying they wouldn't see me.

"Louis's headlamps were still on, and so were the ones on the other car, so I could see pretty clearly what was happening. Right after Louis got out, one of the men—the driver, I think—shot three times. Louis just fell down where he was without a word or a cry. All I heard was a sound like a groan or a gasp. The man who shot him checked Louis like he wanted to make sure he was dead. He said to the other man, 'We got him. There's some blood on the car, but we'll clean it up good when we get there.' Then he reached in Louis's pocket and took his billfold. 'I'll take this one,' he said. Then he got in Louis's car and drove off. The other man followed in their car. I got a good look at the two of them. It wasn't the Klan, Moose."

"How do you know?"

"They were colored men—young, maybe in their early twenties. I guess they were just robbers and they picked us because Louis was driving a nice car."

"So you were out there on the highway with robbers and Klansmen and no way to get home?"

"I hated to leave Louis, even though I knew he was dead and there was nothing I could do. At the same time, I knew I had to get out of there. I was afraid to go too far from the highway and get lost, and I was afraid to stand up and be seen. I just snaked along in the grass, heading east toward Knox Plains. Once in a while a car would go by, but I thought nobody saw me until an eastbound car pulled over just in front of me. I heard a car door open. It wasn't the same car Louis's killers were in, but I was sure it was another robber or the Klan come back, or somebody else out to kill me for the fun of it. There was no doubt in my mind that this was my night to die.

"I stopped still as a stone, but the driver must have seen me in his headlamps, because he walked right to me. I just crouched on the ground, waiting for somebody to shoot me or something. Then I heard a redneck voice say, 'Don't stand up. Git in the back of my car. It's rat here. Jes' crawl in the backseat and lay down flat on the flo' there.' I didn't know whether he had a gun. His voice seemed gentle for a killer's, but I was too scared to think, so without saying a word, I crawled in through the open door. The back door slammed shut, and the driver got in and pulled back onto the highway. He said, 'Jes' stay down back there 'til I say different.'

"Well, for the next hour or so, I crouched in that backseat, wondering who this was and where he was taking me. If he planned to kill me, why was he taking me someplace else to do it? I'd heard stories about how sometimes the Klan liked to take colored men off and cut off their privates or torture them for a while before they killed them. I figured I was on my way to a Klan rally, but I thought if I got up and fought this man who was driving, he'd kill me right there, or maybe I'd cause a wreck that would kill us both. And somehow, no matter how bad things looked, I wanted to hang on to life as long as I could. I figured if I was supposed to live through this, God would give me my chance if I just waited for it.

"Finally, the car left the highway. I could feel we were on another dirt road. After a few minutes, the car stopped. I raised up, but it was pitch black. I heard the man open the car trunk. He must have taken a lantern out, because in a minute there was a little light. The back door opened and I got out. The man said, 'Come on with me to the barn.' I thought that was where the Klan was waiting to torture and kill me, but it was quiet. I expected to hear whooping and hollering from liquored-up Klansmen, but all I heard was some frogs croaking away in the distance. I started to just turn and run, but getting shot in the back didn't make sense either. Nothing I could think of made sense. I walked with him to the barn and stood there shaking while he opened the barn door. No one was in there, but when he held the lantern up, for the first time he could see my face and I could see his.

"He asked me, 'Ain't you Will Lindsay's boy, Barnett?' Then I realized who had kidnapped me. It was Junior Potts. He told me we were at his sister-in-law's farm about twenty-five miles east of Knox Plains. Miz Lucille's sister needed some money, and Mr. Junior was bringing it to her. On his way he passed that Ku Klux Klan bunch with their robes and torches, then he saw a colored man—me—crawling in the grass and figured I must be running away from them. That was why he told me to get down in the back of his car. He was driving me to safety, but he didn't want the Klan, if they came back that way, to see that he had a colored man in his car.

"Old Mr. Junior said, 'If there's one thing that Klan hates worser than a colored man, it's the white man who'll he'p him. If they'd caught us, I'da been the first one they'd wanta lynch.' Anyway, Mr. Junior hid me out in that barn until the next day. On his way back to Dallas, he dropped me off just outside town. He said he'd take me on home, but he didn't want the Klan to catch him in the colored part of town."

"Why did he take that chance?" I asked.

"Two things. Mr. Junior said colored people had always been good to him—I guess he mostly had Miz Pendergast in mind—and he said his daddy taught him that a real man will always fight fair. He said he couldn't stand that Klan, because they're just a bunch of bullying cowards. They hide behind masks, gang up on people, and shoot them in the back. There's not one among them who's man enough to fight fair.

"Moose," Barnett said as we approached the house, "you've got to swear you'll never tell anybody that I was with Louis when he got killed. You've got to swear in blood."

"Why?" I demanded. "You're the only one who saw the men who killed him. You're the only one that can bring them to justice."

"That's right, and they don't know I'm in the world. If word gets back that somebody saw them, they'll find me and kill me for sure."

"What about Ma? She's been nearly crazy since you didn't come home last night. We have to tell her."

"No, we don't. We're not going to tell her and we're not going to tell Pa, either. The best chance we have of keeping the secret is not to tell anybody. Don't make me sorry I told you. Come on, swear in blood."

"Oh, Barnett, that's silly. We haven't sworn in blood since we were about ten."

"This is important," Barnett declared. "I won't believe you unless you swear in blood." He took a pocketknife out of the glove compartment.

I stopped the car a few feet down the road from the house. Barnett took the knife and pricked my middle finger. Then he did the same with his own. We touched our bloody fingertips together, and as the scarlet stream flowed down our hands, I solemnly stated, "I give my oath in blood that I will never tell that Barnett was with Louis Wilson when he was killed." As I wiped the blood from my palm I told Barnett, "You know I'll keep your secret, but we've got to tell Ma and Uncle Will something."

We sat there and made up a story about Barnett's taking the long way home from the picture show to dodge some robbers and getting so worn out from running that he fell asleep under a tree on Mr. Power's farm around daybreak and didn't wake up until Sunday afternoon. It wasn't much of a story and I was embarrassed to be a part of it, but it was all we could come up with on short notice.

"Uncle Will will figure out that we're lying," I predicted. "He's got that chickydee-whick, you know."

"Aw, if that chickydee-whick was worth a cuss, it'd have told him where I was last night."

Ma was so thrilled that Barnett was back home and okay, she never questioned the puny explanation. She just hugged him and kissed him, laughing and crying at the same time. I even believe I saw a tear slip down Uncle Will's cheek. Finally, Ma must have smelled the sweat and cow dung and who knows what else on Barnett. "I'll draw you a bath, baby brother," she told him. "Then I'll put supper on the table."

While we were eating, Uncle Will told us that Reverend Longley had called to let us know that the two dead strangers had been identified. They were laborers from Arkansas. They'd heard about the oil strikes in Knox Plains and had come to town hoping to find work in the oil fields. He told us something else, too. They each had three *K*s carved on their chests, indicating that the Ku Klux Klan had killed them. Everybody assumed the Klan killed Louis, too, even though there were no *K*s on his chest.

CHAPTER TEN

Louis' death hung like a pall over our usually cheery community. This second shooting death within the Galilee Baptist Church membership came like a sucker punch as we reeled from the shock of losing Seck Nesbet to a mysterious and violent death. Even the weather took a peculiar turn. The bright Indian summer we had had just days before turned suddenly into the bleakest of winters. The temperature dropped and the sky turned the hateful gray of a lead bullet.

I dreaded the unavoidable trip to the Wilson house to express our condolences. I never liked such visits. I knew that Louis's open coffin would be on display in the living room, and I'd be forced to face the shell of a person I had once talked with, laughed with, argued with, knowing that we could never again share an opinion, a thought, or even a smile. I always felt uncomfortable staring at someone who couldn't stare back. This time I felt guilt as well. How could I face the Wilsons, knowing that I had information about Louis's death that I would not share with them? I couldn't bear to look at the waxen face in the casket, even though it bore little resemblance to the Louis I had known.

Lula Pendergast had taken over the Wilsons' kitchen, frying chicken and serving it up to visitors along with an array of vegetables and desserts women from the church had brought. She had left Mr. Joe Ollie to run the boardinghouse. Nate Jackson was close by, assisting however he could. Even though Mr. Nate wasn't much of a cook, he responded quickly to "Git me two mo' chickens out the ice box," or "Find me a pan to put these here butter beans in." She saw me and gripped me for a long time in a tight, silent hug. Then just as abruptly, she went back to her chickens. "Seem lack God done cussed us mo' than he blessed us, puttin' money on the colored side of Knox Plains," she said. "Seem lack we was gooder off when we was all po'. Kin I fix you a plate, honey?"

The kitchen was full of the best cooking in Knox Plains. This would be a great party, I thought, if we had gathered for some other reason. No one would have had more fun in this splendid collection of food and folks than Louis.

As visitors came and went, Amos and Cora Wilson floated through their house like sleepwalkers, speaking and acting without logic or purpose, looking directly at people without seeing or hearing them. Ordinary household chores were either neglected completely or mindlessly done and redone.

The Nesbet sisters sat in a corner to themselves, no doubt reminded of their own troubles. Since their sister-in-law sold the ground from under their feet, they were forced to share a room at Mrs. Pendergast's, which I heard Mrs. Pendergast was letting them have for almost nothing. Because they no longer had room for Rosetta, the Nesbet sisters were making arrangements to send their niece to live with a cousin in St. Louis.

I noticed that neither Lorraine nor Wesley was there, and asked where they were. "I b'lieve Wesley's out back. Lorraine say she had to go out for a bit. She'll be back d'rectly. If you wants coffee, there's some in the kitchen," Mrs. Wilson said, repeating an offer I had turned down less than a minute earlier.

I found Wesley in the gazebo. "How are you doing?" I asked.

"How do you suppose?" he answered, with a smile that was empty of joy or mirth.

I hated that I was so bad at finding the right words in situations like this. "You and your family are in my prayers," I offered.

Wesley ignored my greeting-card expression of sympathy. "She's gone!" he spat angrily.

She? Was he so confused by grief that he was calling his brother "she"?

"I knew that little half-white Jezebel didn't want nothing from my brother but money. She got what she come for, now she just took off." I figured out that he meant Lorraine.

"Your mother said Lorraine had gone out for a while."

"Yeah. For a long while, and she took Pa's twelve thousand dollars with her. I checked the safe. It was open and empty. I called up Dan Johnston over there at the bank. Louis's account was closed this morning. That money's gone, and so is that she-devil Lorraine. All I found in that safe was this." He snorted with disgust as he handed me a sepia photograph in a cardboard frame. It was Louis and Lorraine posed against a photographer's backdrop of a garden in front of an opulent antebellum house. This must have been one of the photographs they had had made the day Louis introduced me to her. Lorraine, flawless and regal, was looking at the camera, but Louis's eyes were on his lovely companion. He looked like the proudest, happiest man on earth.

Miss Sadie wasn't well enough to join the other mourners at Amos and Cora Wilson's new house or to go to Galilee Baptist Church for the funeral. At her request, Cornelius Creasy and his staff brought Louis's coffin to the old house the afternoon before the funeral so Miss Sadie could sit with Louis one last time. I came by while Louis's body was there. When I realized Miss Sadie was having a private wake with her grandson, I told Miss Eddie Mae not to disturb her; I'd come back. But Miss Eddie Mae urged me go in and sit with my old friend.

In the gloomy room, heavy with late afternoon shadows, Miss Sadie sat silent and expressionless. I squeezed her hand and lightly kissed her forehead. She looked long at my face as though searching for the answer to a riddle. Finally, she spoke. "What make folks so mean?" she asked rhetorically. "How come the devil git holt of some folks so bad they don't care what kinda wickedness they got to do, long as they gits what they wants?"

Miss Sadie had known a lot of sorrow in her life, and certainly death was no stranger to her. She had buried five husbands and three children, two as infants, but somehow the loss of her beloved grandson seemed something outside of nature and God's ever mysterious plan. Her other losses had come in hard times, when poverty dominated and most people like her, even after slavery had officially ended, were viewed as mere possessions, often with less value than a good plowing mule or a strong riding horse. Sudden or violent death didn't seem out of place in that context. But this loss had come in times of prosperity, perhaps because of prosperity.

Mixed with her sorrow was a terrible anger that someone had thought so little of what she loved so dearly, that the beautiful boy she had helped bring into the world, rocked as an infant, and nursed through childhood diseases, whose boyhood laughter had been the joy of her life, whose early stumbling recitals of ABCs and multiplication tables had been her personal wealth, meant nothing more to someone than a chance to vent some racial anger or maybe just steal a few dollars and a car.

For weeks after the burial, Miss Sadie distanced herself from the people around her as she tried to reconnect with God, to understand why He could allow something that brought so much pain and no discernible good. "I done heard all my life that the Lord work in mysterious ways, His wonders to perfo'm, but I don' see no wonders here, Roos'velt. Try as I may, I can' b'lieve no good could ever come out of this here wickedness."

When I came by to read to her, Miss Sadie only wanted to hear the Bible. She asked for such dark passages as the sufferings of Job. "'Know now that God hath overthrown me, and hath compassed me with his net,'" I read. "'Behold I cry out of wrong, but I am not heard: I cry aloud, but there is no judgment. He hath fenced up my way that I cannot pass, and he hath set darkness in my paths. He hath stripped me of my glory, and taken the crown from my head. He hath destroyed me on every side and I am gone and mine hope hath he removed like a tree.'"

It puzzled me sometimes why Miss Sadie wanted the Bible read to her. There didn't seem to be a passage that she didn't have memorized. She knew exactly the words I would be reading before I read them.

Miss Eddie Mae would meet me at the door, saying, "My ma's down today," and Miss Sadie would mutter, "Ah stays down."

One day when I came by, she seemed cheerier. She seemed finally to have snapped out of her melancholy. I said, "I'm happy to see you so perky, Miz Sadie."

"Don't you tell," she whispered, "but I got the good news las' night." She smiled at me as though we were two little children up to some devilment. "The Lord done told me he comin' for me, he comin' to take me home. I's gonna see Louis soon, and my husbands: Tom, Cyrus, John, Charlie, and my third husband. What was that boy's name? Anyway, I's go' see 'em, and my little lost babies, too. And I's gonna see the Lord face to face, praise His holy name." She carried on as though she were planning a big trip to New York or across the ocean to Paris.

"And He done give me another blessin', Roos'velt," Miss Sadie went on. "He done drained the poison and anger out of my soul. You know the worstest thang can happen to a body is you let yo'se'f git all fill up with the poison of hate. That's worser than grief, worser than pain, worser than slavery. I knowed a man named Rufus way back when. His master was kilt in the waw, and the old lady, she couldn't control no field han's, so she jes' let 'em all go. Well, old Rufus, he knowed blacksmithin' and got to makin' a pretty good wage after he got free, but he didn't never smile, nawsuh! Years after slavery was over and done wid, he was still mad 'bout he used to be a slave. Didn't have a smile or a kind word for nobody, colored or white. I looked at ole Rufus one day and I say to myse'f, 'You know, Rufus ain't got no human master no mo', but he jes' as much a slave as he ever been. Now he a slave to his own bad feelin's.' I was 'bout to git jes' like ole Rufus, but the Lord done brought me out of that. He done he'ped me to accep' His will.

"I was laying up in the bed las' night, couldn't sleep, couldn't thank of nothin' but po' li'l Louis and why he had to die lack that. I jes' couldn't still the hate fo' them mens what killed him. I was mad, Roos'velt. I was jes' plain mad, and ya know what come to me?" A little smile broke across her wrinkled black mouth. "Somethin' you read to me way back years ago, somethin' I hadn't thought about in I don't know the day when. Somethin' that say when you's a Christian, sometime you go' be axed to believe what's unbelievable, you go' be axed to love what's unlovable, and you go' be axed to forgive what's unforgivable. And you cain't do none of that by yo'se'f. But the glory of Jesus Christ is that wid Him you can do all that. He gimme that blessin' last night, and now I's gonna meet my precious Jesus and thank Him to his face."

I was stunned to hear someone speak of death with joy and anticipation. At the same time, I was almost panicked at the thought of losing this wise and dear friend. I felt some precious thing was slipping away, and I was powerless to pull it back. "Miz Sadie, are you sure? Maybe you're just feeling this way because of your grief for Louis."

She gave me a look that pitied my lack of understanding. "I'm sho', son. I'm on that bright road home. I can feel the damp dew of the Jordan. I'm goin' to that place where ever' day is Sunday, ever' month is the month of May, and ever' year is the year of Jubilee." She closed her eyes and smiled a faraway smile as though she were already there. "Now would you please read me that Hunnard-an'-Twen'y-Firs' Psalm?"

This time, she had asked for a passage of scripture that I knew without looking. "I will lift up mine eyes unto the hills, from whence cometh my help," I started to recite before I had found the page. "My help cometh from the Lord, which made heaven and earth . . ."

At home, I found Nate Jackson and Uncle Will sitting together in the front parlor, the late autumn chill having finally driven them from the front porch to the warmth of the season's first hearth fire. Their friendship was like the fire itself, familiar and comfortable yet bright with energy and color, constantly revealing new shapes and patterns. All of Mr. Nate's oil money hadn't changed that. I sat with them for a while. Mr. Nate said, "Ya know, Will, when you ain't got no money, you thanks money kin fix ever'thang. That sho' was what I thought. Rat this minute I reckon Amos'd give up ever' cent he got to have Louis back. I know cain't nobody do nothing 'bout what done happened, but I gots to know jes' what did happen. You got anythang in them roots and what-not that can tell me that?"

Uncle Will took a draw on his pipe and stretched his peg leg. "Even the chickydee-whick don't know ever'thang," he said. "And what she do know, she don' always tell all at one time. She don' like to tell 'bout killin' and dyin' 'til she ready to tell. Ya know, I los' my family back in Mississippi when I was jes' a young buck. Thas how I got the chickydee-whick in the firs' place. All my kin was wiped out when some low-down skunk poisoned the well when we uz all at Grandpappy Floyd's back fifty or mo' years ago."

I'd heard that story about Uncle Will's family all being poisoned at a family reunion, and I never believed it for a second. I was appalled that Uncle Will was still pushing his tall tales in a community torn up with real grief, but I'd begun to suspect that in his old age Uncle Will was no longer able to distinguish between the yarns he'd been telling and real life. Maybe he'd actually started to believe in the chickydee-whick.

Uncle Will continued his story. "We had jes' pull the wagon into the yard, when Cou'in Charlie come up and say Aint Susie cain't find her good hatbox nowheres. Allst they could figga was she musta lef' it at the train depot. So ever'body else gits off the wagon and I goes by m'self down to the train depot to look for the hatbox. Never did find it. When I got back to the house, I fount ever' last body there stretched out dead. It were the saddest funeral in the hist'ry of the county— twen'y-three coffins and I was the onliest mourner.

"Well, I set out from that day to find who done it. Couldn't no-body tell me nothin'. Then one day somebody say, 'Go see Ole Man Mordecai. If'n he cain't tell you, it ain't to be knowed.' They tell 'bout a house way off in the wood. There wasn't even no road goin' out there, but somehow or 'nother I come up on it after while. It wasn't nothin' but a li'l fallin'-apart shack, weeds all growed up around it. I didn't see nobody there. Long about then a voice from under a shade tree say, 'What you want?' It 'uz Ole Man Mordecai. He was so black, you couldn't even see him sittin' there in the shade.

"Well I was young and fulla vinegar, so I says, 'You 'pose to know ever'thang, you tell me how come I'm here.' Well, he rared back and laughed like the devil. 'You come to me 'cause you wants to larn who kilt yo' kin,' he say. 'What you got fo' me?'

" 'What you mean, what I got?' I axed him. He say, 'I got special powers. You don't know what I know for nothin'. Seem lack this here wo'th 'bout a hunnard dollas.' I say, 'I ain't got no hunnard dollas.' He say, 'Well, gimme twen'y dollas, then.' I say, 'I ain't got no twen'y dollas.'

So he say, 'What 'bout that twen'y-dolla gol' piece yo' pappy give you rat after the waw?' There wasn't no way he coulda knowed 'bout the gol' piece 'cept he had powers. My pappy give me that gol' piece in secret. I got no ide' if he earnt it, fount it, stole it, or what, but didn't nobody know 'bout it but me and him."

"Did ya give it to him, Will?" Mr. Nate asked.

"Sho' I did, and Ole Man Mordecai, he give me the chickydee-whick for it. He larnt me how to read it, too. He say he warn't long for this worl' an' that's how come he sell me the chickydee-whick for a twen'y-dolla gol' piece. Now he wouldn't've sol' the chickydee-whick to jes' anybody, but he knowed I was the seventh son of a seventh son, bawn wid a veil over my face.

"I went to the chickydee-whick ever' day for 'bout six munts. She wouldn't tell me who kilt my kin. Then one day she spelt out 'T.R.,' plain as day. Somebody tell me that was fo' Tom Rivers. Come to find out Rivers was a mean ole coot who'd been fightin' wid my pappy fo' years over some lan' up by the creek. Ole Rivers was out to see my pappy couldn't get that lan', and none of his kin could claim it neither. When he fount out the whole family was go' be at Granpappy Floyd's fo' Sunday dinner, well he up and poison Grandpappy Floyd's well. He meant to kill us all, an' he got ever'body but me. He wasn't go' res' til he got me, too, and sho' nuff I looked up one day and there's Rivers wid a shotgun pointed rat at me."

"Did he shoot at you, Uncle Will?" I asked.

"Naw. He didn't shoot *at* me. He shot me. I run all the way to the railroad tracks wid a slug in my left leg. Hopped a freight with nothin' of my own but a piece of ole cracklin' bread I had in my pocket fo' dinna and the chickydee-whick. I didn't git off til we was in Oklahoma. By then the leg was so bad they had to take it off at the knee. I ain't been back to Mississippi to this day."

I had heard Uncle Will tell another story in which the Wabash Cannonball took his leg off. In fact, his stories often contradicted each other, but nobody seemed to notice that but me and maybe Ma, who would sigh, "Oh, Uncle Will," when the story got really outrageous. In all this I had never developed a clue as to how and why the chickydee-whick was supposed to work. Maybe the jar really did go back to before the Civil War, but I knew the roots were not the original ones. I had seen Uncle Will change the chickydee-whick's roots from time to time. Whether the strange talisman's magic was supposed to be in the jar itself or in some spirit that lived inside it, I never knew. I did notice one thing about Uncle Will's stories: they always seemed to leave his listeners feeling better than they did when they sat down.

CHAPTER ELEVEN

Ma took great pleasure in going through the morning mail. When Barnett or I got back from the post office with the day's deliveries, she poured herself a cup of warmed-over coffee and started a treasure hunt through the stack of envelopes for letters from her many friends across the country. Most were people she had met in college and kept in touch with over the years. She truly hit the jackpot when there was something from Phyllis Dyson, a classmate from Fisk who had become a professional dancer, then married the owner of a Harlem nightclub. Mrs. Dyson didn't write often, but when she did, the letter was a long one, filled with lively stories about life in New York. One letter had a photograph of Mr. and Mrs. Dyson. He was at the club's piano and she was sitting on top of it in a satin dress with her legs crossed and her skirt halfway up her thighs. They looked so fancy and prosperous it would have been easy to believe that they owned New York.

Sometimes Ma would laugh out loud as she read her friend's comical narratives of the assorted Jazz Age characters who came and went in her life. An endless parade of flappers, musicians, bootleggers, and dandies spent their evenings in Mr. Dyson's nightclub. It was a world where gangsters operated freely and Prohibition laws were honored more in the breach than the observance. The letters detailed a glamorous life of men and women in high-fashion clothes, dancing the latest steps and smoking cigarettes from long, slender holders. I'd have given a mule just to be able to sit back and watch it all for an evening.

While Mrs. Dyson seemed to love New York's nightlife, she also had a serious intellectual side that thrived on the city's rich cultural climate. She especially loved the proliferation of Negro arts in what people were now calling the Harlem Renaissance. Her gifts to Ma were always books. She sent plays, poetry, art and photography collections, fiction, essays, just about everything. Ma's flighty New York friend sent Christmas gifts in March or sometimes April, and birthday gifts nowhere near Ma's birthday, but the fact that these presents came completely unexpectedly made them all the more delightful.

Every letter included an invitation to come to New York and "help some of these rich colored men spend their money." Ma read me a section of the latest Mrs. Dyson missive: "Honey child, we have to get you to New York to see some jazz bands and blues singers, and downtown to one of these Broadway musicals. I'll take you to Madam Walker's salon first so they can fix you up to go out on the town."

"Yeah," Ma snorted, "I know what she means by 'fix you up.' She wants to get me in there and let those women bleach and bob my hair. That'll be the day!" Ma loved reading about all those folks putting on the Ritz in New York, but she really had no desire to put on a short satin skirt and wave a feather boa in some man's face.

Further into the letter, Mrs. Dyson brought up another favorite topic of discussion. "I read in the newspaper that they've started work on that monument to your hero. I don't know which amazes me more, that they actually are going to carve the faces of four presidents into the side of a mountain in South Dakota or that your favorite president, Theodore Roosevelt, is one of them. I'll grant you that President Roosevelt accomplished some good things, but I just can't see where he belongs up there with Washington, Jefferson, and Lincoln." Ma, of course, was already well aware of the carving of Mount Rushmore. She interpreted the inclusion of Roosevelt as final evidence that Old Rough and Ready was generally regarded as one of America's greatest leaders. Ma and Mrs. Dyson had debated the greatness of Theodore Roosevelt since their college years, when the Spanish-American War hero was in his first elected term as president.

Through my early boyhood, I thought of women as quiet, homey people like the women at Galilee Baptist Church. Ma was the only woman I knew who seemed to have much interest in politics. The letters between her and Phyllis Dyson offered my first clue that for some women, their first interest wasn't what was going on in the home. Then in 1924 a peculiar thing happened. Texas elected a woman governor, a lady named Muriel Furgerson. Now, I had never heard of a woman being governor, or anything like that. Just four years after a constitutional amendment gave women all over the country the right to vote, Muriel Furgerson became the second elected female governor in the United States. Wyoming had voted in the first just five days earlier. When I heard the news, I thought, *That's the craziest thing I ever heard of.* But then I remembered that my ma was about the smartest, most level-headed person I knew, and she was a woman. I could see her running the state with no problem. Another thing that made me warm up to Mrs. Muriel Furgerson as governor is that the first thing she wanted to do when she took office was run the Klan out of Texas.

Some people said that Muriel Furgerson was governor in name only, that the Democrats ran her for office because her husband, the former governor, was now ineligible because of a felony conviction. Whichever Governor Furgerson was actually in charge seemed to have meant it about the Klan. The group didn't disappear completely in Texas, but during the first year of Muriel Furgerson's administration they became a lot less active and a lot less open. There were even a few court convictions for some of the more blatant illegal activities, but in a state still nursing its Civil War wounds, there was no way the courts or the law enforcement officials would come down too hard on white Southerners terrorizing those they saw as enemies of "the Southern way of life."

Southern justice, even when it was relatively just, was often informal and personal. A sheriff or a judge would sometimes visit the offender at home and say something like, "Now, Billy Wade, I don't want to hear about you doing nothing like that again or I might just have to lock you up." If Billy Wade had half a lick of sense, he got the idea. That was pretty much how the Klan was handled in most of Texas, and in most places it worked. Of course, you're always going to have some hotheads who won't act right no matter what.

Joe Ollie Harkwell told me in the strictest confidence—the same way he passed this information along to every other colored person in Knox Plains—that in a sort of under-the-table way, the men who killed the laborers from Arkansas had been identified and made to answer for their crime. Of course, the punishment was far from adequate to pay for cold-blooded murder. No one was hanged, did prison time, or even went on public record as a criminal, but the killers were hit where they were already hurting—in their bank accounts. The murdered men had wives and children back in Arkansas that they had hoped to take care of with the money they earned in the oil fields. The murderers were made to do what their victims had been unable to: provide for the colored laborers' families.

In seems an informant, someone who had been with the group that night, came forward and told Judge Davis Calhoun, a Texas superior court judge, that the Knox Plains Ku Klux Klan had killed two men that he knew about, and some of the group may have murdered the third man, too. The killers were just who we all thought, old Knox Plains gentry—Willis Dayton and his buddies.

Years of listening to the prissy town gossip had taught me that while Mr. Joe Ollie often added his own flounce to a story, he never flat-out lied. And when I thought about it, the story he told fit Barnett's like pieces of a jigsaw puzzle. Mr. Joe Ollie told me every detail about the person who came forward except his name. Refusing to reveal his source was Mr. Joe Ollie's gesture of loyalty to his employer.

The informant went to Judge Calhoun's house one Saturday afternoon to set the record straight. Amazingly, Mr. Joe Ollie was actually in the room when the judge and his visitor were talking. Mr. Joe Ollie was sitting in the corner by the breakfront, polishing Mrs. Calhoun's silver. They took no more notice of him than they did of Judge Calhoun's hunting dog, Pete, who was napping near the door.

Here's the story as Mr. Joe Ollie revealed it. The informant told the judge that he didn't want to see his friends go to jail for what they did, but he hoped the judge could somehow influence them to never do anything like it again. The fellow said he felt so bad about what had happened he couldn't sleep, and he thought if he could keep it from happening again, at least that would be something. "I could see it if they was bad niggers—you know, the kind always looking for trouble anyways," he told the judge, "but these men, well, they was just looking for work to take care of their families, and ain't that what a man's supposed to do?"

The young informant in Judge Calhoun's sitting room said he had never been on a Klan raid before, but the others had insisted he come along that night because he had to learn sometime "what a white man has to do to protect what's his." He said the group went out to the barn and got all liquored up before they went off. The newcomer, it seems, didn't drink, so when the others offered him whiskey, he took only a token sip and passed the bottle on.

"By the time we were ready to go out, they was pretty drunk and talking about how they was going to find some niggers and teach 'em not to mess in white folks' business," the confessor reportedly said. He expected their targets to be black men who had done well in the oil strike and had the audacity to remain in Knox Plains, flaunting their wealth in front of their former bosses. But drunk as they were, they recalled the understated but very serious warning from Pennant Oil's Mr. Sullivan: "I'm not expecting any problems between this council and our local partners, but should such problems arise, Pennant Oil is prepared to deal with them."

All they were looking for that night was some assurance that they still had control. They could find that assurance by making some powerless colored man plead for his life. But according to the former

Klansman's story, as recounted by Mr. Joe Ollie, instead of pleading for their lives, the laborers, who knew they were about to die anyway, called the night riders spineless cowards without the guts to take on a colored man unarmed and dared them to put down their guns and fight like men. Instead, one of the Klansmen fired, killing first one man then the other. That was when Judge Calhoun's informant turned his horse around and headed back to the main road. It was his horse Barnett had heard on the narrow path some fifteen minutes before the other men, who apparently stayed to carve Ks on the men's chests. Mr. Joe Ollie quoted Judge Calhoun's mystery guest one final time: "I never been so ashamed of nothing as I was to be part of them. I mean, I been close to them men all my life and all that, but the nigger was right. What kind of men get guns and gang up on a man that's got none?"

Judge Calhoun never revealed his source, but he did tell his good friend Walt Preston, himself a retired judge, what he had done about the situation. Again, Mr. Joe Ollie was only a few feet away, this time polishing the judge's hardwood floors. Judge Calhoun told Judge Preston how he quietly visited each of the offenders and explained, "I believe in white supremacy myself, and we got to control the niggers if we're gonna have a community where we can live in peace. But you can't go around killing niggers just for being niggers. That's wrong. If you kill the ones that are acting uppity and making trouble, that sends a message to the others, but if you start killing the ones that are behaving, you're going to get all of 'em stirred up, and that's no good. I personally would never send a white man to jail for killing a nigger, but y'all killed niggers that hadn't done anything wrong, so you were wrong and you need to pay for it." He assessed a dollar amount from each of the men on a monthly basis. He learned who the laborers were and arranged to send an envelope with cash to each of their families every month for years to come. It wasn't much of a penalty for murder, but it appeared that the Klansmen who killed those innocent laborers were going to pay a higher price than the men who killed Louis.

One day in the store, Barnett admitted to me that he had wheedled Mr. Joe Ollie into telling him the name of the man who revealed the killers to Judge Calhoun. It was Eli, Willis Dayton's seventeen-year-old son. I was shocked. Barnett said he had been, too. He told me, "I just keep thinking this must be some kind of trick. After all, Eli is a Dayton, and the apple doesn't fall far from the tree."

"Oh, I don't know," I mused. "Every now and again an apple falls, hits a slope, rolls down a hill, bumps against a rock, bounces over the creek, and winds up a long, long way from that tree."

Before 1927 was over, the Grim Reaper had swung his feared scythe into the congregation of Galilee Baptist twice more. Miz Sadie's prophecy of her own death was fulfilled quietly the Sunday after Thanksgiving. One part of my heart was sorrowful, but at the same time I felt a victorious rush, like when one of your teammates steps on home plate for the winning run.

Early in December, Ella Nesbet slumped into her seat in the parlor of Mrs. Pendergast's boardinghouse for what everyone assumed was an after-dinner nap. When Mrs. Pendergast gently shook her shoulder and asked wouldn't she be more comfortable in her room, she discovered that the sixty-one-year-old woman had silently slipped from this world to the next. Dr. Billups said it was most likely a heart attack, but I believe her heart was simply broken, broken by the loss of her beloved brother and the home he and his twin had lovingly built for them.

The Nesbets were never ones to display much affection, publicly or privately, but in their own way, the Nesbet sisters had loved Mr. Seck dearly. Most people saw him as a sour, stingy old man, but his sisters, Ella especially, knew he could be loving and giving to anyone who met him on his terms. His stinginess toward his young bride was a stubborn reaction to her greedy demands. In fact, he would have given her anything had she not demanded everything as her right. After a lifetime in his house, both Ella and Violet knew that all you had to do was approach Mr. Seck with "Brother, if you could see your way clear, I'd really like to have . . ." and he'd grant almost anything. But if you insisted that he give you something because you felt it your due, he'd go cold and hungry himself before he'd let you have a coin or a crumb.

PART FOUR

GOING TO KANSAS CITY

After a Saturday-night adventure that almost cost him his life, Barnett was willing to spend his evenings at home for a while. The most excitement Barnett and I had was slipping off to the Jackson house to listen to reels. Wright had gotten himself a Victrola and all the latest records by Ma Rainy, Bessie Smith, and lots of other blues singers.

These records were called reels, both by those who enjoyed them and those who denounced them as "the devil's music." The combination of sensuous rhythms and suggestive lyrics shocked respectable communities. When Bessie Smith sang, "I want a little sugar in my bowl/I need a little hot dog in my roll," there wasn't much doubt what she was singing about. Some of the good Baptists would get up in church on Sunday morning and announce that they did not allow drinking, card games, dancing, or reel playing in their houses. Curiously, they often named the popular singers and their latest blues songs during the diatribe.

Wright Jackson's favorite was a song called "Going to Kansas City." It seemed to spark his desire to see what life in the big city was like. Soon after school let out for the 1928 fall break, Barnett and I were minding the store one afternoon when Wright's pink LaSalle pulled up to the gas pump. As I filled his tank, Wright seemed deep in thought.

Just as he was about to get back in the car, he stopped and looked straight at me. "Hey, Moose," he asked, "you and Barnett ever been to Kansas City?" He knew darn well we hadn't.

I shrugged. "We're going one of these days."

"How 'bout nex' week?"

We just stared at him. He had to be joking.

Our silence shocked him. "You gots to think about it? I'm talkin' about takin' you to Kansas City, someplace li'l ole Barnett Lindsay and li'l ole Roosevelt Moose O'Malley wouldn't never get to go, and you gots to think about it?"

Barnett jumped right on it. "Sure, Wright, we want to go. You mean it, don't you? You're not just messin' with us?"

"Hell, like I ain't got nothin' to do but mess with such as you. I'm leavin' first daylight Monday mornin'. You goin' or not?"

Ma didn't like it. Our going to Kansas City for a week meant she didn't have help in the store, not that it was anything she and Uncle Will couldn't handle. She didn't think Kansas City, or any big city for that matter, was a fit place for young men not out of their teens. And she didn't trust Wright Jackson as far as she could fling him against an east Texas twister. But she could tell we wanted to go so bad that even if she said no, we might just go anyway. Her control over Barnett had been slipping away for years. Now she feared I might rebel, too, so she reluctantly consented.

We didn't ask Wright why he wanted us to come with him. We figured we knew. First of all, he was going to Kansas City to show off how much money he had. Showing off was about all Wright ever did after his daddy got rich, and we figured he wanted to do it in front of someone who could come back with him and tell the whole town. And there was another reason. We had road maps in the store to help folks who got lost, and Barnett and I had learned to read them. I don't think Wright Jackson had ever seen a road map. There was no telling where he'd wind up by himself.

I didn't quite believe we were really going until early Monday morning, when I saw the pink LaSalle coming up the road. I was wide awake with excitement. I had never even been to Dallas, let alone Kansas City.

Even in Kansas City, the pink LaSalle turned heads, especially when people saw three black fellows in it. As we pulled over to the curb to decide our next move, someone shouted, "Hey, good-lookin'!" We looked up, and Wright and Barnett saw a pretty, smiling light-brown-skinned girl. I saw trouble in a flapper dress and silk stockings.

She strutted over to the car, swinging a little silk purse. "Where you boys headed?" she asked.

"We wants to go to the bes' hotel in Kansas City," Wright told her, grooming himself as best he could with his bare hands. We had been driving for two days on dusty roads and had slept in the car. "Don't matter what it costs."

She looked thoughtful. "That would be the West Wind, but you boys don't want to go there. They're not too nice to our kind. Let me take you someplace where you'll be real comfortable and you'll have a good time, too."

That put a huge grin on Wright's face. I couldn't catch Wright's eye to signal that maybe a little caution was in order. He was looking only at that pretty little café-au-lait with the lip rouge and spit curls. "All right. That sound like where we wants to go," he said. She told us her name was Mamie as she hopped into the seat next to me. Even after seeing all those girls who moved into Mrs. Pendergast's boardinghouse, I still was shocked at such boldness from a female.

She took us to a hotel called the Palace, which, though nowhere close to a palace, was still pretty nice. Wright got a room for himself and another one for Barnett and me to share. As we started toward the stairs, Mamie whispered to Wright, "There's a speakeasy 'round in back. Why don't you join me there after you get cleaned up? Just go down the alley behind the hotel to the gray door with the little diamond-shaped window. Knock three times, then when somebody comes to the door, say, 'Tommy sent me.' " She turned to Barnett and me. "You boys can come, too, if you want."

In the hall just outside our rooms, I said, "I don't believe it. There's a speakeasy here."

"I don' know what that is," Wright admitted. "I jes' wanted to see some mo' of that cute li'l Mamie. Where she invitin' us anyhow?"

"It's a drinking place," I explained.

"That ain't agin' the law here?" Wright asked, puzzled.

"Sure it is," I said, proud to be the youngest but most knowledgeable among us. "That's why we have to do that whole 'Tommy sent me' thing. Are you really going?"

Of course he was going. He was ready to follow little sweet-smelling Mamie to the gates of Torment. When Barnett and I were alone in our room, I said, "I don't think we ought to go to that speakeasy. We could get in trouble."

"You're such a goody-good!" Barnett shrieked. "Are you planning to never have any fun in your whole life?"

"The trouble with trouble," I answered, "is that it usually starts out as fun."

"That sounds like something Miz Davenport would say. I might as well have come to Kansas City with her."

I thought of Barnett and our sixth-grade teacher slipping off to Kansas City together and laughed out loud at the image. "Do you think Miz Davenport would share this room with you?" I smiled and raised my eyebrows suggestively.

Barnett laughed, too. "You're out of your mind, Moose. Come on, just for a little bit. We won't drink or do anything wrong. I just want to see what it looks like."

In the alley behind the hotel, we found the gray door easily. The little diamond-shaped window had a dark red curtain across it. Following Mamie's instructions, Barnett knocked three times. Someone peeped from behind the curtain, and a voice that made me want to turn around and leave asked, "What is it?"

"Tommy sent us," Barnett answered. I wondered if it was okay to say "Tommy sent us." The code Mamie gave was "Tommy sent *me*." The door opened anyway. Inside, people were playing cards and drinking. A piano player was pounding out a song I'd heard on one of Wright's reels.

Wright was already at a table with Mamie and some white man. They were all drinking whiskey, smoking, talking, and laughing. When we walked in, Mamie turned to the tall chocolate-brown man who was waiting tables and said, "Lincoln, make these boys comfortable at that table over by the wall. Get them whatever they want."

"Two Coca-Colas," I said, which caused Lincoln to break into a grin that stopped just short of a laugh. There were several card games going on, but Barnett couldn't keep his eyes off one in the far corner of the room. There were black men in fancy suits playing cards and laughing while heavily made-up women in satin and feathers leaned over them, joining in the laughter and refilling their glasses from a bottle of whiskey on the table. They were all smoking cigarettes, even the women.

As we sipped our colas, Barnett seemed more and more fixated on that table in the corner. Finally, he said to me, "Moose, I'm going to see if there's a johnny crapper back there." I thought that was odd because he'd just been to the toilet before we came downstairs. What was even odder was that when he got about halfway across the room, he turned and came back to our table.

"Let's go for a walk, Moose," he said with an urgency that suggested he wasn't just in need of a breath of fresh air. I nodded and walked with him toward the door. As we passed Wright's table, I said, "We're gonna take a little look around town. We'll be back in a few minutes."

Wright waved a small acknowledgment. We could have gone to Venus for all he cared. Barnett didn't speak until we were at least a hundred feet from the building. "Moose," he said. "I recognize two of the men at that table back there. They're the men who killed Louis Wilson."

"What! Are you sure?"

"I'm positive. But that's not all. The two women with them are Lorraine Dupree Wilson and her friend Fancy. Fancy, by the way, sure wasn't acting like the mother of a young child. I think Lorraine and that man she's all over planned to kill Louis right from the start."

"But he was her husband." I realized how innocent I sounded even as I was saying the words.

"We've got to get Wright and get out of town—tonight! The men never saw me that night out on the highway, but Lorraine and Fancy will recognize us and Wright."

We hurried back to the speakeasy, and I went through the "Tommy sent me" thing again while Barnett stood watch. I was hoping I could signal to Wright without the others noticing me. But when I got inside, Wright was gone. So were Mamie and the white man who was with her. I looked all over the room. The killers were still at the back table with Lorraine and Fancy. They never looked my way.

I caught Lincoln as he passed by me with drinks for another table. "Do you know where the man we were with went?"

"Nope. They just got up and left a few minutes ago." I had a feeling that would have been his answer whether he knew anything or not.

When we walked around to the front of the hotel, we noticed that the car was gone, too. We had no idea where to start looking. Besides, there were cold-blooded murderers just a few yards away from us, so we went back upstairs and locked ourselves in our room. "There's something else I didn't tell you earlier," Barnett said. "I saw a car parked outside the hotel, and I'm almost certain it was Louis's. At first I thought it was a black Pierce-Arrow, but it could be dark blue. I looked inside. There's a radio, and a little hole just above the running board. It looks to me like a bullet hole.'

From time to time, we opened our hotel-room door slightly and peeked out, hoping to catch Wright coming back to his room. After a couple of hours, Barnett said, "You know, I wish we'd gotten something to eat before we shut ourselves in up here."

"I'm hungry, too, but those men in the speakeasy will kill us a lot faster than starvation will."

After a while our weariness from the long road trip won out over our anxiety, and Barnett and I both fell asleep. The first light of day was easing into the window when I opened my eyes. My plan was to wake Wright and get on the road before the rest of this crazy town woke up. Still in my bedclothes, I went out in the hall and tapped on Wright's door. I had to knock several times before he answered. Finally, he said, "Mamie?"

"No. It's me, Moose."

"What you want, Moose? It's early. I ain't had much sleep. Go on back to bed. I gots a surprise for you boys later."

"We've got one for you, too. But I think we'll save it until we're on the road."

He opened the door slightly. "We can't leave just yet. I've got bidness to take care of."

"Business?"

"A little somethin' I set up last night. Gimme another coupla hours. Then 'bout eight o'clock, I'll buy you boys some breakfast and go show you my surprise." He closed the door again and refused to reopen it.

Even though I could have used a little more sleep, sleep wouldn't come. I waited about an hour and a half, then I woke Barnett to confirm that what we'd seen the night before hadn't been a bad dream. "Wright's in his room," I said, "but he won't get up until eight."

"Did you tell him?"

"No. First of all, I swore in blood that I wouldn't tell about the killers. And I was afraid to tell him about Lorraine and Fancy being here. After all, Fancy took his daddy's money by lying about Matt. And while he doesn't know Lorraine is all kissy-face with the man who killed Louis, he does know that Lorraine left town with the money Louis's daddy gave them to buy a house. Remember, Louis was Wright's best friend."

"Great day in the morning, we're in a pickle, Moose. What are we going to do?"

"Well, I've been lying here thinking about it since early this morning. I think we should talk Wright into heading back to Knox Plains any way we can. Then, after we're a hundred or so miles down the road, we can tell him that Lorraine and Fancy were in Kansas City and they were with some men we think are dangerous. We don't have to tell him they killed Louis."

About then, there was a knock at the door. Without thinking at all, I opened it. I was shocked to see Wright standing there bright-eyed and fully dressed. "I thought you was the one rarin' to go," he said. "Come on, git dressed. Let's get us some breakfast."

I wasn't ready with an argument for leaving town quickly, so I just blurted out, "We don't want any breakfast, Wright. Let's just go on back to Knox Plains."

Wright laughed. "The big city too much for you two hayseeds? Come on, I didn't git no supper las' night. I wants me some breakfast, even if you don't want none."

We dressed and walked cautiously down the stairs. The lobby was a quiet contrast to the bustle of the night before. I looked around, studying every face. I saw only one person I recognized, a thin, nervous-looking man in a shiny suit who moved quickly around the lobby, sucking deeply on a cigarette and holding brief conversations with the desk clerk, the doorman, and the bellhops. We went into the hotel restaurant and sat down. There I saw another familiar face. Lincoln, the waiter, was now serving breakfast.

Wright ordered a big breakfast of flapjacks and syrup, ham, eggs, biscuits, and sausages, with coffee to wash it down.

"I'll have the same thing," Barnett said.

When I added, "Me, too," Wright laughed so hard I worried he'd draw somebody's attention.

"I thought you boys wasn't hongry," he said, and laughed some more.

"Wright," I started in a faltering voice. "We saw some people last night that I think are dangerous. We want to go home."

"You boys jes' sked 'cause you ain't never been nowheres. Wait 'til you sees what I done. You go' fall over when you sees this."

After breakfast we got in the car to go see Wright's surprise. He was grinning like a kid at his own birthday party as we drove along a down-town street that dead-ended at a magnificent building with white marble steps and thick white columns. He parked right in front of the building. I looked up and read the words above the columns: Carnegie Public Library.

Wright took bold strides up the marble steps while Barnett and I walked cautiously behind him. He headed right to the center of the main reading room. Barnett and I stayed near the door. "Awright, listen up. I'm Wright Jackson, the new owner of this here buildin'," Wright announced loudly. "I plans to start right now turnin' it into a dance hall. Y'all kin have all these books. I don't care nothin' 'bout 'em. But you gots to get 'em all out of here by Frid'y mornin'. That's when my men'll be in here to tear out all these she'ves and start buildin' the bandstand."

I never saw a group of people look so shocked. Books dropped. Jaws went slack. Eyes bugged. Still, their amazement was nothing next to mine. When someone finally moved, it was the tiny gray-haired white lady behind the check-out desk. She walked quickly out of the room, stealing furtive glances at Wright as she made her exit. She returned seconds later with a mousy little bald man in a brown suit. "Now, see here, fellow," the man said, comically retaining his library whisper. "We generally don't have any trouble with you coloreds here in Kansas City. If you'll just leave quietly, I believe we can forget about this incident. If not, you leave me no alternative but to refer the matter to the police." He folded his arms across his chest and rolled up and down on the balls of his feet as he waited for compliance.

I liked that "leave quietly" idea. Wright didn't. "I don't thank you understands, mister. I owns this place now, and I plans to make it into a dance hall. I don't want no trouble. I jes' wants y'all to get yo' stuff out of here."

The man didn't try again. He turned and walked out of the room. Wright beckoned Barnett and me inside. Talking just to us he said, "Mamie and Jack, that white fellow was with her, said if anybody built a colored dance hall in Kansas City, they'd make a million dollars the first year, guar-ron-teed! And that's jes' what I'm fixin' to do." He kept babbling on about his plans for the building, not letting either of us work in a word of protest.

Within five minutes, there were uniformed men walking toward us. There was no way to pretend we weren't with Wright. We were the only black people in the room. "Okay, boys, the fun's over," said the big one as he clamped a thick hand on Wright's shoulder. One grabbed my arm and another got Barnett. I read my escort's badge. It said, "Kansas City Police Department." They marched us down the street to the city jail, which turned out to be just a block away.

After the three of us were alone in a cell, Barnett asked, "Wright, what the hell was that about?" Barnett didn't curse much. Ma wouldn't stand for it. But I believe if cursing was ever justified, it was at that moment.

"I bought that big ole buildin' las' night, Barnett. I swear 'fo' God I did, from that Jack Taylor fella was with Mamie. He say his daddy lef' it to him when he died 'bout three munts ago, and he jes' wanted to sell it. He say he didn't wanna keep it 'cause it made him feel sad, thinkin' 'bout his daddy and all. That's why he give me such a good price on it. He wrote me out a deed on the spot. Looka here." He pulled a folded sheet of paper from his pocket. Across the top, a childish hand had written "Deed for white building at the end of Missouri Street." Further down on the paper were the words "Sold this day Winsday 15th of Sep. the yeer of our Lord 1928 to Right Jackson for 15 thosand dollers." At the bottom, it was signed "Jack Taylor." It was sad. Even Wright's name was spelled wrong.

I let out a deep breath. "Wright," I said. "I think they were playing a joke on you. That building is the public library. It belongs to the city, like the Knox Plains library does."

"Naw," Wright protested. "Ain't no joke. Ain't no joke atall. I give that fella his money.'

My breakfast was curdling in my stomach. "What money?"

"The fifteen thousand, like it say on the deed."

"Oh, Wright," Barnett moaned. "I've read about men like him. They're called grifters or confidence men. They get you to trust them, then they take your money."

"I got a deed right here."

"You've got a piece of paper right there," I countered.

"If this was jes' some man I met in the street, I'd say you could be right, but Mamie introduce us. She say she been knowin' Jack Taylor all her life," Wright argued weakly. "I know wouldn't no colored woman he'p a white man steal a colored man's money."

"Not where we come from," I pointed out, "but I'd say that in the last three or four years, I've learned a lot about what some colored women will do."

THIRTEEN

None of us had ever been to jail before, and we had no idea what you do to get out. The only people in Kansas City we knew were Lorraine and Fancy, the last people on earth we wanted to see. Early in the afternoon, we were trying to decide what our next move should be when our jailer came in and announced that our lawyer was there to see us. With the jailer was a well-dressed young man with dark curly hair and a neatly trimmed mustache. Although we had never before seen him or heard of his existence, we each silently decided that he might be our only ticket out, so we said nothing.

The jailer let him into our cell, locked the door, then walked away. "I'm John Elliot Singer," the lawyer said, offering his hand. "I know you weren't expecting me, but I thought maybe you could use some help about now."

"How did you know about us?" Barnett demanded.

"Surely you're joking," the man responded with a slight chuckle. "Every colored person in Kansas City, and probably a good many of the white ones, too, are talking about how three colored men in a pink car tried to take over the downtown library. I just had to come see what it was about."

"You sayin' the whole town talkin' 'bout us, and then you, some young white lawyer, gonna come he'p us?" Wright asked, developing a suspicious nature about fifteen hours after he could really have used it.

"First of all," Mr. Singer answered gently, "I'm not white. I'm colored, like you. I really am a lawyer, and I think I can help you if you want my help. If you don't, just say so and I'll leave now."

It was hard to trust anybody at this point, but what choice did we have? We told him our sad story. Although clearly amused, Mr. Singer was making a polite effort to keep a straight face. "What in the world were you doing with fifteen thousand dollars in cash on you, anyway?" he asked.

"Well, somebody tol' me I'd need a heap of money if I was going to Kansas City, so I figured fifteen thousand five hunnard ought to do it."

"I should say," the lawyer answered, shaking his head in amazement. "When did you last see these people?"

"You means Mamie and Jack?"

"Yes, them."

"Well, Jack, he left with the money 'bout 'leben o'clock. Mamie come up to my room for a little while."

"What time did she leave?"

Wright looked embarrassed. "I guess I was ti'ed from the trip. I dropped off whilst she was in the room. When I waked up, she was gone."

"But she didn't take your remaining money?"

We all stared at Wright as he checked his billfold for the first time that day. Of course it was empty.

"How did you pay for breakfast?" I asked.

"That fella Linkcom say I could jes' write my name on the bill and pay it when I pay fo' the rooms. Lord, y'all, I ain't got no money lef'."

"That's going to present us with a little problem. It's okay if you don't pay me. After all, you didn't exactly retain me. But I talked to the police, and they seem to think that the judge will let you go with a fine for disturbing the peace. But you do have to pay it."

"How much would the fine be?" I asked, though I don't know why. I had less than five dollars.

"Probably just ten or fifteen dollars each. We could try explaining that you, Roosevelt and Barnett, were pretty much innocent bystanders. We could even try explaining that whole business with the confidence man, but it'll just depend on what the judge is willing to believe. However, if you tell the judge that you met this Taylor in a speakeasy, that could make matters worse. After all, those places are illegal."

Even though Barnett and I had been about as innocent that morning as two bystanders could be, I didn't have the heart to turn my back on Wright. He looked like a kicked kitten.

"Do any of you have an account with a major bank back in Texas?" Mr. Singer asked. "Maybe I could arrange a funds transfer through a local bank."

Wright, who with some justification felt responsible for this whole mess, explained his family's good fortune in the oil business and offered to try getting money from the account he held jointly with his pa and his brother.

The police sergeant agreed to release Wright into Mr. Singer's cus-
tody for a few hours. Barnett and I were left in the Kansas City jail. A
bright red sun was low on the horizon when Mr. Singer came back,
without Wright. The jailer unlocked the door. "Come on," Mr. Singer
said. "You're free to go."

"Where's Wright?" I demanded.

"I'm not sure. We got First Missouri Bank to wire Mr. Jackson's
bank in Texas. Within an hour, they wired back and said there was less
than fifty dollars in that account."

"There must be a mistake!" Barnett exclaimed. "The Jacksons are
millionaires."

"Not anymore, it appears. The money Wright took out before he
left for Kansas City just about cleaned out the account. The report
from the bank said there hadn't been a deposit to it in more than a
month. My guess is that the Jacksons' oil wells are exhausted. I followed Wright over to a used-car dealer, where he sold the LaSalle for
three hundred dollars. He paid the hotel bill and his fine and yours and
gave me some money to buy your train tickets back to Texas.

"He said, 'Tell the boys to go on back home without me. Tell 'em
don't look for me. Ole Wright'll be okay.' I think he was deeply embarrassed by the incident and doesn't want to face you or anyone from
back home. I got your bags from the Palace. You're welcome to spend
the night at my house. There's a train to Texas leaving tomorrow morning. It goes to Fort Worth and Dallas. From there you can take the
Shreveport train that stops in Knox Plains."

We certainly didn't have a better plan, so we got in Mr. Singer's
Cadillac and went home with him.

The house looked simple from the outside, but once I got inside, I
was awed. We stepped into an anteroom where I saw fine wool carpets,
a handsome mahogany table, a cut-glass lamp, and richly framed paintings that made me feel as though I had entered a mansion. Every piece,
every color, every detail in the room looked as though it had been
chosen with great care. I'd met many people who probably had far more
money than Mr. Singer, but I'd never met anyone who could make a
room look this nice.

"If you'll wait in the library, I'll let my housekeeper know I have
guests," Mr. Singer said. The word *library* made me a little queasy, but
we followed him through a huge set of double doors to our right. He
closed the doors behind him and left us in a book-lined room that was
as handsomely appointed as the anteroom. As we each sank into an
overstuffed leather chair, I heard a girl's voice scream, "Floozy!
Floozy!"

The library doors flew open, and there stood a girl about my age. She stopped just inside the doorway and seemed to be staring at my feet. Then she said in a softer tone, "Oh, there you are, Floozy," as she stepped forward and scooped a large, long-haired silver-gray cat from under my chair. Although she was possibly the prettiest girl I'd ever seen, her appearance horrified me. Less than a foot from me was one of the creatures I feared more than any on earth—more than poisonous vipers, bloodthirsty mountain lions, or rabid wolves. She was a light-skinned Negro female. By this point I was convinced that someone had left the back door to hell unlatched, and a legion of demons in the form of light-skinned women had slipped out.

She stroked the arrogant-looking creature in her arms for a full minute before she took notice of Barnett and me. "Hello," the girl said, her voice now almost musical. "Are you Elliot's friends?"

Elliot? I was puzzled for a second, then I recalled that Mr. Singer's name was John Elliot.

"He's been helping us out, actually. We had a little problem this morning down at the public library." Before I could continue, she started laughing so hard she lost control of the cat.

"You're the boys who tried to take over the library," she shrieked. This time she was so overtaken with laughter she had to sit down. She pulled a handkerchief out of her pocket to wipe tears of mirth from her face. "What on earth were you doing?"

I really didn't feel like telling the story again, especially to this rude young woman. Fortunately, Elliot Singer returned at that moment. "I see you've met my sister Betsy," he said.

Betsy jumped in before I could answer. "We didn't exactly meet yet." She gently extended a soft little hand. "I'm Elizabeth Singer—Betsy." She explained that she lived with her brother so she could attend a private academy for girls there in Kansas City. In the small Missouri town they were both born in, there was no school blacks could attend that went beyond eighth grade.

A gray-haired medium-brown woman in a starched and pressed navy dress and an immaculate white apron entered the room from a side door. "Are you ready for me to serve, Mr. Singer?" she asked.

"Yes, thank you, Mrs. Jacobs."

Even though the house had electric lights, there were candles on the dining table. There was also a small arrangement of fresh flowers. I had read books about people who lived this way, but I had never seen such elegance in real life. Over dinner I learned that my host had a law degree from Harvard, where he had been the only colored man in his class.

"How in the world did you get into Harvard?" Barnett asked.

"Our mother knows some wealthy white people in New England who're very sympathetic to the plight of colored people in this country. They got me into a prestigious boys' school near Boston and arranged for a large church there to pay all my expenses. I was the only colored boy there, too. I worked very hard because I felt the honor of the race was sitting on my frail shoulders. I finished second in my class, and some of my teachers helped me get into Harvard, first as an undergraduate, then as a law student," he recounted.

"The truth be known, I've always wondered if they would have been willing to do all that for me had I been just as smart, just as well mannered and just as hardworking, but with dark skin. My looking like a white boy was very convenient for them. They were able to satisfy their social consciences without alarming anyone. These people would invite me over to their homes from time to time. If some of their friends or relatives dropped by while I was there, they introduced me as 'a deserving young man we're helping though school.' They might or might not mention my race. They knew which of their guests would praise them for helping a colored fellow and which ones would be appalled.

"I've noticed that white people who make an effort to help or hire colored people often choose ones no darker than themselves. It creates a dilemma for those of us on the receiving end. On the one hand we want to say, 'Just a minute, here. You do realize that there are many dark-skinned coloreds who deserve a chance, too?' But we know that might cause them to withdraw their help."

My attention was divided between listening to Elliot Singer and trying to figure out the baffling assortment of silverware. Betsy kept looking at me with a smile that was more a suppressed giggle. I got the idea that she wanted to laugh out loud at me and would as soon as I was out of her presence. Her brother didn't seem to notice.

After dinner, Betsy went to her room to study, and Barnett and I had coffee with Mr. Singer in his library. We told him all about what had been going on in Knox Plains, about the oil strikes and Louis and Mr. Seck. As we were finishing our coffee, Betsy came into the room. She gave Mr. Singer a little kiss on the cheek and said, "Good night, Brother." She turned to Barnett and said, "Good night." Then she looked at me, let out a silly little laugh, and quickly left the room.

That night in the guest room I asked Barnett, "What's the matter with that girl? She sure has bad manners for somebody raised in an educated family and going to a fancy private school."

"She likes you," Barnett said simply.

"So what would she do if she didn't like me, empty a slop jar on my head?"

The next morning at breakfast I studied Betsy, secretly looking for clues that would tell me whether Barnett was right. But there were none. At the breakfast table she thumbed through an algebra book, then suddenly announced that she had to go or she'd be late for class. She brushed past me on her way out of the room, and I picked up a light floral scent that stayed with me the rest of the day.

At the train station, Mr. Singer gave me a card with his address and telephone number. He also gave me ten dollars so Barnett and I could have dinner on the train. "We don't need this much," I protested.

He smiled. "I see you've never bought dinner on a train."

Elliot Singer was right about dining-car prices. They were astoundingly high, particularly considering that the porter made Barnett and me sit behind a putrid green curtain so the white diners wouldn't have to look at us while they ate.

"I wonder what would happen if I jumped up and snatched that curtain down," Barnett mused. "Some delicate little white lady would clutch her husband's arm and scream, 'Oh, Beauregard, there's darkies in heah!' " Barnett assumed a comical falsetto voice and an exaggerated Southern accent. " 'I cannot digest my repast with darkies present.' "

"Will you stop playing," I admonished. "They're gonna throw us out of the dining car." But a few minutes later I whispered in the same falsetto, "Lawdy, Beauregard, the next thing we know, they'll be lettin' African monkeys sit up heah with civilized folks."

"I think they already are," Barnett whispered back, and we both laughed.

Turning serious again, Barnett asked, "Where do you suppose Wright went? He didn't have much money left, and he doesn't know anybody in Kansas City."

"I imagine he'll feel sorry for himself for a while, then he'll come on home to Knox Plains," I answered, though in fact I had no idea what Wright would do. I had no idea what I would do if I were in his shoes.

FOURTEEN

Barnett and I had agreed that our first mission when we got off the train would be to go tell Mr. Nate about Wright. We didn't even call Ma. We just took a taxi to Mr. Nate's house. He saw us pull up and fairly ran to meet us as we came up his walkway. "Oh, Sweet Jesus!" he cried. "Somethin' done happen to Wright. Somethin' done happen to my boy."

"Wright's not hurt," I quickly assured him. "At least, he wasn't the last time we saw him. But something did happen."

Inside the house, we retold the story of our adventure in Kansas City, carefully editing out the part about Lorraine, Fancy, and their men. Mr. Nate just listened, shaking his head from time to time.

"You know," he said. "All that time 'fo' the money came, I was sorriful not 'cause I didn't have nothing, but 'cause I didn't have nothin' to give my boys. An' all that time there was somethin' I could have give 'em and I never did. I could have give 'em some common sense. I could of talked to 'em 'bout how thangs is in this worl', how there's folks who'll make out like they like you jes' so they can take what you got. 'Course befo', we didn't have nothin' for 'em to take. I'da thought Wright woulda larnt som'thin' 'bout fancy women after he seed what happened to Matt and Louis and po' ole Secon' Tim'thy. Still and all, I wish he'd come on home. I ain't mad at him. I's mo' mad at myself. If'n he was to come up that walk rat now, I'd do lack that paw Jesus talk about, the one who had two sons and the one son took off and spent a mess o' his paw's money on foolishness. I'd hug him and put a fancy robe 'round him an' kill us a ole fatted calf."

As low as Mr. Nate was, I hated to hit him with more bad news, but I had it to do. "Mr. Nate, there's one more thing. The money Wright took to Kansas City was just about the last you had in that bank account. The bank says you've got less than fifty dollars left."

Mr. Nate's face registered no surprise. "I was sked of that. I was sked the way them boys was goin', they was go' use up all that money. But them boys was havin' so much fun, I jes' hated to stop 'em. They work so hard all them years, trying to git a cotton crop outta that lan'. Lawd, they worked hard. I figgered they was due somethin'." He looked up at us and could see that Barnett and I were baffled that he was taking the news so calmly.

"I'm kinda shameface to say it, but after I seed the boys—Wright 'specially—tho'in' money 'round lack that, I figgered I best to put some where they couldn't get at it," Mr. Nate revealed. "I gots a nice little chunk set aside where can't nobody get to it but me. Yet and still, them wells ain't go' keepa spewin' out that oil forever, so I'm gonna take some while I gots it and do something I always wanted to do.

"When I was jes' a li'l bit of a li'l boy, I used to sneak downtown when they was buildin' all them buildin's you see down there now. I used to hide in that ole tall grass and watch. Them white mens didn't like no li'l pickaninnies standin' 'round watchin 'em, so I had to hide. I loved to look at them big machines, them big cranes and whatnot. 'Course now, they didn't let colored work the big machines, colored could jes' dig ditches and spread gravel and like that. But, oh, man, I loved them big machines.

"An' when the circus come to town, the bes' part for me wasn't the show. The bes' part for me was lookin' at 'em put up them big tents and the rides. Shoot, I'd rather watch somebody puttin' up a Ferris wheel than ride on one any day. You know it's funny, me sittin' here talking to you boys 'bout stuff I ain't never talked to my own boys 'bout. Anyhow, that's what I'm go' do. I'm go' start me a heavy 'quipment comp'ny, and if white won't let me do no work for them, I'll work for colored. Plenty of colored buildin' thangs nowadays."

While we were talking, Matt drove up in the remaining pink LaSalle. We let Mr. Nate tell him about Wright in his own way. For one thing, I was afraid if I told the story too many times, I'd let the part about Lorraine and Fancy slip. Matt didn't say anything until his pa had finished. Then he turned to Barnett and me. "I guess you thank Wright pretty dumb to fall for that, huh? Wright ain't dumb, he jes' innocent, lack I was. We come up around folk that might be peculiar in one way or 'nother, but mos' of 'em, not countin' that Allycation Council bunch, wouldn't jes' set out to lie to you and steal from you. But I swear 'fo' God, there's folks out there'll shoot they grandma for the change she got in her apron pocket. I b'lieve Wright know that now. Wright gonna be okay, you'll see."

Matt gave us a ride to the house. We told Ma yet another version of the Kansas City story, one that excluded not only Lorraine, Fancy, and their friends, but the fact that we had gone to jail. It was the kind of thing that would upset her. After supper I went to my room and wrote to Elliot Singer.

Dear Mr. Singer,

I wanted you to know that Barnett and I got home safely. Thank you again for letting us spend the night at your house and for buying our dinner on the train. You were definitely right about meal prices on trains. I don't believe I could charge a man that much for a pork chop dinner unless I was holding a gun on him.

Ma and Uncle Will didn't say much, but I could tell it was a relief to them that we were back. You'll be glad to hear that Wright's family isn't broke after all. His pa put some money aside to buy a construction company. We're all hoping that will work out for him. If he gets it going, it'll be steady work for Wright's brother Matt and for Wright, if he ever comes back.

I've been thinking more and more about the killings here in Knox Plains. It's bothering me that nobody seems to be making any real effort to find the killers and bring them to justice. Everybody's assuming the Klan killed Louis, and around here people think of getting killed by the Klan as sort of like getting struck by lightning. It's just something that happens, and there's nothing anybody can do about it. Since Gov. Furgerson took office (I guess you've heard that we have a woman governor) some Klansmen have actually been tried and convicted, and that attitude is slowly starting to change.

As for poor old Mr. Second Timothy Nesbet, every instinct I've got says that trashy wife he took had something to do with his getting shot. She sold the land right from under Miss Violet and Miss Ella and didn't even stay around for Mr. Seck's funeral. I never heard of such low-down behavior from a woman before.

Football practice starts up next week. The first game is September 25, even though school doesn't start again until November. (I told you, didn't I, that we're on this crazy schedule where we go to school in the summer and are off for two months in the fall?) Anyway, Barnett and I are both on the football team. I'm little, but I make up for it by being smart and fast. We're really excited because the new school has a nice football field with new bleachers and a locker room. To me the most exciting thing about our new school is the chemistry lab. I'm going to be a research chemist. Did I tell you that? I dearly love mathematics and science. Both are like working puzzles. It's so much fun knowing that there's an answer and trying to find it. I get such a great feeling when I solve a really hard mathematics or science problem. It's better than scoring in a ball game, really.

A lot of people, even my teachers, are saying that a colored man can't be a scientist in this country. I asked one of them, "What about Dr. George Washington Carver?" and he said, "That's one. One is about all white folks are going to allow." We'll see.

Say "Hi" to Betsy for me.

Your friend,

Theodore Roosevelt "Moose" O'Malley

About two weeks later I was thrilled when I picked up the mail and found a letter from Kansas City addressed me.

Dear Moose,

May I call you Moose? That seems to be what people close to you call you, and I'd like to be counted in that number. Please call me Elliot.

I've been very busy these past few weeks. Kansas City is an interesting place. It's rapidly becoming a modern American city, but there is still a lot of the old frontier town to it, too. The clash between those two cultures has created lots of legal disputes. I imagine that you know what I mean, since Texas is experiencing similar problems.

Yes, I did read that Muriel Furgerson had been elected governor of Texas. Some people are saying that her husband is the real governor and that Mrs. Furgerson is just a front for him. From all I've read about her, however, they may be mistaken. In any case, she and her husband are in agreement about the Ku Klux Klan, so things should get interesting on that front.

I'm very proud of your decision to become a research chemist. You will be a good one. As for those people who keep telling you that a colored man can't be a scientist, I wish I could grab every one of them—especially teachers and others who are supposed to be leading our next generation—who go about discouraging ambition in young colored people and tape their mouths shut. They do our race more harm than all the Ku Klux Klansmen put together. I've wanted to be a lawyer for as long as I can remember, and I wish I had a nickel for every time I heard, "A colored man can't be a lawyer" or "The country's not ready for colored lawyers." I could retire today with the money I'd have. I didn't let them discourage me, and don't you dare let them discourage you. If the country's not ready for smart, ambitious colored people in professional positions, it had better get ready.

Incidentally, give me the name of that lady who was married to Mr. Nesbet. I have a lawyer friend in Dallas who may be able to find out something about her. I'm making no promises, but it's worth a try. My friend in Dallas isn't colored, but he's a good man who's never let me down. We were classmates at Harvard. His name is Robert Sternberg. I'll get a letter off to him as soon as I hear from you.

Betsy's fine. She's having a good year at school.

With warmest regards,
Elliot

I wrote back and told Elliot everything I knew about Sally Lee Nesbet. I don't know whether she did anything illegal or not, but I hoped there was something she could be sent to jail for. I sure hated to see somebody behave as wickedly as she had and just get away with it.

A month later, I got a short note from Elliot.

Dear Moose,

I promise a full letter as soon as my schedule permits. I did want to tell you, however, that my friend Bob Sternberg thinks he may have learned something interesting about your Mrs. Nesbet. I'll tell you all about it as soon as he has confirmed the information he received.

With warmest regards,
Elliot

The next time I was alone in the store with Barnett, I decided to bring up something that had been on my mind. "Barnett, I haven't forgotten that I promised never to tell what you know about Louis's death—"

"And you'd better not forget," he snapped. "You swore in blood."

"I know, and I'm not going to break that oath, but I think you should tell Elliot what happened. He's really interested in helping us. It keeps me awake at night that those people just killed Louis and got away with it. Louis was our friend. Wesley is our friend. I can't even look Wesley in the eye anymore. Can you imagine how mad he'd be if he knew that we knew something about his brother's death and just weren't telling? But I'm not talking about telling just to make me feel better. I really think Elliot can do something. Do you understand what I'm saying?"

"Do you understand what *I'm* saying? The people who shot Louis are ruthless, heartless murderers. If they'd kill him for money, don't you think they'd kill you and me to keep us quiet? We don't need to go after these people unless we're durn sure we can see them hanged, or at least put in prison. If you shoot a wildcat, Moose, you have to shoot to kill. You can't live with a wounded wildcat."

PART FIVE

CHEMISTRY LESSONS

CHAPTER FIFTEEN

The football team at Booker T. Washington High School of Knox Plains, Texas, had an incredible 1928 season. We were so amazing that the coach from Knox Plains High, the white high school, asked if he and his team could come watch our games. Our coach said he would allow it only if the arrangement were reciprocal. Finally, the two coaches agreed that each team could come watch the other for free, but only if they came as a team. No player could attend a game at the other high school alone, even if he bought a ticket.

Football games at our school were never scheduled at the same time as those at the white high school, a habit left over from the days when both schools used the same field. The white team came to every Washington High game, and they weren't disappointed. A bad game was one that we won by only a single touchdown. We never lost, and Barnett and I were the star players. The cheerleaders had a chant that went: "O'Malley, O'Malley, he's our man, if he can't do it Lindsay can. Lindsay, Lindsay, he's our man, if he can't do it nobody can."

Both of us were natural athletes, but Barnett had the advantage, since he was big and strong in addition to being fast and keen-eyed. In the summer, we both played second-string baseball with the Knox Plains Black Prairie Dogs, and as everybody around there knew, being second string with the Black Prairie Dogs meant you were good enough to be starting lineup for the New York Yankees. I was sure that some of our starters were as good as Babe Ruth and Ty Cobb put together. The Prairie Dogs' starting lineup got a small salary now that the team could afford to pay them, but being on the bench just meant you got five free passes to each game and two free hot dogs and a drink at the refreshment stand.

Girls threw themselves at Barnett and me without shame. Just about every day at school, some girl came up to me and said, "Moose, I baked you some tea cakes" or "Moose, I made this gingerbread just for you." They were cute, too. At least most of them were, but what with football practice, going with the team to all the white high-school games, working in the store, and spending time in the chemistry lab, I didn't have much time for a social life. Barnett found time. I rarely saw him without four or five girls hanging around him, listening to his football stories and carrying on like he was Jim Thorpe or Paul Robeson or somebody. He took a different girl to the moving-picture show every Saturday night. Some Saturday nights I'd go, too, but I never asked a girl to come with me. I'd just go with whichever girl Barnett had along as an extra. He'd say, "We're going to the moving pictures Saturday with Annie Laura and Christine. Which one do you want to walk with?"

"Which one's darker?" I'd ask, knowing that he paid close attention to about every girl at school.

"Christine."

"Okay, I'll walk with Christine."

"The blacker the berry, the sweeter the juice, huh, Moose?" Barnett would chuckle. But the truth was I was attracted to girls of every color and too shy to talk to any of them, let alone touch them. I just felt safer with dark-skinned girls.

Mr. Daniel started coming over to the house to give me special chemistry lessons since I had advanced far beyond what was in the textbook. I was really flattered by the interest he was taking in my education. He asked me if I had money set aside for college, and I explained that my pa had taken care of that before he died. One of the few times with my pa I clearly remembered was when we were sitting on the front porch and he said, "Moose, you're smart like your ma, and you need to go off to college like she did. I put some money away so you could do that." I had never asked him or anyone else where the money was, I just assumed that when the time came, someone would produce it.

"I have to go to college, Mr. Daniel," I told my teacher. "Most of the boys around here will become laborers when they get out of high school. I'm not big enough or strong enough to be any good at that. Besides, I love science. I don't want to give it up." Mr. Daniel told me that I had mastered chemistry that most people didn't study until their second year of college, so I knew I could get into college with no problem.

One evening after Mr. Daniel and I had finished up and I had gone to get ready for bed, I was still thinking about a chemistry problem we'd been working on. I hadn't been able to think of a solution at the time, but something hit me as I was brushing my teeth. I rinsed my mouth out and went back into the parlor to ask Mr. Daniel what he thought of my solution. Sometimes he stayed and had coffee and cake with Ma before he went home.

Mr. Daniel wasn't in the parlor or the kitchen and neither was Ma. I looked all over the house, but I saw no sign of her. Finally, I heard voices on the front porch. I opened the door, and there was Mr. Daniel with his arm around Ma. Although they were just shadows in the darkness, I was sure I saw Mr. Daniel kiss her. I was enraged. What was he doing? This wasn't some tramp, this was my mother. All this time I'd thought Mr. Daniel liked me and wanted to help me with my education, but all the old snake wanted was to make a dishonorable woman out of my mother. And what was the matter with her, standing there like she liked having his arm around her? I slammed the door hard so they'd know I'd been there and didn't like what I'd seen. Two of the people I felt closest to in the world had betrayed me. I would never get over this.

I went upstairs to my room and slammed that door, too, even though there was no one else close enough to hear it. Barnett was out visiting one of his many girlfriends, and Uncle Will's bedroom was on the first floor because his false leg made it hard for him to walk up and down the steps.

I was burning with anger. My education was going to have to end that day. There was no way I was going back to Booker T. Washington High School and face my hated new enemy, Mr. Daniel. There was another science teacher, Mrs. Verna Poss, but she taught general science and didn't have that special love for chemistry Mr. Daniel had. In the one class I had taken from her, I caught her making scientific errors from time to time. They were small errors, but I just didn't have the respect for her I had had for Mr. Daniel. Next year there would be no way to avoid him, not if I wanted to take advanced chemistry. And I'd been looking forward to his advanced chemistry class for three years. Now, with one move of his lecherous arm, he had snatched away all my dreams. I wanted to knock him in the head with the fireplace poker.

About five minutes later, there was gentle knock at the door. I knew it was Ma, coming to explain away her wanton behavior. I wanted to ignore her, but I knew I couldn't, so I huffed, "Come in."

The door opened and Ma walked in, but I kept my face turned to the wall. "You seem upset," she said.

"How long have you and Mr. Daniel been carrying on behind my back?" I demanded. She laughed. She actually laughed. "Excuse me," I responded indignantly, "but I don't find anything funny."

She sat on the edge of my bed and gently touched my hair. "I wasn't laughing at your feelings, darling, it's just that you sound like a husband who caught his wife with another man. Edgar Daniel and I have been friends most of our lives. His wife, Essie, was one of my closest friends in high school. After Essie died, Edgar and I became closer, and, yes, lately we've started keeping company. He's a fine man, Roosevelt. You should know that. Look at the way he takes the time to help you with your science."

"Yeah, just so he can see you," I huffed.

"Come on, that's not fair. He's been helping you since you were in the sixth grade. Essie was still living, and they were happily married. He wasn't thinking about me then."

"Well, I'll tell you what I think." I finally turned around to face her. "I think you're just a convenience to him. He wants a woman to court, and he comes over here all the time anyway, so it might as well be you." I was reaching desperately for some crime to charge Mr. Daniel with.

"It's nice to know you think so highly of me," Ma answered.

Her sarcasm slapped me in the face like a winter wind on a January morning. I realized for the first time how ugly I was being. "I didn't mean it that way," I said. "I'm sorry."

She was silent for a minute, then she said, "Roosevelt, always be careful what you say, especially to the people you really care about. It's easy when you're angry to say hurtful words that you don't mean, but it's a very selfish thing to do, because you're thinking only of yourself and how you feel, and not about how your words make the other person feel. Sometimes those hurtful words can live on long after you're over your anger. Once you say something, you can no more call it back than you can gather up dust you've turned loose in the wind."

I apologized again. I was sincerely sorry I had hurt Ma's feelings, but I didn't feel any better about this thing with Mr. Daniel. "Why didn't you and Mr. Daniel tell me?"

"We were going to. In fact, that's what we were talking about on the porch. He wants to take me to supper at Mrs. Pendergast's on Saturday."

"Ma," I said, "I know you're not like those ladies at Miz Pendergast's, but I don't want other people thinking you are."

She laughed again. "I don't think there's much danger of that. I know people are saying that some of the women who board with Lula are gold diggers and women of easy virtue, but having supper at Mrs. Pendergast's doesn't make me one of them. Lula Pendergast is a respectable church-going woman who makes people behave when they're under her roof, but she can't help how they act when they're not.

Besides, if I were going after a man for his money, I don't think Edgar Daniel would be at the top of my list."

I don't know which scared me more, the idea that Mr. Daniel might not be serious about Ma at all, or the idea that he might be very serious. "Are you and Mr. Daniel thinking about getting married?"

"Things are nowhere near that far along. We really just decided we had feelings for each other. To tell you the truth, I never gave much thought to remarrying. There were some things I loved about being married, and others—though I loved your daddy like the Lord loves a righteous heart—that I'd just as soon live without. As my mother used to say, 'Sometimes I believe I'd rather do without the eggs than put up with the cackling.' But then she turned around and married Uncle Will after sixteen years as a widow, so you never know.

"But I'll tell you one thing, Roosevelt, I'd never keep company with a man who didn't like you and respect you and who you didn't like and respect in return. That was one reason I thought things could work out with Edgar. I thought you and he were fast friends. Was I wrong?"

"No, Ma, you weren't wrong. I believe I'll go on to sleep now." But I didn't. After she left my room, I sat up reading—anything but chemistry—until I heard Barnett's heavy footsteps on the stairs.

I walked into Barnett's room just seconds after he did. "I need to talk to you," I said.

"Can it wait? I've got some homework, and I'd really like to get to bed."

"I thought you were doing homework at Eleanor Simpson's house."

"We really didn't get that much schoolwork done," he said, flashing me a knowing grin. "Eleanor's really sweet on me. Trouble is, her sister Margaret likes me, too, and they're both cute."

"I don't want to hear about that right now. This is important. It's about Ma."

Barnett's grin was gone in an instant. "What's the matter?" he asked urgently. "Is Sister sick or something?"

"No, she's not sick. She's seeing another man."

"Another man?" Barnett knitted his eyebrows. "Who's the first one?"

"Her husband, of course—Pa."

"Moose, your pa died in 1921 on a cattle drive. He was thrown against a rock when his horse stepped in a chuckhole."

"I know that, but that doesn't mean he's not still her husband."

"Yes, it does. Have you ever listened to the marriage vows? They say 'til death do us part.' That means when one of them dies, the marriage ends. But who is Sister seeing?"

I could barely bring myself to speak the name. "It's Mr. Daniel. She calls him Edgar," I said.

"Mr. Daniel? The science teacher?" Barnett was laughing with genuine delight. "They sure pulled one over on me. I'd see them in there having cake and coffee. I thought Sister was just being nice to him because he was helping you with your chemistry. She was being a lot nicer to him than I thought."

I shoved Barnett so hard he stumbled into the chifforobe. "You take that back," I screamed. "Don't you talk about my ma like that!"

"Hold on," Barnett said, pulling himself to his feet. "I didn't mean anything. Don't forget, she's my sister. I'm happy she found somebody. I'm just surprised, that's all."

"I'm surprised, too. I always figured there were two kinds of women— trashy women like those light-skinned harpies who moved in at Miz Pendergast's and decent women like Ma who never thought about a man except their husband. I thought I knew what Ma was like," I muttered. "Now I'm living in the same house with a woman I don't even know."

"Would you like me to get a shotgun and go over to Mr. Daniel's house and demand that he state his intentions?" Barnett asked sarcastically.

Uncle Will seemed to like Mr. Daniel, too. He told Ma he was glad she'd found somebody while she still looked like something. Even the chickydee-whick approved. I seemed to be the only one with reservations.

Ma did seem happier over the next few weeks. She joked more, picked herself out some new dresses from the catalogue, and even bought a new electric lamp and made some lace doilies to brighten up the living room. Now that things were out in the open, Mr. Daniel sometimes came early and had supper with us before he and I went to work. Other times Mr. Daniel came by just to see Ma. At school he acted exactly like he had before.

The movie that everybody had been talking about for months, *The King of Kings*, finally came to Knox Plains, and Mr. Daniel took Ma to see it. They had to wait in line to get into the movie theater. As it turned out, the people waiting right behind them for the colored balcony were Calvin Springfield and his parents. Calvin was also in Mr. Daniel's chemistry class, but he hated it and was barely passing.

Monday morning before class started, Calvin walked over to my desk and said loud enough for everybody to hear, "Well, I guess I found out why you always get As in here. I figure I'd get As, too, if my ma was the teacher's lady friend."

The room fell silent, with everyone staring at me. People already knew Mr. Daniel was giving me special lessons at home; suddenly the resentment multiplied. If I hadn't been the quarterback on Washington High's incredible football team, I don't think I'd have had a friend in the school. But every Saturday afternoon that I threw a long, pretty pass right into Barnett's waiting hands and he took it down the field for a touchdown, I won them all back. Besides, everybody really knew that I earned every A I got in science. I was making As in everything else, too, and my other teachers had no reason to give me special treatment.

Still, this business with Mr. Daniel was getting embarrassing. I know Ma was enjoying keeping company with him, but I was going to have to ask them to stop. I had made my mind up to talk with Ma when I got home, but something else claimed my attention. I stopped at the post office after school to get our mail, and there was an envelope from Kansas City. I didn't even wait until I got home. I opened it there in the street. It was a Christmas greeting from Elliot and Betsy. Along with it was a newspaper clipping and a letter from Elliot. The clipping headline announced: "Colored Couple Arrested on Prohibition Charge." The story read:

> A colored transient and his female companion were arrested outside Dallas yesterday evening for violation of the Prohibition laws. They were caught attempting to transport whiskey into the city. Dillard Lester was stopped by Texas Rangers as he attempted to drive a truck filled with Scotch whiskey to a location on the south side of the city. The liquor apparently had been smuggled across the Mexican border.
>
> The female called herself Sally Lester.
>
> Ranger E. W. Flynn, who made the arrest, said the two were known to the police, as they had been arrested a number of times in Texas over the past 12 years for an assortment of petty crimes.

I quickly moved on to Elliot's letter.

Dec. 13, 1928

Dear Moose,

    If the information Bob Sternberg has put together is correct, the Sally Lester mentioned in this story is the same woman who was married to Mr. Nesbet there in Knox Plains. Apparently she and Mr. Lester had been making their living picking pockets, shoplifting, and operating little confidence games. Now that they have advanced to major crimes, the Texas Rangers are eager to put them in jail for a long time. If one of those crimes is murder, they could even hang.

Bob believes that she has been married to Mr. Lester for about 15 years, which means she was never legally married to Mr. Nesbet. If we can prove any of this, at the very least, Mrs. Lester could go to jail for bigamy, and she would be forced to give the money from the land sale to Mr. Nesbet's rightful heirs.

I wonder if it would be convenient for you and Barnett to come to Dallas one day during your Christmas break and give a statement to the Rangers who are handling the Lester case. Anything you can remember about the evening Mr. Nesbet died would be helpful. They also are interested in talking to the doctor and nurse who attended to Mr. Nesbet. I believe the Rangers plan to talk to your sheriff if they haven't already. I would say the Lesters are in a great deal of trouble right now.

If you find you can get to Dallas, contact Bob Sternberg at this address. He will get you to the right people.

> Robert E. Sternberg, Esq.
> 63 Spencer Road
> Dallas, Texas

It is my hope we can all see that justice is done. People like the Lesters are a cancer on our race. They rob decent colored people in more ways than one. Not only do they steal from honest colored people who are struggling to get ahead in a country that refuses to give them fair treatment, but they fuel the prejudices of those who believe that colored people are morally inferior, robbing us of our dignity as well as our money. I hope to see them get what they deserve. You see, Moose, I love justice the way you love science. There seems to be so little of it for our people. I became a lawyer in the hope that in some small way, I can change that.

Give my love to your family. Betsy's school break starts Friday. She will be going home to spend Christmas with Father and Mother. I have lots of work to do here, so I'll probably join them Christmas Eve and stay through the weekend.

Have a wonderful Christmas and a happy new year.
> Warmest regards,
> Elliot

That evening, I studied the greeting from Elliot and Betsy. Maybe it was my imagination, but the card seemed to smell faintly like Betsy did when she brushed past me that morning we left Kansas City. I put it over the mantle with our other Christmas greetings, but late that night I went and got the card, and in the dark I sniffed it until I was sure that something of Betsy had clung to it and traveled the long dusty road from Kansas City to my nostrils.

The card, with Elliot's letter, arrived on Thursday, December 16. Our last classes before Christmas break were the following day. However, Barnett and I would not be able to think of ourselves as free until Saturday evening, because Saturday afternoon the Washington High School football team would play Smith Avenue High School from Fort Worth for the Colored Conference state championship.

SIXTEEN

When the last classes ended on Friday, most of the school ran whooping into the streets, ready for two weeks of holiday parties and freedom. The Washington High football team headed to the field for a final practice. The season was over for Knox Plains High. They'd made it to the playoffs, but lost the first game. Still, they sat in the stands during our practices, along with a few girlfriends and relatives of our team members.

To everyone's surprise, the practice went badly. There were lots of bad throws, dropped balls, and failed passes. Passing is often the weakness of a high-school football team, and even the Washington High Tigers, good as we were, were only mediocre at it. Even Barnett, the team's best receiver, didn't complete a pass all afternoon. We were weary from the hard work we had put in since August, and it was starting to show.

To make matters worse, Barnett twisted his ankle, and we weren't sure whether it was just some minor but painful injury or something serious enough to keep him out of the game. Without Barnett, we'd lose for sure.

On the way to the locker room, Barnett limped up to me and threw his big muscular arm around my shoulder. "Don't worry, Moose," he said. "It's like they say about weddings: if the rehearsal is a disaster, the wedding will be beautiful."

Still, for the first time all season, I worried about the Tigers. Maybe we just didn't have another game in us. On the other hand, maybe the Fort Worth team was as played out as we were. After all, they, too, were at the end of a long season, and they had a two-hour bus ride ahead of them. At least we were playing on our home field. After practice, Ma let me bring the whole team over to the store for free Coca-Colas. It had been planned as a pregame victory celebration, but victory now didn't seem as inevitable as it had before.

I got the first serious case of pregame jitters I had had since my first game as a starter. It took me a little longer than usual to fall asleep Friday night. Finally, I said to myself, *Moose, it's just football. It's just a sport. People play it for fun. People watch it for fun. Nobody's life depends on this. The worst thing that can happen tomorrow is that the Tigers wind up being the second-best colored high-school team in Texas, and that's not too bad.*

Saturday afternoon at game time, I looked up to see the stands packed with people. Among them were the Knox Plains High School team and their coach. They must have gotten there early, because they were right up front on the fifty-yard line. Barnett's ankle was still bothering him, but he said he could play. "A real man is always willing to play hurt," he declared. My spirits were up by kick-off time. Once we started playing, however, my frustration began building. We had never played a team this good. Well into the second quarter, neither team had scored. Then right at the end of the second quarter, we managed a field goal. At half time we were leading three to nothing. I was feeling pretty good, even though we had never had to work harder just to get on the scoreboard. I made a mental note to go over after the game and congratulate the Fort Worth team for being such formidable opponents. They were really making us work for this victory.

Early in the third quarter, things turned around. Just two minutes into it, Smith Avenue scored a touchdown, and my heart sank to the bottom of my stomach. Their try for a two-point conversion failed, but that didn't make me feel much better. The Washington High Tigers had never played better, but we had met our match.

With less than a minute on the clock, the score was still six to three in their favor. We had the ball, but we were on our own ten-yard line. I tried a couple of plays that almost always worked for us, but Smith Avenue's defense was the best I'd ever seen. When we called for a time-out, there were five seconds left on the clock and we had the ball, but we were still ninety yards from our opponent's goal line. Another field goal would have at least tied it, but from the opposite end of the gridiron, a field goal was out of the question. It looked like Washington High was about to be officially declared the second-best colored high-school team in Texas.

When play resumed, I did the only thing I could. There was no time to look for a receiver. Even if I had been sure of one, we were at the wrong end of the field. We were dead. I just threw the ball in a classic pass-and-pray maneuver. An instant later, I heard wild cheering, which I assumed to be the Smith Avenue fans celebrating their victory. But the cheering was too loud to be coming from the handful of supporters who had made the trip from Fort Worth. Then I spotted a black-and-gold blur sprinting down the side of the field. It was Barnett, and he was carrying the football. He was moving through the Smith Avenue defense like they were tin figures on a child's toy football field. Even though the clock had run out, the game wasn't over until the play was completed. The screaming got louder. People in the stands jumped out of their seats and ran to the edge of the field. They were witnessing a miracle, and they wanted to get as close as possible. By the time Barnett got to Smith Avenue's twenty-yard line, there was nobody near him. When Barnett crossed the goal line, people were leaping three feet into the air. They were hugging everybody around them—friends, relatives, and total strangers. Some woman grabbed Reverend Longley and kissed him on the mouth.

I looked out and saw the Knox Plains High team running toward us. For a second I thought the white team might be jealous that we had had a more successful season and were planning to hurt us, but no such thing. They couldn't have been more jubilant if they had just become state champions themselves. In fact, they were screaming, "We won! We won!" Then they did something that I had only seen in the moving pictures. It was the only time in real life that I actually saw a crowd carry their hero on their shoulders. Some of the white football players picked Barnett up and circled the field with him. Then some of them decided to pick me up, too. Soon they were carrying any Washington High player they could get their hands on around the field. The spontaneous celebration seemed to go on for nearly half an hour.

People in the crowd were reaching up and rubbing our jerseys, our shoes, whatever they could get their hands on. Everybody wanted to touch the heroes, to have a little bit of the miracle rub off on them. Some were gathered around me, but mainly it was Barnett's day, as it should have been.

We showered and dressed in the locker room. When we got to the house, there was an extemporaneous party going on. People had gone home and gotten whatever they had fixed to eat that evening and were putting it all together for the ultimate potluck supper. I looked across the table and saw beef stew, fried chicken, chicken and dumplings, pork chops in gravy, stewed corn, black-eyed peas, greens, piles of biscuits and cornbread, cakes, pies—anything you could imagine. Ma was making coffee and hot chocolate. She had given Mr. Daniel the key to the store and sent him and some boys from the high school to get all the soda pop they could carry. Nobody was bothering to keep track of what was being brought out. *It's going to take me a month to get the books straight again*, I thought, but I quickly put that worry aside and joined in the festivities.

There were people who I had never seen at our house before. I was surprised to see Walter Bridges, the star running back of Knox Plains High. He had a hunk of cake the size of a brick and was laughing it up with one of the fellows from our team. There were other people I had never seen before at all. Everybody seemed determined to tell their own version of the story, how the amazing play looked and felt to them. Nate Jackson said, "And when Roos'velt th'ew that ball, I say, 'Oh, Lawd, here it come. Them boys is go' be tow up to lose after all this.' I shet my eyes 'cause I couldn't stan' it. Then I heared ever'body jes'a hollerin'. I open my eyes, an' there's ole Barnett Lindsay tearin' down that fiel' lack the hounds o' hell—'scuse me, ladies—was after him. He look lack somethin' not o' this worl'. Tell you de truth, I b'lieve them Fort Worth boys was sked to touch him."

Even Uncle Will, who hadn't gone to the football game, was having a good time. He was so proud of his son, he could have popped open. He spent the evening telling tall tales of amazing moments in sports that he was probably making up as he went along. I sure don't believe he ever met "Cool Papa" Bell or Rube Foster, let alone played baseball with them, but everybody was having great fun listening to the stories anyway.

As the party progressed, I sat back and watched Mr. Daniel and Ma without emotion for the first time. They seemed genuinely good together. They delighted in helping one another, they found lots to talk about. They made each other laugh. I had to admit that my objections had been nothing more than a selfish need to keep Ma and everything at home the same, even as I explored my own new horizons.

It must have been past ten o'clock when the last of the self-invited guests went home. Although I had been so keyed up when the game ended that afternoon I thought I'd never sleep again, I was out like a bear in hibernation seconds after I got in bed.

I woke up early Sunday morning and lay there thinking about what had happened. How could Barnett have possibly run the length of the field with a sore ankle without anybody stopping him? Had the Smith Avenue team been so sure of victory that they had completely let their guard down? Had Barnett been so energized by the fact that he'd actually caught that unlikely pass that he turned into some sort of superman, strong enough to run right past or right over anyone in his path? No, I decided, it was more than that.

I went to Barnett's room, sat on the edge of his bed, and gently touched his shoulder. "Moose," he said, shaking away sleep, "what day is it?"

"It's Sunday morning."

"Then the game's over and . . ." He cocked his head and looked straight at me, trying to focus his still-sleepy eyes. "I didn't dream it?"

I shook my head. "You didn't dream it. You ran seventy-five yards for a touchdown and won the game in the last five seconds."

"That seems so outrageous, I was sure for a second that I must have dreamed it."

"If you did, we had the same dream."

"And we're still dreaming," Barnett said, reaching up to his nightstand to caress the ball he had carried to victory just fifteen hours earlier.

"Barnett, what happened out there yesterday was a miracle. I have never so clearly seen the hand of God in something. Miracles always happen for a reason. Until yesterday I thought of sports as just entertainment. Now I realize they're a metaphor for life itself."

Barnett scooted up unto a sitting position in the bed. "Moose, what are you talking about?"

"You and I have been scared to try to bring the people who killed Louis and Mr. Seck to justice because we're sure we can't win, because there are too many things working against us. First of all, we're up against ruthless professional criminals who know a lot of tricks we've never heard of and don't mind killing anybody who's a problem for them. We've also got the fact that the Texas Rangers are all white, and a lot of them don't care whether colored people kill each other—they're not going to help us or protect us."

"That's what I've been trying to tell you."

"Well, what God was trying to tell us yesterday is that long shots can come through, that even when everything seems to be working against you, you can still win, and when it's important, you've got to try. What we were fighting for yesterday was just a little ole football championship. God wants us to fight for something much more important—justice."

Barnett stared at me from under his knitted eyebrows. "You got that out of a football game? Moose, you're crazier than I thought."

"How do you explain what happened yesterday?"

"I don't know. I looked up and the ball was coming straight at me. When I reached up, it seemed to just land in my hands. I looked out and saw a clear path through the forest of football players, so I headed for daylight. I ran as hard and as fast as I could. I don't even remember having to knock anybody out of my way. Not only was my ankle not hurting, I forgot that it had been bothering me before."

"And you don't think that was God's doing? The message is so clear. We thought we couldn't possibly win. The chances were about a zillion to one, but we tried it and we won."

"And if it hadn't worked," Barnett pointed out, "all that would have happened is that somebody else would have won the state football championship. There was never any chance Sister would wind up crying over our bullet-riddled bodies. If we get involved in trying to bring murderers to justice, that's exactly what could happen."

"If good people are scared to do what's right, bad people will always win. You know, what Edmund Burke said is true: 'The only thing necessary for the triumph of evil is for good men to do nothing.' "

"That's easy to say when you weren't the one who saw Louis Wilson shot in cold blood. You weren't the one who was crouched down in that ravine, watching them drag Louis's body around like it was just a sack of cattle feed or something. I've never been that scared in my life. You know, if somebody had found me hiding over there, they probably would have asked, 'What are you doing out here, white boy?' That's how scared I was."

I was tickled that Barnett never lost his sense of humor in all this.

"Listen," I said, "I know that Louis's death was pretty upsetting for you. It was for me, too. But that Sally Lee woman and her boyfriend or husband or whatever he is are in jail. The police just need some more evidence to put them away for a long time. They deserve to be put away for a long time after what they did to the Nesbets. I know you don't care for Miss Violet. She's not my favorite person, but she and Miss Ella didn't deserve what happened to them. And Mr. Seck sure didn't deserve what happened to him. We can leave the Louis Wilson thing alone for right now. Let's just go to Dallas and tell the Texas Rangers what we know about the night Mr. Seck was shot."

Barnett was silent for a minute. Then he said, "Let me think about it." He jumped up and went down to the bathroom before I could argue anymore.

There was a downright celebratory mood at church that morning. The place was packed with the regular worshipers and the folks we called C-and-E Christians because they only came to church at Christmas and Easter. People were still buoyed up from the state championship win, and with Christmas just a week away, the choir sang a cheery selection of carols, and the Dorcas Ladies' Handicraft Circle passed out fruit and hard candy to all the children.

The only dark corner in the sanctuary that morning was the one where Violet Nesbet sat. I had never seen a more forlorn-looking creature. She wore the same defeated expression I had seen on her face since the day of Mr. Seck's funeral. Miss Violet had never been exactly a walking festival, but where before she just seemed strict and humorless, she now seemed saturated with a deep sadness. I don't think even a Ham Smiling would have brightened her mood. She just huddled in her corner of the church pew as if everything safe in the world had gone away. I noticed that Barnett's attention wandered to her several times during the service.

After dinner, a few boys from school dropped by to relive the championship game with us with yet a few more retellings. This was clearly going to be a story that would be told around Knox Plains for years to come. Barnett was laughing it up with his buddies, but I knew him well enough to know that he wasn't feeling as chipper as he was acting. Something was on his mind, and I hoped that meant he was thinking about what I had said to him that morning.

The shortest day of the year was just two days away, and evening shadows were starting to fall even though it was only five-thirty. Our friends headed home, knowing it would be dark and cold soon. After they left, Barnett and I stayed out on the porch in spite of a sharp December breeze stirring around us. Barnett looked at me like he was waiting for me to resume my argument from that morning, but I let him speak first. "Moose, I don't know whether you're right about all that message-from-God stuff or not, but you're right to say we ought to try to help Miss Nesbet. Maybe we should at least go talk to Elliot's lawyer friend in Dallas, get a feel for what he's like. If there's some way we can help without pulling down too much trouble on ourselves, I'll go along."

"That's the way to talk," I said brightly. "I knew you weren't a coward."

The word hit him like a fist across his jaw. "Coward?" he shouted. "What kind of coward plows through an army of five-hundred-pound linebackers like they were first-graders lined up for recess?"

I called him on his hyperbole. "Five hundred pounds?"

"At least," he insisted. "There wasn't a man out there who wasn't part Brahma bull. You just call that white lawyer over in Dallas. Tell him we'll be there whenever he says."

SEVENTEEN

CHAPTER SEVENTEEN

Monday morning after breakfast, I called the Dallas operator and asked her to put me through to Mr. Sternberg. "Moose!" he shouted, like we were old friends. "Elliot told me you might be in touch. I'm glad you called. Can you get to Dallas Thursday? A lot's happened since that newspaper clipping. Dillard Lester and Sally Lee are set to appear before a judge on that Prohibition charge." I knew that the possession and sale of alcohol was a federal offense, but I also knew there were state laws against it, too. Mr. Sternberg explained that state and federal officials had agreed to get the state charges heard first, since the state of Texas had more serious charges—things like armed robbery—to try Lester on.

"They know Sally was involved in these, too, but he's the one they're really after," the Dallas lawyer continued. "She's been called as a hostile witness by the prosecution, but I understand that she plans to refuse to testify, since the Fifth Amendment says a woman doesn't have to testify against her husband. That's where we can muddy the water a little. If she produces evidence that she has been legally married to Mr. Lester all this time, that means she can't have been legally married to Mr. Nesbet. If that's the case, no matter how Mr. Nesbet died, she has no right to inherit his property. I want you to be there. Later, when this thing goes to trial, the prosecution might even call on you and Barnett to testify."

"Let me talk it over with Barnett," I said. "I'll talk to you again soon. Will you be around, or are you going to be visiting family for Christmas?"

He chuckled. "My family doesn't celebrate Christmas, Moose. We're Jewish. We've already had Hannukah, so just call whenever you'd like."

"Oh, I . . ." I started trying awkwardly to word an apology.

"It's okay," said the voice at the other end of the phone. "It's not as though I hadn't noticed that most people in this part of the country are Christians. Call me when you decide what you're going to do."

Barnett didn't really want to go to Dallas, but he hadn't forgotten that he'd given me his word. He agreed that we could go over and talk to Mr. Sternberg in his office. We told Ma a half-truth about why we were going to Dallas. We said there was an investigation going on regarding Mr. Nesbet's death, and the state officials wanted to talk to us, since we went to the crime scene that night and were at the clinic when he died. At first she wanted to know why the state had taken an interest in this crime when there had been so many others in the area that had gotten little more than a cursory investigation. Barnett smiled his charming smile and answered, "I guess we'll find that out in Dallas."

The late December weather was mild, as it often is in Texas. The day we drove to Dallas was so pretty I wished we'd been going for fun instead of on a mission I felt bound to by honor. Mr. Sternberg had told us that the hearing as set for eleven o'clock, so we left early. Because Barnett was driving, I got to look around at the awesome sunrise, with pink and yellow wisps of cloud painted against a baby-blue sky. *God gave us such a beautiful world,* I thought. *Why do humans have so much trouble living in peace here?*

We only had to stop twice to patch tire blowouts, so we reached Mr. Sternberg's office before ten o'clock. We walked over to a blonde woman at the front desk. "Good morning," I said, "we're—"

"—Moose and Barnett!" shouted the short, dark-haired young man who had just walked out of a nearby office. "Come on in. I'm Bob Sternberg." He shook our hands, which seemed to alarm the blonde woman slightly. As soon as we were in his office, Bob Sternberg closed the door between us and his secretary's curious eyes.

After we had exchanged pleasantries, Mr. Sternberg said, "This morning Lester and Sally are being brought before Judge Milner for a preliminary hearing to set bond. In deciding how to proceed, the judge will pretty much listen to whoever he wants to. I have no official role in this, I just want to watch and see what happens. I want you there, too, so you can confirm for me that these are the same people and fill me in on whatever you know about them."

We walked the one block to the courthouse, where Mr. Sternberg sat with us in the colored balcony that overlooked the courtroom. Even from that distance, we easily identified both Dillard Lester and Sally Nesbet when the Rangers escorted them in.

At first, the proceeding seemed routine, with an assistant district attorney explaining to the judge how they were caught with a truckload of Scotch whiskey. The large quantity suggested this was no small-time operation. It was fairly common, the assistant D.A. noted, for gangsters to ship whiskey legally from Europe to Mexico, then smuggle it across the border into the United States, but such an operation was expensive, requiring thousands of dollars in financing. It was not an enterprise for a small-time black crook. "Either these nigras have committed some other crime to get the money for this one," the state lawyer proclaimed in a deep Texas drawl, "or there's somebody big backing 'em up. I think you need to lock these two up until we get to the bottom of this."

The old judge looked directly at Lester. "What have you got to say?" he asked.

"Your honor," said Lester as he fired a look of contempt toward Sally. "I don't really know this woman. She paid me ten dollars to drive a truck from Brownsville for her. She told me it was filled with Mexican cloth. I'm just a po' working man, trying to earn a dollar where I can."

Sally's eyes blazed and her cream-colored complexion reddened. "You bastard!" she screamed, shocking me with language I'd never before heard from a woman's mouth. "This is all your doing. How the hell can you stand there and say you don't know me? You married me when I was just fifteen. You took me away from my no-account daddy, and then you turned out to be no better than him. You forced me to steal and grift and sell my body to any nasty mule skinner with two dollars."

Suddenly, she was no longer addressing Lester, but anyone and everyone who cared to listen. Maybe her plea was going out to God himself. "I started drinking before I was even sixteen, just to get through the day. After a while I was drinking so much I didn't know what I was doing anymore. This time in the Dallas jail is the first time I've been completely sober for more than a day or two since I left my daddy's house."

Then she stopped and looked straight at the judge and said, "I want to tell you everything now. I want to tell you about poor old Mr. Nesbet, too. I don't care what happens. I don't care if y'all lock me up for the rest of my life. I can't go on with this son of a bitch." As she spat out this latest profanity, she used the back of her hand to wipe away the tears and mucus running freely from her eyes and nose. If she had had a lawyer, he probably would have stopped her, but the court hadn't appointed one yet, because up to this point the charge had only been violation of Prohibition law. So Judge Milner said, "Go ahead and say what you've got to say."

She told the judge how Lester had heard about the oil strikes in Knox Plains and how they had traveled there separately and she had moved into a boardinghouse to look out for a mark, an unmarried colored man with money. "What I didn't know," she hissed as she shot Lester a look of pure hatred, "was that this lousy bastard was bringing in some more of his women at the same time. I know that woman calling herself Lorraine Dupree and the one who called herself Fancy LeBlanc were two of them. One day at that boardinghouse, I heard those two bitches laughing at me behind my back."

The judge warned her to watch her language, but he didn't really seem to care. Like the rest of us, he was eager to hear what the ranting woman had to say. Sally sniffled loudly, then resumed her story.

A few days after they arrived in Knox Plains, Dillard told her he had picked Mr. Nesbet as their mark. When she protested that Mr. Nesbet was much too old for her, Dillard said that was exactly why he'd chosen him. Sally was supposed to smother him with a pillow one night, and people would just think he'd just had a heart attack. She tried it, she said, but he woke up and was stronger than she thought. Mr. Nesbet started to struggle, and Sally lost her nerve and let go of the pillow.

He had made so much noise he woke his two sisters. Sally managed somehow to convince them that Mr. Nesbet had just had a bad dream, but she knew she couldn't try that a second time. The next day, Sally went by the pool hall and slipped Lester a note telling him to meet her after dark down by the baseball field.

There she told Lester how she had botched the murder attempt, and he slapped her around, causing the bruise we saw the day Mr. Nesbet died. He told her she was stupid and worthless and he should have left her with her drunkard father. Sally swore she couldn't stay with Mr. Nesbet and his two odd sisters anymore. She started telling him how strange they all were and how stingy Mr. Nesbet was—how he even brought his cow down to the baseball field every day to graze instead of buying feed for her. By the time she called Dillard from the store the next morning, he had had an idea.

"So that afternoon," Sally continued, her story now coming out in short gasps, "just as Seck was about to leave and get his cow, I played like I was suddenly feeling passionate toward him."

"Passionate?" the judge asked.

"Yeah, I had to act like I felt passionate toward him. I had to get really drunk so I could stand to go through with it. I kept him busy in the bedroom until the sun started going down. That way, Lester could hide in the shadows and shoot Seck when he came for the cow." I noticed for the second time that this woman referred to her husband by his last name. I knew some black women who, determined to give their husbands the respect that the rest of the world denied them, referred to their husbands as "Mr. Smith" or "Mr. Jones," but I never heard one of them refer to the man she was married to simply as "Smith" or "Jones."

Sally started crying again. "I never wanted to kill anybody, not even that queer old man," she wailed. Everybody's attention was on her, giving Lester the chance to grab a deputy's gun from its holster. He shot the hysterical Sally twice before anyone could stop him. She let out a sharp little cry before she fell in a crumpled heap on the polished wood floor.

"Worthless whore," Lester muttered through clenched teeth. He kicked Sally's lifeless body as a bailiff took back the gun and handcuffed the prisoner in a single motion.

The judge ordered the courtroom cleared of all visitors, so along with a handful of colored curiosity seekers who had joined us in the balcony, we filed down the narrow wooden stairs that led directly to the street.

As we walked back toward Mr. Sternberg's office, I made an observation that made Barnett laugh. "She sure did use nice English for someone with her background," I commented.

"No one on earth but you," my uncle said, "would think of a thing like that at a time like this."

"I've seen situations like this before," Mr. Sternberg noted. "Usually, when men use women in their confidence schemes, they teach them proper English and society manners so their victims will believe they're dealing with polished, refined women. Most men won't believe that a woman with fine manners would stoop to criminal acts, so they're taken in more easily."

"My gosh!" I said. "You mean there've been other cases like this?"

"Not exactly like this, but wherever you find large sums of money, you'll probably find thieves, prostitutes, and would-be killers. Money just seems to bring out the worst in some people."

"What's going to happen now?"

"My guess is Dillard Lester is going to hang for shooting his wife. I don't think they'll even bother to try him for killing Mr. Nesbet. The courtroom murder is easier to prove, and you can't hang a man but once."

"Are you sure they'll hang him? Around here the law doesn't especially care if a colored person kills another colored person. They'll send you to jail for a few years, but they only hang you if you kill a white person."

"That's pretty much true," Mr. Sternberg admitted, "unless they have some other reason for wanting you dead. Lester's been causing problems around here for a long time, and both state and federal officials want him out of the way. They would have settled for sending him to prison, but if I know Judge Milner, he'll consider it a personal insult that someone would commit a murder in his courtroom, with him sitting right there on the bench. Lester will hang for that alone."

I had thought that I could only be happy to see the world rid of a sorry, worthless woman like Sally Lee, but her courtroom speech made me feel sorry for her. Then Mr. Sternberg pointed out that her death might make it harder to prove she'd had no right to Mr. Nesbet's money.

Before we left Dallas, Barnett kept his promise to tell Mr. Sternberg what he had seen the night Louis Wilson died.

PART SIX

TUSKEEGEE SUMMER

TUSKEEGEE SUMMER

EIGHTEEN

Near the end of my junior year, in 1929, the school board finally dropped the absurd schedule we'd been following, where classes began in July and were interrupted by a two-month break in the fall. My senior year would start right after Labor Day and continue until Christmas vacation, with two days off at Thanksgiving. It turned out to be a really lucky break for me, because soon after we heard about the new schedule, I got a letter from Elliot.

Dear Moose,

I have come upon what I believe would be a great opportunity for you, if your school schedule permits. My father's friend Dr. Cedric Benedict teaches at Tuskegee Normal and Industrial Institute, the college in south Alabama started by Professor Booker T. Washington. Father and Dr. Benedict attended Atlanta University together. This summer, Dr. Benedict is conducting a two-month summer program in science and mathematics for exceptionally accomplished colored high-school students. I thought of you immediately. You will recall that Dr. George Washington Carver does his research at Tuskegee. He may agree to give at least one lecture during this program. That alone would make the program worth attending.

I took the liberty of writing to Dr. Benedict about you, and he said he would be honored to have you in the program. Each student is asked to pay a small fee to help cover room, board, and learning materials. I would be pleased to pay this cost for you, as well as your train fare to and from Tuskegee.

It is money I am happy to spend, especially knowing that the beneficiary is smart, hard-working, and ambitious and will take full advantage of this special opportunity. Education is crucial if our people are ever to reach equality with the rest of America.

There are many issues on which the late Professor Washington and I did not agree, but he was right about one thing: Negro people must find ways to become valuable to American society if we are to be accepted.

Before you start believing that my motives are purely altruistic, I must confess that I have a selfish reason for asking. Betsy has been invited to participate in the program. Father is eager to have her take advantage of this opportunity, but he and Mother worry about sending her to south Alabama, where we don't know anyone except Dr. and Mrs. Benedict. Betsy is rather headstrong and outspoken, and we are afraid that she will get into trouble in a place where race relations are only slightly better than they were during slavery. It would make my parents, and me, feel much better if there were someone there who could look after her closely. I know that Dr. Benedict will take an interest in her well-being, but I imagine he will be very busy with the program. You would have my unending gratitude if you could do me this favor.

Moose, I want you to be there to look after Betsy, but I also want this opportunity for you. No one as promising as you are should be denied the chance to succeed. Please contact me as soon as you have decided.

Your devoted friend,
Elliot

Right after I got my dictionary and looked up *altruistic*, I threw myself across my bed to consider Elliot's offer. It was more than generous. I would be less than a friend not to accept, especially after all the kindnesses he had shown me. I would love to go to a real college campus and study advanced science and mathematics with real college professors. More than anything I would love being on the same campus with Dr. George Washington Carver, and maybe having the chance to meet him, or even work with him. I could not have come up with a more perfect opportunity if I had dreamed it up myself.

But could I stand two months of close association with Betsy? Up to this point, the worst I could say about her was that she seemed to be making fun of me, but I couldn't dismiss her skin color. Essentially, every light-skinned young woman I had ever met was bankrupt of moral character. They were all out to take everything they could, and they simply didn't care what they had to do to get it or who they hurt in the process. The lighter they were, the more evil they were, and Betsy looked almost white. Just being in her presence gave me chills.

I had never told anyone, even Barnett, how I felt about these women. He just thought I was more attracted to dark girls. He didn't know my feelings ran much deeper than that. I never told anyone because I realized how irrational it was. I thought of myself as a scientist. I was supposed to believe in the logical and provable. While my feelings toward light-skinned women could not be explained, let alone justified, by reason or through empirical science, they were as real to me as any element on the periodic table.

Ma, Uncle Will, and Mr. Daniel were overjoyed to hear about the offer. Barnett was happy for me, too, even though it would be the first time we were apart for any length of time. How could I tell them that I didn't want to go because a little hundred-and-fifteen-pound girl scared the stew out of me? So I wrote to Elliot and told him I'd be delighted to be part of Dr. Benedict's program.

The material that came directly from Tuskegee explained that the fee we were paying covered only a small portion of the cost of running the program. A grant from a large corporation covered much of it, and the college was putting in the rest. Each student would be required to work two hours a day on campus as well. I was told that I would help serve breakfast in the faculty dining hall.

If there's any place hotter than south Alabama in the summer, the devil is holding it in reserve in case he runs out of room in Hell. I had always heard that two places could be the same temperature, yet one would be far more uncomfortable than the other. After I stepped off the train in Tuskegee, Alabama, I believed it absolutely. I saw a thermometer that read ninety-seven degrees, yet it was the stickiest, most uncomfortable ninety-seven degrees I'd ever experienced. There was an awning covering the white side of the platform, but the colored side was exposed to the merciless sun. I took my hat off and wiped the sweat from my forehead with my handkerchief. I was fanning myself with the hat when a cab with a colored driver pulled up. "My guess is you's looking for a ride to the school. That right, son?" the driver asked.

"Yes, sir," I answered. "I need to get to the Tuskegee campus."

He put my bag in the back and opened the door for me. "You mus' be mighty set on gettin' a education, you goin' to school in all this here heat," he commented.

"If I'd known it was this hot, I might not have come," I answered honestly. "But I'm in a special math and science program for high-school students. I hope I get to meet Dr. Carver."

"Oh, yeah. I knows 'bout Dr. Carver," the driver boasted. "He 'bout the smartest colored man in America, an' that prob'ly make him the smartest man in America." He cackled out loud at his own quip.

"I heard that Thomas Edison offered him more than a hundred thousand dollars a year to come work for him, but he said he'd rather stay here and do his own research at Tuskegee."

"You don't say?" The car was kicking up clouds of red dust as we moved quickly down the narrow south Alabama streets. "Well, I takes my hat off to him then, 'cause I'd sho' take it. But then I don' reckon there's nothing no white man would pay me no hunnard thousand dollars to do."

When we arrived on the campus, I went straight to my dormitory so I could bathe and change clothes. In the room, I saw evidence that my roommate had arrived, though no one was there. A beaten-up brown leather suitcase bore a tag that read, "W.C. Cooper, Dothan, Alabama." On the table between the two beds there was a family photo of an almost comical collection of unstylishly dressed colored people posed awkwardly in front of a weather-beaten wood-frame house. Next to the photo was a painted and decorated cigar box. A narrow slit had been cut in the top, with the words "Grammar Box" written just above the slit.

When I went outside again, it was almost five o'clock and the temperature had dropped a little. The campus's billowing shade trees also brought some relief from the heat. I strolled toward the building the driver had pointed out as the dining hall. I saw other young men and women heading there as well. They looked as young, awkward, and uncertain as I was sure I did. As I looked them over, I was surprised to see a white girl up ahead of me, talking with some other students. Then she turned, and I realized it was Betsy. I had hoped to avoid her for a while, even though I was essentially being paid to look after her. She must have seen me, since she turned and walked toward me. Remembering the rules in Grandma O'Malley's etiquette book, I walked straight past her. Then I heard her yell, "Moose, are you blind or you ignoring me deliberately?"

"I was just giving you the chance to ignore me if you wanted to. That's what a gentleman is supposed to do." I thought she'd know that, since she went to that fancy private school and all.

"Why on earth would I want to ignore you?" she demanded. "Moose, you can be so queer sometimes."

Several boys had been hanging around her. One of them looked at me and laughed out loud. "You sure don't look like you'd be called Moose," he said. "You're a little small for a Moose." Some of the others laughed, too, but Betsy knew how to confer instant triumph in that social battle. She slipped her arm through mine and said, "Come on. Let's find a table." Walking away with the best-looking girl present was an unchallenged victory.

Most girls I knew hated summer heat. It frizzed their hair and made a sweat-streaked mess of whatever face paint they put on. But Betsy was prettier than ever. The summer sun just seemed to make her radiant.

In the dining room, eager brown-skinned boys in white jackets brought our supper. It was served family-style. The boys in the white jackets put bowls of food on the table, and we passed the dishes to one another as though we were at home. The food was tasty but portions were small, and there was very little meat. It was as though word hadn't reached south Alabama that the World War was over and there was no longer a need to ration food. "Hey, there's something in my chicken and dumplings," shouted one young man at my table. "Wait a minute! I believe it's an actual piece of chicken!" His jest made the room explode with laughter.

As our servers were putting down our bread pudding, Betsy turned to me and asked, "Would you like to go with me after we finish and meet Dr. Benedict?"

I didn't want to go anywhere with her. I wished she'd leave me alone. "Dr. Benedict is your father's friend from Atlanta University. Is that right?"

"Yes. He's in charge of the program here. He lives about two miles from campus. It's a pleasant walk. It won't be dark yet for a couple of hours."

"I'm rather tired from the trip."

Betsy laughed. "You talk like some old lady instead of a strapping young farm boy. My mother could make the walk easily."

I was shamed into it, but as we walked toward the front entrance to the campus, I muttered, "I've never lived on a farm."

She was right, the walk was pleasant. The streets were lined with tall oak and magnolia trees thick with leaves that shaded us from the late afternoon sun. "Moose," she said after a long silence, "I hope you don't mind my asking, but I'm still curious about the library incident. I'm sorry I laughed before. I really wasn't laughing at you and Barnett. I was imagining the looks on those white people's faces. Elliot wouldn't tell me much. He can be tiresomely ethical about not repeating anything his clients tell him." I told her the whole story of our trip to Kansas City, including parts I didn't intend to tell. Betsy was so easy to talk to I found myself opening up to her before I realized it. *I could like this girl,* I thought, *if she were just darker.*

Dr. Benedict was a tall, handsome, fiftyish man who was impeccably neat even in casual clothes. His lovely house reminded me bit of Elliot's home in Kansas City. His wife was a slightly plump, pleasant woman who probably had been a real beauty in her youth. She brought us all bowls of sherbet, a wonderful treat I had never had before.

The conversation was even more of a treat. Apparently Dr. Benedict had been good friends with Booker T. Washington and had many charming stories about the famous educator. "I remember once several of us had a meeting that was supposed to start at ten o'clock in Professor Washington's office," Dr. Benedict recalled. "He had walked into town on an errand that morning and was late getting back, which certainly wasn't like him. Professor Washington placed great value on punctuality and was never late, nor did he tolerate tardiness in others.

"It was a crisp fall day, but when he got back to his office, Professor Washington was sweating and had his coat and tie over his arm. 'Why, Professor Washington,' we were all saying. 'What in the world happened to you?' He explained that on the way back to the campus, a white woman called to him from her front porch. 'Come here, boy,' the woman had said. 'I've got some wood that needs chopping in the back.' Well, Professor Washington said he just answered, 'Yes, ma'am,' and followed her to her backyard, where he chopped a big pile of wood. She offered him a nickel, but he turned it down.

"He was just telling us this when his secretary came in. She whispered just loudly enough so those of us in the room could hear, 'Professor Washington, there's a white woman out here who says she needs to see you.' Professor Washington said to us, 'Gentlemen, please excuse me a moment. I seem to have a visitor. I believe this will only take a minute.' The white woman walked in and looked nervously around her, then she said, 'Please excuse me, Professor Washington, I didn't realize that was you I stopped on the street. My servant girl told me who you were and I rushed over to apologize.'

" 'That's quite all right, ma'am,' Professor Washington said graciously. 'I'm always happy to do a friend a favor.' The last thing that woman did before she left was hand Booker an envelope and say, 'Please accept my small donation to the school.' We opened the envelope after she left. There was a hundred dollars in it. Now, a hundred dollars was a nice bit of money back then. In fact, we wouldn't turn it down today." Dr. Benedict, laughed, obviously enjoying his memories.

"If you want to get an argument going among the faculty on this campus, you just raise the question of whether Professor Washington did the right thing in chopping that woman's wood," he told us.

"Well, of course, he did," inserted Mrs. Benedict. "What else could he have done?" Like many successful colored men, Dr. Benedict had a light-skinned wife. Sally Benedict wasn't really white-looking, she was a coffee-with-milk color that might have suggested an Egyptian, a Mexican, or one of those Caddos who lived in Knox Plains. From time to time I glanced at her and wondered whether this seemingly gracious and devoted wife sat alone in the dark at night, plotting evil that Dr. Benedict's brilliant but innocent mind could never imagine.

"There's a rule that all students in the high-school program must be back on campus by eight o'clock, and even I cannot override it," Dr. Benedict declared. "I hate to chase away good company, but I'm afraid it's time for you to go."

"Give them a ride, Cedric," Mrs. Benedict pleaded. "Don't make these nice young people walk back to campus." Dr. Benedict dropped Betsy at her dorm, then he drove to the other side of the campus, where the boys sleep. I returned to my room and met my roommate for the first time.

"You must be Theodore," he said in a polished but pronounced drawl. "Mah name's Dubyah Cee Cuppa." I remembered the name from the suitcase tag: W.C. Cooper.

"Ah'm from Dothan. Where're you from, Theodore?"

"Knox Plains, Texas," I answered. "It's about forty-five miles from Dallas. And please, don't call me Theodore. I prefer Moose. But if you don't want to call me Moose, call me Roosevelt."

W.C. was only a little bigger than I was, and his wire-frame glasses made him look scholarly. He was awed when I told him I had visited Dr. Benedict at home. He started treating me so respectfully that it made me uncomfortable. "Ah just put ma thangs down when Ah came in. If you'd rather have this bed, Ah kin move them," he said. "It makes no difference to me at all."

"That's okay," I answered. "It makes no difference to me either. You already have your things in place, just leave them." My eyes fell again on the painted cigar box, so I asked him about it.

"Don't bother about that," he said with obvious embarrassment. "It's something ma brother and m . . ." he hesitated, "my brother and Ah do. We both know how to speak English correctly, but we live around people with terrible grammar, and sometimes it makes us forget. So Ah made a penalty box. Anytime one of us makes a grammar mistake, we have to put a penny in the box. At the end of the month, we give the money to the church. Ah'd thought Ah might git a roommate who'd like me to use the grammar box to help him improve, but Ah see you don't need any help. Ah feel that correct grammar is real . . . really . . . important to help our people get ahead, don't you?"

"You're right, W.C.," I answered. "I like your grammar box. I'm willing to do it, if you promise to make me pay up anytime you catch me using poor grammar."

"All right," he said, then he gave me a devilish grin. "You just used an unnecessary preposition. There was no need to say 'pay up.' 'Pay' would have been sufficient." He waved the box in front of me until I dug a penny out of my pocket and dropped it in.

I amazed W.C. again when I told him my father had been a cowboy. "A colored cowboy? I never knew there were colored cowboys," he admitted.

"You'd never know it from watching the moving pictures, but when my pa was working the range, about one cowboy out of every four was colored."

I reported to my job in the faculty dining room at five forty-five the next morning. As I walked across the dew-sprinkled campus, I was happy I'd been given an early-morning job. I loved that time of day, especially in the summer, when the sun came up early and the air was cool and pleasant for a short time. If someone was going to make me work in a kitchen in the summer, early morning was certainly the best time. Mr. Vincent, the food-service supervisor, told me that my job would be to put fresh tablecloths, napkins, silverware, cups, and saucers on the tables. Then I was to make sure each table had salt and pepper and sugar and cream. I was to serve coffee until seven forty-five, then I could have breakfast in the kitchen with the rest of the dining-hall staff before my first class at eight-thirty. On Mondays, students were allowed to stop work at seven-thirty so we would have time for a quick breakfast before the mandatory eight o'clock convocation.

Not all of the people I worked with were fellow students. Some were permanent workers, most of whom were older colored men and women, supplementing the modest pay they were drawing as servants someplace else. I quickly learned that these permanent workers were the people who could help you if you got in a jam. I had set the tables and put out the salt, pepper, and sugar. I returned to the kitchen for cream. I saw a dozen or more little cream pitchers arranged and waiting on a large tray, but no cream to fill them. I couldn't find Mr. Vincent, so I looked in the large industrial Frigidaire. Still I saw no cream. The faculty members teaching eight-o'clock classes would be in for breakfast any moment. I turned around and saw a little white-haired, dark-skinned man in a white jacket. "Do you know where I can find the cream?" I asked him.

"Here you are, son," he said gently as he handed me a large, cool pitcher.

"Thank you," I said with a relieved sigh. I quickly poured the thick white liquid into the smaller pitchers and placed one on each table as faculty members walked in. When I got back to the kitchen, Mr. Vincent was standing just inside the door. He swapped my tray for a coffeepot and told me to start pouring. After I had served the first round of coffee, Mr. Vincent swapped my empty pot for a full one and told me to stand in the dining area in case someone wanted a refill. The faculty members were chatting socially as other servers put plates of food on the table. Then one woman sipped her coffee and made a face. "The coffee tastes strange this morning," she said.

"It certainly does," added the man next to her, "but I don't think it's the coffee. I believe it's the cream."

"Yes, I believe you're right," agreed another diner. He dipped his spoon directly into the cream, then sipped from the spoon. He wrinkled his brow as he moved the substance around in his mouth. Finally, he said, "It does have an off taste—not unpleasant, like cream that's soured—just odd in some way. Actually, it tastes a little like . . . a little like . . . peanuts."

Everyone in the room turned and stared at the little black man who had given me the offending substance. "Dr. Carver!" one of them exclaimed in an accusing voice.

The little man smiled. "Okay," he said. "But next time it'll be good enough to fool you."

Much to my astonishment I got a letter from Barnett. Ma had drilled into both of us the need to observe such social niceties as letter writing, but the drilling didn't take as well with Barnett. Now, obviously, he had managed to get a letter written and mailed. I was amused, however, to see that he had made no effort to follow proper letter-writing form.

> Moose,
>   It's pretty dull around here this summer. Without you here, minding the store is pretty boring and lonely most of the time. It's gotten so I miss Miss Violet standing over me while I measure her "company" flour. She comes in once in a while to buy something like a bar of Ivory soap, but she always speaks softly and goes straight about her business. I'd like to just give her the soap, and I've tried to refuse her money, but she absolutely won't leave the store with something unless she pays for it, even though I know she has very little money these days. To be honest, I miss her old feistiness.
>   How's Betsy? I know you prefer those girls who look like they got off the boat from Africa last week, but you have to admit, Betsy's pretty cute, even if she is "light, bright, and dang near white."
>   Have you met Dr. Carver yet? I'm nowhere near as science-crazy as you are, but he's one scientist I'd love to meet.
>   Take care of yourself, you old rascal. I'll see you in a few weeks.
>   Barnett

Barnett's letter reminded me that I had resolved to go spend some time with Dr. Carver. After all, I might never get a chance to meet a great scientist again. Ordinarily, I would be much too shy to approach such a famous man, but the fact that he had involved me in his little prank made me bold enough to go see him. On Wednesdays we had no afternoon classes, so I decided to walk over to Dr. Carver's lab after the midday meal and see whether I could engage this brilliant scientist in conversation.

I was nervously rehearsing my greeting to him as I walked toward the lab. "Good afternoon, Dr. Carver," I planned to say. "I'm the student you switched the cream on in the faculty dining room." No, that would sound as though I were accusing him. Surely he wouldn't want to talk to me after that. "I'm the student you met in the faculty dining room" would be much better, but maybe that wouldn't be enough to make him remember me.

I was muttering to myself and looking off into space as I walked along the narrow campus pathway. I ran smack into someone and almost knocked him down. It was Dr. Carver. "Oh, my goodness," I cried when I realized what I had done. "I'm sorry, Dr. Carver, please excuse me, I'm . . ."

"The young man from the faculty dining room," he noted with a pleasant smile. "You got away before I could apologize to you that morning."

"No apology is necessary, sir. I was honored to be part of your experiment. I tasted that imitation cream. It was very good. I believe you're very close to having something that no one can tell from the real thing." He smiled and nodded, so I continued. "My name is Roosevelt O'Malley. I was just coming to see you."

"About the cream?"

"Oh, no." Then I realized he was joking. "I've always wanted to meet you. I think you're the greatest scientist in the world. Greater than Thomas Edison, sir."

"There are many who would disagree with that," he chuckled. "But what did you want to see me about?"

Now I truly felt foolish. "I didn't want anything special," I admitted. "I want to be a scientist, too, and I just hoped you would spend some time with me and tell me about your life and your work."

He nodded again. "I'm walking over to the administration building. You can walk with me if you want to."

"Yes, sir." I couldn't believe I was getting my dream in spite of my clumsiness. "I'm really sorry about running into you."

"Yep," the great man said. "I saw you walking along talking to yourself, but I just couldn't get out of your way." He must have seen how embarrassed I looked, because he added, "I do it all the time myself, son. Sometimes, I don't even see the world around me. I'm just walking and talking with my God. A lot of people say that you can't be a scientist and believe in God, but I don't see how anybody can study science and not believe in God. The more I study, the more I believe. To look at this complex and perfectly ordered universe and think it all just happened by accident is like looking inside a clock, with all its springs and interlocking wheels, and still refusing to believe there is any such thing as a clock maker."

"How did you get interested in science?" I asked.

"I don't know," he answered. "I don't remember a time when I wasn't interested in the world around me—what makes the trees grow and the river flow. I wanted to know it all. You know, by the time I was any size, slavery had officially ended, but nobody around where I lived seemed to take much notice of that. It was probably after the Emancipation Proclamation that I was traded for a horse. That's right," he said, noting my astonishment. "I was traded for a horse. It wasn't much of a horse, either, but I was a sickly little thing, and I guess they figured they'd never get much work out of me. I was raised on a farm owned by a German couple, and they noticed that I had a way with plants, so they just let me fiddle around in the garden as much as I wanted."

"How did you get interested in peanuts?"

"Well, you know I've done a lot of work in crop rotation. That's an agricultural technique that involves alternately planting a crop that strips the soil of nutrients and one that restores the nutrients. The soil here in the South was pretty thoroughly damaged during the war. When I say the war, I don't mean the Great War, I mean the one folks around here like to call the War Between the States. Peanuts are pretty good for restoring soil after cotton has robbed its goodness, but the question then is, what do you do with all those peanuts? So I started developing new peanut products. I've had some interest in them. There's a fellow in Battle Creek, Michigan, who's been selling my peanut butter as a health food. I tell you, son, if there's one sure way to keep people from buying a food, it's to label it 'health food.' I don't think peanut butter will ever catch on with the general population.

"How did I get interested in peanuts?" he pondered, searching for a more philosophical answer to my question. "One night I was just sitting under the summer sky, nobody out there but me and God. So I asked God if He would show me the mysteries of His great universe, and God said, 'Now, George, the universe is mighty big and you're mighty small.' So I said, 'Well, God, could you just show me the mysteries of a peanut?' and He said, 'Now, George, that's more your size.'"

Dr. Carver continued his astounding biography as we walked into the administration building and down several hallways, finally reaching an area marked "Business Office." Dr. Carver walked over to a scarred old counter where a young woman was going through a file cabinet. "Excuse me," Dr. Carver said. "I'm Dr. George Washington Carver. I teach science here. I'm here to get a paycheck, please."

"I'm sorry, Dr. Carver," the young woman said respectfully, "but payday isn't until Friday. The checks won't even be ready until tomorrow afternoon."

He looked carefully at the woman. "You're new here, aren't you?" he asked.

"Yes, sir," she said. "I was hired this summer."

"Unlock that little drawer right there at your left hand, and look in it for me," he instructed. Puzzled, she did as he asked. She was astonished to find at least a dozen paychecks, each made out to Dr. George Washington Carver. "Just give me any one of them," he said. Then he turned to me and explained, "I don't take a check until I really need it. I figure the school needs the money more than I do, but right now I've got some bills to pay, so I thought I'd better get over here and get a check."

I had made a new friend. Dr. Carver even allowed me to visit him at home now and then. Sometimes I took W.C. or Betsy along. Sometimes they both came with me. Dr. Carver let us sample his peanut butter and some of the other products he had developed from such lowly Southern crops as peanuts and sweet potatoes. There seemed to be no end to his talents. Dr. Carver was an excellent cook and a magnificent painter. He worked entirely in paints he had made from clay dug out of the Alabama hills. His "canvas" was paper made from peanut shells, and the works of art were displayed in frames made from dried cornhusks. When I asked what had inspired him to make paint and other things from the "worthless" clay of Alabama's hills, he smiled and quoted Sadie Brown's favorite psalm: "I will lift up mine eyes unto the hills from whence cometh my help. My help cometh from the Lord who made heaven and earth." For Dr. Carver, life was a single flowing tapestry on which art, science, and religion blended seamlessly.

One evening as we were walking back from Dr. Carver's house, W.C., Betsy, and I got into a lively discussion of W.E.B. DuBois's vision for colored America as compared with Booker T. Washington's. "Booker T. Washington's ideas are an embarrassment to all American colored people," W.C. insisted in a drawl that deepened when spiced with emotion. "He as good as said we don't care whether we get to vote or not. And everyone praises him for saying there's as much dignity in tilling a field as in writing a poem, but you don't have to think about that too long before you realize that whites will take that to mean that colored people should be content to till fields and never bother about writing poems, or doing anything else that would demonstrate intellectual ability."

"I agree that Professor Washington was far too limited in his scope, but to understand his philosophy, you have to understand his perspective," noted Betsy. "The man was born a slave. Even when white people were gracious toward him, they still treated him as an inferior. Thomas Jefferson said it is self-evident that all men are created equal, but in the South where Professor Washington lived and worked, everyone behaved, and still behaves, as though it were self-evident that God made whites superior. Dr. DuBois has a Ph.D. from Harvard. He has lived and worked around white people who respected him as a man and a scholar. That has to make a difference in the way he views the world."

I greatly enjoyed my two friends' discussion. They were the only people my age I'd ever met who were intimately familiar with the writings of Booker T. Washington and W.E.B. DuBois. My mother had read Washington's *Up From Slavery*, DuBois's *The Souls of Black Folks*, and other books and essays by these men as well as the works of many other prominent writers of the time, and we often discussed ideas and philosophies, especially with regard to the direction the Negro in America should take.

When we reached Betsy's dorm and were saying good night, she asked, "Would either of you boys like a kiss?" We were both dumb with shock. Then she reached into her pocketbook and produced a handful of little Hershey's chocolate candies in silver foil. "Elliot sent me a box of treats," she added innocently. "I had almost forgotten I had them. Here, please help me eat them."

She must have noticed how flustered I was, because she asked, "What's the matter?"

"Nothing," I said. "I'm just delighted that you have my favorite candy. We sell these in the store, but we call them 'silver tips.' "

When W.C. and I got back to the room, his breathing still hadn't returned to normal. He fell backward onto his bed with a deep sigh. "Boy, oh, boy!" he exclaimed. "Ah just about fainted! Ah thought she was going to kiss us, both of us. Ah've dreamed about kissing Betsy since the first time Ah saw her, but Ah knew she wouldn't want to kiss an ole country coon like me. Boy, oh, boy, oh, boy!"

I stared at my roommate, who was rolling back and forth on the bed in ecstasy at the mere thought of kissing Betsy. "I didn't know you were attracted to her," I said.

"Any boy that's not attracted to Betsy is . . . something's wrong with him. Moose, she's beautiful. She looks like one of those women in the moving pictures. Don't tell me you don't want to kiss her."

"I never thought about it," I lied.

Each week started with a Monday-morning convocation in the chapel. The door was locked promptly at eight o'clock. The penalty for not attending was dismissal from the program. Although Booker T. Washington had died in 1915, his spirit lived on in the culture and values of the school he founded. Professor Washington had believed in discipline and punctuality. He had been determined to break young black people of the casual attitude toward time that had developed in the fields, where there were no clocks or watches.

The convocation included a brief devotion with prayer, scripture, and a hymn. Someone, usually Dr. Benedict, gave a short inspirational message and read the week's announcements. At the third Monday-morning convocation, Dr. Benedict's final announcement was that there would be no classes that Thursday. Instead there would be a picnic in the grove, with entertainment from local bands and choirs and fireworks at dusk. With genuine emotion swelling his voice, he added, "Our nation turns one hundred fifty-three years old on Thursday, so let's remember that this is not just a day for fun and frolic. Independence Day is a time to reflect on God's blessing that we live in a free nation."

The holiday sky seemed a brighter blue than any day before. Tiny wisps of cloud waltzed gracefully across the sky, and even the temperature seemed more bearable. The festivities in the grove started early in the afternoon, with games, music, and what appeared to be an unlimited supply of lemonade and hand-cranked ice cream. In a stylish green-and-white print dress and a broad-brimmed straw hat, Betsy looked like one of those rose-cheeked modern girls out of Ma's women's magazines.   She found W.C. and me and invited us to join her and the Benedicts on a blanket under the trees. Dr. and Mrs. Benedict had wisely camped where they would be in the shade all afternoon. W.C. walked all the way around the Benedicts to the far end of the blanket so he could sit next to Betsy.

The abundance and variety of picnic foods made it hard to believe that the same people who put the stingy little servings on the dining-room tables every day had provided the feast. About five o'clock Dr. Benedict went up onto the temporary platform that was draped with red, white, and blue banners. He told us all to stand as two students came forward with a large American flag. He led the Pledge of Allegiance to a flag whose age was evident not only in its frayed edges but in the number of stars. There were only forty-six. Since two additional states had joined the Union in 1912, I knew the flag was at least a year older than I was.

After the Pledge, a choir took the platform and sang a nonstop selection of patriotic songs. As they filled the air with "America," "America the Beautiful," and "The Star Spangled Banner," the picnickers sat in reverent silence. Some actually had tears streaming down their cheeks.

"Why do you suppose colored people love this country so much?" I asked those around me. "We've probably been treated about as badly as you could imagine any group of people being treated in their own country, yet no one recites the Pledge of Allegiance with more sincerity. No one sings patriotic songs with more emotion. No one shows more honor to people like George Washington and Abraham Lincoln."

There was silence for a minute, then Mrs. Benedict responded. "I don't think it's what America is or has been that colored people love, it's what America has promised to be. We hear phrases like 'land of the free,' and 'brotherhood from sea to shining sea,' and we are enraptured by the ideal of what America is supposed to be striving for. In our minds we catch a glimpse of an America where everybody is equal and nobody is judged by who his parents were or where he came from."

Dr. Benedict's voice came out of the deepening afternoon shadows. "This country was founded by people who were weary of seeing others get respect and privilege just because their daddy was the Duke of Such-and-Such or the Earl of So-and-So. They wrote into our most scared documents the idea that God created all men equal and gave all men the same basic rights. But it's easier to have ideals than to live by them. Some of the very men who were formulating these ideas owned slaves and took advantage of fellow humans in other ways. The very Declaration of Independence, with all its lofty notions of freedom and justice, was written by a slave owner and refers to the people who were already in North America when the Europeans arrived as 'merciless Indian Savages.' "

"Does that mean the Declaration of Independence and the Constitution are not worthy of our respect?" W.C. asked.

"Oh, I don't think so." A new voice had joined the discussion. Up to that point I hadn't noticed a young white man sitting on another blanket just beyond the edge of the Benedicts' blanket.

"Have you young folks met Mr. Barry?" Dr. Benedict asked. He completed the introductions, then explained, "Mr. Barry teaches American history to the freshmen here at Tuskegee."

"Ah don't mean to be rude, Mr. Barry," W.C. declared in a voice that was genuinely without hostility, "but it's easy for you to be unconcerned about America's failure to live up to its ideals. After all, you're in the dominant group."

"I didn't mean that I'm unconcerned, W.C. I'm very concerned. But I'm also concerned that we as a nation not throw away worthy ideals because human frailty has kept us from living up to them. While colored people are certainly suffering the ill effects of this problem, it's an American problem, one that should concern all of us. As far as I'm concerned, the phrases 'liberty and justice for all' and 'all men are created equal' represent a covenant between this country and its citizens. It is a promise that has not been kept, but every American of goodwill should devote his intelligence and energy to seeing that it is kept, because the promise of freedom, justice, and equality for all *is* America. Without it there is no America. Without it, we're just a collection of people living on a big stretch of land between the Atlantic and Pacific Oceans. It is our devotion to a common set of principles and ideas that makes us a nation."

"You're not from Alabama, are you, Mr. Barry?" Betsy asked, setting off a wave of laughter in the group.

Mr. Barry laughed harder than anybody. "No, Betsy," he answered, "I'm from Maine. Does that make me a maniac?"

"No," Dr. Benedict teased. "But I'm not quite sure we're ready to eliminate the possibility."

CHAPTER TWENTY

Over the course of the summer program, Dr. Benedict invited Betsy to dinner several times and always included me in the invitation. Of course, I accepted. I hadn't lost sight of the fact that I was supposed to keep an eye on her, especially when she went off campus. Since I could always count on good food and stimulating conversation at Dr. Benedict's house, it wasn't a tough obligation to meet.

On the last Sunday morning we would spend at Tuskegee, Betsy found me in the chapel and sat with me during morning worship. The Benedicts sat right across from us. After the service, Mrs. Benedict insisted that we come home with them for Sunday dinner. Rumor had it that the student dining room was again serving its almost chickenless chicken and dumplings. I was sure that the fare at the Benedicts would be far better.

It was another very hot south Alabama afternoon, maybe the hottest we'd had all summer, so I was grateful to be able to ride with our hosts instead of walking. Soon after we arrived, I discovered we weren't the only guests. Within a few minutes a middle-aged couple walked in, and we were introduced to Dr. and Mrs. Harry Comstock. Dr. Comstock taught history on the campus, but had no summer classes. He was spending his break doing independent research, so Betsy and I were meeting him for the first time. Alice Comstock was a tall, slender, patrician woman with the elegance and bearing of a queen. Her skin was velvety black, like Barnett's. Despite the fact that she must have been nearly sixty years old, she had barely a wrinkle and was so flawlessly beautiful I found myself staring at her. Dr. Comstock would look at his beautiful wife and smile once in a while. He seemed proud just to be by her side.

At the dinner table, Dr. Benedict and Dr. Comstock chatted about campus goings-on. "That young man I met this summer who was finishing up his Ph.D. at the University of Chicago, did you decide to hire him?" Dr. Benedict asked.

"McDuffie? He'll be joining us this fall. We were lucky to get him. Right now the college just isn't paying these bright young instructors what they're worth. McDuffie took the job because he just got married, and he needs to be sure of an income, even a modest one."

"I didn't know he was thinking of marriage. Who is his bride?" Dr. Benedict wanted to know.

"Oh, like all these successful young colored boys, he had to go out and find himself the closest thing to a white girl he could get without being lynched. I believe she's from Atlanta, Georgia. No offense, Sally," he said to Mrs. Benedict, "but I believe that the fact that every success-ful colored man feels like he has to have a light-skinned wife is evi-dence that most of us still believe that the Negro race and everything characteristic of it is inferior."

"Well whether you believe it or not, Harry," Dr. Benedict huffed, "I married the smartest, kindest, most loving woman I could ever hope to meet. I would have married her had she been the color of tar or the color of snow. And by the way, I had the opportunity to marry several young ladies much fairer of complexion than Sally, but I chose to marry the woman I love." He said this last with dramatic flair, as though reciting lines in a play.

"Again," Dr. Comstock added defensively, "I meant no disrespect. If I spoke any criticism, it was directed at McDuffie. He once told me he wouldn't keep company with a woman unless he could see blue veins in her arm."

"You know," Dr. Benedict mused, "everyone assumes that ambi-tious colored men marry light-skinned women because they really want white ones. But they live in a society that would never permit them to take a white wife. There are other explanations, of course. In many instances the colored people with good educations and good jobs are light-skinned because they're the ones white people favor. Few people know this, but Professor Washington's father was white. He probably would never have gotten the opportunities that led to his founding this school had he been pure African. So light-skinned girls often come from the colored families with education, polish, and a little money, and isn't that the kind of family an ambitious young man wants to marry into? No man of distinguished accomplishments wants to marry a washerwoman."

Dr. Comstock puffed up like a blowfish. "Alice comes from a family with money and education. She and her two sisters all went to college. There are certainly no washerwomen among them," he countered. "Her father made quite a bit of money in Chicago with small businesses he was able to buy over the years. He had a barbershop, a restaurant, and a clothing store in the colored district. Her people are all quite dark— and proud of it."

"I didn't mean to suggest that this was an uninterrupted pattern," answered Dr. Benedict. "I believe your lovely wife's family illustrates my point rather than refutes it. Successful colored men were eager to marry her and her sisters because they wanted to have polished, educated wives who would be assets to their careers. Skin color is incidental. It's just that more often than not, the women with poise, social graces, and education are also light-skinned.

"Of course, people have individual reasons for their preferences, too. We're very complex creatures, we humans. We might like or dislike a particular physical type because of a relationship earlier in our lives that we don't even remember. For example, someone may have had a plump grade-school teacher who was really mean. That person might grow up disliking plump ladies without realizing that it had anything at all to do with that grade-school teacher.

"In fact, I once knew a fellow named Leon who had a light-skinned mother and a dark-skinned father. As it happened, the father was a harsh man who beat his wife and children and never showed them any affection at all. The mother protected the children as best she could and showed them the love and encouragement the father never did. The mother's family—the children's grandmother, aunts, and an uncle— also light-skinned people, were very loving to the children and taught them to laugh and to believe in themselves. Leon was dark like his father, but he grew up disliking dark-skinned people and would never keep company with a dark-skinned woman. He married a woman that you would almost take for white. I believe that Leon's preference for light-skinned women had more to do with what had happened in his own family than it did with the values of the larger society, colored or white."

"Are you trying to say that dark-skinned men are all harsh and mean?" Dr. Comstock asked.

"Of course not," Dr. Benedict answered with an exasperated sigh. "You have missed my point, as usual. In that particular family, the cruel father happened to be dark. It could just as easily have happened the other way around."

"I know what you're saying," Dr. Comstock chuckled. "You're just so serious about all those psychology books you read that I love to get you going."

Mrs. Benedict served chicken in cream sauce, but unlike the student dining room's dishes, hers contained pieces of meat large enough to be recognizable as actual chicken. At the end of the meal, she brought out a tall cake piled high with heavenly white icing, and more of that wonderful frozen concoction called sherbet. As we were finishing dessert, Dr. Benedict abruptly rose from the table and said, "Excuse me just a moment," then he walked quickly out of the room.

The rest of us moved to the parlor, where the conversation again turned to social chitchat. "So, did you two meet this summer, or were you keeping company before you came to Tuskegee?" Dr. Comstock asked Betsy and me.

I hastened to correct his error. "Oh, no, sir, no, no," I said, waving my hands to add emphasis. "She and I are not keeping company. We have no interest in each other in that sense. Miss Singer is just my friend's sister. I don't even think of Betsy as a girl. I'd never even consider taking her out." I turned to see Betsy's face red with mortification. My denial, it appeared, had skirted the ragged edge of insult.

The astute Mrs. Comstock helped me cover my faux pas by changing the subject. "So you're from Texas, Moose," she said pleasantly. "I've never been there, but I understand it's lovely country. What part of the state are you from?"

I gave her a few travel-guide facts about east Texas, realizing that her inquiry had come more from good manners than an actual interest in Knox Plains. As I talked, I glanced at Betsy from time to time. She was staring straight ahead, her countenance stripped of even the faintest hint of a smile.

"What's become of Cedric?" Dr. Comstock asked after a few minutes. I suddenly realized it had been about fifteen minutes since Dr. Benedict excused himself from the table.

Mrs. Benedict went to check on him. In a few minutes she came back and reported that Dr. Benedict sent his deepest apologies, but he was suddenly overtaken by stomach pain and nausea, probably from a combination of the heat and rich food. "Is everyone else all right?" Mrs. Benedict asked anxiously. We all assured her that we were fine.

Dr. Benedict appeared at the doorway, looking slightly green. "I'm so sorry," he said. "I'm from Massachusetts originally, and this Alabama heat gets the best of me every now and then. Usually, if I lie down for a couple of hours, I'm all right again," he assured us.

"Well, you go lie down then," insisted Dr. Comstock. "We were about to leave anyway. Alice and I are due at a Founders' Day program at church. We can't be late. Alice is on the program."

"We need to get back to campus, too," I said.

"It's much too hot to walk," Dr. Benedict noted. "Harry, can you give them a ride?"

"Ordinarily, I'd be glad to, but the campus is in the opposite direction, and we really need to be at church a little before four o'clock."

Sinking into a chair and stroking his ailing belly, Dr. Benedict asked, "Moose, do you drive?"

"Yes, sir, I do," I said, unsure why he was asking.

"Good. I'd ask Sally to take you back, but she doesn't drive. You can take my car. I'll walk to the campus in the morning."

"I can give you a ride," Dr. Comstock offered, eager to be of help after all. "I'm going there first thing in the morning to interview some graduate students who are looking for teaching-assistant positions."

Dr. Benedict handed me his car key. "Then the matter is settled," he pronounced as he walked unsteadily back toward his bedroom. "I wish I could say the same for my stomach."

We had just pulled away from the house when the outspoken Betsy shrieked, "They might have taught you a lot about chemistry back in Texas, but they sure didn't teach you anything about good manners. I have never been so humiliated in my entire life!"

"Humiliated?" I echoed. "What in the world did I do to humiliate you?"

"You made it sound as if the idea of a boy being interested in me was laughable, as if I were just about the most unattractive creature on earth." Out of the corner of my eye, I could see tears streaming down her flushed cheeks.

"All I did was tell the truth. All I said was that we weren't keeping company," I protested.

"Oh, no, that's not all you said." Her voice went up about an octave on the word *all*. "You said, 'I don't even think of Betsy as a girl. I'd never even consider taking her out.'" She turned my words into brickbats and threw them back at me.

"I was just trying to straighten out a misunderstanding," I said meekly.

"Well, I don't think anybody misunderstands now," she screamed. "I think they all realize that you find me ugly as a troll."

"I don't find you ugly as . . . I don't find you ugly," I said. I had no idea how to make this right. I wasn't sure there was anything I could say. I just wanted to get back to campus as quickly as possible.

The road that led from the Benedicts' neighborhood to the campus was all but abandoned that Sunday afternoon. I didn't see another vehicle until an Alabama State Patrol car pulled out behind me and turned its siren on. The siren startled us so that our argument was momentarily forgotten. "He probably just needs to get around you. Pull over to the side of the road," Betsy suggested.

"No, he's not going around me," I said as I pulled over. "He probably thinks you're white and wants to know why you're sitting next to me."

The state patrol car parked behind me. A big, red-faced state patrolman walked around to my side of the car. He glared at Betsy and me for what seemed like at least a minute. Then he spoke. "You're in a mighty big hurry this afternoon, ain't you, nigger? Where you goin' with this woman?"

Betsy answered for me. "We're summer students at Tuskegee, sir. We're on our way back to the campus. Dr. Cedric Benedict was kind enough to lend us his car."

He walked around the car and studied Betsy carefully. He looked at the tips of her ears, then he said, "Lemme look at yo' han's."

She put her hands out the window and sat motionless as he examined the palms and the fingernails.

There are a number of myths about how you can tell whether a person has Negro blood. Southern whites believe that colored people are totally different creatures, and the distinctions are so dramatic that anyone could tell the difference from a mile away. Mistaking a colored person for white or vice versa is as embarrassing for one of them as mistaking a cat for a dog. Of course, they've made their task more difficult by deciding that anyone with a drop of Negro blood is exactly the same as someone of pure African ancestry. I figured that he was looking for signs of Negro blood in Betsy. Betsy apparently figured it out, too. "I'm colored, sir. I swear it," she said.

"'Course you are," he spat. "Anybody kin see that. I stopped you because this boy over here was going over the speed limit." He shouted through the car at me, "Speed limit's fifteen miles an hour th'ew heah, boy. You remember that when you drive in ma patrol area."

I don't know what came over me. This was clearly a situation that called for a "Yes, sir." The trooper felt foolish that he had made a mistake about Betsy's race, and he was trying to save face. If I had just said, "Yes, sir," he probably would have let us go. Instead I said slowly and angrily, "I was not speeding. I was only going fifteen miles an hour."

"If I say you was speedin', you was speedin', nigger. Don't get smart with me, you'll get your ass whupped," the state trooper growled.

Slowly, softly, and in an absolutely even tone, I pronounced the words, "No, sir, you're wrong. I was not going faster than the speed limit." Betsy grabbed my arm. She was shaking her head pleadingly.

The trooper was incredulous. "What did you say, nigger?"

I answered in a clear, loud voice. "I said I wasn't speeding."

"Boy, you do want your ass whupped." The trooper's voice registered as much surprise as hostility. "I 'uz jes' go' give you a ticket, but look like I need to learn you some Alabama manners. Git out of that car!"

Betsy jumped out of the car faster than I did. She rushed over to the trooper and stared into his eyes, searching, it appeared, for a glimmer of human compassion. "Please don't hurt him," she begged. "We're both leaving the state in a few days. You won't have any more problems from us. If you want us to pay a fine, I'll be glad to do that. Just tell me how much you want." She reached into her little silk purse and astonished me and the trooper with the wad of five-dollar bills she pulled out. "Here, here!" she screamed, tears rolling down her cheeks. "Here's a hundred dollars. Just please don't hurt him."

I hadn't been afraid for myself, but now I was afraid for Betsy. The trooper glared contemptuously at both of us for what was probably only a few seconds but seemed much, much longer. I thought of Barnett, and the night he came across the Klan rally and was sure he was living his last few minutes. That was the feeling I had, except there was no fear, just a deep regret that Elliot had trusted me and I had let him down.

The trooper reached over and snatched the money from Betsy, but I let my breath out only when he walked back to his patrol car and started the engine. He pulled around us and yelled as he passed, "Crazy niggers!"

As soon as he was gone, Betsy screamed, "What were you doing? You could have been killed! He could have just shot us both and covered it with some kind of lie so he'd never even miss a day at work!" She threw her arms around me and sobbed loudly. She was shaking so hard I was afraid she'd get sick.

Still hugging me tightly, she whispered, "Moose, promise me you'll never do anything like that again. There's nothing to be gained from taking these people on. Killing you would just be an afternoon of fun for them, and I'd lose you forever, my precious." She took my face in both her hands and kissed me. My nostrils filled with the same floral scent that had haunted me after our first meeting. Part of me wanted to simply push her away, but it was as though I'd fallen under one of those spells Uncle Will talked about. Another part of me wanted to stop time so I could hold on as long as I lived to the exquisite feeling I had at that moment. Conflicting emotions wrestled inside me until common sense, at least for a moment, got the upper hand.

"Stop, Betsy," I commanded as I pulled back from her. "You're acting and talking out of your head. You let that man upset you, so you don't know what you're doing or saying." Slowly and silently she separated from me, walked around, and got back in the car.

Without speaking again, I got into the car, restarted the engine, and very slowly drove down the little unpaved road that led to campus. As we turned onto the college grounds, I asked, "Where did you get all that money?"

Without a hint of emotion she answered, "It was our train fare home."

"Our train fare?"

"And our food money for the trip back."

At that point all I could do was laugh. "The trooper was right," I said. "We are crazy niggers."

TWENTY-ONE

When I got back to my room, I was struck by the irony that Elliot had sent me to south Alabama to protect Betsy, and she wound up saving my life. On top of that, I now owed him a hundred dollars, but I had no idea how we'd get home, let alone how I'd repay him.

I don't think I understood how much danger I had put myself and Betsy in until I told W.C. the story. He was bug-eyed with amazement. "Golly-durn, Moose!" he exclaimed. "Don't you know around here colored boys have been killed for way less than that! This is south Alabama, boy. You hear stories all the time about some po' colored boy gettin' lynched because he forgot to say 'ma'am' to a white woman, or some such foolishness. These crackers don't play! Don't you ever forget yo'self like that agin. You jes' don't know how lucky you were. Some of these soda crackers around here would have taken Betsy's money and shot you, and raped her in the bargain. We gonna have to send you on back to Texas before you git yo'self and somebody else killed."

That night after we had gone to our beds, W.C. spoke into the dark room. "You know, Moose," he said, "Ah was brought up Christian, and we were taught that we are all God's children, and brothers and sisters in Christ, but it's real hard for me to believe that somebody like that state trooper is actually a child of God—you know, like you and m . . . Ah are. It's real hard . . . really hard . . . to thank of him as a brother."

"I know," I answered. "I was lying here thinking that very thing. It reminds me of something an old friend once said to me. She said that when you're a Christian, sometimes you'll be asked to believe the unbelievable, love the unlovable, and forgive the unforgivable, and you just can't do that by yourself. That's why we need Jesus."

All night my mind went back and forth, pondering what fit of madness made me defy a man who hated me enough to kill me just for the physical traits I was born with, and wondering what had possessed Betsy to kiss me and call me precious. I guess anybody in his good mind would have focused on how he almost got killed, but I was thinking more about the kiss. As I recalled the excitement I felt holding her in my arms, I could see how all those wicked women were able to rob otherwise sensible men back in Knox Plains.

The next morning as I was serving coffee in the faculty dining room I saw Dr. Benedict, looking perfectly healthy again. He beckoned me over to his table.

"I guess you saw your car outside, sir. Here's the key," I said as I fished deep into the pocket of my white serving coat. "And thanks again." I poured him some coffee, then I started to walk away.

"Wait," he said. "Betsy called me last night. She told me what happened." That statement alarmed me so, I almost dropped the coffeepot. I thought he meant Betsy told him that she and I had kissed. Why on earth would she tell him a thing like that? I could feel my face flushing with embarrassment.

"I'm really sorry, Moose. I should have driven you back," Dr. Benedict continued, and I realized he was talking about the encounter with the state trooper.

"No," I shot back. "You were too sick. It's all my fault, being all stubborn like that. I could have gotten myself killed and Betsy raped or something. I was awake all night thinking about it. I can't believe I did something so stupid. And to make matters worse, Betsy had to give him our train fare to get us out of the mess I made."

"Moose," he whispered, pulling me down into the seat beside him, "what you did is perfectly understandable. I know how it is. You can play along with these people maybe ninety-eight percent of the time. But once in a while—and you never see it coming—you have to assert your humanity. You have to say in some way, 'Damn it, I'm human just like you, and I won't be treated this way.' Don't worry about the money. I'm going to the bank as soon as it opens, and I'm replacing Betsy's cash. After all the things Nelson Singer did for me back at Atlanta University and in the years since then, this is the least I can do for his daughter. And for one of the most promising young men I've met in a long time."

I was flattered that he considered me promising and that he was as concerned about me as he was about Betsy, and in some odd way I was flattered that he felt close enough to me to say 'Damn it' around me. I started to thank him for giving us the money to get home, but before I could open my mouth, we both saw Mr. Vincent looking very annoyed. "Better get back to work," Dr. Benedict whispered.

The session ended Wednesday at noon. Several times I saw Betsy in class or from a distance, but she didn't seem interested in talking to me. There was a closing banquet Wednesday evening, with Dr. Benedict as the featured speaker. When I walked in, Betsy was already seated at a table that had no vacant chairs, so W.C. and I found seats somewhere else. During a lull between dessert and the program, I caught the now familiar fragrance of Betsy's perfume. She had walked over and was just behind my chair. She leaned over and whispered, "I got our train tickets home. We'll be together as far as Dallas, from there we take separate trains. Dr. Benedict offered to drive us to the station, if that's okay." I nodded, and she turned and walked back to her chair. I watched her sway through the arrangement of tables in a beautiful silk dress that was the perfect blue to set off her hair and skin. Betsy wasn't just lovely, she was a very high-class girl.

The afternoon before the closing banquet had been overcast, bringing the temperature down a little and making the evening a bit more livable than most summer evenings in Tuskegee had been. When the program ended, I pressed through the crowd to find Dr. Benedict to thank him for the kindness he had shown me and to congratulate him on his fine speech. I stood to the side while a number of others came up to greet him. When he was alone, I stepped forward.

"Moose," he said, "let's go for a walk. I don't have to hurry home. Sally is at a church function tonight, and somebody there will give her a ride home."

A light, cooling breeze came forward to meet us as we strolled along the narrow campus pathway. We were far from the banquet crowd when Dr. Benedict spoke. "I'm really happy to have gotten to know you this summer. I meant what I said in my remarks this evening. When I meet young people like you, it encourages me that the future of our race is in good hands."

In his speech that evening, Dr. Benedict had talked about the future of black America. He prompted a question that had been on my mind for a long time. "Realistically, Dr. Benedict, where do you think we're headed as a race?"

"Well," he answered, "Dr. DuBois says that race will be the biggest issue America will face in the twentieth century. He's probably right. By the end of this century, things will be a lot different for colored people than they are today. In my lifetime, I've seen a number of things actually get worse for us. A lot of doors that were open to at least some of us after the Civil War have been slammed shut and locked. When President Wilson segregated some of the government agencies that had been integrated, he set us back a good fifty years. Seems I can't pick up a newspaper without reading about lynchings and race riots. This whole issue has the potential to destroy America, and that would be a tragedy. The stinging irony would be that a nation founded on the concept of equality and justice could be destroyed by the refusal of its people to treat one another with the dignity and respect that we publicly insist all humans are entitled to."

Dr. Benedict had mentioned something that had bothered me for a long time, and I told him so. "I don't know how America will solve this problem, but we had better find a solution soon. There's a fable my father used to read me; you may have heard it. It's about a father who had seven sons who were always quarreling with each other. One day the father challenged each of them to break a tightly bound bundle of seven sticks. Each son tried and each failed. After the boys finally gave up, the father took the sticks and said, 'I'll show you how to break them.' He untied he bundle and easily snapped each stick one at a time. 'You see,' he told them, 'if you stick together, no one can defeat you. But if you quarrel among yourselves, any outsider can quickly defeat you.' That's the way I see America and Americans. If we keep fighting among ourselves, we make ourselves an easy target for any outside enemy looking to conquer us."

In the dim light along the main campus paths, I saw Dr. Benedict nod thoughtfully. "But I've seen a lot of things get better, too," he added, resuming his train of thought. "I went to New York last fall, and I visited the part of Manhattan they call Harlem. I saw lots of our people living well. I saw educated, well-dressed people you'd be proud to claim as relatives. I saw Negro art forms thriving and earning a level of respect they'd never had before. Writers, painters, and musicians were being openly admired by many people, colored and white, for their talent and innovation. At the same time, I was discouraged to see nightclubs that featured Negro performers and Negro musical forms such as jazz and blues open only to white customers. Negroes could perform and serve there, but they could not be seated as customers."

"That's amazing," I replied. "I've heard a little about what's going on in New York because my mother has a good friend who's married to the owner of a Harlem nightclub. She has written to my mother about her frustration over those clubs that won't allow colored people in as customers. She says the colored performers work there because they pay much better than her husband and other colored club owners can. Do you think we'll ever see the day when we're just treated like everyone else?"

Dr. Benedict let out a heavy breath. "Other ethnic groups have come to this country and been treated badly, but they've managed to overcome it in a few generations. When the Irish began arriving in the 1840s, they were treated almost as badly as we are, but these days in many American cities—Boston, for example—the Irish have a great deal of political power."

I chuckled to myself at my luck. The part of me that wasn't Negro was Irish. My heritage managed to incorporate two ethnic groups that were both thoroughly despised in America. Dr. Benedict went on earnestly. "Jewish people were treated shamefully when they first came to this country—many are still treated unfairly—but many are now bankers, college professors, business executives, and so forth. Some of them have acquired a good deal of wealth and are highly regarded in their professions.

"Of course, I am overlooking the obvious. While many newcomers were singled out for their distinctive language, accent, customs, dress, and so on, those characteristics can vanish in a generation or two. Some people of, shall we say, unpopular ethnic origins even change their last names and blend successfully with the general population. But we have the distinct disadvantage of high visibility. Our physical traits are hard to miss. No matter how well we speak and dress, no matter how much education and talent we possess, we still have a huge barrier to break through.

"And then, of course, we were the only group to reach America's shores in chains. Slavery is such a deep shame to this country that for white Americans to admit we're as human and worthy as they are would be to admit that they—or at least their forebears—had committed a serious sin before both God and man."

"But slavery has been over with for more than sixty-five years," I argued. "Most of the people associated with it are dead, or at least very old. Why can't we just let the past go, and do what we all know is right from this day forward?"

Dr. Benedict sighed again. "It's too bad that most people aren't as logical as you are. It would be a better world. But most of the time people's hearts are at war with their heads, and generally their heads don't stand a chance. I've heard many otherwise intelligent people offer the most illogical arguments to support what they believed emotionally even though they knew it made no sense at all."

CHAPTER TWENTY-TWO

T W E N T Y - T W O

Early Thursday morning, true to his word, Dr. Benedict picked us both up and took us to the train station. We were to arrive in Dallas at seven that evening. Betsy would change for a seven-fifty train going north to Kansas City, and I would take the eight-ten going east to Shreveport, stopping in Knox Plains. Other than saying, "Good morning," Betsy didn't speak to me until Dr. Benedict had driven off. "Well," she said, as we settled into our seats in the colored car, "it's been quite a summer, hasn't it?"

"It sure has," I answered. Just sitting next to Betsy was giving me a rush of excitement that I wanted very much to ignore. On the long train ride, we chatted about classes, plans for college, and even Dr. Benedict, but we never spoke of the afternoon we borrowed his car. Like me, Betsy was a year ahead of her class and was about to enter her senior year in high school. I was impressed when she told me that Elliot wanted her to go either to Radcliffe or Vassar after she graduated. She said he doubted they could find white people willing to give her the type of help Elliot had gotten, since even their liberal white New England friends didn't feel very strongly about college education for girls. So Elliot had set up some investment portfolios to pay for Betsy's education at a prominent women's college.

I told Betsy that the best I could hope for was one of the state Negro schools in Texas. "They may not be very prestigious," I told her, "but you'd be surprised at what a high-quality education is available if you really want to go after one. My dad left some money for my college tuition, but I don't know how much. He died years ago, and the cost has gone up, so I doubt there's enough for one of those fancy New England schools. I'll probably go to Rio Vista State." Right after I spoke, I realized what I had done. I had always referred to my father as "pa," but just then I'd called him "dad," because that was the term Betsy used for her father.

Late in the afternoon I called the porter over. He was a handsome medium-brown-skinned man who carried himself with almost as much dignity as Dr. Benedict did. "Excuse me, my name is Roosevelt O'Malley. We'd like to have supper in the dining car, if that's possible," I told him. I knew he'd have to set up a table for us separate from the other diners.

"Let me see what I can do," he answered. About twenty minutes later he came back and said, "Your table is ready, Mr. and Mrs. O'Malley. Just follow me." He turned and started walking down the narrow aisle before I could correct his error. Then I remembered how angry Betsy had gotten before when all I was trying to do was straighten out a misunderstanding. I decided to let it go for the moment.

He seated us behind a curtain that was the exact hideous shade of green as the one Barnett and I had been seated behind on our trip from Kansas City. I imagined an entry in a railroad supply catalog: "Colored diner curtain. Available in putrid green only."

The porter handed us menus and walked away. That same expression—the one that looked like a suppressed giggle—she had had the evening I first met her was dancing in Betsy's eyes. "I never realized it was that easy to get a husband," she said.

"I don't know what's the matter with him," I grumbled. "Can't he see we're much too young to be married?"

"Oh, Moose," she said. "Don't be so serious. He's obviously very busy. He probably never looked at us that closely. I think it's funny."

Not long after supper, we arrived in Dallas. I walked Betsy to her train. I half hoped she'd decide to kiss me again, but instead she squeezed my hand, looked into my eyes, and said softly that she hoped to see me again soon. If I had kissed her good-bye, that would have been the moment, but I lost my nerve and just wished her a good year in school and walked away. I stood on the platform and watched her train pull away until I realized that I only had a few minutes to catch my own. I got to Track 23 with thirteen minutes to spare, but there was no train at the platform. When it hadn't pulled in by eight o'clock, I began to worry. There was no one else on either the white or the colored end of the platform. Was the train late? Had it left already? Was it leaving on a different track?

The information window was a good three-minute walk away, and the train was scheduled to leave in ten, so I hurried over as quickly as I could. When I got there, a man in a brown suit was already talking to the information clerk. The inquiry seemed to go on forever. I believe someone could have taught me to build my own train in the amount of time it took. While they were talking, a middle-aged white woman walked up to the window. When the clerk, a little pink prune of a man with rheumy blue eyes, finally finished helping the man in the brown suit, he turned to the middle-aged woman and said, "Yes, ma'am. May I help you?" Pointing out that I had already been standing there for five minutes would only have annoyed the two of them and delayed things even further. All I could do was hope nobody else walked up, since he clearly wasn't going to help me until there were no more white people waiting to be served. She started asking about a trip to New York that she apparently was planning to take around Christmas. She argued about the fare. She argued about the schedule. She argued about the route. I decided she wouldn't be satisfied until the railroad gave her a special train that left when she wanted and took the route she wanted for the price she had decided was fair.

I kept telling myself that there was nothing I could do to hurry her along. I didn't want to risk losing control the way I had that afternoon in south Alabama. When she finally walked away from the window, it was about eight minutes after my train was scheduled to leave. I no longer felt like shouting at the little man. There was no energy left in my voice or my body. "Sir," I said wearily, "I have a ticket to Knox Plains on the Shreveport train, which was supposed to leave at eight-ten, but there was no train on Track 23 at eight o'clock. Could you tell me whether it's in yet and when it will leave?"

He gave me a hateful look that I had in no way earned. "Wasn't no train on Track 23 'cause there wasn't s'posed to be no train on Track 23," he snarled, then turned and started straightening his rack of schedules.

I was afraid that if I spoke above a whisper, all my anger and frustration would come out and I wouldn't stop until I had done something that landed me in the Dallas jail. I took a deep breath. "Could you please tell me when the next train leaves for Shreveport?" I let the breath out, then added, "Sir?"

"Eight-ten, Track 23," he said, without looking at me again.

"Eight-ten?"

"Eight-ten A.M." he shouted at me. "That means eight-ten in the morning. Ain't but one Shreveport train leaving here a day, and that's at eight-ten in th' morning." Then he muttered under his breath, though he obviously wanted me to hear him, "And some folks want to let these monkeys vote when they can't even read a train schedule."

Obviously, when Betsy bought our tickets, she thought both trains left Dallas that evening. Now I would have to remain in Dallas until morning. I didn't want to spend the night at the train station. For one thing, another interaction like the one I'd just had would drive my patience to the breaking point. I had heard that there was a hotel in Dallas run by black people, but I didn't know the name of it or what street it was on. I sure wasn't going to ask the information clerk about it. I asked a few people in the colored waiting room, but they, like me, were just passing through and didn't know anything about it.

It occurred to me that I knew someone in Dallas, Bob Sternberg. I didn't think he'd be able to help me, but a telephone call was just a nickel, so it might be worth a try. Besides, I needed to hear a friendly voice. I dug his business card out of my billfold and called the home phone number he had written down. He answered on the second ring. "Mr. Sternberg," I said. "This is Moose O'Malley. I'm sorry to bother you, but I seem to be stranded in Dallas for the evening, and I was wondering whether you know of a hotel where I could spend the night." I explained the details of my predicament, but I didn't tell him about the rude and unhelpful information clerk.

"I tried to call you at home a couple of weeks ago, but Barnett told me you were in Alabama for the summer. Listen, why don't I come get you? I've got some things to tell you, and you can stay here for the night if you want, though we don't exactly have a guest room anymore. My wife and I had a baby back in February and we turned the spare room into a nursery. We're looking for a larger place, but right now we're a little cramped. The sofa's not too bad, though. I've slept on it a time or two myself when I was up working late."

"Are you sure?" I asked. "I don't want to put you and your wife to any trouble, especially if you have a new baby in the house."

"It's no problem. Just stand in front of the station. I'll be there in about ten minutes."

Mr. Sternberg's house was nowhere near as modest as he had made it sound on the phone, but there were just two bedrooms. A third room that might have served as a bedroom had long since been made into an office and law library.

Esther Sternberg was a tiny dark-haired woman with a pretty face. She seemed a bit frazzled by all the chores associated with caring for an infant, but she was nonetheless a gracious hostess. She made me a chicken sandwich and poured me a big glass of cold milk to go with it. Bob Sternberg brought us each a slice of cake and milk for himself, then he sat with me at the table. "Moose," he said, "the reason I tried to contact you this summer was to tell you that they did execute Lester McDaniel. I'm not a big fan of capital punishment, and I think it's applied in a lot of situations that don't warrant it, but it's hard to argue that this was a better world with McDaniel in it."

I thought there must have been some big news story that I had missed while I was absorbed in campus life. I washed my bite of cake down with a swallow of milk and asked, "Who is Lester McDaniel?"

"Sorry, Moose," he answered with a foolish smile. "I forgot that you haven't been keeping up with the case like I have. The man you knew as Dillard Lester was actually Lester McDaniel, from somewhere near Baton Rouge, Louisiana. You remember how Sally kept referring to him as Lester, and we just thought that for some reason she preferred to call him by his last name. He was the leader of a group of thugs who've been involved in every sort of theft and con game you can imagine. His gang was a lot like the ones up North run by Al Capone and John Dillinger, except on a smaller scale. Someone told me McDaniel was a big admirer of Dillinger's; whether or not that's true, he was every bit as ruthless. We don't even know how many people he killed or had killed. Dillard Lester was just one of many aliases McDaniel used."

For a fleeting second, I took some bizarre pride in the fact that colored people had their own big criminal gangs just like the white ethnic groups did. But I realized that unlike white gangs, who were admired by some for their brains and boldness, gangs like McDaniel's would only be seen as further evidence that black people were inferior morally and in every other way.

"There's something else that will interest you. Sally wasn't the only person in Knox Plains who had ties to McDaniel. Just about all those women you told me about were working for him, as were a lot of the men around that pool hall."

I wanted to ask why all the women were light-skinned, but I didn't think it was a question a white person would understand. White people never seem to notice that we're not all the same color.

He answered my question, however, without its ever being asked. "It seems that McDaniel recruited young women, some as young as thirteen and fourteen years old. He trained them to take men's money any way they could, even if it meant killing them. Often these young women had one white parent and one colored parent and weren't especially wanted by either family. They were quick to take up with someone like McDaniel who seemed to care about them. Because many of these women looked almost white, he could use them in cons against both white and colored men.

"Someone explained to me that the women were easy bait for colored men who are attracted to fair skin. I believe that men everywhere are drawn to women who are unusual in some way for their population group. Around here, for example, a blonde woman will capture attention with her unusual hair color. But in a place where most of the women are blonde, a dark-haired woman will turn heads. For a similar reason, McDaniel often gave his women French names and told them to say they were from New Orleans. That made them seem exotic."

Now he had really fueled my curiosity. "I know Lorraine Dupree and Fancy Leblanc were working for this man. Who were some of the other women?"

He got up from the table, and through a mouth half full of milk and cake he said, "Hold on a minute." Mr. Sternberg went into his home office and returned seconds later with some papers.

"Let's see," he said. "There's a Betty Southern, also known as Renee LaBonte."

"That's the woman Mr. Simon bought all the jewelry for," I gasped.

"And an Annie Battle, who was calling herself Danielle DuMonde."

"The woman who was supposed to marry Mr. George but cleaned out his bank account and left town!"

"There's a Dorothy Reid. She's Fancy LeBlanc."

"The woman who claimed that Matt Jackson got her in the family way."

"Well she was arrested in Kansas City along with a woman named Ruth Betts, the woman you knew as Lorraine Dupree. Apparently between big thefts and con jobs, they picked up money through simple prostitution, pickpocketing, that sort of thing. Ironically, it wasn't one of their big heists that got them arrested. They were doing a little everyday theft, with one of them distracting a man while the other took his money. It appears they were caught with their hands in the wrong man's pocket. They were trying to rob Edwin Arthur Wilde, a man with a lot of quiet political clout in Kansas City. He virtually controls the colored vote there. You never saw his name in the paper, but he figured heavily into putting a lot of people in public office. He was so angry he didn't stop until what was left of McDaniel's gang was rounded up and taken to jail. They had been in scrapes before, but McDaniel always found a way to get them out. With McDaniel dead, they had no one working for them on the outside.

"The police investigation led to the arrest of Bobby James Taylor and Perry Lee Printis. Ruth Betts, who is now cooperating with the police, confirmed they were the shooters. They're to be tried for the murder of Louis Wilson, and she's the principal witness against them. Betts is in prison herself, but she'll avoid the death penalty by testifying against Taylor and Printis, who were the actual triggermen."

This new information was coming in almost faster than my brain could process it. I had long since given up on the idea that anything would ever be done about Louis's death. Even in my relatively short life, I had had to accept injustice so often that I had come to expect it. Finally, my head cleared enough to formulate a question. "When is the trial?"

Again, Mr. Sternberg studied his papers. "It's set for . . . September fifteenth. That's not far off, is it? At the Van Zant County courthouse." I vowed to myself to be there.

Exhausted from a long day of travel, I had no trouble falling asleep on Mr. Sternberg's narrow settee. He had to wake me the next morning to be sure I didn't miss my train.

Esther Sternberg prepared breakfast, then left her husband and me at the table while she went to tend to the baby. While we ate, I asked Mr. Sternberg a question that had occurred to me the night before, after he'd gone to bed. "How certain is the prosecutor that he can actually put this Bobby James Taylor and Perry Lee Printis in prison? Do they have any evidence other than the women who'll be testifying?"

"I understand some other gang members are going to testify, too. Of course, Taylor and Printis will insist that they're lying. There's one piece of physical evidence, but that, too, will come down to who the jury believes. The Texas Rangers confiscated some weapons, including a pistol of the type that was used to shoot Louis Wilson. They also have Louis's car, which was in Printis's possession. There was no denying that it was the same car, because it's a custom-made vehicle. But Printis contends that he bought it from a man named John. When asked about a bill of sale or a receipt, he went into his I'm-just-a-simple-colored-man-and-I-don't-know-about-all-that-white-folks-papers-and-legal-stuff act. The frustrating thing is that the jury, which of course will be all white, probably already believe that colored people do everything casually, leaving no paper trail. It won't seem odd to them at all that 'John' just handed over the car in exchange for some cash.

"There's one other thing, but it might not help much. The Rangers found a bullet embedded in the framework of the car. It's the same type that was used to kill Louis and probably entered the car as those men were shooting at him. But that's all we can prove. We know it's the right type of gun and the right type of bullet, but we can't prove that it's the same gun."

I thought a minute, then said, "Maybe we can."

"Not a chance," my lawyer friend answered. "Guns these days are mass-produced on an assembly line, like automobiles. The parts are standard and identical. When they build one, they make a thousand just like it."

"Mr. Sternberg, do you know anything about ballistics?"

He pulled his eyebrows together quizzically. "Ballistics? I have no idea what you're talking about, Moose."

"Ballistics is a relatively new branch of science. Wait a minute, I'll show you." I opened my suitcase and dug out what was now a pretty dog-eared copy of *U.S. Science*. Just before I left for Alabama, the July issue had arrived. I threw it in my suitcase, and during my stay at Tuskegee I read it over and over in my dorm room. The article I wanted to show Mr. Sternberg was called "How the Police Are Using Science to Fight Crime."

"You can read this yourself, but basically what it says is that all firearms have markings, little irregularities, on the inside of the barrel. They call it 'rifling' and it's as unique as a fingerprint. When a bullet is fired, it takes on the special markings of the gun it was fired from. What the police investigators do is fire another bullet of the same type from the gun they think was used in the crime, then they magnify an image of that bullet and an image of the one from the crime and compare them. If the markings on the two bullets match, the police know they have the gun that was used in the crime. The proper term for it is *ballistics*. According to this article, the first time the police actually used ballistics to solve a crime was in 1925," I explained.

I handed Mr. Sternberg the magazine and he quickly read through the relevant part, then looked up at me. "I'm not sure the Texas Rangers have ever heard of this."

"Is there some way we can find out?"

"I'll call the Ranger office here in Dallas." In the other room Mr. Sternberg made a brief phone call, then reported that no one who could help us was in yet. "I'll call later today, but you have to realize this is a long shot. Even if they test the bullet they have, all it means is that the bullet lodged in the car was fired from that gun. They still can't prove Taylor and Printis shot Louis Wilson. For that, we'd have to have the bullets from Louis's body, and he died two years ago."

Mr. Sternberg seemed lost in thought as he drove me to the train station. Finally he spoke. "I have a confession to make," he told me. "All my eager-young-lawyer instincts tell me to take on Pennant Oil for turning over Mr. Nesbet's mineral rights to Sally without questioning her right to inherit them. But I know they acted in good faith. It was all just an unfortunate mistake. There's a fairly straightforward way to approach this, and after giving it a good deal of thought, I've decided that taking the sure route might be better than taking the noble one. Challenging Pennant Oil in court and winning might set some legal precedent that could be helpful in the future, but there's always the risk we could lose. I frankly think it might be difficult to make our case without Sally Lee Lester. Her testimony would probably have nailed the case down, but she's dead now. The surer route would be to approach Pennant directly and get them to do the right thing."

"But do they care about doing the right thing?" I asked.

"I think they at least care about their image enough not to want to appear to be siding with criminals like Lester McDaniel. I don't know whether you know William Sullivan, but he's a vice president at Pennant Oil, and the Knox Plains project was assigned to him from the beginning. He and my father have been friends for a lot of years, and I hope you'll believe me when I tell you that Bill Sullivan is genuinely interested in treating everyone fairly. In all honesty, I also have to tell you that he was raised in the South and probably can't bring himself to believe that colored people are truly equal to whites, but he does firmly believe that it's wrong to mistreat anyone, colored people included. I'm fairly sure I can approach Bill privately and see what he'd be willing to do for Mr. Nesbet's sister. I gather she's not a young woman. A quick settlement would be most beneficial to her."

I was back in Knox Plains by ten in the morning. Since I had never been away from home alone for such a long time before, I expected a big homecoming, with Ma and Barnett waiting down at the station to welcome me. I looked around when I got off the train, but I didn't see either of them. I had assumed that when they checked the train schedule and found out there was only one train in from Dallas, they would realize that I was on the Saturday morning train, not the Friday evening train. But no one was there. I collected my bag and started walking home. Then I heard a voice call out, "Roosevelt!"

It was Mr. Daniel, standing by Ma's car. His voice, however, was not joyous. It was as serious as I'd ever heard it. "Mr. Daniel!" I yelled, suddenly fearing that something was very wrong, "Where's Ma? Where's Barnett?" Nearly every ugly possibility was flashing through my brain: Ma was sick, or Barnett injured. Or maybe something bad had happened to both of them. Then Mr. Daniel put one arm around my shoulder and told me the one thing I hadn't guessed at. "It's your Uncle Will, Roosevelt. He took ill suddenly. We think it's his heart. Your mama was up all night with him. We took him to the hospital early this morning, but they haven't been able to tell us much."

Mr. Daniel never said the word *death*, or anything related to it, but his voice was so grave there was no missing the implication. We went straight to Prairie Memorial Hospital and parked in the small lot behind the building, then walked through the little side door that led straight to the black section. What they called the "colored ward" was actually a medium-sized room with a translucent eggshell-colored curtain that separated the men's side from the women's.

It had been many years since I had been inside the hospital, and I was surprised to see that it had changed so little. After the oil strike, practically everything available to black people in Knox Plains had been improved—the schools, the ballpark, the churches. I assumed that the hospital had been fixed up, too, but I suppose in all the excitement of prosperity, people didn't think too much about it. Sickness and death were too readily associated with the old life of poverty and despair that Knox Plains's black population was all too eager to leave behind. On the wall there was a floor plan labeled "New Prairie Memorial Colored Wing to be completed in 1928." But 1928 had come and gone without the first spade of dirt being turned.

Uncle Will looked worse than I had expected. Normally a slender man, he was now a little black sack of bones. His eyes were sunken and his skin looked ashen and lifeless, like that of someone already embalmed. I took his bony hand, damp with cold perspiration, and whispered, "How're you doing, Uncle Will?"

"Daylight," he said with slight surprise in his feeble voice. "I tell you, son. Look like we gonna have to send for the two-headed man." I almost laughed in spite of the gravity of the situation. Uncle Will always said the only one more powerful than the seventh son of a seventh son born with a veil over his face was a two-headed man. He closed his eyes and slipped back into semiconsciousness. Ma wrung out a washcloth in a small pan near the bed and gently wiped sweat from Uncle Will's forehead. Barnett sat off to the side in a straight-backed chair, looking like a lost little boy. Over the years I had seen so little parent-child interaction between them that at times I'd forgotten Barnett and Uncle Will were father and son.

"Are you doing all right, son?" Ma asked without looking up.

"I'm fine. Why didn't somebody let me know?"

"His condition just turned serious yesterday. We thought at first he might be having a bad reaction to the heat, but now it looks much more significant." After a while Ma told Mr. Daniel to drive me home so I could rest from my trip. "There's some ham in the icebox," she added. I don't remember Ma ever leaving me to fend for myself in the kitchen. She tried to get Barnett to go home and eat something, too, but he just shook his head and insisted he wasn't hungry.

The house was dark and solemn. Usually it smelled of furniture polish and familiar foods cooking in the kitchen. When I opened the door, I was greeted by a disagreeable medicinal odor. I rushed to the little room below the stairs that had been Uncle Will's home for as long as I could remember. It was strange to enter the tiny fortress. I honestly couldn't remember going in there more than three times in my life. Ma was the only person other than Uncle Will who regularly did so, and she went in only to change his bed, deliver and collect laundry, and tidy up a bit. Uncle Will's unmade bed looked as though he had just gotten out of it. The door to his small wardrobe was open, and I could see several freshly pressed shirts hanging where Ma, no doubt, had left them. Outside that room, Uncle Will was the most sociable person you ever met, but his room was his private world, and others just weren't welcome. Now he was too sick to care that his sanctuary had been invaded.

I hadn't slept very comfortably on Bob Sternberg's sofa, and I'd been looking forward to a nap when I got home. Now I wasn't tired at all. I made a ham sandwich for myself and another for Mr. Daniel. We ate in silence, then I asked, "Would you drive me back up to the hospital? I think I ought to take Ma and Barnett something to eat."

I spent the rest of the day in Uncle Will's hospital room, searching his frail body now and then for signs of improvement, but he looked as though he was slipping further and further away. As the last light of day faded from the window, Dr. Dobbs walked in. Prairie Memorial did not extend hospital privileges to black doctors, so Uncle Will was under the care of a young white doctor. Dr. Dobbs seemed like a nice enough fellow, but he obviously had too many patients and got around to the colored ward only at the end of a long and tiring day. Still he seemed patient, caring, and respectful with Uncle Will. As I watched him check my ailing relative, my fear that he might not lend his best effort to saving the life of an old black man subsided.

The routine was the same for about a week. None of us would leave the hospital for more than a few hours. Once a day at separate times, each of us would go home, bathe, rest, change clothes, and bring back food for the others. A simple sign on the store's door told those who didn't know that we were "Closed Until Further Notice." I didn't think Uncle Will was really religious, but I prayed for him anyway.

Then one evening after Dr. Dobbs finished his examination, he turned to Ma and said, "Lil, I think we've done everything we can for Will. I'm going to let you take him home in the morning."

Ma was completely taken aback. Uncle Will was obviously no better. "What are you saying? Are you sending him home to die?" she demanded.

Dr. Dobbs seemed to be avoiding her eyes. "There comes a time when nothing can be done for a patient that can't be done at home, so there's no real point in spending the money to keep him in the hospital."

"If you think I can't pay—" Ma started, but Dr. Dobbs interrupted her.

"I'm telling you the same thing I'd tell anybody with a relative in his condition. He's in very poor shape. I personally doubt he'll live more than a few more days, and whether or not he's in the hospital will make no difference. All we can do here is make him comfortable, and you can do that at home. Most people prefer to spend their last days there, with friends and family around."

The words "last days" hit me like a sharp pain. Dr. Dobbs was telling us that Uncle Will was close to death. The town's lone ambulance would only carry white patients, and Uncle Will was far too ill to sit up in a car. So our already heavy hearts were weighed down even further when we had to take Uncle Will home in Cornelius Creasy's hearse.

Ma had bought a big electric fan and set it up in Uncle Will's room. Its steady hum created a cadence for the sickroom, where everything moved slowly and methodically. Ma was Uncle Will's devoted and uncomplaining nurse. She would sit for hours, trying to give him nourishment in the form of oatmeal reduced with milk. As more than half of each spoonful ended up on Uncle Will's chin or his chest or the pillow, Ma patiently wiped away the spill and tried again. "Come on, Uncle Will," she'd urge. "You can't get better if you don't eat."

August had ended and we were in the first days of September when late one night we all agreed that for the sake of our own health, we should all try to get a few hours' sleep. Although it had been almost midnight when I went to bed, I awoke long before dawn. I turned on the small electric lamp next to my bed and looked at the clock. It was not quite three-thirty. Common sense told me that I should go back to sleep, get all the rest I could for the day ahead. But anxiety filled the room the way smoke fills a burning house. I was completely in the grip of some undefined dread. I knew I would not be able to sleep again until I had checked on Uncle Will.

With great reluctance, I descended the stairs. Uncle Will's door was slightly ajar. The room was dark and silent. There was no hum from the electric fan, but I thought maybe Ma had turned it off before she went to bed so Uncle Will wouldn't catch a chill. Stepping just inside the doorway, I listened for the sound of labored breathing, but there was only silence. I listened harder. In the stillness, I should have been able to hear even normal breathing, or perhaps the sound of a sick man turning in his sleep. I stood by the door for several minutes, but I could detect no signs of life. My mind was finally forced to name the dread that had awakened me and forced me down the stairs. I was afraid that sometime between the hour when exhaustion had forced us all to bed and now, Uncle Will had breathed his last.

Instead of going over to Uncle Will to confirm my fear, I turned around and went to the front parlor. Ma and Barnett had essentially been awake for days when they finally went to bed. They were at last getting the sleep they very much needed. Should I wake them to tell them about an event against which all humans are powerless? If Uncle Will were dead, he was no less dead than he would be in the morning. Maybe the sensible thing to do would be to let them sleep. Then another thought hit me. Maybe Uncle Will was still alive but had slipped into a coma. Maybe I should be on the phone to Dr. Billups that very minute.

I heard movement on the front porch. It was far too late for visitors, but the footsteps were too heavy to be an animal. If it was a burglar, he sure had bad timing. In the Irish folklore Pa used to tell me about, a banshee—a spirit from the afterlife—comes to collect the soul of the newly deceased. Was what I heard some specter from the great beyond, coming for Uncle Will? Then I remembered that banshees always wail. I couldn't hear any wailing, but maybe it was a sound that only the dying person could hear.

I was immediately ashamed of my late-night imagination. Of course there were no banshees. If there were, surely the Bible would have mentioned them. But the Bible did mention an angel of death. Was that the mysterious visitor on the front porch? I tiptoed to the window and slowly pulled back the curtain. In the bright September moonlight I saw a distinctly human shape against the front porch column. Although frail and slender and clothed in some loose-flowing garment, the figure was clearly male, not a female banshee.

If the man outside was a burglar, I told myself, he would have tried to get inside by now. It was probably some poor soul whose car broke down on the road, and he was afraid to approach strangers in the middle of the night to ask for help. It was only the odd shadows that made his clothes look like celestial robes. Once I had convinced myself of this, I cautiously opened the front door.

The shadowy figure approached me, and when I turned on the porch light, I saw a face that looked like death itself. The eyes had sunk so far into the skull that they seemed to have disappeared. The cheeks, too, were just hollow indentations.

I was close to slamming the door when the phantom spoke. "Daylight," he said, "lemme in. I woke up wid my throat all dry. I's goin' fo' the kitchen and I got all turnt around." It was Uncle Will, or Uncle Will's ghost. I still wasn't sure.

With his unmistakable peg-leg limp, he walked past me and into the house, where he slid with a single liquid motion into a chair. "Git me some waw-ta, son," he snorted. Still baffled by what I had just seen, I went to the kitchen and came back with a glass of water. He drank greedily, not taking the glass from his lips until he had drained it completely. "Li'l bit mo'," he gasped, and handed it back to me. He downed a second glass almost as eagerly. This had to be some fatigue-induced crazy dream. For the last two days, Ma had used a meat baster to force water, gruel, or pot liquor into Uncle Will's mouth to keep him from dehydration and starvation. She worried that he was reaching a point where he would no longer be able to swallow. More and more we had spoken of burial arrangements and notification of the few kin who would want to come and pay their last respects to Uncle Will.

"What's going on, Roosevelt?" Ma was awake. She scurried down the steps in her bathrobe. Barnett was right behind her. When she saw Uncle Will sitting in the chair, she stopped as if she had hit an invisible brick wall. She and Barnett were dumbstruck for a full minute.

The haunt-like figure in the chair spoke again. "Jew Baby, I do' know what time o' the day or night it is rat now, but I sho' could use somethin' t'eat." Ma just stared, still unable to believe her eyes. "Jes' anythang'll do," he assured her, "some aigs, whatever you got." We hadn't cooked or bought food since I returned from Alabama. We had lived on food brought by neighbors and friends from church. The Dorcas Ladies' Handicraft Circle had pretty much adopted us. Ma headed toward the kitchen. As she reached the doorway, she turned and looked one more time to be sure the hungry ghost was still there.

Disbelief hung in the air as we sat around the kitchen table and watched Uncle Will eat a huge meal of rewarmed food. His bony hands worked quickly to push vegetables and meat onto a fork with a cat's-head biscuit, then shovel the food into his mouth.

At last we put the miracle man back to bed and returned to our rooms. As I happily climbed the stairs, I laughed to myself that Uncle Will, the greatest con man I knew, had managed to somehow con death.

PART SEVEN

SOW THE WIND, REAP THE WHIRLWIND

SOW THE WIND, REAP THE WHIRLWIND

T W E N T Y - F O U R

I thought I would sleep for days. I thought we all would, but early the next morning I was awakened by an urgent rap at the front door. More energized than anyone existing only on catnaps for more than a week should have been, I bounced down the steps and jerked open the door. There, looking unbelievably comical in a starched white apron and a tall white chef's hat, stood Mr. Joe Ollie. He spoke before I could even say "Good morning."

His voice softening to a sickroom whisper, Mr. Joe Ollie said, "I jes' wanted to tell y'all we go' bring plenty of bobby-cue by here soon as it's ready. I'm doin' the cookin' m'self, so you know it's go' be good."

"Who's having a barbecue?" I asked.

"Aw, now Roos'velt, long as you been goin' to Galilee Baptis' you know we been havin' a bobby-cue over there ever' Labor Day. What make you thank we ain't go' have one today?"

"Labor Day? Is today Labor Day?"

"Bless yo' l'il heart, y'all been so busy wid Mr. Will, you do' even know what day it is." Then he gave me a one-armed hug like he used to when I was a little boy. I hated it then, too. He leaned even closer and whispered, "How Mr. Will doin' this morning?"

I gently pulled away. "He's better," I said. "He's a lot better. We think he's on the road to recovery."

Mr. Joe Ollie looked as if he didn't believe a word but admired my brave optimism. "Really," I insisted. "He was up last night, walking around, eating."

"You sho' you didn't jes' have a dream, Roos'velt? I seen Mr. Will jes' day 'fo' yestiddy. He was bad sick. I done been aroun' a lot of sick folks, Roos'velt, and Mr. Will was 'bout as close to the Promise' Land as anybody I ever did see. I'da guessed he wasn't go' make the night. Why he—" Mr. Joe Ollie stopped abruptly and gave one of those startled white-eyeballs-against-black-skin double takes that white moviemakers loved to capture on film.

I turned around and saw the subject of our conversation walking toward us. "Good morning, Uncle Will," I sang out triumphantly. "Mr. Joe Ollie came by to remind us about the Labor Day barbecue at church."

Uncle Will hobbled forward and grabbed Mr. Joe Ollie's limp hand. He shook it with a politician's vigor and said, "Well, Joe Ollie, you know I don't get out much, but I 'spec' you'll see Lil and the boys over there."

Mr. Joe Ollie was uncharacteristically speechless. He nodded and finally said, "Yes, suh, Mr. Will, yes, suh." As he walked away, I knew that we wouldn't have to tell another soul in Knox Plains that Uncle Will's health had returned. Within the hour everyone would know.

After breakfast I decided it finally was time to proceed with the chore of visiting Miss Nesbet to tell her that the man who killed her brother had been hanged. I had no idea how she'd take the news, but I thought she had the right to know. I decided not to mention Bob Sternberg's attempt to straighten out the loss of her property. Even if he succeeded, it would probably take so long that Miss Violet would be dead or too old to care by the time she was granted some actual money. Things seemed to move slowly in the white people's world of law and business, especially in matters that benefited black people.

At the boardinghouse, Lula Pendergast was busy getting ready for the big annual end-of-summer party on the church grounds. As flustered as she was, Mrs. Pendergast was in a wonderful mood. Already dressed for the barbecue in a bright summer print, she hugged me and invited me in. "You look beautiful, Mrs. Pendergast," I said.

She gave me her old sassy grin, "I know it," she answered.

"I came by to see Miss Nesbet," I explained.

"She's out yonder on the verandah, havin' coffee. I made her go out there and enjoy this beautiful late-summer day. I'm go' cheer that woman up yet."

Out on the verandah, I told Mrs. Nesbet what I knew about Sally's death. She listened with great interest, her weary eyes fixed on my face as I went through the sordid tale. Now and again she would stop me and ask a question. She wanted every detail she could get about the wicked people who had plotted and carried out her brother's murder, then stolen her inheritance. She registered surprise but no particular joy at learning that Sally had met her dreadful fate and that her co-conspirator met his soon after. I finished by telling her that some other people in Lester McDaniel's gang would be tried the next week in Van Zant County.

Miss Violet looked thoughtful, then spoke very slowly. "I think I just figured something out. After Seck passed on, I asked Nurse Holmes to tell me what it was like at the end, since I couldn't be there with Brother." She shot me an accusing look. "Nobody came for me. And I wanted to find out what I could. Mattie Holmes told me everything she remembered, but one thing she said made no sense. While they were working on Second Timothy, he said the same words two or three times: 'Cold truth, cold truth.' I studied on that and studied on it. What in the world did my brother mean by 'cold truth'? But now I know he was telling us who killed him. He wasn't saying, 'Cold truth,' he was saying, 'Gold tooth.' That low-life who killed him had a gold tooth. If he'd known that sorry wife he took was in on it too, he really would have had reason to say 'Cold truth.' "

I looked up and saw Mrs. Pendergast in the doorway. "Miss Violet," she said, "looks like you got another visitor." A tall gray-haired white man in a business suit walked out from behind her onto the verandah. When he turned toward us, I realized it was William Sullivan, the Pennant Oil vice president. Miss Violet recognized him, too, even though it had been years since he'd come to the humble house she had shared with Mr. Seck and Miss Ella to discuss the deal that would make her brother wealthy.

"Well, Violet," he said in his heavy Texas drawl, "it looks like we made a mistake concerning your brother's property. It was an honest mistake, and I believe it would be in everybody's best interest to settle the matter outside the courts. All the court will do is drag everything out and make some lawyers rich. I propose we come to an agreement between us and call it done. I want you to know, Violet, that we had no idea what kind of woman your brother's wife was, or that she had left you destitute. At Pennant Oil we try to deal fairly with everyone, colored and white alike, and we want to deal fairly with you now. I've got a piece of paper here for you and me both to sign. It says that Pennant Oil will restore to you the property rights that Sally Nesbet illegally sold to us and that you in turn will not take us to court.

"What you will receive is a good deal of money in the form of Pennant Oil shares. Once a quarter, you will receive a check for the dividends on those shares. I believe you will find the quarterly checks more than enough to live comfortably. The details are here in the agreement."

Miss Violet slowly took the paper and, showing no emotion whatever, carefully read every word. Mr. Sullivan made one nervous gesture after another, folding his arms, looking around him, checking his pocket watch as Miss Violet took her time with the two-page document. Finally, she looked up into Mr. Sullivan's somber blue eyes and said, "All right. I'll sign it."

A smile of relief crossed his face as he handed Miss Violet a pen. When she returned the paper to him, he blew softly on the new signature to set the ink. "Thank you, Violet. I knew you were a smart woman and we could settle this matter without a lot of fuss. I took the liberty of having the company clerk write you a check for the last two quarterly dividends." He handed her a check folded in half, and to everybody present he mouthed an awkward, "Now y'all have a good Labor Day, y'hear?"

Mr. Sullivan had driven away in his car before Miss Violet looked at the check. After she read the amount, she gave the closest thing to a smile I'd seen on her face in years. "Roos'velt," she asked, "how'd that white man know 'bout me? Who told him Second Timothy's sister was entitled to the money that worthless hussy ran off with?"

I summarized the story. "That time I went to Kansas City with Wright Jackson, I met a colored lawyer who said he might be able to help us. He put me in touch with a white lawyer in Dallas who was able to straighten everything out. I didn't tell you because I wasn't sure that Dallas lawyer would be able to do anything. I figured you had seen enough disappointment in your life. You didn't need me building up your hopes just to have them knocked down again."

Still smiling her faint smile, she nodded, squeezed my hand, and softly whispered, "Thank you." Right at that moment she reminded me of Miss Sadie.

I had one more errand before I, too, stopped by the church picnic. Somewhere between worrying about losing Uncle Will and wondering what I'd say to Barnett if we did, I had had a thought that might help convict Louis Wilson's killers. For some reason I remembered Mr. Creasy's odd little collection of death souvenirs, the small casketlike boxes filled with tiny objects that had ended people's lives. If the old undertaker liked to keep such mementos, maybe he had saved the bullets from Louis Wilson's body. If so, they could be the very pieces of physical evidence we needed to tie the accused men to the killing.

I didn't want to admit that many years ago I had snooped uninvited through boxes in Mr. Creasy's business office, so I took another approach. From a comfortable leather chair in his private office, I asked the dignified gentleman, "Mr. Creasy, did you by any chance keep the bullets you took out of Louis Wilson's body? I believe they could help convict his killers."

Mr. Creasy wrinkled his forehead. "No, son," he answered. "I wouldn't have kept anything like that. It would have gone out with that day's garbage."

I thought maybe Mr. Creasy was embarrassed by his macabre hobby, so I tried again to make him understand how important those bullets were. "Please think carefully about what might have happened to the bullets, Mr. Creasy," I pleaded. "If there's any way we can produce them, it could bring some very ruthless men to justice." I explained ballistics. I explained how the bullets could be scientifically tied to the murder. Again I beseeched him to turn the bullets over to the Texas Rangers.

Again he shook his gray head. "I'm sorry, son. There's just no possibility that the bullets are still around."

The deal with Pennant had made Miss Violet a substantial shareholder in the midsize oil company. Once a quarter, as Mr. Sullivan had promised, she received a dividend check that more than supported her modest lifestyle. Independent again, Miss Violet bought a small, simple house. Unlike the one she had shared with her siblings, this house had running water and electricity. The surviving Nesbet heir could have afforded many more luxuries, but a lifetime of frugal living had instilled habits that Miss Violet could not change no matter how large her bank account grew.

She went back to shopping at the store, never dropping her practice of watching carefully to make sure she got her money's worth on every purchase. She still would not buy a piece of clothing or a household item without asking dozens of questions. What's it made of? Who made it? Does the company have a good reputation? Is there one just as good that sells for a lower price? But she no longer drove me crazy with her chary habits. I was delighted to have the old Violet Nesbet back.

TWENTY-FIVE

The trial started on a Thursday morning. I suppose most high-school students taking a couple of days off for such a reason would have lied about the absence. I went straight to my teacher, Mr. Tredway, and told him I planned to attend the trial. "Oh, go ahead," he sighed. "We both know you could take a month off and still be ahead of the rest of the class." Barnett planned to go, too, but he didn't say anything to Mr. Tredway, figuring it's always easier to get forgiveness than permission.

We got to the courthouse by seven-thirty, and already it was uncomfortably hot outside. The proceedings were to begin at eight, but the visitors' galleries—both the white one and the colored one in the balcony—were close to full. Barnett and I took the last two seats together in the balcony. As eight o'clock approached, a few latecomers decided to stand against the walls rather than leave. I noticed a number of people from Knox Plains, but there were just as many that I had never seen before.

Warm air in the courtroom rose to make the balcony even more stifling. People eagerly reached for the fans from Cornelius's Funeral Home, even the ones with broken handles. Not long before the trial began, the door to the colored balcony opened, and heads jerked around in surprise to see a white man enter. It was Bob Sternberg. He walked over to us. "Barnett, I need you to come with me," he whispered.

Barnett didn't move, He wasn't going to give up his precious seat without good reason. "What is it?" he asked.

Mr. Sternberg lowered his voice even more. "Richard Collins, the prosecutor, tells me that Taylor and Printis have concocted some story that Ruth Betts is lying about them because they refused to pay her for prostitution services. It's malarkey, but they can prove that she has worked as a prostitute, so the jury just might believe it. We can't take a chance that they'll go free. Barnett, you're the only eyewitness. We need you to testify."

"Oh, no," he protested. "It's much too dangerous. If you put me on the stand, I'll claim I was never there. I'm not going to get my head shot off."

People sitting around us were trying to pretend they weren't interested in what we were saying, though you only had to look at their faces to know they were riveted to every word. I didn't care. "Barnett," I whispered, "you have to do this. We owe it to the Wilsons not to let Louis's killers go free when you have the power to put them away. Don't turn coward on me again."

I had said the magic word. Barnett shot me an angry look, then got up and walked away with Mr. Sternberg.

It was a few minutes after eight when Judge Robinson banged his gavel and called the proceeding to order. Assistant district attorney Collins immediately asked permission to approach the bench. He and a stocky middle-aged man in a dark suit walked up to the judge. My guess was that the other man was the attorney for the defense. I figured that Collins was adding Barnett's name to the prosecution's witness list.

In his opening statement, the defense attorney, whose name was Dean Nutchell, said that the two accused men were laborers, laundry workers at the Palace Hotel in Kansas City. He said that he would demonstrate beyond any reasonable doubt that both men were in Kansas City at the time Louis Wilson was killed and that the two witnesses against his clients were such liars that if those women told you the sun was shining, you'd better go get your umbrella.

Richard Collins apparently had decided Barnett must now be his trump card. He told the jury that he had a witness who would not only establish that the defendants were in Texas on the night of the killing, but that they were on the very road outside Knox Plains where the killing took place and that they were in fact the killers. As for the women who would testify, they were, he acknowledged, no Sunday-school teachers. These women were indeed thieves, prostitutes, and of the lowest moral character. "These women are not angels, gentlemen," he said, "but let me remind you that there are no angels in an adventure that was clearly plotted in hell."

I glanced across the colored visitors' gallery and noticed for the first time that Amos Wilson was sitting alone in a far corner, watching with a face as expressionless as that of a figure carved in ebony.

Lorraine, or Ruth Betts, as she was known in the courtroom, wasn't on trial because she and the woman we knew as Fancy had already pled guilty to conspiracy to commit murder, as well as a number of other crimes, and were there as witnesses for the state. The women appeared in the courtroom without the face paint, fancy clothes, and fashionable hairstyles I had known them to wear. They were still very pretty women, especially Lorraine. With no face paint, dressed in a simple cotton shift, her hair pulled back in a plain bun, she was in some ways more attractive than she had been all dolled up. The flirtatious smile was gone from her lips and her eyes. She looked somber and defeated.

She testified that Lester McDaniel had told her about a little town in east Texas where oil had been found on land belonging to some uneducated, unsophisticated black people. He said that it would be easy to go in and romance one of the men, then leave town with some of his money. No one would be hurt, he had assured her. These were people who had never had money and wouldn't know what to do with it. They were better off poor. "We hadn't worked out all the details," she explained in a soft, sincere voice. "I was just supposed to stay around town and look for a mark. I met Louis Wilson my very first day. I had taken a room at the colored boardinghouse."

"That would be Lula Pendergast's boardinghouse?" the assistant district attorney interrupted.

"That's right," she confirmed. "Louis came in for supper with his friend Wright Jackson. I suspected by the way they were dressed that they'd gotten lucky in the oil strike. When I heard them order the most expensive steaks on Miss Lula's menu, I knew that they were among the newly rich colored in Knox Plains. I sashayed over to their table and said something like, 'You boys look mighty handsome this evening.' I could tell they both liked the looks of me, but Louis was really thunderstruck. His eyes told me he'd follow me to the jumping-off place. I knew right then Louis was my mark. He invited me to join them for supper and almost fell over his own feet making room for me at the table. I was all coy and demure and said, 'I wouldn't normally sit with men to whom I haven't been properly introduced, but Miss Lula seems to know you, and I know Miss Lula to be a fine Christian lady. And I am rather lonely being here in town all by myself like this. I think the company of two good-looking gentlemen is just what I need tonight.'

"I handed them some story Lester made up about my being in town because of an asthma problem. It sounded ridiculous to me, but they went for it. Back in my room that night, I laughed my head off at how innocent these people were. You could tell them anything and they'd believe it." There was more astonishment in her voice than mockery.

"After that," she continued, "Louis came by the boardinghouse every day to see me. He brought me little gifts—candy, flowers, perfume, that sort of thing. And he took me to the moving pictures and for rides in his Pierce-Arrow. He wanted to have supper with me every night. Sometimes I would tell him I had other plans, just to keep his interest piqued. Lester taught me that trick. When I told him we couldn't have supper together, he looked like a child on punishment. When I told him that I would see him, he was as happy as a puppy turned loose in a butcher shop." She let out a tiny laugh that made spectators scowl and whisper among themselves.

Quickly reassuming her somber tone, the woman picked up her narrative. "I just meant to get him to buy me some jewelry or something, but before I knew it he was talking about marriage. I told Lester, and he said, 'Go on and marry him. We can probably get a lot more money that way.' Well, I didn't want to marry that bumpkin. Perry had promised to marry me after we got rich, and I still expected that to happen." I supposed that she meant Perry Lee Printis, one of the men accused of killing her husband. "But Lester said it would be okay, since I wasn't marrying him under my real name. We'd be back in Missouri when Perry and I got married, so no one would know or care about the marriage in Texas. I swear to God, neither one of them ever told me before Louis and I got married that they planned to kill him. It was a surprise to me when Louis's daddy gave us twelve thousand dollars in cash for a wedding present. I told Lester I just wanted to take the money and get out of Texas, but he said that wouldn't work because Louis was so crazy about me he'd never stop looking for me, and since we were married, the law would help him. The last thing on earth we wanted, Lester told me, was to have the Texas Rangers after me."

The woman I had known as Lorraine Dupree told the crowded courtroom that McDaniel instructed her to start acting a little cross around her husband, to get on his nerves a bit, so he'd start wanting an evening away from her. When he expressed his exasperation, she would say, "Maybe it would do us both good to have an evening apart. I'd like to stay home and do some reading and needlework. Maybe you'd like to go to the pool hall or to that new juke joint. I hear they have a good jazz singer on Saturday nights." She casually mentioned an evening at the juke joint again and again until Louis thought it was his idea.

"When Lester told me he had decided they'd better kill Louis, at first I said I couldn't go along. But he got mad and slapped me and said if I didn't do what he wanted, he'd kill me. I believed him. I wouldn't be the first woman who worked for Lester McDaniel to be found dead somewhere."

The woman Louis Wilson had loved—in Shakespeare's words, not wisely, but too well—was on the stand for more than an hour. Her story fit what I already knew about the night of Louis's death, and I believed she was telling the truth. I also believed that she was truly sorry about all that had happened. Though I had little sympathy, I no longer despised this woman. It was possible that she, like Mr. Seck's wife, was more Lester McDaniel's victim than his confederate. The law had already judged her guilty of many things, and I was confident that God, who knows all, would judge the rest.

In his cross-examination, Dean Nutchell was brutal in attacking her character. He made certain that the twelve white men who sat in the jury box did not forget that this was a woman who slept with and even married men for money, who used her feminine charms to rob men, black and white, of their hard-earned cash. This was a woman who respected neither man's laws nor God's, a woman who had told lie after lie to continue her ungodly, criminal lifestyle. "Is it not true," he asked with the trembling voice of a preacher reaching Sunday-morning crescendo, "that had you not agreed to cooperate with the state of Texas, you might have hanged for your own crimes?" She nodded and said that it was true. "Did you not testify before this court that you allowed your friends to slaughter your husband because you were afraid for your own life?"

She softly whispered, "Yes."

"Then, Ruth or Lorraine, or Mary or Susie, or whoever you really are, how on earth," he demanded rhetorically, "do you expect these twelve intelligent men to believe that you would not now lie to this court in the interest of saving your worthless life?"

Dorothy Reid, or Fancy, as we knew her, took the stand to provide more details about Lester McDaniel's operation. She admitted that at McDaniel's insistence she tried to get Matthew Jackson to marry her. When it became clear that that wasn't going to happen, she lured him into bed, then pretended to be pregnant. The false pregnancy was originally intended to prod Matt into marriage, but as a backup strategy, she claimed to need money to go to a home for unwed mothers. When Nate Jackson offered her the astonishing sum of ten thousand dollars, she took it so fast it would make your head swim.

Again, the defense attorney made much of the witness's bad character and corrupt lifestyle. "Lies and deception are her stock in trade, gentlemen," he said to the jury. "You see sitting before you as wicked and immoral a Negress as has ever stained the great state of Texas with her presence."

Her testimony was intended only to confirm that Taylor and Printis both worked for McDaniel and took orders from him. It would be

Barnett's role to nail down the details of the actual shooting for the jury. Between Fancy and Barnett there were other minor witnesses, men who knew McDaniel from his hours in the pool hall, a man who had hauled guns and whiskey for McDaniel in south Texas, women who had picked pockets or sold their bodies to make money for him.

Barnett took the stand about three-thirty that afternoon. For more than forty minutes Barnett recounted the story of the night Louis Wilson died. He told how he and Louis had gone out for a night of fun that had turned into a night of terror. As Barnett testified, I wondered how Dean Nutchell would discredit him. It was easy to make the jury suspicious of testimony from the other witnesses, who all had lengthy criminal records. Except for that silly arrest in the Kansas City library, Barnett's record before the law was spotless. It was not uncommon for lawyers trying to shoot down the testimony of a black witness to fuel the popular belief that all colored people are liars. In this case, however, it was a strategy that could blow up in the defense attorney's face.

When Nutchell's turn came, he questioned that Barnett could see so much with so little light and from a distance sufficient for him to remain undetected. He questioned that Barnett could positively identify two men that he had seen once more than two years earlier. He even planted the notion that Barnett might have shot Louis in a jealous rage over his friend's new wealth. Then he raised another issue. "Barnett, would you please tell me and this jury why after you had seen your good friend shot to death you did nothing. I believe under the same circumstances, my first move would had been to contact the sheriff when I got to a telephone."

Barnett looked ashamed. "I was afraid," he answered. "The killers hadn't seen me, and they didn't know I had seen them. I figured if I talked to anybody, word would get back to them and they'd come kill me."

"Well," said Nutchell to the judge in a voice that the last person in the back of the courtroom could hear, "we had a woman this morning who said she let some boys kill her husband because she was scared. Now this boy says he didn't report the murder of his best friend because he was scared. Looks to me like we got us a whole bunch of scared niggers here in Van Zant County." The whole courtroom laughed at poor Barnett, including most of the black visitors. As soon as the courtroom settled down, Judge Robinson declared the trial in recess until Friday morning at eight.

When we were back in the car and on the road back to Knox Plains, I admitted to Barnett, "I think they're going to get off. That Mr. Nutchell seems to be doing a pretty good job of making every one of the state's witnesses look ridiculous. People are already half inclined to believe that colored people all lie for the fun of it. Mr. Nutchell knows that, and he's subtly working it for all he can get."

Barnett was quiet for a minute, then he said, "I'm not supposed to talk about the case at all because I could be recalled as a witness, but I'll say one thing to you in confidence, then I'll shut up. Collins has another witness coming up tomorrow that I don't think Nutchell will be able to dismiss so easily."

TWENTY-SIX

CHAPTER TWENTY-SIX

The second day of the trial, I arrived about forty-five minutes earlier than I had the first day, but the visitors' gallery was no less crowded. Word of the drama being played out in the Van Zant County courthouse had spread all over the community, and anyone who could get away from work or other responsibilities was there to witness the most excitement the area had seen since the oil strikes.

By quarter after seven, the small courtroom was both crowded and hot. As eight o'clock approached, conversations subsided in anticipation of the start of official proceedings. But the old courthouse clock struck eight and nothing happened. There was no sign of the judge or the lawyers for either side. Barnett went straight to the witness room, so I sat in the balcony visitors' gallery with a collection of longtime acquaintances and total strangers.

Here and there, I held brief conversations with those around me. Suddenly, the side door burst open and lawyers from both sides stormed in. The bailiff shouted a resonant, "All rise!" and within seconds the judge walked through the same door.

As soon as the courtroom was called to order and we were back in our seats, the judge explained that the proceedings had been delayed while he discussed in chambers the prosecution's request to add witnesses to the list. "After a discussion that involved Mr. Nutchell and Mr. Collins, I decided that we will hear from two additional witnesses," he announced.

I didn't have long to wait to see who the first of the surprise witnesses was. About ten o'clock, Mr. Collins called her to take the stand. I just about toppled over the balcony when Mrs. Ruby Nell Creasy came forward.

She was a small, quiet woman who almost never appeared in public. Like most people in Knox Plains, I knew Mrs. Creasy more through rumor and gossip than through any personal interaction. She never gave you a chance to know her. She was almost the only woman at Galilee Baptist who didn't belong to the Dorcas Ladies' Handicraft Circle, and she never volunteered for charity bazaars and the like. The Creasys' housekeeper, Mrs. Queen Esther Moore, did the shopping for the household, and even Miss Queenie insisted that her employer's wife seldom spoke to her.

Mr. Joe Ollie once told me that Ruby Nell Creasy had been born to a white girl who lived out in the country. When the girl's family realized the baby's father was black, they set about looking for a black family to give little Ruby Nell to. Cornelius Creasy and his first wife, Julia, took the child, but never went through a formal adoption. Mrs. Julia Creasy died when Ruby Nell was fourteen. Within the year, the man who had been Ruby Nell's father became her husband. Other local sources told me that while his first wife was still living, Cornelius had more than once sneaked down the hall at night and slipped into Ruby Nell's bed. Julia caught him, they said, and it was the shock and heartache that killed her. Officially, she caught her shoe in a carpet tack, tripped down the stairs, and broke her neck. But I was told that the reason she didn't see the same loose carpet tack she had stepped over many times before was that she was blinded by tears after catching her husband in a horrible act of incest and betrayal. When I asked Ma if that was true, she answered, "Don't gossip, Roosevelt. It's not becoming, especially to a young man."

I believed the stories about Mrs. Creasy were probably true because she was much younger than her sixtyish husband and seemed so melancholy and withdrawn. The family lived in a stately white-columned house high on a hill. The one time I had been inside it was when Miss Emma, Cornelius Creasy's daughter by his first wife, married. I was awed by the polished marble floors, the rich mahogany furniture, and the life-size oil paintings of family members. The Creasys were a brown-faced version of the classic well-to-do Southern family. But all the beauty and comfort that money could buy could not erase the faraway look of deep, deep sadness that haunted Ruby Nell's lovely eyes. That morning in the courtroom she looked as she always did, quiet and forlorn. I studied her comely profile and wondered again if all that I had heard explained her withdrawal from the human race.

It was Mr. Collins, the assistant district attorney, who called Mrs. Creasy to the stand. The viewers were silent as she spoke, as curious as I was to learn why this undertaker's wife had been called as a witness. I could have understood the prosecution's calling Mr. Creasy. He, after all, had received Louis's body and prepared it for burial. He might have unique insights into Louis Wilson's death. But what, I puzzled, did his wife have to offer?

The assistant district attorney opened with the routine items. "Would you give us your name, please?"

"Ruby Nell Conyers Creasy."

"What is your occupation, Ruby Nell?"

Her voice was soft and girlish. "I'm a secretary and bookkeeper at my husband's business."

"Who is your husband, Ruby Nell?"

"My husband is Mr. Cornelius Creasy."

"What is your husband's business?"

"He owns Cornelius's Funeral Home on South Heartland Road in Knox Plains."

"Do you happen to recall whether your husband took charge of the body of Louis Wilson on or about October 14, 1927?"

"I recall that he did."

"Do you recall the cause of Louis's demise?"

"He died of a gunshot wound."

"Did your husband or someone working for your husband remove bullets from Louis's body?"

"Yes."

"Do you have personal knowledge of what became of those bullets?"

"Yes, I kept them in a box in my office."

"How did you get the bullets?"

"I took them out of the waste bin in the embalming room."

"Are you certain the bullets you took are the same ones that were removed from Louis Wilson's body?"

"Yes. Louis Wilson was embalmed on Sunday afternoon. No other bodies had come in since the waste was taken out to be burned Saturday. Later Sunday evening the Texas Rangers released two other bodies, also gunshot victims, to us, but that was after I took the bullets out of the waste bin. I remember that after Cornelius finished with Louis Wilson, he came home and had some dinner. The mortuary is just a short distance from our house. While my husband was eating, I walked down to the mortuary. That was when I got the bullets."

"Tell me, Ruby Nell," the assistant district attorney's voice was gentle and avuncular, "what made you decide to take these bullets out of the waste bin and keep them?"

Mrs. Creasy stared at her feet within the tight confines of the witness box. After a long pause she looked back up at the district attorney and answered, "I like to keep small things that led to people's deaths, like bullets, and objects people choked on or impaled themselves on, just to remind myself how fragile and precious life is and how little stands between this world and the next. You see, my mother—or the only mother I ever knew, the first Mrs. Creasy—caught her slipper on a carpet nail and fell headlong down the stairs to her death. A carpet nail. Who would have thought a tiny thing like that could end the life of such a strong and beautiful woman." She started weeping as though Julia Creasy's death had been the week before rather than some twenty-four years earlier.

Returning to her testimony, Ruby Nell Creasy said she overheard me telling her husband that the Texas Rangers needed those bullets to help catch Louis Wilson's killers. Instead of telling her husband about her strange hobby, she went straight to the Texas Rangers with the bullets and a note that she had inserted in the little satin-lined box along with them. It said, "These bullets were taken from the body of Louis Wilson, a man killed in a robbery Oct. 13, 1927."

In his cross-examination Mr. Nutchell tried to make Mrs. Creasy seem eccentric to the point of being not quite sane. She was certainly a very odd person, but her calm, lucid answers to Mr. Nutchell's rapid-fire questions demonstrated that she was indeed quite rational.

Mrs. Creasy was followed on the stand by Mr. Philip Gilbert of the Texas Rangers, Austin office. He worked in the crime laboratory there and had been brought into the department in 1926, he said, because of his knowledge of ballistics. He was from New York originally. Mr. Gilbert's testimony took more than two hours as he explained ballistics in the type of detail I would expect from a graduate-level college course. Even with my keen interest in science, I found Mr. Gilbert's testimony tedious. He had charts, graphs, and drawings and went over each of them in exhausting detail.

The jurors looked like ranch hands, dirt farmers, and other simple, uneducated folks. They were all white men, of course, and their ages varied widely. One fresh-faced blonde fellow looked barely old enough to serve on a jury, and a scruffy gray-haired man who seemed well past sixty reminded me of a stock character I'd seen in dozens of western movies—the oddball trail cook. The others represented about every age group in between.

As the lengthy ballistics testimony went on, the men in the jury box screwed up their faces, straining to understand the detailed scientific information. My fear was that the jurors would be suspicious of testimony given in a New York brogue or simply become so confused by scientific terms that they would discount the testimony entirely. Apparently that was the defense attorney's hope. In his cross-examination he asked questions that were clearly designed to further bemire already muddy waters. He scoffed at the whole suggestion that there was a reliable way to determine which gun a bullet had come from. "Do you mean to tell us," Mr. Nutchell demanded of the ballistics witness in a mocking tone, "that you can just look at a bullet and tell for a fact what gun it came from? Tell me, Mr. Gilbert, can you also look at a young girl and tell which boys have kissed her?" While the spectators were laughing, he turned sharply to the jury. "Isn't science amazing?"

The defense offered as its principal witness Mr. Theo Jericho, a greasy-looking light-brown-skinned man whose hair was slicked down with heavy pomade. A loose-fitting glossy gray suit hung like a curtain on Mr. Jericho's slender frame. His hand-painted tie with its splashes of purple and yellow was just a little too gay for the courtroom setting. Mr. Jericho said he was manager of the Palace Hotel in Kansas City and employed the two men on trial in the hotel's laundry room. I looked at him carefully and vaguely remembered seeing the nervous little man moving around the lobby of the Palace. At one point, Mr. Jericho took a packet of cigarettes out of his pocket, but the judge told him he wasn't allowed to smoke on the stand. Now and again during his testimony, he reached into that same pocket, then quickly withdraw his hand. He stirred nervously in his seat and occasionally milked the bright-colored tie as he testified.

When asked whether he had seen any indication that the men on trial were part of a gang or engaged in criminal activity, Mr. Jericho let out a little laugh that sounded artificial even from the balcony. "Oh, no," he answered, "these men are just simple laborers. They wouldn't know anything about all this gang mess these folks are talking about. I think if one of them heard a gun go off, it would scare him half to death." The emaciated little man seemed to really enjoy the laugh he got with that line.

During the cross-examination, the assistant district attorney asked Mr. Jericho how he supposed two laundry workers happened to have a custom-made Pierce-Arrow. The witness shifted from one narrow hip to another and insisted he had never seen such a car and knew nothing about it.

In his closing remarks, Mr. Nutchell launched into an emotional tirade on how scientists were forever coming up with one cockamamie concept after another. "One year everybody's reading about some new half-witted idea these scientists have come up with, and the next year they've tossed that one out and replaced it with some other bubble-brained notion. Gentlemen," he urged, "there is no substitute for plain old common sense. And common sense shows that these Texas Rangers couldn't figure out who killed Louis Wilson and that made them look bad. So they decided to lay it on these poor laundry workers here."

Elliot once told me an old saying among trial lawyers: "When the law is against you, pound the facts. When the facts are against you, pound the law. When the law and the facts are against you, pound the table." Nutchell was pounding the table.

Although the defense's efforts to discredit the ballistics testimony were weak and illogical, I had no idea whether the jurors would be willing to invest the mental energy necessary to understand ideas far beyond their schooling or whether they would prefer to trust an emotional plea from a man whose family had been part of their community for generations. I studied their faces as they retreated to the jury room to deliberate. Their expressions offered no clue as to what they were thinking.

My experience taught me that people were willing to believe or disbelieve all sorts of things. Uncle Will's steady flow of "patients" were happy to pay what little money they had for completely worthless potions and treatments. Over the years, I had met people who believed in haunted houses, fortune-tellers, horoscopes, good-luck charms, and bad luck brought on by black cats, broken mirrors, and hats tossed casually on beds.

For many, science and religion were thrown carelessly into the same box of life-and-death mysteries as an assortment of superstitions, and believing or not believing was a matter of personal persuasion. Sometimes even people who called themselves Christians or regarded themselves as educated believed, for no apparent reason, in something completely outside the body of convictions they claimed to subscribe to. You could never know what was in people's heads or predict what behavior it would translate into.

Shortly after the jurors retired to deliberate, the judge declared a dinner recess. He warned all present not to stray far from the courthouse, as he wanted no delays when he reconvened court.

Outside I found Barnett, and we went to look for a place to eat. The only thing nearby was the Courthouse Square Cafe. Just below its sign reading, "Real Texas Barbecue" was another smaller sign that said, "Colored Service at Window in Rear." We walked around to the back and found to our dismay a long line at the window. Their policy was probably the same as most other restaurants in the South: they served black customers only after no white customers were waiting.

We got in line, which after five minutes hadn't moved at all. Ahead of us were nearly all the black people who had been in the courtroom. Witnesses, defendants, and spectators all stood together in line. Just behind Mr. Amos Wilson was a chain-smoking Mr. Jericho, who shuffled nonstop in what almost amounted to a little dance. A few spectators had been smart enough or frugal enough to bring box lunches. They were already camped under shade trees, enjoying their picnics. Then I looked up and saw Bob Sternberg beckoning to us. He had bought sandwiches and tall, ice-cold colas for all three of us and had even staked out a shady spot on the low fence surrounding the courthouse square.

"What do you think the jurors will do?" I asked as I unwrapped the waxed paper that held my sloppy barbecued-beef sandwich.

Mr. Sternberg shook his head and swallowed the bite of sandwich in his mouth. "I've practiced law for a number of years now, and even before I went to law school, I used to sit in on trials to see how they went. One thing I've learned is that you can never predict what a jury will do."

As it turned out, even the people at the very end of the line had time to eat. We had been outside nearly two-and-a-half hours when word reached us that court was reconvening. Even then, it took an additional twenty minutes to get everyone back in their places. The judge called the courtroom to order and announced that the jury had reached a verdict. The room was silent as the twelve men filed back into the jury box. "Would the jury foreman please rise," the judge said, and the scruffy sixtyish gentleman sprang to his feet.

"Read the verdict," the judge instructed.

"On the charge of murder, we find the defendant Bobby James Taylor guilty as charged. On the charge of murder, we find the defendant Perry Lee Printis guilty as charged." From the balcony, I could see no particular reaction from the two men or their attorney.

The old judge cleared his throat. "Soon," he said in an even, controlled voice devoid of even a hint of emotion, "bright fall colors will cover our lovely countryside, our senses will delight in the refreshing first breezes of autumn, and shortly thereafter families will enjoy one another's company as they come together to celebrate Thanksgiving and praise God for sending a bountiful harvest. Then will come Christmas, when we will celebrate the birth of our Lord as we sing merry songs, feast upon the season's most succulent foods, and delight in gifts from loved ones. And after that, we will look into the last starry night of 1929 and watch as a new decade begins on January first. We will stand filled with wonder and excitement at what that decade might bring." He paused. "But you, Bobby James Taylor, and you, Perry Lee Printis, will not see any of this. I sentence you both to hang by the neck until dead, this sentence to be carried out at the earliest practical date."

That was when the two reacted. Like everyone else in the court-room, I suppose, they had never considered the possibility of a death sentence. Usually the penalty for killing a black man or woman was no more than a few years in prison. I wasn't sure what had inspired this judge to be far harsher than was customary. Maybe he just didn't like the looks and attitudes of the arrogant and unctuous defendants, who throughout the trial had stared contemptuously at everything and ev-erybody around them, including the judge himself.

Both Taylor and Printis jumped to their feet and started forward as if to attack the judge. Guards standing no more than a foot from each were ready. They restrained the men and swiftly dragged them, writh-ing and protesting, from the courtroom.

I wondered as I walked to the car that afternoon what had caused the jury to find them guilty. Had the jurors understood and believed the ballistics testimony? Had they seen the judge's disdain and decided to yield to what they read as his judiciary opinion? Had they assumed that black men accused of a crime were always guilty, if not of the crime they were changed with, then of something else they should be pun-ished for? If it was the ugly racist traditions of the South that led the jury to find Bobby James Taylor and Perry Lee Printis guilty, then it was one more instance of the right thing being done for the wrong reasons.

The store always seemed either to bustle with activity or be almost unbearably quiet. The quiet days gave me a chance to read or talk to Barnett. On one particularly slow Tuesday afternoon in late October, Barnett had gone to the post office and I was reading when Mr. Joe Ollie ran in out of breath. "You had the radio on this afternoon?" he asked.

"No," I answered. "Is something going on?"

"There was somethin' on Miz Lula's radio sound' real important, but you know that ole piece of radio she got kept going in and out on me. I thought maybe you knowed 'bout it. They say somethin' about a big sto' in New Yawk fallin' down. You know anythang 'bout some kinda sto' they got in New Yawk where they swaps and sells animals? They say somethin' 'bout the farm animals was fallin' out and a bear was runnin' loose. It sho' musta been a big ole mess, they gettin' all that worked up."

"A store in New York that sells farm animals? And a bear running loose?" I said. "That doesn't make any sense."

"Sho' don't. New Yawk's a great big ole city. What they doin' wid a buncha animals runnin' 'round in a sto'? But that what they said. Well, git the radio on, git the radio on. It's jes' 'bout time for the news to come on."

The sound came up just as the announcer was saying, "Officials at the New York Stock Exchange have confirmed that stock prices have been plummeting all day, with numerous stock failures this afternoon. They are calling it the most disastrous trading day in stock market history. In Wall Street's bear market, billions of dollars in open-market values have been wiped out. Hysteria is sweeping the country as speculators watch one after another of their investments get completely wiped out. Late this afternoon, the stock market virtually collapsed."

As the announcer babbled on with news of the financial crisis, Mr. Joe Ollie looked triumphant. "I told you!" he shouted. "Jes' like I say—some sto' in New York fallin' down and a whole buncha animals is gettin' messed up."

I didn't know what they meant when they said the stock market had collapsed, but I was fairly sure Mr. Joe Ollie was off base. I had read about the stock market in school, but it didn't mean anything to me, so I forgot most of what I had learned. About then, Ma and Mr. Daniel came in to get some Coca-Colas. "Do you know anything about the stock market?" I asked neither one in particular.

"What about it?" Ma wanted to know.

"The radio says the stock market collapsed. Stock prices plummeted, and some speculators have completely lost their investments."

Ma's face was rigid with shock. "Which stocks?" she asked. "Did they say which stocks?"

"From what I could understand, almost all of them either went way down in value or are completely worthless."

Without speaking another word, Ma went to the telephone. I heard her ask the operator to connect her with someone in Dallas. Mr. Joe Ollie looked more confused than ever, so I gave him as compact a clarification as I could. "Big businesses sometimes sell small pieces of the business to people they call 'investors' or 'speculators,'" I explained. "If the business makes money, those people make money. If the business does badly, they lose money. They call those pieces of the business 'stock.' It has nothing to do with livestock."

"Mr. Harrison," Ma all but screamed into the receiver, "what's going on?"

Her voice sunk to a tone of utter despair as I heard her say the word "No" over and over. "What about RCA?" she asked. "U.S. Steel? General Motors?" There was a long pause, then she said. "I guess I'd better sell for whatever I can get." Another long pause followed. "I see," she said in a barely audible voice. "I see. Thank you." Then she hung up and dropped into a chair, crying. Her face showed the kind of grief you see when a beloved family member has died.

At that moment, Barnett walked in. He saw Ma doubled over in anguish, threw the mail on the counter, and rushed over to her. He probably assumed, as I would have, that someone had died. "Sister," he cried, kneeling to her level, "what's wrong? What's happened?" He turned to us and repeated the question. "What happened?"

We mutely shook our heads. Then Ma looked straight at me and spoke. "Oh, Roosevelt, I'm so sorry. I'm so sorry, baby. I've done a terrible thing. The little bit of money your pa left for your college education wasn't nearly enough to pay for four years of college. I added to it when I could, but it wasn't building up fast enough. And I had to use some of it to pay the doctors when Uncle Will was sick. My friend Phyllis Dyson in New York—you remember her, she and her husband have a nightclub—she wrote me that white people up there were getting rich overnight investing in the stock market. She said the demand for American goods was growing so fast around the world that all the big American companies were making piles of money. She and Ross, her husband, were thinking, 'Why should white people be the only ones making money hand over fist?' So they invested some money and made ten thousand dollars in three months. She told me I could double, even triple my money by buying stock in big growing companies like Radio Corporation of America, U.S. Steel, and General Motors. I don't know anything about investing, but Phyllis seemed to know what she was talking about, so I got in touch with Palmer Harrison, a broker working out of Dallas, and had him buy some stock for me."

She took a handkerchief out of her pocket and wiped her nose, then she went on, her normally strong, confident voice breaking and faltering. "At first, I just had him get me a few shares in U.S. Steel. I knew lots of people were buying cars all over the world, and I knew that meant a steel company should do well. Well, the stock went up and I made some money, so I used that money to buy stock in more companies. I made even more money. It was getting to where it was really fun. I felt like those rich white speculators in New York. Pretty soon I had tied up the money for your college and my own little savings in stocks. I even cashed in the Liberty Bonds your pa bought during the World War. It was going so well I expected to have enough to send Barnett to college, too, even though he never particularly wanted to go. I started reading the financial pages in the paper. There were some ups and downs in the market, but all those big New York financiers kept saying the fluctuations weren't important because ultimately the market couldn't go anywhere but up."

She stopped again to sob over her folly. "My ma always told me there's something wrong anytime you see wealth without work. I've got a college degree, and Ma with her eighth-grade education was smarter than I'll ever hope to be." She resurrected another of her old heroes. "And President Roosevelt always said speculating in the stock market is no better morally than betting on card games. Oh, how could I have been so foolish?"

I wasn't angry with Ma at all. In fact, I was impressed that she had done something so daring. If she had told me about it while she was doing it, I probably would have encouraged her and had fun right along with her. My ma, the She Wolf of Wall Street.

Not only had Ma not told any of the family about her investments, she hadn't told Mr. Daniel either. Now she was convinced that this would stand as final proof that she was stupid and that Mr. Daniel, who was always praising her intelligence, would stop seeing her. She began avoiding Mr. Daniel, rejecting him before he could reject her. He was clearly baffled as to why the woman he'd been seeing nearly every day was now too busy even to go for a walk or have a cup of coffee at Mrs. Pendergast's.

Finally, he came to the house one day and simply refused to leave until Ma came out and talked with him. "Hello, Edgar," she said in a very formal tone. "I'm sorry, but you've come at a bad time. I'm much too busy to receive company."

"It always seems to be a bad time, Lil, so it looks like if I'm going to talk with you at all, it's going to have to be at a bad time."

Ma's face was rigid and her eyes seemed focused on something far away. "If you've come to tell me that we can't see each other anymore, I understand. You don't owe me any explanation." The statement seemed so odd to Mr. Daniel that a laugh escaped his throat in spite of the serious expression on his face.

"Have you lost your mind?" he asked. "Why would I keep calling and coming over here if I didn't want to see you? It looks to me like *you* don't want to see *me*, and I do feel you owe me an explanation."

"Edgar, you thought I was smart because I went to college. Now we both know I'm nothing but an educated fool. Don't waste any more of your time on me."

"Lil," he whispered softly, "I know that what happened was a blow to you, but haven't you been reading the papers? You are far and away not the only person who lost money in the crash. Men with Harvard degrees and twenty years' experience on Wall Street have lost their life's savings. The country is full of people who were rich as Solomon and are now dirt poor. You're probably the smartest woman I've ever met, and nothing that's happened has changed my mind about that. Count your blessings, Lil. You've still got the store. You've still got your home. And more than that, you've got people who love you. And I'm one of them whether you want me to be or not. Lil, not only do I want to waste some more time with you, I want to waste the rest of my life with you. I love you, Lil. Let's get married. Whatever the future brings, I want us to go through it together."

Ma opened her mouth to speak, but only a tiny animal sound would come out. She threw her arms around Mr. Daniel and held him tightly for several minutes. He pulled apart from her, looked her straight in the eye, and said, "I'm still waiting for my answer. Will you marry me, Lillyun Elaine Patterson O'Malley?"

She bit her lower lip and nodded. "Yes, Edgar Allan Poe Daniel, I will."

Early that December they had a small wedding at Madam Lula Pendergast's Boarding House, which was already festooned with Christmas greenery. Actually, it was a double wedding. Mrs. Pendergast and Nate Jackson—who I had no idea were seeing one another—decided to get married in the same ceremony. Mr. Daniel, whom I started calling Papa Edgar, moved into our house, as he had sold his in a fit of grief after the death of his first wife. He had lived ever since in one of the larger and more isolated rooms at Mrs. Pendergast's.

Papa Edgar offered to use the money he had left from the sale of the house to send me to college, but he learned to his dismay that his savings, along with those of other depositors, had been frozen until the economy settled down. It seems the bank's investments also were tied to Wall Street. When the bank finally agreed to release the money, they were only paying ten cents on the dollar. The country's whole financial structure was in disarray. We became so used to bad news that it no longer had much impact. What was left of Papa Edgar's savings was far too little to finance a college education. After he told us, he just shook his head and philosophized, "Blessed is he who expecteth little, for he shall not be disappointed." I decided all I could do was take a job for a few years until I had earned the money for college. I still wanted to be a research chemist. Plenty had happened to slow me down, but nothing was going to stop me.

The football season my senior year was a good one, but not a championship year like the one before it. It didn't matter. Nothing could top the 1928 season anyway. After the last class before Christmas break, I was leaving the schoolyard when Coach Dickerson called my name. "O'Malley," he said. "Let me talk to you a minute." He broke into a trot until he caught up to me. "We had a special guest at our last game, Coach Charles Rutledge from Rio Vista State College. He's looking for players for next year, and he expressed an interest in several of you fellows, including you and Lindsay. You may be invited to try out for the Rio Vista team. If you make it, you'll be given full scholarships. I know you've been concerned about paying for college, so there could be good news in this for you."

I couldn't believe it. Just as I had resigned myself to putting off college until I could afford it, the clouds parted and the bright rays of opportunity broke through. Of course I would be invited to try out for the team. Of course I would make it. I knew a gift from God when I saw one.

In the months to come, I became all the more grateful that I could play football. I heard that most of the boys who were looking for work at home or even in Dallas or Fort Worth were finding nothing. It seems the stock market crash had been the stone that hit the nation's financial pond and was now leaving ripples everywhere. The American economy seemed to be getting worse every day, and when the economy was bad for white people, it was disastrous for the rest of us.

Over the next few months I watched the crash take its toll on my hometown in many ways. Even people who had never heard of the stock exchange let alone invested there were nonetheless stripped of their life's savings. Banks failed, returning little, if any, of their depositors' money. Those lenders still in business were foreclosing daily on mortgages and other loans. People who had gone from rags to riches a few years earlier were back in rags again. Just about everybody in Knox Plains was forced to accept a lower standard of living. People were desperately trying to sell off the expensive cars, clothes, and furnishings they had bought during boom times, but no one was interested. Those who finally found buyers were greatly disappointed to get only a fraction of what they had paid for jewels, furs, appliances, and automobiles.

The first icy winds of winter brought with them a wave of economic problems that made it clear that hard times had settled in on the nation. Knox Plains was in a choke hold as well. Half the town had learned that the fat bank accounts they had enjoyed months earlier were all but worthless. Sales at the store dipped dramatically. There were so few purchases of perfume, jewelry, and Cuban cigars that we cut our wholesale orders of such luxury items to practically nothing. Men quit buying Cuban cigars and began regarding an occasional North Carolina cigar as an indulgence, and women returned to dressing their hair with petroleum jelly instead of fancy pomades from New York.

In a sense, those of us who had known hard times before had an advantage. We knew how to scale down, conserve, reuse, mend, and do without. People like the Daytons seemed unable to figure it out. Little things like walking to church in your sturdy work shoes, then changing into your dressy ones once you got there never occurred to them.

A few people surprisingly took comfort in the return to the simple life. Many who had grown up with the use-it-up, wear-it-out, make-it-do mentality were uneasy with a life of plenty. But many more missed a life in which they didn't have to count pennies or dress their children in underwear made from old flour sacks. A cartoon folk character in a

Negro newspaper that we subscribed to summarized the situation with a rhyme:

> Mr. Lincoln done freed the Negroes,
> Mr. Ford done freed the mule.
> Now, Mr. Hoover he done freed the working man.
> There ain't a thang left for nobody to do.

Poor Glenda Gibley had taken to affluence as though she had been to the manor born. While the other Gibley girls didn't seem to mind the family's return to simple living as much, it was Glenda's personal humiliation. She had started keeping company with a student from Rio Vista whose father was an Austin doctor. A handsome, articulate young man, Glenda's suitor planned to become a doctor himself. Glenda was starting to envision a future as his wife. She watched in anguish as her father sold all four of the grand pianos for far less than their original market value. Most of their nicer pieces of furniture were sold, too. They still had the house, but with cash in short supply, it quickly fell into disrepair.

One day at the store, Brenda was telling me that Glenda's young man had been by for a visit the evening before. As he rose to leave, he asked, "Do I hear rain outside?" and before Glenda could stop him, he pulled back the curtain, revealing a piece of cardboard that had been put in place of a broken windowpane. The young gentleman was greeted with the upside-down image of the Morton's Salt girl under her umbrella. He quickly let go the curtain and said nothing. Glenda was mortified. Brenda and Linda laughed half the night about the incident.

The good times vanished like a crazy dream for most people, but an unlikely few had the good sense or the good luck to come out ahead. Miss Violet Nesbet was one of them. It seems that Pennant Oil was one of the few American corporations that had come close to holding its value during the stock market crash. Because Pennant had been regarded as a small-time player in the oil industry, the Wall Street financiers who had artificially inflated the value of many other stocks hadn't bothered with it. So while the company had had its worst year in over a decade, it was faring much better than most of corporate America. Quarterly dividends were down, but they had not vanished as many companies' had. No one was sure how much the closed-mouthed Violet Nesbet had, but many suspected she was as financially comfortable as anyone in Knox Plains.

Another was Mr. Nate. While he no longer had the bottomless money pit he'd enjoyed during good times, he had built a sound business that continued to turn a profit even after the Great Depression was well under way. He and his new wife both had a good deal of business sense, and even though the lean days reduced the profits on the construction business and the boardinghouse-restaurant to the slimmest of margins, they enjoyed a relatively comfortable life in which they were able to support and care for each other. They seemed happier than ever—especially after their Easter surprise.

TWENTY-EIGHT

I was walking downtown by the train depot early on Good Friday when I saw a tall, dark man in a preacher's collar. I barely noticed him, since many strangers get off the train to stretch their legs during the brief stop in Knox Plains. He seemed vaguely familiar, but I figured he just looked a little like someone I knew. Then a voice I clearly recognized called out, "Moose!"

"Wright!" I screamed. "I thought I'd never see you again. What are you doing disguised as a preacher?"

He laughed his old familiar laugh. "It ain't no disguise," he said. "I heard the call. I'm a Baptist preacher now. Last time you saw me, I'd sunk 'bout low as somebody could. That ole prodigal son didn't have nothing on me. I'd done tho'd away all my daddy's money and got you and Barnett put in jail. It was jes' a messed up sit-cha-a-tion. I tell you, I was jes' too shamefaced to face the family or anybody. But now I done made my peace wid the Lord, and he done forgive me for ever'thang. Now I reckon it's 'bout time I made my peace wid my family, too. I heard tell Pa married up wid Miss Lula, and Matt and Dolly done set the date. Ain't that a hoot?"

I was about to ask how he had gotten news from home if he'd broken off all connection with his friends and family, when a neatly dressed light-brown-skinned woman in glasses walked up to Wright and said, "Sweetheart, I don't see any colored taxis. Let's just walk. It's not that far."

A boyish grin broke across Wright's face. "Baby," he asked, "you know who this here is?"

The woman and I stared at each other. Recognition hit us both about the same time. "Moose!" she shrieked.

"Rosetta?" I knew it was her, but I could hardly believe it. I had never seen anyone change so. She was still plump, but she had lost lots of weight and was handsomely dressed in a tailored blue suit that made her look like a woman executive. Her hair was stylishly and becomingly arranged under an attractive hat that matched the suit. And she was wearing glasses that fit. Rosetta was almost pretty.

"This here is my new bride," Wright announced. Then he backed up and told me the story of his adventures since I last saw him in Kansas City. "When I wasn't doin' no good in Kansas City, I got on a freight train and wound up in St. Louie. Somebody tol' me there was work there, but I wasn't doin' no good in St. Louie neither. I jes' walked the streets hongry and wo' out. Didn't have no idea what to do nex'. Ya know there jes' ain't no work these days. I was walkin' through a colored area and I could smell some food, smelled like Miss Lula's on Sunday afternoon. I was next to a church where they was havin' all-day singin' and dinner on the grounds. Them church ladies was puttin' out the food on big long tables back of the church, and one of them looked up and caught me peepin' through the hedges. I started to run off, and she say, 'Hey, you want somethin' t'eat?' I say, 'Yeah, but I ain't got no money.' She say, 'You don't need none. Jes' come on 'round through the gate rat there.'

"Mercy, they had a spread out there—ham, stew beef, chicken, and any kind of vegetable you could thank of. Cakes and pies like you ain't never seed, and fo' different kinds of home-churned ice cream. I git hungry now jes' thankin' 'bout it." Wright laughed with pure delight. "The preacher there was a fellow named Jonas Crabtree—ain't that a name?—but he was the nicest fellow I met since I left Knox Plains. And his wife, she was as fine a Christian woman as I yet met. Well, they hadn't spoke a dozen words to me when Reverend Jonas up and say, 'Look like you need somewheres to stay tonight. Me and Clorine be happy to have you. Our place ain't much, jes' the li'l pars'nage over there, but I believe we could make you a li'l mo' comf'table than you'd be on the street.'

"You know, I come near to sayin' no? By then I was so down on myself I believed I didn't deserve nothin'—not a crumb or a rag, let alone a comf'table bed. But they took me in and made me part of the family. I did mo' church-goin' than I had ever did in my life. We was at ever' service, of course, 'cause he was the preacher, and ever' evenin' we had family Bible study wid Reverend Jonas and Miss Clorine and their young'uns. The folks in the church was like boys what took in a stray dog. First one and then the other would come by wid clothes or food or somethin' for the stray. At first I was jes' goin' 'long 'cause ever'body was so nice, but after while I started wantin' to study the Lawd's word. I find myself readin' that ole Bible when Reverend Jonas and Miss Clorine wasn't even at home. Pretty soon I knowed I wanted to be a preacher, too. I wanted to serve folks and serve the Lawd."

As intriguing as all that was, he wasn't getting any closer to the answer I wanted most. How in the world did he wind up married to Rosetta? Wright must have seen the question on my lips, because he quickly said, "At first Reverend Jonas wasn't too sure I for real wanted to be a preacher. He say a lotsa young men thank they wants to preach 'cause ever'body look up to the preacher and have him to supper all the time and whatnot. 'Sides, when you's the preacher, you don't have to do no back-breakin' work to make a livin' like mos' colored men gots to do. He told me one time he heard Professor Booker T. Washington speak, and one thang he say was that a lotsa men gits out behind the mule trying to plow they field and say, 'Lawd, this sun's so hot and this groun's so hard, I believe I done been called to preach.'

"Well I had a time makin' him b'lieve it was the Spirit moved me to want to preach and not 'cause I was sked of hard work. So he starts givin' me preachin' lessons and tellin' me how to put a sermon to-gether. Sometime he'd let me write up a sermon and try it out on him and Miss Clorine. 'Bout all he'd ever say when I got through was, 'You gittin' there. You gittin' there.'

"Then one Sunday mawnin' back January of las' year, Reverend Jonas wake up wid a fever and sweatin' like a pig, couldn't hold no food on his stomach or nothin'. He say he got to go to church anyhow 'cause ever'body lookin' to him to preach. Miss Clorine say, 'You ain't goin' nowheres, sick as you is. I'll call Reverend Winters. He ain't got a church rat now. I'm go' see if he'll come preach for you.' Reverend Jonas say, 'You know he in Hannibal this week.' Then Reverend Jonas's red runny eyes move slow over to me. He say, 'Wright, you reckon you ready to git up in front of First Street African Baptist on a Sunday mawnin'?' I say, 'Ah'm ready.' He say, 'Preach that prodigal son one. You got that one down real good.'

"So I got up and preached that January mawin' and I preached from the heart. I told them folks Jesus's story and then I told 'em my story. I told 'em I had strayed from my pa and ever'thin' he taught me, but the Lawd will reach out and bring you back if you let him. Sometime he got to take all your worldly goods jes' to git yo' attain’tion, but he'll bring you on back home if you lets him. I was so wrapped up in preachin' I didn't pay much mind to who was sittin' out there, but I did jes' barely notice one young lady I hadn't never seen at First Street African befo'. She look like I knowed her, but I couldn't quite place her.

"Well you can figger the res' out for yo'se'f. Rosetta come up after service and made me know her. We started gittin' together right reg'lar. Jes' friends at first, you understand. 'Fo' long I say, 'This here is a special lady. She smart, she pretty, and she understand how I is, 'cause she growed up same place I growed up.' Jes' 'bout a munt ago Reverend Jonas do the honors and make us man and wife."

I couldn't wait to get home and tell Barnett. I knew he'd roll on the floor laughing.

Later I heard that Violet Nesbet invited Wright and Rosetta to live in her new house. She even gave them the big bedroom and moved into a smaller one down the hall. She had a lawyer draw up a will leaving them the house, but she made certain that Rosetta had no less right to the property than Wright had.

Wright couldn't find a full-time preaching position in our community, so he, like his brother Matt, went to work at his pa's new construction company. But he was always ready to fill in at Galilee Baptist when the preacher was unavailable on Sunday morning.

After the news about Wright and Rosetta had made the rounds, the gossip circuit got quiet for a while. Then Mr. Joe Ollie came in with a bombshell: Ruby Nell Creasy had left her husband and was living at the boardinghouse in the room that been Miss Violet's until she regained her inheritance. Even Mr. Joe Ollie had no idea what had happened between Mr. and Mrs. Creasy. "I come in one day and Miss Lula she say, 'Joe Ollie, git that room at the top of the steps ready, the one where Miss Violet used to stay, we got us a new boarder.' Well, you coulda knocked me over with a feather when I seen it was Miz Creasy."

I was certain that the trial and all the secrets that had come out because of it had had something to do with it. The only other person I knew to ask was Miss Queenie. "All Ah knows," the aging housekeeper offered, "is they was off in the back room havin' private talks ever' time I looked up. I didn't hear no yellin' and screamin', nothin' lack that. They was jes' all the time talkin', talkin'. Ah'd cook they food, but they didn't come in to eat at the same time. He might eat a few l'il bites, she barely touched nothin'. Next thang Ah knowed, Miz Creasy had her bag packed." Miss Queenie delivered that last word with the force of a door slamming, so I questioned her no more.

As the school year drew to a close, we were all busy as Barnett and I prepared to take final exams and Papa Edgar prepared to administer them. Ma was running the store so we could give schoolwork our full attention. One night when he was working at the kitchen table, I asked Papa Edgar, "What's gonna be on that final chemistry exam?"

"Wouldn't you just love to know," he answered, but we were both joking. He knew I had no need to cheat, even if I had had the character to consider it. Happily, the principal at Washington had faith in our integrity, too, and expressed no reservations about allowing me to take a class from the man who was now my stepfather.

The day exams ended, we were all in a sunny mood. Papa Edgar walked through the front door just a few minutes after Barnett and I got home. "I have an idea," he announced. "Why don't I treat us all to supper at Lula's so Lil won't have to cook tonight. Uncle Will, if you don't feel like going, we can get Joe Ollie to bring you a plate."

"I don't need no plate," Uncle Will responded. "There's some veg'able soup in there from th' other night. It's 'bout all I wants anyway." Since his illness, Uncle Will had slowed down even from the unhurried pace he had kept before. His appetite had diminished proportionately.

When Ma came in from the store, Papa Edgar sang out, "Put on your glad rags, darlin', we're going out on the town." To Ma's protest that we couldn't afford to eat out, Papa Edgar answered, "You've got thirty minutes to get ready, or the boys and I are going without you."

Madam Lula Pendergast's Boarding House and Restaurant was still a pleasant place, but nowhere near as exciting as it had been in its glory days when oil-rich men ordered suppers fit for European royalty and beautiful young women in satin, lace, and French perfume smiled and swayed and told funny stories to get their attention. Other than Miss Lula's boarders, there were only a few diners. As we walked past the main dining table, where the boarders by tradition sat, I looked out of the corner of my eye for Ruby Nell Creasy, but she wasn't there, even though Mr. Joe Ollie was already bringing out the family-style platters of food.

Within a few minutes Mrs. Creasy walked in shyly and was moving toward the boarders' table. To get there she had to brush past ours. I didn't know whether good manners dictated speaking to her or allowing her the privilege of speaking first. Ma didn't hesitate. "Good evening, Mrs. Creasy," she said. "How are you?"

"I'm just fine." Her voice was low and childlike. Mrs. Creasy looked over at the boarders' table as though it were a train that had already pulled away from the station. There was still plenty of food, but she probably would rather go hungry than cause even a small disturbance by joining a meal already in progress.

Ma seemed to have assessed the situation along with me. "Would you like to join us, Mrs. Creasy?" she asked. "We haven't gotten our food yet."

I expected the timid little woman to shake her head and slip from the room in the same apparition-like fashion with which she had entered. Instead she answered, just above a whisper, "If you're certain I wouldn't be a bother, I'd like very much to sit with you."

Papa Edgar didn't have to get Mr. Joe Ollie's attention. Mr. Joe Ollie's eyes had been riveted on our table from the second Mrs. Creasy approached us. At the first hint from my stepfather, Mr. Joe Ollie came running over with an extra chair and place setting. As she took her seat, Mrs. Creasy looked up at Mr. Joe Ollie's eager face and said, "I'll just have some soup and crackers tonight, if that's all right." Then she turned to Papa Edgar. "It's been paid for, Mr. Daniel. I pay Mrs. Pen . . . Mrs. Jackson weekly for my room and board here." The rest of us chose the family-style dinner, which meant Mr. Joe Ollie brought out dishes of whatever Miz Lula had cooked that evening and we shared as if we were at home. The selection was especially good that evening and included fried catfish and many of my other favorites.

I had looked forward to a fun evening with the family. With school over and graduation just days away, I knew Papa Edgar, Barnett, and I could openly joke about things at school that we had had to be discreet about before, since we were students and he was a teacher. At first we were restrained and mindful that we had a guest, but after a few minutes Barnett was no longer able to contain his high spirits. "Just think, Moose, we might never again get to hear Mr. Hughes say, 'I believe the bell has sounded,' or Miz Joel say, 'Everyone here is well acquainted with the rule against gum chewing.' "

I think every teacher on earth has some stock phrase that he or she repeats so much that it becomes a joke among the students. Barnett had so perfectly imitated the tone and inflections of the two teachers he was mocking that we all chuckled.

Papa Edgar laughed harder than any of us, then he asked, "All right, what do I say that the students make sport of me for?"

Barnett and I looked at each other, then we said in unison, "Put your materials in order and prepare to begin class."

"I say that all the time?" Papa Edgar asked with an amazed grin.

We both nodded. "All the time," Barnett confirmed.

We looked over and saw Mrs. Creasy laughing with us. I don't believe I'd ever seen her smile before, let alone laugh. After that the mood at the table was so festive it was almost silly. We kept cracking jokes and piling our plates. Even Mrs. Creasy abandoned her just-soup notion and put a pork chop, some greens, baked squash, and cornbread on her plate. She was laughing like a drunk woman at some wisecrack Barnett had made, when she looked up and saw something that drained her expression of mirth. We all turned in the same direction. Standing at the dining-room door was someone none of us had seen for years, Cornelius Creasy's daughter Emma. She scanned the suddenly silent room until her eyes fell on Mrs. Creasy, then she walked straight to our table.

We all greeted Emma warmly, as though she had just popped in for an impromptu visit. Emma apologized for interrupting our supper and asked Mrs. Creasy if she could speak to her in the parlor as soon as she was done. "If it's about your father," Mrs. Creasy answered coldly, "I don't believe we have anything to discuss." She added, "Right now, I'm having supper with my friends," as if we got together socially on a regular basis.

Emma's voice dropped to a murmur. We could still hear her, but the rest of the room could not. "Ruby Nell," she whispered, "I came here all the way from Texarkana. Please give me just a few minutes of your time."

Then with more emotion than I had ever before heard in her voice, Mrs. Creasy said impatiently, "Just say it, Emma. What do you want?" I thought how strange this was. Emma was Mrs. Creasy's stepdaughter, but Emma was the older of the two.

Emma pulled a chair over from a nearby table. I scooted closer to Barnett to make room for her. "Papa is distraught, Ruby Nell. He doesn't know what to do without you. He's been calling me long-distance every night. I finally got so worried about him I got on a train and came down here.

"Please come home. I know he hasn't done right by you. He never did right by Mama or me either. But you have to understand how he was brought up. His pa was dreadful to his ma and to all the women in the family, so Papa never learned how women need to be treated. He always thought that if a man provides a nice comfortable home for his wife, which was more than his pa ever did, that was enough to make him a good husband. He thought that if a woman had lots of nice things, she had no right to ask anything else from her husband—understanding, affection, or even fidelity. And if the man brought home the bacon, he felt his wife should mark his bill 'Paid in full.'

"He knows better now, or at least he's learning better. He wants you back more than he's ever wanted anything in his life. He loves you, Ruby Nell, he just never knew it before you left. If you go back to him now, he'll do anything you want. I know he will."

Her speech completed, Emma Creasy Owens looked straight into her stepmother's soft brown eyes and anxiously waited for a response.

"Why do you care?" Mrs. Creasy asked.

"Because I know that deep in his heart he's a good man. I love him in spite of all the mistakes he's made. I think you love him, too."

Ruby Nell Creasy looked down for a long minute, much the way she had in the witness box, then she gazed straight into her stepdaughter's eyes and asked, "Emma, do you know what it's like to have a man just handle your body anytime he likes, whether you want him to or not? Do you know what it's like to have somebody treat your body like it was his old shoeshine rag? Something he used when he got ready for it and then threw in a corner until next time? Do you know what it's like to be fourteen years old and scared to death, with absolutely nobody to turn to? Do you know what it's like to have no choice about any of it because you simply have no other place to go?

"I've spent the past twenty years ducking everybody in this town because they all think I'm some kinda tramp for marrying your pa just weeks after his wife died. They all act like everything that happened was all my fault and none of his. I've asked myself a thousand times what other choice I had, and I still don't see one. I've kept it to myself for all these years, and I don't know why, but I just couldn't keep it in anymore."

Emma's voice was tender as she asked, just above a whisper, "What do you want from him, Ruby Nell? What would you like him to do?"

Mrs. Creasy shut her eyes and shook her head. "I don't know what I want. I guess I just want him to understand how I feel and try to care a little bit. He doesn't even have to say he's sorry. I just want him to quit acting like he hasn't done anything wrong."

Emma reached over and touched her stepmother's shoulder. She smiled a twisted little smile. "He's a man, Ruby Nell. He's never really going to understand, but he does care, and he's truly sorry for the hurt he's caused you."

The two women had been talking as though they were the only two people in the room. They both looked around as if suddenly recalling that others were present. Embarrassed to have shared so intimate a moment, Mrs. Creasy smiled awkwardly and said, "Thank you all for a lovely evening. It has been most enjoyable, but I believe I should be getting home. My husband is expecting me."

PART EIGHT

A NEW PLANET

TWENTY-NINE

To no one's surprise I was class valedictorian. Glenda Gibley was a fairly distant second, and Barnett wasn't far behind her. We marched in the same robes the class ahead of us had worn, and the four classes ahead of them. Even though the school secretary said she had taken the robes out of storage several days before graduation and aired them out, mine smelled musty, and I was glad to get out of it.

The day after graduation had the same quiet and slightly melancholy feel as the day after Christmas, now that the flurry of activity had abruptly come to an end. The June 1930 issue of *U.S. Science* had lain unopened in my room for almost two weeks. I took it with me to the store in anticipation of a slow day. Almost every day had been a slow day since the economic downturn settled in. Business picked up a little as people bought clothes and small gifts for graduation, but otherwise we were barely making a profit. I had plenty of time to read.

Artwork on the cover depicted the solar system with nine planets and the words "Another Planet?" splashed across it in bright red. I was intrigued. Several years ago I had read an article claiming that an American astronomer named Percival Lowell had found evidence as early as 1905 that a ninth planet existed out beyond Neptune. I had followed the debate in *U.S. Science* and other publications. Learned scientists had argued that such a planet was impossible. The sun's gravitational pull could not possibly hold a body that was two-and-a-half, maybe three billion miles away. The June 1930 issue of *U.S. Science* carried the astounding news that another American astronomer, Clyde William Tombaugh, had confirmed the existence of this distant sphere. The new planet was called Pluto. A Pluto year, the article said, was more than 245 earth years.

I walked outside and gazed into the atmosphere as if there were some way I could see the evidence on my own. The discovery thrilled me because I had believed from the first that this ninth planet existed. I would have been willing to believe that there was a tenth planet or even an eleventh one. A scientist must never assume that what has already been established defines the limits of what is or what can be. As I followed scientific developments, again and again I saw the impossible proven possible, the theoretical proven to exist after all.

Maybe that explained my optimism about the future of colored people in this country. Over and over I heard people say that black people can't do this or will never have that because white people won't allow it. I'm sure that while slavery was still legal in the United States there were people who insisted it would never end. But to my way of thinking, if there could be a ninth planet that we'd never seen before, there could be peace, respect, and fairness among people, even though we hadn't yet seen it.

In mid-July, Barnett and I both received letters inviting us to try out for Rio Vista's football team in two weeks' time. It was exciting to think that Barnett and I would not only be at the same college, but we'd be playing football together just like we did in high school. Maybe we'd wind up as star players there, too.

In spite of the highly charged atmosphere, tryout week was a lot of fun. There were some great guys competing, many more than the team really needed. Only one player in four would be picked, but that didn't stop the fellows from having a good time together. Barnett and I were especially relaxed. We knew how good we were. We had led our high-school team to three exceptional seasons. There was no way we weren't going to be among the chosen.

Coach Rutledge was terrific, too. He took a personal interest in each of us, and at the end he said we had all done a fine job and he was going to have a tough time picking his team. We ate a final breakfast together before we all went home to await his decision. At the breakfast Coach Rutledge got up and made a few parting remarks. "If we choose you," he said, "you'll get a letter in about two weeks. Then you'll have to report back here for practice about a week later, so be prepared to move quickly. If you don't report for practice on starting day, your name will be dropped from the roster, an alternate will be selected, and you will lose any athletic-scholarship money set aside for you. Do you understand?"

"Yes," we all answered in unison.

Two weeks later to the day, a letter arrived from the Rio Vista State athletic department. It was addressed to Barnett. It read:

Dear Mr. Lindsay,

I am pleased to inform you that you have been selected as a member of Rio Vista State College's football team for the coming academic year. You have been awarded a full athletic scholarship as well. This includes tuition, room and board, books and other academic materials, and a small weekly allowance for incidentals. You will room in Carson Hall with the other athletes. You are to report at noon on Monday, August 29, to the locker room adjacent to the practice field, where you will be issued a practice uniform. Then the team will have dinner together in the Carson Hall dining room before we start afternoon practice. Congratulations on being chosen to join the Rio Vista Wildcats.

Sincerely yours,
Coach Charles Rutledge

"Wow," Barnett said. "They're even giving us a weekly allowance. Did your letter say the same things?"

"Mine didn't come today. I guess they didn't mail them all out at the same time. It'll probably be here tomorrow or Monday."

"They must be sending them out in batches. If they'd been paying attention, they would have noticed we're at the same address and just sent our letters in the same envelope."

"Yeah," I said. "They could have done that and saved some postage."

Every day I eagerly checked the mail, but there was no letter from Rio Vista State. Finally, I decided to call Coach Rutledge and tell him I hadn't gotten get a letter. I called the only office on campus that was open that time of year, the administration building. A secretary told me that Coach Rutledge was on vacation. When I asked whether he had gone out of town or maybe could be reached at home, she snapped, "I don't believe that's your business, young man."

"I'm sure the letter just got lost in the mail," I told Barnett. "It's a good thing yours came, so we know when and where to report. You remember what Coach Rutledge said, 'If you're not here for the first day of practice, your name will be dropped from the roster.' I sure don't want to be dropped from the roster."

Our train to Rio Vista was scheduled to leave early on August twenty-ninth. I had slept poorly the night before and probably wouldn't have made it without the rest of the household pushing and prodding at every step. Ma and Papa Edgar were up early. By the time I was on my feet, Ma had cooked a big breakfast and Papa Edgar had come back from his errands. When Ma saw me still in my bathrobe, she screamed,

"Roosevelt, will you hurry up. We're due at the train station in an hour."

Papa Edgar had picked up the previous day's mail at the post office. "There're some letters here for you, Moose," he said. He had started calling me "Moose" as part of his effort to gain acceptance as my stepfather. I took the small stack and saw on top letters from some relatives, probably wishing me well in college. There was something from Rio Vista State, too—at last my acceptance letter from Coach Rutledge, no doubt. There would be time to read it all on the train. I tossed the mail into the small satchel I'd carry with me and quickly finished dressing. I had eaten a little more than half my breakfast when Barnett pronounced it time to leave. Still chewing a last bite of buttered biscuit, I dashed out the door and climbed into the car next to him. We each had a midsize suitcase. Most of our college clothes were in footlockers that would be sent by train later before cool weather set in.

Our train was already at the platform when we got to the station, so Barnett and I quickly said our good-byes to Ma and Papa Edgar. Uncle Will had stayed at home. Not even an occasion like this could lure him away from his comfortable world, which was now no larger than the first floor of Ma's house and the porch outside it. As we pulled out of the station, Barnett started to read. I fell asleep and woke once when the conductor asked for my ticket and again when Barnett elbowed me to tell me we were approaching the station.

The train pulled in at about ten-fifty. Soon after we got off, a neatly dressed young black man came up and asked, "You fellows on the Rio Vista football team?"

"That's right," I said.

"Okay, I'm Bobby. I'm a senior at Rio Vista. Get in the Ford over there. Let me check to see if anybody else on the team is here, then I'll drive you to campus. I have to hurry right back. There's another train due in at eleven-forty."

He came back a few minutes later with two huge guys from Louisiana. I was the only small person in the car, so it was a tight squeeze. Fortunately, the ride to the campus was a short one. Bobby dropped us at the practice field and headed straight back to the train station.

As soon as we stepped inside the locker room, another young man told us to go to our left and line up for our practice uniforms. He looked me up and down and asked, "Aren't you kind of small for a football player?"

"Quarterback," I answered simply.

"Okay. Go get in line. Give the fellow behind the counter your name, and he'll issue you a practice uniform."

When we got to the counter, there were two lines. One had a sign above it that said, "A through M"; the other, "N through Z." The first line was much shorter, and Barnett had his uniform in a couple of minutes. He came over to me and said, "It's too hot and crowded to stay in here. Just meet me in the dining hall after you get your uniform."

It was another five minutes before I reached the counter. "O'Malley," I told the well-built young man behind it. He looked at his list, then said, "Spell that."

I sighed. O'Malley was not a hard name. "O-apostrophe-M-A-L-L-E-Y."

He looked up at me. "You're not on the list."

"Maybe they made a mistake," I suggested. "My uncle and I tried out together, and his last name is Lindsay. Since we're in the same family, they probably thought we were both named Lindsay. Would you check to see if there's a Theodore Lindsay or a Roosevelt Lindsay—maybe a Moose Lindsay?"

He gave me a very odd look. Then he went over and checked the "A through M" list. He came back and reported, "There's only one Lindsay on the list, a Barnett Lindsay, and he's been checked off. He's already picked up his uniform."

"I don't understand," I told him.

He looked me dead in the eye. "Did you receive a letter from the school saying you had been picked for the football team?"

"Well, no, but . . ."

"Then you didn't make it. Move away from the counter. I've got a lot of football players still waiting to get their uniforms."

I moved slowly away and watched as the big muscle-bound fellow behind me stepped up and announced, "Williams. Norris Williams."

"Got you right here, Norris," said the same young man who had had no uniform for me.

I felt poleaxed. How could they pick Barnett and not me? We were partners. We were a unit, like a set of salt and pepper shakers. How could they pick the pepper and not want the salt? There had to be a mistake. This couldn't be right. As I started out the door, I saw Coach Rutledge. Finally, I thought, a chance to get all this straight.

As I walked toward him, his expression made it clear that he recognized me. "O'Malley," he said, "what are you doing here? Classes don't start for another two weeks." This was the final confirmation. There was no mistake. I hadn't made the team.

"I thought I was supposed to be here for football practice," I mumbled sheepishly.

"Didn't you understand that only those who got letters were supposed to report?" He lowered his voice so he wouldn't embarrass me.

"I thought when Barnett made the team, that meant I'd made the team, too. We were sort of paired together in high school."

He touched my shoulder with an avuncular tenderness. "O'Malley," he said, "you and Lindsay are both fine football players. I wish I could use both of you, but the truth is, at a hundred and forty pounds you're too little. You're a good quarterback, but with your size, you can only play quarterback. I don't need another quarterback right now. But I've got several positions Lindsay might fit into."

As I walked away from the football complex, I felt as though I had been sucked away from the world I knew to a distant planet, a hot airless place without life, without hope. I had never before in my life failed at anything. I had always made top grades in school. I had won every competition I ever entered, from spelling bees to oratory contests. I had always been among the first picked for every sports team I tried out for. Now it was as though all the little failures I had successfully dodged all my life had come together in a huge, heavy ball and dropped squarely on my unsuspecting head.

It occurred to me that I probably would have been accepted at Tuskegee. Dr. Benedict, and maybe even Dr. Carver, might have helped me get a scholarship. But I had been so sure I had everything worked out at Rio Vista that I hadn't looked into any other possibilities.

But even as I trudged along the dusty campus pathways, dragging beside me my heavy, awkward suitcase and the burden of my first real defeat, I had more immediate problems. I was counting on the football scholarship to pay my expenses. Without it, I couldn't afford to go to school at all, even though I had been accepted. And even if I'd had the tuition money, classes didn't start for another two weeks. The regular dormitories and dining hall wouldn't open until then. Only Carson Hall, where the football players lived and ate, was open. I didn't even know how I'd eat dinner that day.

As loath as I was to do it, I had to call Ma and tell her to come get me. I couldn't face Barnett. I was afraid he'd make fun of me, or that he'd feel sorry for me. I don't know which would have been worse. I walked aimlessly around campus until I saw a sign that said, "Administration Building." I remembered that it was the one building that was open even when classes were not in session.

I walked inside, into a large carpeted room with high ceilings and oversized windows. There were huge file cabinets along the walls. In front of a closed door was a desk where a stern-looking woman with gray hair was sorting through a stack of papers. She peered over her glasses at me. "May I help you, young man?" I knew that voice. She was the woman who had refused to help me contact Coach Rutledge.

"Yes, ma'am," I said humbly. "I need to use a telephone. It would be long-distance, but I'll pay for it."

"These phones are for official college business, young man. Is this an emergency?"

"Well, yes, it is. I came early by mistake, and I need to call my mother."

"You came early by mistake?" She let the question hang in the air. She wasn't going to help me until she had the full story, and I didn't feel like telling it.

"Please, if I could just . . ."

A round little man who looked to be in his late forties stepped out of the office behind her. "Is there a problem, Mrs. Griffin?" he asked.

"Apparently, Dean Greathouse." Her tone was sharp and condescending. "This young man seems to have been confused about when classes start."

"Is that right, young man?" the dean asked.

"Not exactly."

"Well that's certainly what he told me," she sniffed, annoyed to be contradicted.

"Why don't you come into my office, and let's see what we can do for you," the dean said.

The lady behind the desk let out an audible, "Humph!"

I took a seat in a handsome leather chair in front of a desk that was completely empty except for a telephone and a nameplate that read, "Dr. Montgomery W. Greathouse, Dean of Students."

I told Dr. Greathouse the whole embarrassing story, punctuating it with apologies for my arrogant assumptions.

"You say you've been accepted as a student here?" he asked.

"That's right."

"You're sure about that?" he chuckled.

For the first time since I arrived on the Rio Vista State College campus, I smiled. "Yes, sir." I said. "I did get a letter accepting my application."

"How were your grades in high school?"

"They were excellent, sir, and Washington High School in Knox Plains has very high standards."

"Yes, it does. Believe it or not, I've heard of it. We actually had a mathematics instructor leave here to go teach at Washington."

"That would be Mr. North," I said.

"That's right, and Bill North is as good a young math teacher as I've ever seen. I wish we had something to offer you—I don't like to see any good student turned away—but most of our academic scholarships dried up when the economy went sour. What few we do have are special endowments, and you have to apply early. If your high-school grades are good, you might be able to apply for next year, but that doesn't help you with this year's tuition.

"At this late date, I'm not even sure I could arrange an on-campus job for you. The unskilled positions in the dining room and grounds maintenance are gone. The jobs that are left require special skills. Even if we had something, it wouldn't be enough. It might cover about a fourth of your expenses, but your parents would have to pay the rest."

"My father died when I was eight, and my mother can't come up with that kind of money. All she has is a little store. It was doing fine until the stock market crashed and the bank failed and we lost almost all our savings. A lot of other people around there did, too. When our customers don't have anything to spend, we can't make any money," I rambled. "If it hadn't been for that, Ma probably could have paid my tuition. I know how much the store used to make, because I used to do the books."

Dean Greathouse brightened. "You say you have bookkeeping experience?"

"I've been keeping the books at my mother's store since I was about twelve. She has an auditor go over them once a year, and he always compliments me on what a good job I do." It was nice for a fleeting second to feel good about myself again.

"The bookkeeping office needs some help, but you've got to have a head for figures and you've got to have experience. If you're really that good, I'll give Mr. Whitman a call, but if you let me down, he'll never trust me again."

"I won't let you down, but I don't know where the rest of the money would come from. It's no use. My ma just doesn't have it. Looks like instead of being Theodore Roosevelt O'Malley, research chemist, I'm going to be Theodore Roosevelt O'Malley, common laborer."

"Well, at the very least we can help you get home." Dean Greathouse reached for the heavy black phone on his desk. "What's your telephone number?" He tried to make the long-distance call, but the operator couldn't get through because of problems with the phone line. She told us to try again in an hour. "Come on," Dean Greathouse said, "let's get us some dinner."

He picked up the phone again and recited a number to the operator. "Nettie," he said into the receiver, "set another place. We've got company for dinner." Dean Greathouse rested his chin between his thumb and his index finger. He looked down at the bare desktop, deep in thought. "Why," he asked himself out loud, "does your name sound so familiar?"

CHAPTER THIRTY

Dean Greathouse lived in a little brick bungalow on the edge of campus. As we came up the walkway, the front door flew open and a plump, jolly woman who reminded me a lot of Lula Pendergast greeted us with a big smile. Just for a minute, I forgot my problems as I was seduced by the perfume of fresh-from-the-oven yeast rolls.

"Come on in, son," Nettie Greathouse urged. "I hope you're hungry."

"Now, you're not fixing to give my dinner away, are you, Mrs. Greathouse?" Dean Greathouse teased.

"It's not like you need it," she answered, giggling as she patted his oversized middle. Right away you could see a tremendous affection between these two people. They seemed to match, as though she were the sugar dish and he the cream pitcher in the same tea service.

"I hope I'm not imposing, ma'am," I inserted earnestly.

"No, no, son. You're doing us a favor. Do you have any idea how long Dr. Greathouse and me would be looking at this ham if we didn't have somebody to help us eat it? This is just its second day on the dinner table, but long about Thursday we'll be going to the highways and hedges to find folks to help us finish it up," she chuckled.

"Abraham Lincoln was about right when he said, 'Eternity is a ham and two people,' " Dean Greathouse added with a grin.

Along with the ham, Mrs. Greathouse put a big bowl of steaming collards and another bowl of sweet potatoes that glistened with a heavy brown sugar glaze on the neatly set dining table, but it was those heaven-sent rolls that made me add a loud "Amen" to Dean Greathouse's prayer of thanks. For the next few minutes the food claimed all of our attention. Both the Greathouses piled their plates high and urged me to do the same. "We got plenty, honey," my hostess assured me. "Just help yourself."

The first plateful of food was just a warm-up exercise for this couple, who obviously shared a passion for hearty meals. They each quickly cleaned their plates and went on to second helpings. After she finished her second serving of candied sweet potatoes, the roly-poly little woman announced, "I made a peach cobbler." She turned to me and added, "It's Willie's favorite."

"Is he your son?" I asked politely.

"Oh, no," Dean Greathouse laughed. "The only child we have is a daughter, Ellen. She's a senior at Spelman this year. She went back to Atlanta early—she's going to be a counselor for the incoming freshman girls. When my wife said, 'Willie,' she meant me."

He saw the puzzled look on my face and continued. "My wife and I grew up together in Montgomery, Alabama, where I was Willie Greathouse. When I got to Morehouse, the fellows started calling me 'Montgomery' because that was where I was from. After a while it started to feel right. I began signing my name Montgomery W. Greathouse. The W is for 'Willie.' I held on to it because that's the name my mother gave me, but I just liked the sound of Montgomery Greathouse."

"Trying to put on airs, if you ask me," his wife commented, but her smile said she was teasing him again.

"One thing about being colored," Dean Greathouse said, lowering his voice as though there might be curious white people lurking outside, "is that none of us have any famous family histories written down somewhere, so we can change whatever we want and be whoever we want."

"Well, being just plain old Nettie Parker Greathouse is good enough for me," Mrs. Greathouse declared. "I've never been much on folks bragging about who their granddaddy or their great-granddaddy was, anyway. What did they have to do with it? If your great-granddaddy was a king or a chicken thief, you didn't pick him. My daddy always used to tell me, 'It doesn't matter how tall your grandma was, you got to grow for yourself.' "

"You're so right, baby," Dean Greathouse acknowledged. "Now where's that peach cobbler?" To me he said, "My wife makes a peach cobbler that'll make you love your mother-in-law."

As she spooned up huge bowls of the mouth-watering dessert, Mrs. Greathouse asked, "Why are you on campus already, Roosevelt? School doesn't start for another two weeks."

Dean Greathouse gave her the short version of my sad tale. "Roosevelt was interested in trying for a football scholarship, honey, but that didn't work out. It's too late to get an academic scholarship for this year. That money was gone a long time ago. This dad-blasted depression we're in has set colored folks back another twenty years." He turned to me. "But I still think some of us will be all right in spite of everything. Dr. DuBois refers to the 'Talented Tenth,' and I don't know whether that's the right number or not, but I do feel that a certain percentage of us will be successful no matter how much segregation, discrimination, and just plain meanness they throw at us. My instinct is that you're one of the ones who'll find a way. I'll help you any way I can. When we get back to the office, I'll give you some applications to fill out in case some money frees up next semester.

"We need to get back pretty soon, too. Mrs. Griffin can't go to dinner until we get back, and she gets pretty testy if I make her late."

When we arrived back at the administration building, Dean Greathouse went right inside to tell Mrs. Griffin she could leave for her break. Barnett was outside, pacing between two massive white columns. He lit into me as soon as we were within earshot of each other. "Great day in the morning, Moose!" he shouted. "Why did you run off like that? You had me scared half to death."

I was forced to acknowledge my embarrassing situation. "I didn't make the team, Barnett. I guess I'm just too little to be a—"

"I know about all that," Barnett interrupted, "but why did you run off without letting me know where you were going?"

"I just wasn't ready to lay my disgrace at your feet, okay? You made the team and I didn't, and I feel like thirty with the three punched out, okay?"

Barnett looked as if he were trying not to laugh. "I don't believe you sometimes," he said, shaking his head. "You were actually embarrassed to face me because I made the team and you didn't? Moose, I've spent my whole life feeling embarrassed because I couldn't keep pace with you at school. And you're my nephew, for goodness sake! This is football. This is a game. It's nothing. You're going to do things in your life that people will remember long after they've forgotten that there ever was a Barnett Lindsay who ran down a field with a piece of pigskin in his hand."

"And just how am I going to do great things with my life if I can't go to college?" I demanded. "Football isn't just a game to me. It was my ticket to a college education. It's easy for you to say, 'It's just a game.' You have a scholarship and I don't. I'm not trying to be mean or anything, but I'm the one who always wanted to go to college. You never cared, especially. It's not fair." I realized how selfish I sounded, so I quickly added, "I'm happy for you. I really am. But I'm just very disappointed for myself."

Barnett looked at the ground. "I talked to the coach. He said that ordinarily, football players aren't allowed to have overnight guests, especially during the season, but he's sympathetic to your situation and said you can sleep in my room for a few nights until you can make arrangements to get home. He's even going to have an extra bed put in there. He really seemed to . . ." He stammered and finally said, "Oh, Moose, if I could, I'd let you take my place in a minute. You know that."

I clapped my hand on his shoulder and nodded. There was nothing he could do. I didn't even blame Coach Rutledge. His job was to put together the best football team he could. He couldn't do that if he was going to be influenced by every sob story he heard.

As we walked back toward the football field, I realized I would now have to face the fellows who had succeeded where I had failed. I'd have to face them first at the stadium, then in the dormitory. I'd have given ten years off my life if I could have just gone straight home.

A few yards from the stadium, Barnett broke the silence between us. "Oh, I forgot to tell you. Guess who I saw in the dining hall? Betsy Singer. She's enrolled here as a freshman this year. She's on campus early because she has a job in the bookstore and she had to come ahead to help set up."

"She's going here? She told me Elliot wanted her to go to Vassar or Radcliffe or someplace like that. She said she had the grades and connections to get in."

"She didn't have any trouble getting accepted to those fancy white schools, but it seems Elliot had her college money invested in the stock market, and, well, you know what happened there. He's not dead broke, but he sure can't pay for any place like Radcliffe now. He can just afford to send Betsy here, and that's if she works to help out. Everything happened pretty quickly, but she wrote you a letter. It probably arrived after we left. She told me she picked Rio Vista because you said it was such a good school. I think she picked it because you're here. That girl's crazy about you, you know that?"

"Well, whether she picked the right school or not, she sure didn't pick the right fellow."

"By the way," Barnett asked, "where's your suitcase? I looked around the locker room for it. Did you take it with you?"

I had to think for a minute before I recalled that my bag was in Dean Greathouse's office. "It's back at the administration building. I'd better go get it." I was happy to have an errand that would keep me away from the football field a little longer.

Back at the dean's office, I was relieved to see that Mrs. Griffin had gone to dinner. I wasn't sure anyone was there. Cautiously, I walked into Dean Greathouse's office and saw him digging through a file cabinet.

When he looked up and saw me, he broke into a grin. "I was just about to call over to the athletic department looking for you," he said.

"Oh, yes, I left my bag here. I'm sorry. I'll get it out of your way."

"I wasn't calling about the bag. Sit down."

I slid into the broad-armed chair, where I was silent and thoughtful for a moment. Then he asked, "What did you say your full name was?"

"Theodore Roosevelt Bullmoose O'Malley."

He pulled a manila file folder out of the drawer and studied it for a minute. "I believe I remember who you are now," Dean Greathouse told me. As he thumbed through the file, his smile grew larger until he was actually chuckling. "Son," he said, "you don't have a thing to worry about. Your tuition and all your expenses have been taken care of."

"Taken care of?" I echoed. That made no sense.

"You remember that I said we had a few special endowments? Well, we got a new one this year, and one of the stipulations was that as long as you and your—your uncle, is it?—are students here, any expenses you have that are not covered through other scholarship monies will be paid out of the fund. You could still take the job in the bookkeeping office and use your salary for spending money," he suggested.

"I don't know how I could have forgotten this," Dean Greathouse continued. "Dr. Meadows—he's the president here—and I were laughing over the name of the endowment. It's called the Timothy and Second Timothy Scholarship Fund. I don't know what that's about, but the lady who gave the money insisted on it. Her name is, let's see here . . ." He thumbed through the papers. "Ah, here it is—Miss Violet Nesbet."

Miss Ella had always been a kind person, so it wouldn't have surprised me that she would do something like this, but Miss Violet? I guess you never really know people as well as you think you do.

Dean Greathouse was bouncing with excitement. "I want you to read the letter we got from her. It's in Dr. Meadows's office. Wait here a minute, I'll get it." The word *letter* prompted me to remember the mail I had stuffed in my bag. I opened the envelope from Rio Vista first. It was the information about the scholarship. Just as Dean Greathouse told me, Violet Nesbet had pledged whatever sum was necessary to put Barnett and me through undergraduate school. Another letter I hadn't noticed before was from Betsy. It read:

Dear Moose,
    I was heartbroken to learn that the financial portfolio Elliot set up for my college education had collapsed in the wake of the stock market crash. Like most Americans we are certainly feeling

the effects of that event. I suppose I should count my blessings. We still have a comfortable home, an income adequate to keep it up, and have even been able to keep Mrs. Jacobs. We are, however, having to keep track of our expenses as never before.

Initially, we decided to postpone college until times were better. But my dear, practical father huffed, "You know, not every colored person in America has to go to a fancy Ivy League college to be successful. I went first to Atlanta Bible Seminary, then to Atlanta University, and I've done just fine." (You may recall that Atlanta Bible Seminary is now called Morehouse College.) At first, Father wanted to send me off to one of the schools in Atlanta, but I remembered that you said a student could get a fine education at Rio Vista and talked Father and Elliot into looking into it. Finally, we agreed that I would enroll there, but we were so close to the registration deadline, we were afraid we might be too late. A friend of Father's laughed when we told him our fears. He said with the shape the economy is in, almost any college will take a paying student, even at the last minute, and when that student has an academic record as good as mine, they'd just about send a car to get him.

I must close now, as I have lots to do before I leave for Rio Vista. If we don't run into one another on campus, please come by the bookstore. I have a job there. By the way, Moose, I won't consider it a breach of etiquette if you speak first.

    With Warmest Regards,
    Betsy

I was rereading her letter when Dean Greathouse came back with Miss Violet's. He wanted me to see what she had written: "I have always been impressed by young O'Malley's character and intelligence." She never told me. "This young man is a true hero."

I left Dean Greathouse's office with a brighter step in spite of the heavy suitcase I was now lugging. I was not even all that embarrassed to face the football players who had seen me in the most humiliating minutes of my life. I did feel rather ill at ease when Barnett introduced me to his roommate—Norris Williams, the fellow who had been standing behind me in line in the locker room and witnessed the whole humiliating scene. Norris was pleasant and polite. If he felt inclined to make fun of me, I saw no hint of it. Within minutes, two fellows arrived at Barnett and Norris's room with an extra bed.

We had laughed and chatted away most of the afternoon when Barnett asked, "Did you go by to see Betsy? I think she'll be really disappointed if you don't."

"That's right, she's working in the bookstore. I wonder where that is."

Norris led me over to the window. "Do you see that grove with the statue of Sam Houston in the middle? Now, do you see the yellow brick building just on the other side of it? The bookstore is in there. Go in through the door on the west side. It's the only one that's unlocked."

I found the building easily. The door was propped open with a wooden wedge to allow the dusty air to flow freely. Inside, the bookstore was a mess. Narrow trails snaked between boxes all over the floor. Most of the shelves were empty and dirty. I spotted Betsy on her knees, cleaning one of the lower shelves. Even in a simple pinafore and a head rag she looked incredibly cute. I just stood looking at her for a minute. Then a fortyish cocoa-colored woman who was similarly dressed and cleaning another shelf happened to look up. "May I help you?" she asked.

"I stopped by to say hello to Miss Singer, but I can come back when she's not so busy."

Betsy jerked around at the mention of her name. She saw me, jumped to her feet, and snatched away the head rag. "Hello, Moose. I saw Barnett in the dining hall. He's looking for you."

"He found me. I don't mean to keep you from your work. I . . ."

"If you can wait, I get off at five. Mrs. Jenkins . . ." She looked at the watch attached to a bob on her pinafore, then turned to the woman. I knew it had to be close to five.

The cocoa-colored woman smiled. "Go ahead," she said to Betsy. "I'll see you tomorrow."

Betsy washed her hands in a little pan near the shelf she was cleaning, then she took off the pinafore and folded it neatly. She carefully removed the watch bob and attached it to the bodice of her dress. My lovely friend stepped through the maze of boxes and, beaming with genuine delight, took both my hands in hers and squeezed them. "It's wonderful to see you, Moose."

"You, too," I said, and I meant it. Intellectually, I had known all along that Betsy wasn't like the women in Lester McDaniel's gang even though she had the same physical features. Now I knew it emotionally, too, and I wasn't afraid of her anymore. I was ready to like her, to truly enjoy her wit, her intelligence, and even her sunny American-girl beauty. In fact, I decided then and there that if I didn't marry Betsy one day, I'd marry someone a lot like her.

"How long have you been on campus?" I asked.

"Just since yesterday. There are about six of us in Vernon Hall now, three freshman girls and three upperclassmen. Mrs. Ryan, the dorm mother, is there, too. She had us all to supper last night, but we ate breakfast and dinner with the football team. The regular dining hall isn't open yet, you know. I don't know whether I can take another meal with those sweaty football players today."

"I guess you know I'm not going to be one of them," I admitted sheepishly.

"Barnett told me. My first reaction was happiness. I've seen some of those fellows who've played college football for a few years. Many of them have half their front teeth knocked out and bumps and scars all over their faces. I'd rather see you keep that handsome face than win all the football trophies in America," she told me. Betsy's gentle, caring smile faded. "Of course, the one part that worries me is your football scholarship. Are you going to be able to go to college without it?"

I told her the crazy story about the Timothy and Second Timothy Scholarship Fund, and she laughed a hearty laugh that reminded me why I liked her so much. She was as graceful and feminine as any girl I'd ever known, yet she could laugh, play, and eat with an enthusiasm that wasn't ashamed of itself, just the way the fellows did. I had never enjoyed being around overly dainty females.

"You deserve to be taken out to supper for that," she said. "Come on. One of the older girls told me about a little place just off campus called The Hut. It's run by a colored couple, Mr. and Mrs. Stewart, who treat all the students as if they were their children. I understand they made a half-hearted attempt at jungle decor that ended up just looking junky, but everybody says the food is good."

"I'd love to take you," I said, "but I won't have any money until I start working."

"I'm inviting you. I have money."

I was shocked. "I couldn't let a girl pay for my supper. My grandmother's etiquette book says—"

Her full-throated laugh interrupted my sentence. "Then let a man pay. It's Elliot's money, and I'm sure if he were here, he would want to take you to supper. Besides, we're not talking about the family fortune here. If there's one good thing about this Depression, it's the way prices have gone down. And this place is really cheap."

I still hesitated.

"I won't tell anybody," she promised teasingly.

The writers of my grandmother's etiquette books would have been appalled, but there was nothing I wanted more than to spend the evening with Betsy, and I couldn't pass up the opportunity. Over supper, she told me another bit of news. "There's a girl in the freshman class from Knox Plains. She's here early to start a campus job, too—in the library. Her name is Glenda Gibley. Do you know her?"

"Glenda Gibley. Sure I know her. We were good friends in high school, but I wouldn't have thought her father had the money to send her to college. They made a lot of money in the oil boom but lost it all to foolish spending and bad investments."

"She told me that. She said her fiancé, who's a graduate student here, is getting his dad to help out. His dad's a doctor, and he's lending them the money for Glenda's college expenses. The fiancé has promised to pay his dad back once he's a doctor himself and he and Glenda are married. Isn't that romantic? He must truly love her."

"Yes, he really must." I smiled to myself at the realization that this man loved Glenda for all her fine qualities and didn't care whether her family had money or not.

Betsy and I had a fine time that evening, laughing at the tacky paper palm leaves and badly made fake coconuts that decorated The Hut, always stopping politely when one of the Stewarts came over to see if we needed anything.

Back at school we strolled arm-in-arm around the campus, enjoying its sprawling beauty in the fading light of a late-summer Texas sunset. We talked about a hundred different things and could have kept going all night, but nine o'clock, curfew for freshman girls, was quickly approaching. In front of her dorm I told her how happy I was that she had decided to come to Rio Vista. And, yes, this time I kissed her.

EPILOGUE
EPILOGUE

Many years after Barnett and I graduated from Rio Vista State College, the Timothy and Second Timothy Scholarship Fund continues to pay expenses for smart, hard-working Rio Vista State students who love to learn but just don't have the money to go to school. Violet Nesbet left a nice endowment, but the fund has other benefactors, too. The Nate Jackson and Sons Construction Company, and Cornelius's Mortuary, for example, are big contributors. And I understand that twice a year, just for old times' sake, the Dorcas Ladies' Handicraft Circle at Galilee Baptist Church holds a Ham Smiling to raise money for the scholarship fund.